A SINNER'S PRAYER

M. P. WRIGHT

ISIS
LARGE
PRINT

First published in Great Britain 2019
by
Black & White Publishing Ltd.

First Isis Edition
published 2020
by arrangement with
Black & White Publishing Ltd.

A catalogue record for this book is available
from the British Library.

ISBN 978–1–78541–884–6

Published by
Ulverscroft Limited
Anstey, Leicestershire

Set by Words & Graphics Ltd.
Anstey, Leicestershire
Printed and bound in Great Britain by
T. J. International Ltd., Padstow, Cornwall

This book is printed on acid-free paper

In memory of Richard "Dickie" Dexter
and dedicated to Jack Peberdy.

Two hombres who have kindly blessed me
with their friendship.

Prologue

Carnell Harris was dead.

In the six years since he'd been murdered, those words had gone through my mind almost every day. Carnell Harris was dead because of me.

Most nights, my old friend waited for me in my dreams, haunting my sleep, always emerging from the same cold world of Cimmerian shade. His restless spirit would return to inhabit my nocturnal reveries; his wraith-like figure standing motionless at the end of the bed, watching me with unblinking eyes; his dark-skinned face waxy and gaunt, his hair a tangle of snakes, tombstone teeth yellowing and wideset, his sagging cheeks patinaed with grey whiskers that looked as stiff as emery-wheel filings.

Carnell's cruel visitations played out the same way each night. I'd hear the faint sound of a music box mechanism click and whirr, followed by a tinkling, distant chime. A familiar tune I remember from the Barbadian home where I grew up. Then, as always, the same words are spoken to me. A command to stir, woken by a voice from my past, a voice of the dead.

"JT, wake up, brutha."

I feel a hand shake my shoulder. I'm still a slave to sleep, my body craving rest. I hear a scratchy striking sound and then a brief susurration before smelling the sharp sulfuric odour of a struck match, and then a few moments later the delicious scent of mild floral incense and burning tobacco. I feel the hand touch my shoulder, again followed by a sharp, burning pain awakening inside of me, running through my upper torso and down my shoulder.

It is always this pain that forces me to open my eyes.

I can see after a fashion, but my vision isn't proper yet. I know I'm in my own bedroom but everything around me is hung in a dense white gauze. A hazy, slow-swirling mist of reefer smoke that impairs my sight and continues to confuse my sluggish mind. Carnell's unwelcome chimera at the foot of my bed is always as clear and present as a Catholic priest preparing to give last rites. The cannabis smoke from the joint he's holding between yellow-stained fingers begins to waft around him, his face becoming blurred by the thick vapour, his once playful features seeming to move with ugly, sinuous wisps.

Despite a strong reluctance, I always call out to the all-too-familiar apparition.

"Carnell?" My voice is hoarse and congested, cracking hard enough that I think my throat will bleed.

"Yeah, JT?"

I try to rise from the bed but a heavy weight across my chest pins me down against the mattress. I fight against the crushing sense of paralysis and slowly lift my arm a few inches off the bedclothes, finally reaching

2

my unsteady hand out towards my friend. "I'm sorry, man. Sorry I let you down."

The thick musky stench of marijuana strikes my face like a fist. Carnell leans forward and shakes his head, the whites of his eyes filled with ruptured blood veins. "Nah, you din't let me down, JT. You ain't sorry either. You let me die. Die out in dat damn cold gutter on ma own."

I hear myself begin to plead my innocence but cannot feel my lips moving. "I . . . I . . . I didn't know . . . Please, it's not my fault. I didn't mean for any of this to happen."

The air around me is breathless, so humid and still and devoid of movement that every line of sweat running down my skin underneath the sheets is like the paths of insects scurrying across my hide. Carnell's mannequinlike head remains perfectly still as he watches me. He puffs on his joint and lets smoke drift from his lips. I feel a pain in my chest like jagged iron twisting its way through tendon and bone. Carnell flips the butt in an arc out into the smog-filled room. "Sooner or later, everyone round you dies, JT. They all in hell, everyone you evah loved, all either burnt up or here rotting wid me."

My eyes are now fully open, but I still cannot focus on anything other than my dead friend. I feel as if the bed under me is beginning to shake and fall. I begin to panic, struggling against the paralysis that forces me to remain motionless. I turn my face towards Carnell and watch in horror as a wet, crimson stain begins to soak through the middle of his shirt, the cotton fabric gluing

3

to his wet skin. Carnell looks up at me, shock etched across his face; his mouth opens and closes and he cries out, his hand snatching at his shirt, tearing the thin cotton fabric open to reveal a gaping wound in the middle of his stomach. Dark rivulets, the colour of burnt coffee grounds, run through his unsteady fingers, the flow of blood quickening. As I lay inert, I hear it splattering on to the floorboards at the foot of the bed frame.

Carnell stares back at me, then raises his blood-soaked hands in front of him, his palms upright, his eyes boring into mine before pointing a thick, callused finger down towards my face. "This is the suffering you gone an' caused me, brutha."

Carnell grunts then staggers forward through the smoke. I watch him cough and sniff then spit a thick wad of crimson-stained phlegm down on to my bedclothes. His head falls to one side, his mouth snapped shut; I watch his body judder as one hand drops towards his stomach. His face distorts in agony as he clenches at the rolls of dense fat below his belly button with his fingers, kneading at the blood-caked skin around the exit of a huge stab wound. Carnell's hand reaches into the gaping hole in his guts, his fingers forcing their way inside his bloated abdomen. I try to scream for him to stop, but my muted outcry is lost in the gathering abyss that envelops me. My friend snatches and tears at his insides with frenzied jerks, wrenching at his intestines. Spittle and blood pour from his mouth. Carnell lets out a deep-throated scream as he finally heaves out steaming lengths of his own

4

decaying, grey-tangled bowels. The stink of boiling offal and faecal matter fills my nostrils; I gag and wretch, warm vomit lodged deep inside my gullet. Carnell's huge body lunges forward, his head sinking to his waist, his frame gripped in a wave of violent fits and spasms. The sound of his wet innards unspooling down on to the floor fills my ears.

Carnell's body remains motionless for what seems like an eternity. Powerless to do anything, I await the torment to continue. When he finally raises himself up, I again see the sucking wound, and the torn, soaked cloth of his undershirt, which flutters in the cavity from the release of air and viscera. When he tries to speak, he sounds like a man strangling in his own saliva.

"Dis . . . Dis is fo' you, bastard!"

Carnell's arms spring forward. I see the glistening underbelly of a black serpent curled up among the remains of his guts, which are cradled in his hands. My friend's fingers splay apart as he throws the snake and steaming entrails on to my chest. Helpless to defend myself, my feet immediately try and kick underneath the sheets, but they feel as if they have been wired together. One of my hands remains locked at my side, the other held up in front of my face like a meaningless, outstretched claw.

The snake remains still, eyeing me before slithering backwards. I feel the warmth of its coiling body through the sheets. I watch as it sinks down between my legs, its lower half nestling close to my groin. Its bulbous head then rises, its grey tongue darting in and out of its mouth as it savours the scent of my fear. The serpent's mouth opens to reveal huge fangs, its head and neck barely moving. I can hear my heart beating savagely inside my head as the creature lunges towards my face.

Before the viper strikes, the room becomes as bright and shattering to my eyes as a phosphorous shell exploding. Carnell and the snake both burst into flame like huge candles. Their bodies glow with the cool white brilliance of a pistol's flare. A huge fire erupts, the sound like the whistle of super-heated air cracking through brick, metal and wood, followed by the resinous popping of everything around me. It scorches all it touches — skin, organ, bone and soul.

In the glare of the maelstrom, for the briefest of moments, I see the faint images of the people I have loved standing in the enraged heat shimmer. Their quivering voices call out to me to join them in their everlasting perdition. Their arms outstretched, blistered hands open, their charred fingers spread wide, awaiting my body to cradle.

I reach out my own hand to join them. Closing my eyes, I feel myself being dragged from my bed and lifted across the flaming room towards them. As I am drawn closer, I feel my skin welt, sear and pustule as the blaze wraps itself around me. I submit to the inevitable, open my mouth, suck in the tinder, sparks and smoke then stretch out my arms and feel myself drawn into the hellfire. As the heat pierces every part of my body, I am forced to open my eyes, but as I do, the burning and the pain subside. I stand in a realm of pitch darkness, the howling conflagration no more. As the veil of

6

blackness slowly rescinds, I find myself greeted by the fragile, unearthly forms of my deceased wife, children and sister. I begin to sob uncontrollably, the relief and joy immeasurable. But as we embrace, my family are violently torn from my arms, and I watch as they disappear into an unknown ether as quickly as they appeared.

I bellow out their names as I fall to my knees and claw at the charred earth with my fingers. I look up and, through tear-soaked eyes, I face a tenebrous void, a chasm of misery, one I know is of my own making.

CHAPTER
ONE

Friday, 13 August 1971

I woke with a jolt, the sheets twisted across my chest, in almost complete darkness. My breath was ballooning in my chest, my naked body sweating. At first, I didn't know where I was. I reached over and turned on the lamp on the bedside table, picked up my watch and brought it close to my face. I snapped my eyes shut briefly then opened them and waited for the world to come back into focus before I looked at the time.

A strip of dawn light showed through a crack in the curtains. I sat up slowly, my head bent down, my jaw clenched tight to keep it from shaking. I threw off the damp sheets and swung my clammy legs out of bed, staring down at the floorboards before getting to my feet. Dragging my ass off the mattress and getting upright felt worse than swimming to the surface in a cesspool full of pus. The effort made my stomach lurch. I got my balance then staggered out of the bedroom and down the hall to the bathroom, where I splashed my face with water, hoping to clear my head. It was like I'd been poisoned. I avoided the mirror, my eyes locked on the edges of the white porcelain washbasin and waited until the grisly nightmare dissolved from inside my head.

Despite the passing of the years, most mornings I found myself locked in the past, reflecting on Carnell's brutal demise and feeling like hell. It wasn't a great way to start the day. My nightmares were a product of guilt and conscience. The guilt refused to release me from its ugly grip, hanging invisibly over my head like a perverse crown of thorns. I secretly lived with my inner tormentors, only allowing them to besiege me while I slept.

I threw off my ugly thoughts and went back to the bedroom, pulled on a pair of trousers and my vest, then made my way down to the kitchen. I filled the battered kettle, lit the gas, heaped three full spoons of Nescafé Blend 37 into my mug and waited for the water to boil. I couldn't start my working day without at least two cups of strong coffee inside of me. The caffeine fired me up to face another day at work and helped settle my frayed nerves.

I sat down next to the kitchen window and looked out on the poky rear garden at the back of the terraced house I now rented on Morgan Street in St Pauls. It was my fourth summer living in the two-up two-down, which was situated right in the heart of our tight-knit black community, and much had changed in my life. Four years ago, I'd been living like a hermit on a narrow beam Dutch barge on Cumberland Basin, close to the port and Bristol city centre. I'd been eking out a meagre living as an off-the-books private detective. That dangerous life was long behind me now, though in

10

truth, part of me regretted giving up such an unusual profession. Although I'd never admitted it to anyone, I'd secretly enjoyed trouble knocking on my door. Living in the shadows and playing the devil at his own game.

There'd never been a cat in hell's chance of returning to my job as a police officer once I'd settled here in Britain. The lofty position I once held so proudly back home on Barbados was denied me from the day I stepped off the boat in 1964. Now in the second year of a new decade, and at the age of forty-eight, I was too damn old to join up again and walk the beat. That and the colour of my skin had prohibited me from getting a foot in the front door at Trinity Road police station to apply for the force when I'd first arrived.

Nowadays, the menial job I held down working as an assistant school caretaker put a roof over my head and food on the table.

Four years ago, I made the decision to trade in the world of lies and deceit, and since then I'd moved from one dead-end job to another — unsettled, unsatisfied, unhappy. I'd been on the payroll at Parson Street Primary School in Bedminster, on the other side of the city, this past eighteen months. The long hours of graft that I put in were in no way comparable to the detective work I'd once undertaken. Sticking my nose into other folks' dirty business had never been a barrel of laughs, but neither was sticking my arm down the U-bend of a boys' toilet to unblock it, or tipping out the ashtrays in the teachers' staff room at the end of the day. On the plus side, I was keeping my head above water financially and my name out of trouble with the law. My caretaker life brought forth little excitement, few mysteries and certainly no dead bodies. It was a safe form of occupation, but one that, in truth, I hated doing and that at times made me feel little better than a sharecropper.

I sank the last of my coffee, raised myself up out of my seat and, with little enthusiasm to face another day sweeping floors, walked over to the sink and refilled the kettle. While it stoked itself up, I went to get myself ready, washing and shaving before I dressed in a blue flannel shirt, navy necktie and my denim overalls. While I was tying my shoes, I heard my six-year-old adopted niece, Chloe, waking noisily in the tiny box room adjacent to my own. I listened as she clambered out of bed, her little feet plodding along the bare boards outside in the hall. I waited for her to stick her head around the door frame and beam her usual wide smile at me. It was a tradition she'd kept up each morning for as long as I could remember. A rhythm to our lives, more satisfying than good music.

"I dreamed, Joseph," Chloe said, then she stared off into space, lost for a moment as she slowly began to walk towards me. I sat back on my bed, held out my arms and caught her by the waist, lifting her on to my knee.

"You did. What about, kidda?"

"I dreamed there was a scary man in the house last night."

A burning sensation struck at my belly and my brow creased. "What kind of man?"

Chloe raised the palms of her hands and opened her eyes wide to say she didn't know. "I didn't see him, just heard him."

"What'd he sound like?"

"Like he was screaming."

"Screaming? I didn't hear no screaming last night," I lied.

I could feel Chloe's eyes on the side of my face. She reached out and touched my cheek with her palm.

"Joseph?"

"Yeah?" I lowered my head and smiled at her.

"There ain't no ghosts in this house, is there?"

I shook my head and listened as her stomach rumbled against my chest. "Only strange noises in this old place come from your empty belly, child."

Chloe laughed and I pressed her against me tightly. She was the daughter of my late sister, Bernice, but still I loved her as if she were my own, so much so that at times it hurt. I looked down at my watch over the top of her head.

"How 'bout we get you some breakfast?"

Chloe nodded silently. I hoisted her up on my hip and carried her down to the kitchen, sitting her in a chair at our blue Formica-topped table. The kettle on the hob bubbled away frantically, a thick plume of steam pouring from its spout. I grabbed a tea towel from the draining board, wrapped it around the kettle's handle and took it off the gas, then turned and leaned against the sink with my arms folded.

"So, what's it to be then?"

Chloe looked across at the pantry door. "Jam."

"Again? Child, that's three days on the trot. You eat much more o' that stuff, you gonna start looking like a strawberry."

I listened to her laughter as I walked across the kitchen and stuck my head inside the larder. I reached in and picked up a tall glass jar of home-made preserve, which had been made for us by her great aunt Pearl. I spun the jar in my fingers, thinking of my elderly relations. I felt myself smile. Chloe called out to me.

"So, no ghosts then, Joseph?"

That burning sensation rose again in the centre of my chest and the smile fell from my face. I turned back from the pantry to face my niece and shook my head at her.

"Ain't no ghosts here, baby girl," I lied for a second time.

As I unscrewed the jam jar lid, I could feel my pulse beating in my throat with the urgency of a damaged clock that was about to run out of time.

CHAPTER
TWO

Parson Street Primary was a red-brick school that resembled a prison more than a place of learning. It stood bleak and foreboding at the top of the Bedminster Road, on the east side of the city. I hated walking through its doors and I dreaded to think what kind of ill feelings it brought out in the children who sat in its classrooms each day. I may have had to grin and bear the gloominess of the old schoolhouse, but I sure wasn't about to let my kin suffer it. Chloe had recently started at Newfoundland Road in St Pauls. Each morning before work, I dropped her off at Uncle Gabe and Aunt Pearl's house on Banner Road, then they took it in turns to take her to school and then collect her later in the day. I picked her up each night after I came off shift. It was a set-up that worked well. It allowed me to clock in and out without any hassle from my employers, who were hot on their staffs prompt timekeeping, and it gave Chloe a sense of routine and family stability. I left her with my kin, with not a worry in the world, happy in the knowledge that I was a working man, versed in floor waxes and bleach — not blood. The only weapon I carried these days was a pocket knife given to me years back as a birthday gift by my good friend and former neighbour, Mrs Pearce. The razor-sharp blade only ever pierced flesh if I nicked my own skin accidently.

I walked into school the same way I did every morning: through the back door. The caretakers' hut sat at the rear of the building, tucked away from both prying kids and, worse still, the teaching staff. The concrete and asbestos prefab, erected during the Second World War, was on its last legs. The old shack was like a sweatbox in the summer and felt like an iced-up fridge during winter. Its dilapidated frame and neglected interior had, over the years, been patched up and nailed back together so many times that there was little left of its original 1940s construct, and like the two caretakers who used it, it was out of sight and out of mind. This suited both the school governors and Bristol City Council, neither of which were eager to stick their hands in their pockets to cough up for a new build.

Friday was the head caretaker's day off. For eight or more hours, I got to be my own boss, and I relished every second of it. For the rest of the working week, my supervisor was Reg Everett. Everett was a 62-year-old waste of space, who spent more time with his mouth glued to his tea mug and chain-smoking roll-ups than he did doing any actual work. Reg was good at handing out orders, and he made sure that I was around to carry out every one that he barked out. Scrawny, lying and afraid of his own footsteps, I didn't trust the man as far as I could throw him.

16

Knowing I was on my own today lifted my spirits. On Fridays, I didn't clock-watch. Never had to worry about ole man Everett and his indolence or the next dirty job he was about to throw my way. For one day a week, I got to put my head down and do things how it suited me.

I hung my jacket on a hook on the back of the door, grabbed a broom and made my way into school and along the echoing tiled corridors to reception to clock in. The time recorder was on the wall next to the staff room and the headmaster's office. As I was putting my card back into the metal rack next to the machine, I heard the click-click of high heels walking towards me. I turned to face the school's sombre receptionist, Shirley Kemp. She was a tall young woman with yellowish eyes and thick, slack lips, which gave her the unusual appearance of looking as though she was about to burst into tears at any moment.

I leaned against my broom and smiled at her. "Morning, Miss Kemp. How's things?"

Shirley returned a brief, nervous smile. "Good morning, Mr Ellington. I'm fine thank you."

"Yeah? Well, if you don't mind me saying, you don't look it."

Shirley gave the briefest of glances behind her, then turned her watery eyes back to me and directed her thumb over her shoulder in a single sharp stab towards the staff room. "She wants you."

"Who?" I looked down the hallway. "You talkin' 'bout Amos?"

Shirley nodded.

I blew air into my cheeks, exhaling slowly. The deputy headmistress was the source of all discord and wasted energy. Haughty and disdainful, Amos hated me because I wouldn't bow down to her position. "What now?"

Shirley shrugged. "I was just told to come and find you."

I rested my broom against the wall and stuck my hands in my pockets. I looked at Shirley and winked. "Right, let's go see what the ole witch wants."

Sarah Amos had been deputy headmistress at the school for more years than she or anyone else working in the place cared to admit. Now part of the furniture, she had become the bane of my working life, considering herself — rather than the council — to be my personal employer. Most of the time, the old harpy stayed out of the way and outta my face, stuck firmly in her lair — an office laid with thick maroon carpets and a huge desk constructed from African ivory wood, with teak shelving installed from ceiling to floor. But every now and then she emerged to make my life a misery.

Today was gonna be one of those days.

When I arrived outside her office, the door was already open. I gave a sharp knock on one of the polished oak panels.

"Come in, Mr Ellington."

I did as I was told, deliberately leaving the door open. She kept her head down, her glasses perched on the end of her pinched nose as she read the contents of a manila folder. She held up her hand and waggled her fingers at me. I stood across from her desk with my arms folded behind my back. For a brief moment, it felt like I was back on the force.

"Deputy," I said.

Amos pointed a finger straight out in front of her. "Door, Mr Ellington."

I looked back at the open door for a moment then shut it. The deputy head was still concentrating on the contents of the file when I returned to the spot I'd been standing in a few moments before. When she finally looked up, her eyes focused on the flock wallpaper behind me rather than on my face, though after a few seconds, she corrected her line of vision and gave me the evil eye. "A rather delicate matter, Mr Ellington."

I cleared a frog from my throat. "Say what?"

Amos shook her head in disdain at my lack of diligence. She repeated herself, just to hammer home the point. "As I said, a rather delicate matter. Yesterday evening, I had a rather disturbing conversation with your superior, Mr Everett."

I felt my heart sink. "Yeah, 'bout what?"

Amos's eyes actually sparkled with anticipation. "Mr Everett came to report that he'd found a rather unusual discrepancy in the caretakers' stockroom."

"Discrepancy? What kinda discrepancy?"

"Bleach, Mr Ellington. Three bottles of Purex bleach seem to have vanished into thin air."

I shrugged, never once taking my eyes off hers. "What's that gotta do with me?"

Amos leaned forward in her seat, eyeing me suspiciously. I was used to it. Most white people I came into contact with liked to keep their eyes peeled on black people, and vice versa. We lie to each other so much that often the only hope is to see some look or gesture that betrays the truth. Amos's arrogant motioning of her fat head towards me before speaking again told me everything I needed to know.

"That's exactly what I'm trying to ascertain this morning, Mr Ellington: if it *does* have anything to do with you."

I held my palms out in front of me then rolled them over so that Amos could get a good look at the back of my hands. "Well, I ain't been taking the stuff home to wash in it, if that's what you're getting at?"

"That's not a very helpful attitude, is it?"

"Maybe not, but it's the truth."

The blood was rising under Amos's pale skin. "Be that as it may, Mr Ellington, I have a duty to follow up such matters, and to deal with them accordingly."

"Deal with 'em any way you like. I'm telling you I ain't took a brass farthing outta this place that didn't belong to me. Only thing I leave here with at night is my damn coat!"

Amos didn't like my bolshie turn of phrase one bit. "I don't think there's any need for insolence or that kind of language, do you?"

A hammering in my ears spurred on my blossoming anger. "Maybe you're right, Miss Amos, but you ain't the one being called a thief."

Amos bit back at me. "I have done no such thing."

"No? Then why the hell you dragged me down here to interrogate me then?"

20

Amos lifted her face to mine, her eyes blazing. "This is hardly an interrogation, Mr Ellington."

"Well, it damn well feels like it. Why don't you call the police? That's what I'd do. When I find out 'bout some crime, I call the police. I don't have anything to hide."

I looked down at the ground and took a breath. I hadn't stolen any bleach, but bluff was all I had left to defend myself. I heard Amos sniff. Maybe she didn't like the smell of my aftershave. Maybe she thought my patter stank. Maybe the bloodhound in her was trying to smoke out the missing bleach.

I looked back up to find Amos nervously leafing through sheets of paper in the manila file. She returned another one of her hard stares. "I hardly think it's a matter for the police."

"Why not? Looks to me like you're accusing me of thieving bottles of your bleach."

Amos folded her arms on her desk blotter. "The city council's bleach, Mr Ellington."

"I don't care who the hell's damn bleach it is, I ain't took it!"

Amos continued to eyeball me. I watched her try to clear her throat. She pinched under her chin with her thumb and forefinger before addressing me again. "Very well. I'll speak to Mr Everett again on Monday morning. See if we can get to the bottom of this unfortunate conundrum."

I nodded in agreement. "Sounds good."

I turned to leave.

"This isn't over," Amos called back after me.

"Too damn right it ain't!"

The sound of me slamming her office door behind me was loud enough to wake the dead.

My day went on at a natural pace. No fire alarms. No plumbing or electrical disasters. No more accusations of theft. It was actually a good day, because after my falling-out with the deputy first thing, she stayed locked away in her hide. She wasn't around looking into everybody's business like she normally did, whether it was teachers or the custodial staff. She often walked into classrooms to make surprise evaluations. That might have been a good idea, but Amos was rude and rough. She loved Parson Street School more than anything, but not a soul there cared for her.

I went about my work, cleaning out the bins in the playground, fitting some shelves in the stockroom at the back of the assembly hall and directing two fellas from an extermination company who had come in to lay bait in the gutters of one of the older buildings to get rid of an infestation of pigeons.

At just after three thirty, a short time after all the children and most of the staff had left for the day, I was outside sweeping leaves and dirt off the doormats at the school's main entrance. I had my head down, with little over an hour of my work day left to play out. I was tired, hungry and looking forward to the weekend.

I never heard the young black woman come through the school gates at the top of the path, heard her footsteps or noticed that she was standing right behind me. The first thing I knew of her presence was the gentle cough she gave to get my attention. I turned and smiled when I saw her pretty face. She could have been no more than eighteen years of age, slim built with deep brown eyes. She was wearing a coral-coloured coat drawn tight around her shoulders, her arms folded across her chest. I watched as she suddenly gave a shiver, her sandaled feet shuffling on the ground in discomfort. I could tell that she'd been crying.

"Can I help you?"

The young girl swallowed hard, embarrassment etched all over her face. She lowered her chin and looked down at the floor when she spoke. Her accent was pure Jamaican.

"Ah was wonderin' if there was a bathroom ah could use, please, mistah?"

I looked inside the school, then back at the girl and smiled again. "Sure, no problem."

I took hold of the big brass handle, swung the door open and held out my hand. "I'll show you where they are."

I walked her the short distance down the main corridor, stopping a foot away from the crimson-painted door of the girls' toilet. "Here you go. I'll be close by to show you back out. Okay?"

The girl kept her chin tucked in low, her red-rimmed eyes unable to connect with mine. She nodded then hurried inside, thanking me as the door closed quickly behind her. While I waited, I busied myself with my broom along the corridor outside. I heard the toilet flush and then running water before the girl stepped out and made her way over to me.

"Thank you."

I stopped sweeping and rested my hand on top of the broom. "That's no problem. No problem at all."

The girl's face brightened a little. She lifted her chin out of her chest to look at me.

"Hard day, eh?"

The girl nodded. When she spoke, her voice crackled uneasily. "Been trying to find myself a job, mistah."

"An' no fool wanna give you one, right?"

Another nod. "Dat's 'bout tha sum of it, yeah."

I looked across at the bathroom door. "None of 'em let you use their toilet either?"

The girl looked back down at the ground, her eyes filming. I began to hold out my arm but was interrupted by a familiar and unwelcome voice.

"What's going on here, Mr Ellington?"

I turned to face Amos. I lifted my palm to introduce the girl. "This young lady here needed to make use of our bathroom facilities, deputy."

"Did she now?" Amos gave the girl a cursory, bitter glance.

I nodded again. "Yeah, she did."

"And you thought it'd be appropriate that this woman make use of our girls' lavatory, did you?"

"I thought it'd be more *appropriate* than her using the fellas'." I looked across at the young woman and winked. Her face broke into the briefest of smiles.

Amos didn't like me winking nor the momentary beam on the girl's face. "Don't be so facetious."

"I ain't being nothing o' the sort, Miss Amos. I'm just doing what I thought was right an' proper."

24

"Right and proper has nothing to do with it. It wasn't your decision to make."

"No? What was I supposed to do, let a young lady take a leak outside in the gutter?"

I watched Amos grimace in disgust. "This happens to be a school, not a public convenience!"

"Yeah, I understand that —"

"I don't think you do, Mr Ellington. We can't have any old Tom, Dick or Harry wandering on to the premises. You, of all people, should know that."

It was that *all people* remark that got me really riled up.

"You gotta problem with this here young woman taking a leak?" Amos's cheek twitched again when I said the word *leak*. I promised myself that I'd use it in her company more often if it caused such a disturbing reaction.

Reigning in my temper, I turned to the girl. "You get yourself off now, child. There ain't no problem here." I took a few steps forward and began to usher her down the corridor with my hand at her back.

She gave me a nervous smile. "Thank you, mistah."

Amos didn't like my belligerence nor my decision to escort the girl off the premises. She tried to block our path, her arm outstretched, palm stuck out in front. I put my back to her, pushed past her arm and guided my charge deftly towards the main doors, my hand cupped under her elbow to keep her moving.

Amos hollered after me, "Stop right there."

I ignored her and carried on, but I heard the old hag's footsteps coming up behind me, her pace quickening. I took hold of the handle and hurried the girl outside, nodding towards the street. "Go."

She hesitated for a moment, so I took a step forward, forcing her to move back up the path. "You don't wanna see what's gonna happen when that old harpy gets to this gate."

The girl's smile grew large. Lord, was she pretty. I winked again. "Go!"

I turned and walked inside, my back to the door. Amos came to a blustering standstill just inches away from me then pointed her finger in my face.

"What the hell do you think you're doing?" Her voice sounded like it was coming up from a well. Dangerous and wild.

My jaw set hard, my hands restless. "Escorting the young lady off the premises."

Deputy Amos's lip curled at my disrespectful tone. "That was also not your decision to make."

I felt my fingers curl up into a fist. "Mebbe not, lady, but I made it all the same."

Amos was about to bawl me out again, but I cut her off before another word could come out of her mean little mouth.

"I just gone an' made anutha decision. You're gonna be needin' to pin back those big ears o' yours. Make sure you get every word I'm 'bout to say."

Her face bloated with red-faced anger. "How dare you!"

"Come Monday morning, you need to start lookin' to gettin' yourself a new assistant caretaker."

"I beg your pardon?"

26

I began to walk back down the corridor, back towards the prefab to collect my coat. "You heard me, woman. I'm through. You can stick your job where the sun don't shine."

I turned back to face Amos. She glared at me in disgust, her body trembling with anger, her mouth wide, unable to find further words to reprimand or rebuke. I called back at her. "An' when you find those three bottles o' bleach, you can stick them up there too!"

Amos looked at me in pure disgust. She took a step backwards, about to carry on walking. I watched as she rubbed her hand over her mouth and mumbled something. Despite her low tone, I heard the two disgusting words she called me.

I should have walked back down the corridor and smacked her across the face. I should have dragged her in the girls' john and washed her mouth out with soap. I should have thrown her sorry bigoted ass out into the street . . . I should have done it all, but I didn't.

CHAPTER
THREE

I spent the weekend keeping Chloe occupied, doing chores around the house and brooding about walking out of a job I could well have done without losing. I had a little money saved up in a building-society account, enough to feed the two of us, pay the bills and keep the wolf from the door for the next couple of months, but I was hardly Aristotle Onassis, and I needed to get myself back into paid work.

Sundays for Chloe and me was all about being with family. After Uncle Gabe and Aunt Pearl had been to church, the two of us would walk the short distance to their home on Banner Road to spend the rest of the day together. While Pearl prepared dinner with Chloe, Gabe and I would walk into town to the Western Star Domino Club and spend a couple of hours playing the *bones* and chewing the fat. Like cricket, West Indian dominoes was a Caribbean national sport. Playing bones had been the connecting tissue to centuries of history, a thread linking slave plantations to black communities all over the world. When Gabe told Pearl that he was "goin' down tha boneyard" it meant he wanted to get outta the house, get a couple a pints of

Dragon stout in his belly and play a game or two of dominoes with other men.

Gabe remained tight-lipped as we walked. I detected a greater air of discontent simmering just below his usual crotchety manner. I'd come clean about what had happened at work with Deputy Amos and the girl on Friday afternoon when I'd picked Chloe up and, although I knew by the look on his face that he was unhappy I'd chucked a perfectly good job away, the old man had kept his council. Gabe was saving his disapproval and rebuke until we were alone.

Benton Barrow, the Star's formidable doorman, was propped up against the wall on his usual high-backed wooden stool outside the main entrance with a cigarette hanging from his lips. Benton had been perched on the same rickety old pew guarding the gambling club's door since the early 1960s. Perhaps ten years my senior, Barrow was an imposing figure, wide and burly with close-cropped hair, greying at the sides. When he saw Gabe and me walk across the street towards him, his face lit up with a beaming smile that belied the Kittitian's often severe demeanour and his reputation for handing out a beating to anyone foolish enough to cross him.

Benton pulled a hefty final drag on his smoke, threw the butt into the gutter and opened out a huge palm in front of him before opening the door. He smiled again, revealing crooked, wide-spaced teeth.

"How you doin', gentlemen?"

Gabe simply nodded at the bouncer and walked inside. Barrow shrugged his powerful shoulders, ignoring my uncle's impatience and grouchy mood. I followed after Gabe, shaking Benton's hand.

"I'm good, Benton. You?"

Barrow held on to my hand, squeezing the blood out of it. He nodded at me a half-dozen times before letting go. "Me aright, brutha. Ain't seen you 'round much, JT. Where you bin hidin'?"

"Just workin'. Workin' all the hours God sends. You know how it is." I heard Gabe suck air through his teeth.

The bouncer stuffed his hand into his jacket pocket, pulled out another cigarette, stuck it between his lips and lit it, then stabbed a finger at my chest. "All that damn wuk gonna send you ta an early grave, JT."

"Ain't that the truth." I watched as Benton blew a thick plume of smoke into the air then began to cough and splutter, then followed Gabe down the hallway that led into the club's inner sanctum. I could still hear Benton hacking as the club's two doors slowly closed behind me.

Inside the Star's main hall, the haze of yet more cigarette smoke dimmed the room. Black men, all of them smoking, sat in various positions of ease around the room. Desmond Dekker's "You Can Get It If You Really Want" was playing on the jukebox. There was a sour smell under the smoky odour. The stink of stale beer coming off the men's breath. I went over to the bar and ordered two pints while Gabe found us a table at the back of the club, away from the dance floor, where most of the regulars were already beginning to huddle over their bones. Playing dominoes in the Western Star was never a quiet pastime, and Sunday lunchtimes were no different to any other day of the week. The clicking, the banging, the shouting, the laughing was all, at times, deafening.

To anyone who'd never witnessed it, the physical enthusiasm of Caribbean dominoes would seem overwhelming, like a football pitch invasion at a chess match. West Indians have two methods of laying a domino down: either flicking it in disgust, or raising it high over their heads and smashing it down on the table like one of those karate fellas who snap planks of wood. The better the domino, the heavier the wallop.

I carried the two glass jugs of stout over to where Gabe was sitting. One of the few ways I knew how to make a foul-tempered old fella happy was to feed him some ale and let him win a few games of dominoes. Neither of those wellworn strategies were going to work for me today though. I sat down across from my uncle, took a sip of beer and watched as he tipped the bones out and spread them in all directions across the table. He sat back in his seat, not bothering to touch his drink. I could feel his cold, pale eyes giving me a withering look before he finally spoke.

"You bin lickin' you mout' too much again, boy."

I lowered my head, shook it and took another slow swig of ale. When I looked back up, Gabe's bearing was still riled and ornery, his eyeballing all the more intense.

"What the hell was I supposed to do, Gabe?"

31

"Fo' a start? You could try tinkin' wid dat foolish head o' yours, 'stead o' unleashing dat nasty temper you got."

"Uncle Gabe, the woman I told you about, Amos — she was a real nasty piece o' work."

"Ain't the first time you met one o' those."

"Mebbe so, but this was different," I answered gruffly.

"Why, cause some rasclat woman vex you? Med sum foolish mutterin's 'bout tha colour o' you skin. You heard it all befo'. Dem kinda folk a' two a penny round 'ere."

"All the more reason to stand up against 'em!"

"All tha more reason ta ignore 'em, if it means you losing a job."

"It was the kinda work I could live without."

Gabe sat forward and hunched over the table. "You gonna live widout the money too?"

I sank almost half my pint in a couple of swift gulps. "I'll find something soon enough."

"Well, you need to. Cause it ain't jus' you dat needs feedin' an' clothin'. You got tha pickney to be tinkin' 'bout too, Joseph."

"Don't you think I know that?"

Gabe shook his head grimly at me. "It ain't what you know I'm worried 'bout. Wha' gnaws at ma guts is whether you can git rid o' some o' dat dotish bad temper befo' you do sum'ting you gonna end up regrettin' fo' the rest o' your life."

"I saw red Friday afternoon for the right reasons, Gabe. I did what I thought was right. The days of me looking for trouble are long gone. You know that, of all people?"

"I don't claim ta know much 'bout anyt'ing. What I do know, Joseph, is you was born ta trouble. Trouble bin you bidness long as I can rememba. Why's trouble gonna stop botherin' you now?"

I didn't have an answer for such an accurate observation. Sometimes the truth hits hardest when it's told to you by those that love you the most. As I finished my drink, I watched the anger in my uncle subside. Gabe drew a handful of dominoes across the table, lining them up on their sides in front of him. He looked up and smiled at me, his eyes glazing with a watery sheen. It was a desperate, sad look, one that sank its pain deep into my insides. Then Gabe took a sip of his ale and leaned towards me in a confidential manner, his hand resting on the back of one of my own.

"It's bad enough Victor causes Pearl an' me such grief widout tha two o' us havin' ta be frettin' 'bout you as well." Gabe sniffed and picked up a domino. He looked at it briefly then slammed it down on the table in front of him. I reached across and gathered up my own pieces, not saying another word. When I looked across at Gabe, he was wiping his cheek with the back of his hand.

It was the first time in over four years I'd heard my uncle utter his son's name.

CHAPTER
FOUR

I was thinking about one kind of trouble when another came knocking at my door early on Monday morning. It was just after nine; I'd got back from taking Chloe to school and was sitting at the kitchen table when the hammering started. It was the kind of persistent drumming that could only belong to the clenched fist of either a debt collector or a policeman. Though I didn't owe a soul a penny, nor had I broken any law, I reluctantly opened up my door knowing that whoever was on the other side of it wouldn't be delivering me any glad tidings.

"Good morning, Joseph."

A man's face stared back at me. It was a face from the past — an unwelcome reminder of darker times. I held on tight to the edge of the door frame, my heart pounding in my chest.

"What you wantin', Detective Inspector Fletcher?"

"It's Superintendent these days, Joseph." Fletcher, his smile loose and amiable, held out a hand. I looked at it but didn't reach out to take it. Not many policemen had offered to shake hands with me. Outstretched hands of the law held wooden truncheons, handcuffs and warrants, but rarely a welcome and never an offer of equality.

"I need to have a word, old son." The policeman closed his hand then opened it to rub his fingertips together. His smile held little friendliness and that was fine by me. I didn't need a friendly white copper in my life right now. I swung the door open, let the man in and we walked back down to the kitchen.

Fletcher was a good example of why most black folk give the police a wide berth. He was a snidey old goat. A man so dedicated to sniffing out the bad in humanity that he could find a dodgy angle at a Monday-night prayer meeting. Fletcher had it on good authority that everybody in the world was crooked, and the more villains he could sling in a cell, the better he'd feel. He was a big, red-faced Bristolian and I hated him. Tighter with kind words than a Parisian waiter with a free bread roll and more devious than Old Nick, the superintendent had, years before, made it his life's mission to get in my face any time he could. But I'd been off his radar for some time, and his visit today was long overdue. I went to the sink, poured myself a glass of water then rested my back against the draining board.

Fletcher was still smiling at me and that made me feel even more ill at ease. He wore a dark grey flannel suit and a white shirt that had yellowed from too many launderings, his regimental tie tied tight at the collar in a Windsor knot. The old copper was getting a good look at the place before his gaze focused on me, his smile not altering in the least.

"Been a while."

"Not long enough."

Fletcher frowned and lost the smile. "Now, now, old son, no need to be like that."

"There ain't? Well excuse me if I ain't jumpin' fo' joy!"

There was the slightest hint of threat in his voice. "Just trying to be genial, that's all."

"Look, man, whatever it is you gotta say, spit it out, cause I ain't got all day."

"Really? From what I hear, you've recently found yourself between jobs. Got plenty of time on your hands, I'd say." Fletcher sniffed the air, his face flushing with an anger he was barely able to keep at bay. "I hear you've been caught with your fingers in the till?"

The penny dropped. "This about Parson Street?"

Fletcher nodded; a gesture followed by a few moments of uncomfortable silence. "I'm afraid it is. On Saturday morning one of my detective constables received a complaint from a Mrs Sarah Amos. Her name ring any bells?"

"Oh, they ringin' alright."

"I thought as much. Mrs Amos informed this constable that she wished to report a matter of theft."

"I bet she did."

"Theft of council property."

"Bleach by any chance?"

"Got it in one, Joseph. Bleach that she accuses you of stealing."

"The woman's deranged."

36

"Maybe so. But she is also a well-respected teacher of many years, a deputy headmistress and the daughter of a retired local MP."

"Yeah, she may be all of that — don't mean she ain't a liar too."

"Be that as it may, a complaint has been made and I'm duty-bound to follow up such allegations."

"You can follow up what you want, I din't steal no damn bleach."

Fletcher nodded. "I don't think you had anything to do with it, Joseph. But I can haul you down to the station and question you about the matter for the rest of the day, or . . ."

"Or what?"

"Or I can wash away this ridiculous accusation very quickly."

I gave him a blank stare. "Oh, I bet you can."

"Let me put it another way. I have a problem that needs solving outside of the public eye. Help me and I help you."

"What kinda problem?"

"One that requires a detective."

I laughed. "Try police HQ. Get one o' your minions to do your donkey work."

"It's not as simple as that. I need a man who has his finger on the pulse with the local ethnics. A man with policing experience — somebody who's used to poking his black nose into other folks' business. A man like you."

"Excuse me, Superintendent, but you must be mistaking me for some other Joseph Ellington. I'm outta the detective game; have been a long time now."

"No, I have the right fella. Once a copper, always a copper, right, Joseph?"

"Not me."

Fletcher began to laugh. "Okay, let's say you used to do favours for folk. The Somerset and Bath Constabulary needs your assistance, and if you know what's good for you, you'll cooperate." The superintendent reached inside his jacket pocket and took out a small black notebook then pulled a chair out from the kitchen table.

"Think of it as doing me a favour. Take a seat, Joseph."

I put my glass on the draining board and did as I was told. Fletcher rested his palms on the table and asked, "What'd you know about Indians?"

I shrugged. "You mean Sitting Bull, Geronimo?"

Fletcher shook his head. "No, I'm thinking more along the lines of the Pakistanis and the like. Folk that have settled over here from the colonies."

"Don't know a thing 'bout 'em."

Fletcher found his smile again. "Shame ... No matter. You see I'd like you to pay a visit to a gentleman by the name of Suresh — Mani Suresh." Fletcher opened up his pocketbook, tore out a page, slid it across the table towards me and pointed at it. "He's a shopkeeper over at Cotham. You can find him at that address."

"And what do I do when I get to this fella's place?"

"Good question. Mr Suresh has a son, Nikhil. Twenty-two years old, works in his old man's corner shop. Nikhil went missing ten days ago. Three days before he was supposed to get hitched."

"Hitched?"

"Married, old son. Suresh and his family had a big arranged marriage set up for their lad."

"Perhaps the son didn't like the idea of getting *hitched*."

"Maybe he didn't. But the fact is, the lad's gone and pissed off somewhere." Fletcher folded his arms across his chest. A thin line of sweat was forming on his brow. "Now, I've got Mr Suresh making daily visits to my station, pestering my lads to go out looking for him. He's telling me I should be dredging the bloody canals and putting posters up around town. He's being a right pain in the arse. My constable has already taken a missing person's report to placate him, but he ain't having none of it. I've had the *i*s dotted and the *t*s crossed on his case, but Suresh is a persistent little bastard, if nothing else." Fletcher gave a heavy sigh. "I haven't got the time or the manpower to go looking for a boy that didn't fancy taking a trip down the aisle, and that's where you come in."

"Me?"

"Yes, you. I told Mr Suresh that I knew a fella who might be able to help him."

"Help him how?"

"Well, I'd like you to go and look for his lad. See what you can turn up."

"Say what?"

The policeman showed me his red gums and gritted his teeth. "You heard me. I want you to get off your black arse and go wear out a bit of your shoe leather looking for this missing Indian!"

Fletcher took a passport photograph out of his notebook and slammed it on to the table next to the piece of paper with the address on it. "This is Nikhil."

I picked up the square black-and-white photo and looked at it. Fletcher appeared a little more subdued. He rested his hand on my shoulder and bent his face down towards my ear. "I know that in the past you've gone after folk that have taken off, people that have gone missing."

I nodded. "Yeah, but that was a long time ago, and this is different."

Fletcher moved away, raised himself back up to his full height and slammed the table top again. "No, it ain't! It's just the bleedin' same, only this bloke happens to live in a different part of town than the rest of your kind do."

I snapped my head round to face him. "Whaddya mean, *my kind*?"

Fletcher ignored my outburst and bulldozered on. "Look, you know the streets, the coloureds who live in these parts, you know where all these John-Johns knock about for Christ's sakes. Indians or blacks, it's all the bloody same to me. You have contacts that my boys can't get to. These fellas, they'll speak to one of their own."

"Their own! You gotta be kiddin'?" I lifted my hand to my face and turned my cheek towards Fletcher. "I know it's bin a while but I ain't become Pakistani since

40

you last hauled me in. I ain't their own. I'm Barbadian, in case you forgot."

"I know what the hell you are, Ellington. You're a bolshie bastard who thinks that just because he once wore the Queen's uniform that he can stick two fingers up to the likes of me. Well, old son, as far as I'm concerned, you're just another dark-skinned bugger with a chip on his shoulder. Well, I'm here to knock that chip off on to the ground where it belongs. Last time I saw you, you were breaking bread with every crook and ponce in the city. You did favours for 'em all. Now you're gonna do this favour for me. Either that or you'll be cooling off in a cell within the next half hour. You hearing me?"

I kept my mouth shut and nodded. Nothing bothered a serving officer like Fletcher more than having to deal with an ex-cop like me, especially one who's had a medal pinned on his chest and frequents with the city's unwashed on a daily basis. I knew the superintendent had me over a barrel. For now, I'd have to go along with his demands.

Fletcher folded his beefy arms again. "Right, so we understand each other, do we?"

I nodded again, staring at the floor.

"Good." Fletcher pointed at the paper in front of me. "Start by visiting the old man. Get some background on this lad, ask the locals a few questions and see if you can dig something up. Look like you're doing something useful and take the fee."

I looked up to see Fletcher smiling at me again. "Fee?"

"Ten quid a day, plus your expenses." Fletcher winked then turned and began to walk out. "Don't say I don't have your welfare at heart, Joseph."

I followed Fletcher back down the hall to the front door. He opened it up, walked out and stood on the top step, looking out into the street for a moment, then turned to give me the once-over, sticking his blustering face into mine again. "Bloody tidy yourself up, will you?"

He strode out into the sunshine before turning to give me another of his smirks. "You need to start looking like a detective again, old son."

The bastard went down the path without so much as a farewell wave.

CHAPTER
FIVE

When the best your day offers you is little more than a
kick in the teeth and the promise of a bucketful of
misery at the end of it, there's not much more a man
can do than wade in and take whatever's thrown at him
on the chin. I'd just been thrown a job I'd not gone
looking for nor had any appetite to undertake, and the
fact that a high-ranking police officer had proffered me
such gainful employment set my teeth on edge.
Superintendent Fletcher wouldn't have crossed the
road to piss on me if I was on fire. Him turning up
outside my gate door like the tooth fairy with some
half-baked missing-person story and the promise of
easy money stank like week-old garbage, but the threat
of a day or maybe longer stuck in some cold cell at
Fletcher's behest didn't fill me with joy.

Telling the copper to stick his job would have been
the smartest move, but heeding my own wisdom had
never brought me a great deal of luck in the past — or
lined my pocket for that matter. I picked the passport
photo up from the kitchen table and looked at the
grainy black-and-white image of Nikhil Suresh and
wondered what kinda trouble, if any, this stranger had
landed himself in, and what the hell any of it had to do

with me. Unable to give the nagging voice in my head the answers it sought, I did what I'd always done when confronted with hard questions I had no way of answering. I shrugged 'em off and soldiered on.

I decided to take the superintendent's thirty pieces of silver, and his advice to tidy myself up.

I was out of my house by eleven. I'd bathed, trimmed my nails and was wearing my best wool suit in two shades of grey, with a white cotton shirt and kipper tie, and my black brogues were spit-shine polished. Only thing I needed was a decent shave, and I knew just the place to go get one.

Twenty-Two Moon Street on the furthest edges of St Pauls was the home of the Déjà Vu barbershop and hairdressing salon. The red-brick, three-storey building sat at the end of a row of terraced houses and was just a stone's throw from proprietor Loretta Harris's own home on Brunswick Street. Loretta was the widow of one of my closest friends, Carnell. Straight-talking and with a fiery disposition to match, Loretta had taken on the barbershop after the previous owner had got himself deep into a gambling debt with my cousin, Victor. Vic, never one to waste an opportunity to benefit from the downfall of his fellow man, quickly snatched the place up, no questions asked, to expand his ever-increasing property collection, which in turn would expand his flourishing criminal empire. He put Loretta in as manger and the legitimate front of the business while his various and many crooked activities went on behind the scenes.

44

Most folk came through the front door without knowing a damn thing. Ladies queuing for their weekly afro tint and the fellas for a quick trim were never the wiser. Meanwhile, on the other side of the joint, the back door was wide open bringing in caseloads of knocked-off booze, stolen cigarettes and Cuban cigars, fancy French perfume and wooden pallets with short hessian sacks stacked a half-dozen high on them, the contents of which only Vic knew.

I liked getting a regular shave at Déjà Vu because it was old-fashioned. Loretta used real barbers' chairs and straight razors sharpened on leather strops attached to each station. There was always good company and often a card game going on in the corner. Women nagged about their idle husbands or the kids, while fellas read their newspapers, discussed the cricket or a horse race and moaned about the rising price of a pint. Hot towels were wrapped around your face and you could close your eyes and relax for a few precious moments. I peered through the glass panel in the door to make sure my friend was there, then headed on in.

Inside, the sweet cologne-smelling room was crammed to the rafters with customers. The Four Tops' "It's All in the Game" blared out from a transistor radio perched on the edge of the counter next to the till. Two female hairdressers and one male barber were lined in a row, each with a customer sat before them. Half a dozen men waited along the far wall, sitting in chairs made of red leather with arms and legs of dark wood.

Loretta rose out of a lead barber's chair and put her hands on her hips. "Well, look what tha fuckin' cat dragged in." She wore a multicoloured smock over a purple crushed velvet jumpsuit, her tight-curled hair raised, bunched up and tied high on her head. She looked me up and down suspiciously and grinned. "What tha hell you dressed like a fuckin' pimp fo'?"

"Job interview," I lied.

"A job! You gotta be kiddin' me. With all that nasty stubble you got goin' on? What damn fool gonna take you on lookin' like you just walked offa skid row?" Loretta laughed then pointed a finger down at the seat she'd just vacated. "Git over 'ere and sit your sorry ass down in dis chair."

I did as my friend ordered. Loretta unfolded a white apron and spread it over me then ran her fingers playfully through my short-cropped, greying hair.

"You want me ta' put you a little colour on dis mop o' yours, Joseph?"

"Colour?"

"Yeah, ta hide some o' this ole-man shit you got goin' on up here. You startin' ta look like Uncle Remus." The barbershop suddenly erupted with laughter. Loretta winked at me.

"Git the hell outta it, woman. Jus' gimme my damn shave!"

Loretta picked up a cut-throat razor from out of a pot and began to sharpen it on the strop next to where I sat.

"I was next!"

The objecting voice belonged to a big-set black fella walking towards me. He had dark brown skin and was dressed in a dark blue Bristol bus-company uniform. He stood over me, close enough for me to get a good whiff of the stink coming off his massive hide; a mixture of three-day-old sweat and stale tobacco smoke. Loretta sniffed the air, ignoring the irate customer and began tying the apron at the back of my neck.

The bus driver took a step closer, his fat gut hanging over the buckle of his trouser belt. "Did you hear me? I said I was next!"

I felt Loretta place her hand on top of the headrest at the back of my chair. When she spoke, there was ice in her voice. "You want a haircut or a shave, you better sit down, brutha."

"Sit down! Shit, I bin sittin' back there fo' the better part o' half an hour," he complained.

In the mirror I saw one of Loretta's work colleagues come forward to nervously chip in. "Sir, did you make an appointment?"

The man snapped his head round to bite back at the young hairdresser. Loretta, having none of it, quickly stepped in to protect her stylist neighbour.

"Dat's okay, baby, dis man here, he don't need no appointment, do you?"

The bus driver turned back to face Loretta, a smile creeping across his face. He looked down at me, clearly impatient for me to climb out of the chair. Loretta put her hand on my shoulder and stuck a steady finger out towards the man's face.

"Befo' you start itching to get you fat ass in dis seat, you best know I got a straight razor in ma hand an' one hell of a bad fuckin' temper."

The bus driver's face twitched and Loretta walked round the chair to go toe to toe with the fella. I could see the man was afraid, but at that moment he was stupid enough not to want to back down.

"I'm . . . I'm jus' sayin' I bin waitin' all this time and this chump, he waltzes on in and you sit him down like he the Duke of Edinburgh!"

"Who tha hell you callin' a chump? Joseph, you want me to take dis sheet off or you gonna beat tha shit outta him with it on?"

Loretta's outburst made it easier on the fella. Two against one meant that he could get the hell out without a mask of shame hanging over him. Loretta raised the cut-throat at her side and took a step forward. The big man began to back up, tripping over his feet to get out of the way of the oncoming blade.

"Git your fat butt outta my place fo' I tear you a new ass'ole!"

I watched straight-faced as the man spun on his heels then ran across the salon, falling through the door and tumbling in a heap into the gutter. Loretta followed, cursing him from a pig to a dog. The bus driver hobbled away down the street, his limbs and extremities still intact, his uniform dusty and his dignity in tatters.

Loretta had me clean-shaven and feeling good in no time. She'd been unusually quiet as she'd worked, doing nothing more than giving me the occasional

48

quizzical look as she lathered shaving cream on my face and ran the cut-throat across my stubbled jowls. After the hot towel around my face had cooled, she anointed the skin around my cheeks and jaw with shave talc and splashed on some Tabac aftershave.

I looked up at her and smiled. "I need to ask you a favour?"

Loretta undid the apron tie at the back of my neck, spun the barber's chair towards the wall and pointed to the door that led out back. "Git your ass through there, Joseph."

I did as I was told and walked into the staff tearoom. Loretta pushed by me and kept on going along the hallway, finally coming to a halt outside another door marked *storeroom*. She kicked at the bottom rail, flicked on the light switch and stabbed her thumb in the direction of the salon's private annexe. Inside the room was an Aladdin's cave of contraband and hooky goods. Loretta leaned back against a row of grey metal shelves laden down with boxes of Johnny Walker Black Label, then gestured her head towards me in a curt and accusing manner. "So, what you playin' at?"

"Playing at?"

Loretta put her hands on her hips, her bottom lip about to curl itself into a savage pout. "Don't gimme any o' your horseshit, Joseph. You come in here dressed up to tha nines. I know you got sum'ting shifty goin' down."

"Like I said, job interview."

"Job interview, my ass. You got wuk at tha school!"

"I lost it."

"You job? How, man?"

"It's a long story."

Loretta looked at me blankly. "Well, let's hear it, then."

I gave a heavy sigh. "In short, some woman called me a black bastard under her breath. I told her to stick her job."

"You bin tryin' to put you doggy in her poky?"

"Whaddya take me for? She's the school's deputy head. She accused me o' stealin'."

I heard a sharp intake of air cut between Loretta's teeth. "You too damn high-minded ta steal — any fool know dat. Mebbe not so righteous not ta lie to you friend though?" Loretta looked me up and down, her hard gaze burning into me. "So, the trute. Tell me, what kinda job you goin' fo', needs you to be dressed up like a dog's dinner?"

"One I already got."

"Doin' what?"

"I been asked to do a little sly work for the po'lice."

"Fo' tha Babylon! You outta you tiny mind, Joseph?"

I shook my head. "I need the cash, Loretta."

"I give you money. You don't tek from tha Babylon."

"The po'lice ain't giving me the cash."

"Then wha' fool is?"

"A detective called Fletcher has put me on to some fella who's gonna pay me to look for his missing boy."

"Wha' fella?"

"Some Indian shopkeeper over at Cotham."

Loretta looked down at the ground, shaking her head. She kicked at the lino with her shoe before setting

50

her crushing stare back on me. "You must be dotish, man! Didn't God give you a brain, enuff ta tell you bein' used as a lackey fo' tha Babylon?"

"It ain't like that."

"It always like dat, Joseph. White po'liceman ain't got no use fo' the black man unless he doin' his dirty wuk fo' him. You of all people know dat."

"It ain't about what I know, Loretta. It's about necessity. 'Bout me bringin' in a wage."

"Wage . . . It's blood money, man."

"Look, you wanted the truth. You just got it."

"Trute, shit! I woulda bin better off settlin' fo' you lies, fool! What's the damn favour you wantin'?"

"I need a motor? Some wheels so I can get about over the next few days."

"You got some fuckin' cheek, you know dat?" Loretta stamped over to a wall cabinet that hung behind a tired mahogany roll-top desk and after rifling through it a while, turned and threw a bunch of keys at me.

"Thanks."

Loretta's top lip curled, the lines on her forehead tightening in exasperation. "I don't want you damn gratitude." She pointed at the keys in my hand. "Brook Lane lock-up. One o' dem's fo' the garage door, other fo' the motor. Bring the damn ting back in one piece or Vic'll have my hide."

I winked at her. "I'll treat it with kid gloves, promise."

The grim look on Loretta's face lifted a little, but she shook her head disapprovingly then clicked her fingers at me. "What 'bout Chloe?"

"What about her?"

Loretta made a huffing sound. "Who'll be lookin' after the damn pickney while you off playin' pretend po'liceman?"

I shrugged. "Same as usual. Gabe picks her up from the school gates and I collect her later on round teatime."

Loretta nodded. "You git stuck, you can bring her over ta me if you like. I can walk the child ta class with Carnell Jr, befo' I start here."

"Okay, thanks. I'll do that." I smiled and turned to leave. Loretta called after me.

"Hey, fool. You need ta remember sum'ting."

I looked back and Loretta and I made eye contact. "Yeah, what's that?"

"Nuthin' spells trouble like a white man knockin' at a black man's door."

True and prescient words that I should have heeded, but which at the time fell on deaf ears.

CHAPTER
SIX

It was just after twelve thirty by the time I'd picked up a car from the small fleet that was lined up in the series of knocked-through garages that unofficially belonged to my cousin, Vic. An E-Type Jag with a gleaming crimson paint job stood out at the front of a row of runabout vehicles, including a Ford Capri, Austin 1100, Hillman Imp and a Mini. I looked at the key in my hand, clocked the familiar symbol etched into the leather fob and walked down past each of the cars until I reached the final motor — a weather-beaten metallic blue MK1 Ford Escort. I smiled to myself then went and pulled open the garage doors.

I looked back enviously at the E-Type for a moment, wishing I could trade in my key for the one that would unlock that stylish beauty. But a flash car like that would have me standing out like a sore thumb and bring me a heap of trouble to boot. Loretta had chosen well on my behalf — a more inconspicuous set of wheels that befitted a man undertaking shadowy business.

I climbed behind the wheel of the battered Ford and started her up, then accelerated out of the lock-up and down the road, taking my covetous desires with me.

I drove over to Cotham with the windows down. Somewhere, in the back of my mind, an alarm bell was going off. It was like the uneasy feeling I get after waking from a nightmare. Loretta had unsettled me with her heavy questioning about Fletcher and his strong-arming me to undertake his dirty work. My worry had no picture, so it was more of a suspicion than fear. At the same time, I was now happy to be driving towards someone else's troubles. The sensation of delight made me smile. It was a grin that represented a whole lifetime of laughing at pain.

I parked the Ford under the railway arches at the top of Cheltenham Road and walked the hundred yards or so down to the address I'd been given on the corner of Cromwell Road. The sign above the shop read *Suresh's Shoe Repairs and General Store*. When I opened up the door, a small bell tinkled and there was rustling behind the wall of hanging shoes which stood between the workroom and the counter. There was a sour tang in the air. The store was less than eight feet deep and just about the same across. The back room was composed of endless shelves cluttered with pairs of shoes tied together by their laces and marked with yellow tailor's chalk. Women's shoes were held together by string. A middle-aged man wearing a long brown overall stood in the small opening that led into the workshop. He looked tired, dishevelled and none too pleased to find me in his shop.

"What you want?"

"Good afternoon. I'm looking for Mr Suresh?"

54

The man peered over his brass-rimmed, half-moon specs at me and nodded. "Yes, this is me. I'm Suresh."

I stuck out my hand. "My name's Joseph Ellington. Superintendent Fletcher instructed me to come and visit you."

A surprised look crept across Mani Suresh's face. "You? You the detective chappy, the one bloody useless policeman tell me about?"

"Enquiry agent," I corrected him.

"You come here to find my boy, yes?"

"I'm here to see if I can help, yes."

"Same policeman. He says you find people." Suresh rubbed the tips of his fingers together. "I pay you, you find my boy?" He walked over to the front door of the shop and locked it, put up his CLOSED sign then gestured for me to follow him. "This way, Mr Ellington."

He guided me through the back of his workshop into a long hallway. The dim corridor led to a stairway lit by small windows at the elbow of each half-flight up. I noticed that the stairs were well maintained and the window panes were clean. There was no dust in the corners or crevices. On the second floor, we entered another faded passageway lined with doors that were sealed with bright tawny varnish.

Suresh led me to the last door on the left side. The door was noiseless as we entered.

Suresh's living room had the same ordered feel about it as the hall. The place was fairly spartan, with its threadbare carpet, blue sofa, a dark red stuffed chair and a wooden coffee table with frosted glass in its centre. Incense sticks burned in a small gold jar, the ash collecting in a heap on the glass table top. The room smelled of a heady mixture of jasmine and Indian spice. Suresh pointed to the armchair.

"You . . . you have seat."

I sat down, took a notebook and pencil from my inside jacket pocket and rested a hand on my knee. Suresh stared at me for a few seconds. I imagined that I was the first black fella he'd had in his house as a guest. I could see that he was struggling to be a host in his own home.

"Why don't you sit down too, Mr Suresh," I said.

He regarded the sofa for a moment before sitting down at the end furthest from my chair. Then he looked at me, his eyes bloodshot with fatigue. "My boy, he brings much shame on my family."

"What kind of shame, Mr Suresh. What is it you think your son has done?"

Suresh squinted at the words as if they were bright, cancer-inducing sunbeams. "Done? I tell you what he done. He make a bloody show of me!"

"How?" I pressed. Fletcher had already given me the bare facts. I needed to hear what I was getting myself into from the horse's mouth.

"Boy should be married by now!" Suresh shook his head. "Wife insisted he find bride. Wedding all planned, paid for. Too much expense. We find a good girl, from decent family. I pay to bring bloody woman from India." He looked down at his worn carpet, grumbling to himself in his own language.

"Nikhil has been gone for ten days, is that right?"

56

Suresh raised his head, fixing me with a confused stare. "How you know that?"

"Superintendent Fletcher gave me a few details. He said that your son hadn't been seen for nearly a fortnight."

Suresh nodded in agreement. "That's right. He lucky I no bloody kill him when he turn up, all the bastard trouble he's causing me."

"Why do you think he's done this?" Suresh stared back at me in dismay. "Run off, like he has?"

Suresh shrugged, the skin around his eyes tightening with frustration. "I no idea? Two day before ceremony, he walks out of shop."

I hesitated for a moment. "And the wedding day was supposed to have been when?"

Suresh grunted. "Friday . . . July the thirtieth. Boy behaving bloody strange all past year."

I wrote the date down in my pocketbook. "Strange, in what way?" I asked.

"Started looking like bastard hippy! Wearing silly bloody clothes. Stopping out till all the hours God gave."

"He ever tell you where he used to go, who he was out with at night?"

Suresh twisted his face away, avoiding my scrutiny by concentrating on the drab wallpaper over the fireplace. He shook his head after he'd thought for a short while. "No. Never tell me or his mother a bloody thing."

"You have any other children?"

Suresh slumped back on the sofa and stared at the ash detritus accumulating on his coffee table. "No, just Nikhil."

I noted that it was the first time that he'd called his son by his first name. "Where is your wife, Mr Suresh?"

He muttered something under his breath, then reached into his overall pocket, took out a packet of cigarettes and lit one. I inhaled the fumes while he pointed angrily towards the living-room door. "Pissed off in bedroom. Been in the bloody thing crying since boy gone. She not coming out if she knows there's a *Shabdkosh* in house."

"A Shabdkosh?"

Suresh sniffed with embarrassment then pointed at my chest. "Yes . . . *Shabdkosh* . . . a black man."

At that moment, for some strange reason, I felt that Suresh and I were of the same race, despite appearances to the contrary. Two men, all too aware of how names, cruel or otherwise, can define how we see the world and those residing in it. I tapped the top of my pencil on my notebook. "I've been called a lot of things in my time Mr Suresh, but never one of those."

Suresh offered me the faintest of smiles. "It not an insult. Just name in Punjabi."

"Your wife, she don't like black men?"

Suresh looked at me warily. "Only man my wife like is her son."

I saw the pain seep up into his icy gaze and changed tack. "Your son, Nikhil — he have any friends I can speak to?"

"Friends?"

"Yeah, somebody he may have confided in?"

Suresh frowned. "I don't know. He always knock about with that bloody little Pakistani *bevakooph*, Kamani."

"Who?"

"Fahad Kamani."

"This word, *bevakooph*, what's it mean?"

"Idiot!" Suresh snapped.

I flinched, glad he hadn't called me that. "And where can I find Kamani?"

"He work as waiter at Taj Mahal in Stokes Croft. Perhaps he can help you?"

"Perhaps." I wrote down the fella's details and looked up at Suresh. He had moved forward in his seat, his expression a mixture of confusion and anguish.

"Can you find my boy?" I heard the child in his voice as he spoke.

"I can do my level best."

Suresh reached round to his back pocket and pulled out a brown leather wallet. He took out three £10 notes and slid them across the coffee table towards me. "Here's down payment your policeman friend told me to give you."

I shook my head. "He's no friend of mine."

Suresh stared back at me dourly. "Me neither."

I reluctantly scooped up the cash and stuffed the notes into my inside jacket pocket, along with my notebook, then rose to my feet. Suresh followed suit, his skinny frame wavering slightly as he lifted himself up off the sofa.

"I'll be in touch in a few days."

Suresh nodded and I walked out of the man's living room, thinking that I needed to go find myself a better job. One where I didn't have to sell my soul to the devil or endure the suffering of others to earn a crust.

CHAPTER
SEVEN

My cousin Vic had often referred to me as the unwilling detective. When I asked him what he meant, he said, "It ain't no profession fo' you. You helpin' out folk causa what's happened to 'em, not fo' the cash!"

"Wouldn't everybody rather be rich than workin'?" I asked.

"Fool, dey tell you that shit, yeah. But most folk in a job like you got, well they kinda driven ta be there, peeking through keyholes an' mixing wid scum."

Well, I was no longer the unwilling detective. I was once again voluntarily heading towards a world of grief and heartache, whether I knew quite what was in that world or not.

On the drive away from Suresh's shop, I wondered how much of the truth I'd actually got out of the man. I'd deliberately kept my time with him short. Sometimes you get more out of a person if you tighten the pace of the conversation but keep your questions loose and not too probing. I knew that I'd have to go back and discuss matters pertaining to his son's disappearance in the coming days so why get the man's back up by jamming him in a corner and grilling him to within an inch of his life? The first thing my old

61

sergeant on the force back home on Bim had taught me was that less was more when interviewing. "Let 'em fools spill tha beans or dig tha own grave in tha own time." It was advice that had stood the test of time.

So, what had I found out from that musty living room?

Well, for one, Suresh was, from the look of his simple home and the small business he ran, not a wealthy man. He had enough dough stashed away to pay me thirty quid for three days' legwork, and he could probably keep coughing up my fee for a good while longer. The man clearly wanted his son found, but there was a deep sense of resentment in the way that he spoke about him and a hell of a lot of anger, which I'd initially put down to him being vexed at his boy going missing and the embarrassment his running off had caused within his family. As for the absent wife? The fact that Mrs Suresh wasn't about had set my teeth on edge. There could have been any number of reasons for the woman choosing to take herself off to bed. I doubted that it was as simple as her being stricken with worry. I guessed her absence had more to do with her high-handed husband than any maternal anguish she may have been suffering.

Black clouds were forming ahead of me, the air cooler as it blew in through the car window. I needed time to think before I made my next move and spoke to the waiter at the Taj. I needed to get my head around both Mani Suresh's problem and sift out the truth from the lies he may have been telling me, and I needed a couple of pints in my belly to make sense of any of it.

★ ★ ★

The Beaufort Inn was tucked away down a narrow side road on York Street in Montpelier. On paper it was owned by Vic, though he rarely ever entered the place. It had been a rough joint even by my cousin's standards, with a long-time reputation for illegal betting, fist fights, bad ale; a second home to every low life and villain in a ten-mile radius. Since Vic had taken it on and put his people in charge, all that had changed — all except for the crooks. Over time, Vic's people had managed to shift most of the undesirables — the drunks, shylocks and grifters — away from the place, but the hardcore mob, the real villains, they weren't going anywhere. Applying a fresh coat of paint might have changed the colour of the pub's appearance, but the dubious clientele was still the same, only now any punter stupid enough to be wanting a punch-up didn't get a chance to raise their fists in anger at the bar. Nowadays, those kinda problems were taken outside, into the backyard, behind closed doors. Out there, standing on the rough cobbles, with the stink of spilt beer, dried blood and the sewer drains creeping up your nostrils, a fella had the chance to calm the hell down or push his luck. Foolishly choosing the latter meant a beating was on the cards before you were slung out into the street.

As I walked across the pub's oval-shaped lounge with its ash-panelled walls and decorative plaster architrave, I was greeted by many familiar faces. Black men and women originating from every island in the Caribbean, of varying ages, each with their elbows at ninety degrees

63

to the chest, all gripping half-filled pint pots or fluted sherry glasses, a convivial family of normally drink-addled individuals who each seemed to spend more of their valuable time supping in the Beaufort than they did doing anything else. That kind of loyalty meant that trade was very healthy, which in turn kept a smile on my cousin's face.

I stopped and offered up the usual pleasantries and shared a joke or two with a few of the regulars before heading for the polished bar that stretched the length of one side of the lounge. Traditional ceramic beer pumps and brass drip trays lined its top, while behind it, a dozen polished optics ran along the wall, each housing the usual hard liquor.

Behind the wall of the bar, in the adjacent room, was a dimly lit snug — my favourite place to hang out and drink. I said good evening to the pub's regular barman, Dutty Ken, ordered a pint of bitter then snuck under the counter flap, headed through into the snug and dropped down on to one of the upholstered benches. I closed my eyes and let my head rest against the wall. Despite all the frivolities going on next door, the little snug was always quiet and calm. It was the main reason I enjoyed spending so much time in there.

I stretched my legs out and let my body relax and listened to the bucketing rain beat down. I thought I heard a rumble of thunder in the distance. A few moments later I was jarred out of my reverie by the sound of glasses clinking together. I felt cold air waft against my face as someone walked past me, then a whiff of cigar smoke. I quickly drew in my legs and sat bolt upright.

"'Ere you pint, JT." Dutty Ken stood over me, a stogie stuck in the corner of his mouth, his jowly face resembling that of a tired-out building. He coughed loudly, handed me my pint then placed a shot glass filled to the brim with Mount Gay on to the table next to me. He began hacking again then gestured at the glass of amber rum with a nod. "Compliments o' da 'ouse."

"Thanks, Dutty." I looked at the stogie in his mouth and shook my head. "Man, didn't I tell ya to stop smoking those damn things. That cigar gonna kill you."

Dutty ignored my berating, still making a sound like an engine that wouldn't turn over. He wiped a tear from his rheumy eye and stared down at me. "You want me ta call Vic, let him knaw you 'ere?"

"Nah, I need to catch up with the man later, in private."

Dutty stifled a cough, took another drag on his black cigar and grinned, breathing in smoke through his teeth. He leaned over to smash the butt into a glass ashtray.

"Okay, JT," he whispered as he headed back towards the bar, his huge shoulders rising up and down as he continued to bark and croup.

I drank my beer without further interruption, my mind weighing up the things Mani Suresh had told me about his missing son, the agitation in his voice when he spoke of him, the AWOL wife, and the easy manner in which he had handed over thirty pounds to a perfect stranger. I didn't know how honest the shoe-mender had been with me, what he may have held out on. All I knew for now was that lies and deceit come easy to some folk. Perhaps Suresh was one of those; perhaps he wasn't. Being told the truth in my business was like swimming in a peaceful lake and suddenly seeing the beady eyes of a crocodile bearing down on you. A rarity yes, but hell, it could happen.

I put the shot glass to my lips and sank the spicy liquor in a single gulp, then sat the jigger next to my empty pint pot. I heard the sound of coughing coming from the other side of the pub, called out Dutty's name and waited for him to show his saggy face on the other side of the bar.

At that moment, I knew only one truth, and that was that I needed another drink.

CHAPTER
EIGHT

People back home on Barbados and right across the Caribbean's many islands have, for centuries, placed heavy stones on the graves of their dead, so their souls would not wander and afflict the living. My cousin Vic had always told me that this was simply the practice of superstitious people. But over the next few hours, I was once again about to learn that ghosts and spirits can hover on the edge of our vision with the density and luminosity of mist, and that their claim on the earth can be as legitimate and tenacious as our own.

It was just after five thirty by the time I'd dragged myself out of the Beaufort, checked in on Chloe back at Gabe and Pearl's and then driven back over to Stokes Croft. I parked across the road from the Taj Mahal and headed down two flights of flophouse stairs at the end of the street to get inside the place. The Taj was below pavement level and was probably once used as cellars. Inside, the restaurant was empty. The room comprised three whitewashed plaster arches with a line of booths along one side, separated by ornate Indian-style stained-glass partitions.

I saw the heavy maroon curtains at the rear of the restaurant twitch. A thin-faced man appeared from behind them and gave me his best front-of-house grin. He was dressed formally, in a dark worsted suit and burgundy knitted tie, his shoes heavily buffed so that the light glinted off the toes. He had the confident swank of a manager rather than one of his minions.

"A table for one, sir?"

I shook my head. "Not this evening, thank you." I stuck out my hand. The man stared down at it for a moment before grasping my palm gingerly and shaking it. I flashed him a smile to try and keep things light. "The name's Ellington. I'm an enquiry agent."

He gave me a quizzical look. Certain of my surname, but unsure of what I actually did for a living and if it meant trouble for him. "Feroze Ahmed, the owner. What can I do for you, Mr Ellington?"

"I'm looking for a man I believe works here at the Taj, a Fahad Kamani?"

"Fahad? What are you wanting with Fahad?" The man's voice was a strange mix. Calm like honey and milk but laced with the spice of suspicion.

"Fahad's name has been passed on to me by a Mr Suresh. I've been hired as a go-between by the police to search for Suresh's son. I believe Fahad and his boy were friends. I'm hoping he can help me out by answering a few questions. He around?"

The Taj's owner looked at me cagily before nodding. "He is . . . but Fahad speaks little English."

"Then would you be so kind as to translate for me?"

Ahmed considered my question for a moment before giving his guarded answer. "If it will help, yes."

He turned on his heels and held out his hand towards the maroon curtains. "This way, please."

Ahmed disappeared behind the curtain and I followed. We made our way down a damp, bare-brick passageway, past an open door, exposing a toxic-looking toilet and hand basin. The corridor came to an abrupt halt at a kitchen at the back of the building. The dank stench of sodden water coming off the walls behind me mixed with the heady aroma of boiling meat and musty spices.

The small kitchen was lit by a bare bulb. The walls were greasy yellow, the floor covered in a pitted brown linoleum. The stained tile sink was piled high with dishes. There was a pan sitting on the four-burner gas stove and the ceiling was blackened by smoke and grease. The back door was flung open and, outside in the yard, a skinny woman, with work-weary shoulders, was sweeping out the spaces between the dustbins with a long-handled broom. She shot me a scowl and went on with her work.

Ahmed stood in the doorway and yelled out Fahad's name. A few moments later, a scrawny kid ran across the yard and stood obediently in front of his employer. Fahad Kamani was dressed in a blood-soaked apron, which in turn covered a yellowing string vest, cream-coloured cords and scuffed brown brogues that looked older than me. His face and bare arms were covered in thick perspiration. Sweat also ran from his forehead, down his cheeks and neck and soaked into the ribbed collar of his vest.

Ahmed spoke to Kamani in their mother tongue, the young man nodding nervously and peering into the kitchen at me as they spoke. He was still looking daggers as his boss ushered him in. Ahmed gestured with a nod towards his employee. "Fahad is from Lahore; we both speak Punjabi."

I smiled, but my expression of friendliness did little to settle Kamani's unease. I held out my hand. The boy opened his mouth to reveal a string of missing teeth, both upper and lower, but he did not say a word. He took hold of my fingers limply and gave my hand a skittish shake. His eyes were almost without colour, small and cagey, clotted with little red veins.

"Hello, Mr Kamani. My name is Joseph Ellington. I'd like to ask you a few questions about your friend, Nikhil Suresh."

A jarred look appeared on his face as soon as I mentioned Nikhil's name. Ahmed began to repeat my question, but Fahad's taken-aback countenance gave more away than any words ever could have. When the young man finally spoke, his voice crackled with fear, and for me the flow of his indecipherable language seemed to go on for ever. When Kamani finished speaking, his boss gave me a rueful smile.

"Fahad wants you to know that he has not seen the man you seek for many weeks. He says that there has been a *taraka-vitaraka*."

"*Taraka-vitaraka?*"

Ahmed nodded. "Yes . . . they have argued. A disagreement between the two of them."

I scratched at my chin and said, "Ask Fahad when he thinks he last saw Nikhil and what their argument was about?"

Ahmed spoke to his employee again. When the two men had finished talking, Ahmed nervously clasped his hands together. He stared down at the floor before looking back at me. "Fahad tells me that it was perhaps three weeks since he last saw this man and their disagreement was of a most delicate matter."

I looked over at Kamani, caught him squarely in the eye and smiled. "Delicate how, Fahad?"

Ahmed repeated my words in Punjabi. The boy swallowed hard before answering. "*Bondu*."

I shrugged at the two men. "What's *bondu*?"

Mr Ahmed coughed into a clenched fist before continuing. "It is an offensive and vulgar word, Mr Ellington."

"Okay, but in what way vulgar?"

Ahmed stared back down at the floor, his embarrassment plain to see. I pushed him for an answer.

"Please, Mr Ahmed . . . what does *bondu* mean?"

Ahmed kept his gaze firmly placed at his feet. When he spoke, his words were full of disdain. "*Bondu* is the name given to a man of few morals, one who lays down with another man."

I felt the heat of my own discomposure prickle around the nape of my neck. "You talkin' 'bout a homosexual?"

Mr Ahmed nodded and took a step back. Kamani, sensing our mutual unease, suddenly moved towards me and put a hand on my forearm, his fingers tightening around the sleeve of my jacket. He began to speak wildly in Punjabi, his voice trailing off into silence then rising to a high pitch. Tears welled in his eyes. I could feel his body trembling as he grasped at my arm. Mr Ahmed reached across to prise Kamani's fingers away from me then drew him back, a few steps away.

"Fahad says he is ashamed of his friend. That he deserves his terrible fate."

"What terrible fate?"

Ahmed hesitated for a moment. He held on to either side of Kamani's arms as he stared down at the ground and sobbed, then cleared a frog from his throat. "Fahad says he saw this Suresh man in a dream three nights ago, that he is now *bhoota*."

"Bhoota?"

Ahmed nodded, his eyes hardening to my question. "The man you search for is with the jinn."

I hunched my shoulders again. "I'm afraid I don't understand, Mr Ahmed."

The restaurant owner swallowed, knowing that his next words were important ones. "He is a ghost. His mortal being is no longer here with us; his spirit lingers with the undead. Cursed."

Kamani looked up, met my eyes and blinked, a tear rolling slowly down his cheek. He began to talk in Punjabi again, only this time one word he spoke made perfect sense to me.

The word was *Moulie* . . .

72

CHAPTER
NINE

Clifton village is where the money is in Bristol. If you've got a bob or two in the bank and live in town, then chances are you make your home in one of the suburb's many handsome Georgian houses. The ornate terraced streets that make up Clifton are the play area of the great and the good. The lush, green downs, which overlook the river Avon and the towering suspension bridge and separate the prestigious area from the bustle of the city and the rest of the riff-raff, has to be the icing on the cake for those who reside within its hallowed grounds.

Known as the Moulie, the Moulin Rouge club also made its home in the upmarket neighbourhood — though its stinking-rich residents preferred to iron over that indelicate fact. The club occupied a former swimming pool off Whiteladies Road and was a long-time resident of the exclusive ward. It had an unsavoury history as a former bingo hall and striptease club and had, in the spring of 1970, reopened as a club exclusively for the use of homosexuals.

If what Farad Kamani had told me was correct, that his friend was in fact gay, then the Moulie would have been one of the very few places in the city that Nikhil

Suresh could have frequented to mix with others like him. If I was to get any closer to singling out the truth of where Suresh may have disappeared to, then my next port of call had to be there. I can't lie: the thought of walking through the doors of that place filled me with dread. Agreeing to take on Superintendent Fletcher's grunt work was clearly going to take me on a far stranger journey than the one I had planned when I'd rolled out of bed this morning. I was starting to regret snatching up those three £10 notes from Mani Suresh. The cash in my pocket now felt wrong, like it didn't belong there. The trio of crisp notes were a little too much like blood money for my liking.

After leaving the Taj Mahal, I drove back to St Pauls and spent the rest of the evening at Gabe and Pearl's. My aunt and uncle had rented the same home on Banner Road since they first settled in Bristol at the start of the 1950s and returning to the bay-fronted Victorian tenement always felt like coming home. The house had been my sanctuary, and now it was Chloe's too.

Walking through my aunt and uncle's front door always conjured up happy memories from our former island life: the smell of familiar food cooking, the comforting chatter of our own patois, the laughter of a family, sharing and loving together. The house was thousands of miles from the azure waters and paradisal sands of Barbados, but Banner Road was, to us, a little piece of home hidden behind British red brick.

74

It was after eight by the time I walked in and kicked off my shoes in the hall. Pearl called out to me from the kitchen as I made my way down the hallway. "That chil', she'll be in bed frettin' fo' you. She gonna be wantin' you ta kiss her go'night befo' you come in here lookin' ta fill you belly."

I headed upstairs and made my way to the back bedroom, stuck my head round the door and peeped inside. Chloe was lying on her side in bed, her eyes shut, the lids gently flickering; a tell-tale sign that she was still awake. A small lamp on the other side of the room cast a weak amber glow across the room. Stuffed animals and dolls were scattered across the floor. I crept in and perched myself on the edge of the mattress, kissed Chloe on the top of her head and whispered, "How you doin', little guy?"

Chloe's eyes shot open, her face filled with a mixture of happiness and puzzlement. She kept blinking at me as though she were waking from a dream. Then she sat up in bed, put her arms around my neck and pressed her head against my chest. I could smell baby shampoo in her hair. Her hand touched the lapel of my jacket.

"Where you bin, Joseph?"

"At work."

"School?"

I shook my head. "Nah, not school. I gotta new job."

"What kinda job?"

"Just helpin' folk out."

Chloe squinted, thinking about what I'd just told her. "That sounds like a good job."

"Beats cleaning up after a bunch o' noisy kids, that's fo' sure." I winked at her then brushed her curls under my palm. I kissed her forehead then laid her back down against the mattress, pulling the sheet and blankets across her chest. As I rose from the bed, she looked up at me from her pillow. "Joseph, will the laughing man be back tonight?"

"No, he ain't coming back. I promise."

I had to look away from her lest she see the lie in my eyes.

CHAPTER
TEN

You can't wake up from a nightmare if you never fall asleep.

After sunset, I drove back out to Clifton Village and the Moulin Rouge feeling irritable and tired. My eyes were heavy, and I had a nagging feeling in the pit of my gut that was telling me I'd have been better off staying back at Gabe and Pearl's place with a stiff drink in my hand rather than trudging out after dark to stick my nose into places I didn't belong. Heavy rain had begun to fall again. On the horizon, a bolt of lightning exploded, its electric talons arcing out in every direction. I parked on the street across from the club, got out my car and pulled my hat brim down over my face.

As I headed over the road, I saw a police car coming towards me. The driver stared out at me, his face a picture of mistrust. Inside, I knew that both policemen were eyeing me up: a black fella, a suspicious character dark as night. A tall man who was in shape enough for one good round before they had the chance to draw a truncheon and beat me to a pulp. I could tell from their fleeting glances that neither officer liked the look of me, but I didn't care, and the swagger in my gait told 'em so. The car slowed to three miles an hour; the pale faces within were wondering if they should stop and roust me. I rolled back my shoulders and stared directly at them. The driver hesitated, exchanged a few words with his partner, then sped off. Maybe it was close to the end of their shift. Maybe they were just too plain tired to be picking on a random black guy with attitude. Probably, though, some real crime had come in over their radio and they didn't have the leisure to bring me under their control.

As I closed in on the doors of the Moulie, I could hear the sound of a trumpet, a trombone and a sax inside. It brought a smile to my face but not to my heart. Standing alone on the pavement outside, guarding the entrance to the private club, was a face I recognised but didn't expect to see. Dinah Henry was a former good-time girl who sidelined as a bouncer on the doors of the Shebeens in St Pauls but rarely went any further to ply her unusual trade. Dinah had spent her life between the street and jail. She was six-foot-two of solid muscle, handy with her fists and a razor-sharp stiletto blade, rumoured to be secreted on her singular person. She stood on the bottom step outside the club, wearing a red long-sleeved dress with a curious lizard-skin look about it and maybe an extra ten pounds since we'd last met. Her face was flat and hard, the skin on her hands and fingers a mass of short white scars. When she recognised me, a cruel grin cut across her blood-red lips.

"Joseph Ellington . . . man, I thought you were dead."

I shook my head. "Nah, that was the other guy."

Dinah's laugh was deep and infectious — like pneumonia. She gave my threads the once-over then focused her full attention on my eyes. "Hell, last I heard, you was sweeping floors fo' the council."

I smiled, ignoring the cheap crack. "How you doin', Dinah?"

"I'm okay, baby. What the hell brings you out here. You lookin' fo' sum'ting special?" Dinah winked and I felt the heat rise across my face.

"I'm lookin', Dinah, but not in the way you be thinkin'."

I took the photograph of Nikhil Suresh out of my pocket and showed it to her. Dinah peered at it, shook her head and gave me a blank look in return.

"Can't say I recognise the fella."

"No? I hear he's a regular face at the club."

"Yeah? Not on the nights I'm workin' this gate door, he ain't."

I raised an eyebrow. "Maybe the man's on the private guest list. Perhaps gets in some other way?" I took two £1 notes out of my wallet, quickly folding them together into a small square. I took hold of Dinah's left wrist and pressed the cash into her palm. She instinctively curled her long fingers around the money and averted her eyes from me for a moment, then pocketed the notes, slipping them inside the sleeve of her frock. Then she stood to one side and nodded towards the inside of the club.

"Pay the girl on the till in the foyer then go ask fo' Perri St Claire at the bar. Take my advice, don't show that photo to no one else other than Perri, you hearin' me?"

I nodded, smiled and began to walk up the steps. Dinah called after me, "How's that long-lost cousin of yours?"

I kept on walking. "Oh, you know, same as he always been . . . dangerous."

It wasn't the two £1 notes I'd just parted with that had got me inside the cloistered world of the Moulin Rouge.

Fear had.

I did as Dinah had instructed. I paid a further £1.50 to the cashier in a cubbyhole, signed the guest book under the name of Fletcher then headed across the plush red-carpeted lobby towards the double doors that led to the dancehall. The doors' wooden handles had been stained black by the pressure of many sweating hands, and the doors themselves opened out into a wide, smoke-filled room that glowed under polished brass chandeliers. The walls that ran down towards the bar were decorated with monochromatic prints of blue nudes, all male, all in various erotic poses. White-clothed tables lined either side of the dance floor. Two thirds were empty. The rest were occupied by white men who stared at each other rather than the black fella who'd just walked in. I clocked that most of the men's companions were young, paid for or willing to be paid, all with fixed ingenue smiles.

The jazz band that I'd heard jamming when I was outside was now nowhere to be seen; instead a woman was playing a grand piano on a low platform at the far end of the room. She looked unreal through the cigarette smoke, like some kind of rag doll. Her face was hidden, her tense bare shoulders slender, the shoulder blades protruding through alabaster skin. Her dark hair poured down on her flesh like tar, turning her uncovered frame a stark white. I didn't like the number she was playing, but it deserved a better audience than the chattering and canoodling one behind me.

I headed across to the bar. Either side of the polished counter were a pair of leather-cushioned booths, both decorated in the same tinted, coarse manner as the rest of the club. Each booth came complete with a brass-topped table, lit by a single white candle in a tall silver candlestick. The booths were sunk back away from the dance floor, offering privacy and seclusion to those choosing to sit within. As I glanced at the booze on offer, I felt the middle-aged waiter's eyes already reaching for me. "What will it be?" he said.

I pointed across to the line of spirit bottles behind him. "Rum, please."

Wooden-faced, he nodded, and I watched as he poured a shot glass full of Lambs Navy. He placed the brimming thimble on a small cream-coloured doily then slid the glass across the bar towards me. I lifted it carefully and took a sip.

"That'll be a pound."

I looked back at the fella, almost choking on my liquor. "Say what?"

"A pound, sir." The "sir" part was certainly for effect, rather than deference.

I took out my wallet, pulled a £5 note out and waved it under the bartender's nose. "I'm lookin' for Perri St Claire?"

The waiter grinned to himself, looked at the clock on the wall behind him then gestured towards the woman playing the piano.

"Perri will be finished her set in another twenty minutes or so."

I waved the fiver at the barman some more. "I'd like to buy Miss St Claire a drink and have a quick word with her when she's finished playing."

He snatched the cash out of my fingers then picked up a fluted glass from the counter behind him. "I'll let the lady know she has a fan waiting for her. You can park yourself in one of the booths."

The barman began to unscrew the cap off a large green bottle then grinned at me. "Perri has expensive taste." He held the uncapped magnum out for me to see the fancy label. "That's a Dubonnet and gin you've just coughed up for."

The man's voice was back-street Bristolian. Guttural and forced. I felt the urgent desire to slap the smirk right off his face but instead held out my hand. The barman looked at my open palm, then up at me and I stretched my arm out across the bar towards him, just to give him a further hint. "My change." I wiggled my fingers. "If you don't mind?"

He sniffed and walked away. I shook my head and watched as he punched angrily at the keys on the cash register then returned with a handful of silver and copper coins. He dropped the loose change into my open hand. I stared down at what was left of my £5 note, whistled and looked back at my leering host. The man's grin had just got a little wider.

"Like I said, Perri's got expensive taste."

I leaned forward to look in the mirror behind the bar and caught a three-quarters' view of Perri St Claire at the piano, her face still hidden by her flowing black mane. Whatever information the pianist may have had for me needed to be pretty damn good. Some juicy titbit or two that was valuable enough to satisfy my prying and console my badly depleted billfold.

Just under half an hour later, I saw the wooden-faced waiter point me out as he sat the gin cocktail down on the piano and the woman turned to look. Her face was still partly masked by heavy grey wisps of cigarette smoke and the club's subdued lighting. Her vague features appeared so small and delicately modelled that her face looked pinched. She made no effort to smile. I raised my chin by way of invitation and knocked back the rest of my rum. Music began to thunder from the club's speaker system and a few couples got to their feet, giving each other awkward looks before making their way to the dance floor.

I watched as the pianist sat motionless for a moment, then lit a cigarette, picked up her drink and walked across to sit down next to me. I saw that in fact Perri St Claire had a slender body, tall and perfect, poised somewhere between thirty and forty with long legs, and feet encased in black high-heeled sandals. Her eyes were the clearest jade, made all the more alluring by the false eyelashes attached to her smokily made-up lids. The skin on her face was smoothed with expensive foundation, the French perfume she wore heady and expensive. But for all her glamour and style, her hands gave Perri St Claire away. They were not the hands of a slender woman, but those of a goalkeeper — a dead giveaway. As was the Adam's apple protruding from her neck. When St Claire spoke, it was with a masculine timbre, the feminine illusion shattered with just four simple words.

"You like my music?"

"Yeah."

"I don't believe you. You're tone deaf, I bet." St Claire looked intently into my face, the bitterness in the voice quickly spreading to the eyes, the lips twisted over the end of the cigarette as the drag queen eyed me. "You a copper? You've got copper's eyes."

I shook my head. "No, but I used to be."

Perri's face became pinched, her — no, his — eyes scanning the room uneasily. "Whaddya mean, *used to be*?"

"I was on the force a long time ago, back in the West Indies."

"And now?"

"And now I do a little private work. Just when I need to put food on the table."

"You mean you're a private detective?"

"Of a kind, yeah."

"And why are you here talking to me, Mr . . .?"

84

"The name's Ellington." I took out my wallet and handed over the photograph of Suresh. "You know this fella?"

St Claire's face suddenly filled with white terror. The drag queen shoved the photo back across the table and got up to leave. I grabbed hold of his forearm, pulling him down on to the seat next to me.

"Take it easy." I held on to his arm, squeezed it a little firmer. "I ain't wantin' any trouble here, Perri. I just got a few questions I need answering."

St Claire tried to wriggle free of my grasp. I held on, applying a little more pressure, my grip tightening, pinching at the skin underneath the bejewelled ballgown. I saw him wince in pain before he reluctantly sank back against the leather cushioning. I kept the pressure on to make sure he didn't try to bolt again.

"Right, let's start over, shall we?"

St Claire scowled at me then inhaled deeply on his cigarette and flicked the ash on to the wooden floorboards under the table. His mutable green eyes suddenly softened, the pupils darting back and forth across the dance floor. "You need to get your hand off me and walk out of here."

"That ain't gonna happen till you tell me what I wanna know."

"Go piss up a rope." St Claire tried to haul himself away from me again. I squeezed harder on his arm, the backs of my knees anchoring my frame squarely to the seat. I dug my fingertips deeper into the fabric of the dress, the flesh beneath contorting under the pressure of my grip. St Claire's nostrils flared and became bloodless, his breathing quickening, his chest rising rapidly, his pinched mouth opening and closing as the pain intensified. I continued to apply more pressure. "You're hurting me, you crazy black bast —"

I saw red and slammed my fist into his stomach, doubling him over. St Claire's cigarette flew from his hand. The butt bounced across the dance floor, the burning tip sending fiery sparks up into the air. St Claire clenched hold of his belly, gasping for air. I pushed him back in his seat again, his black wig slumping across his forehead, my grip on his lower arm tighter than ever. I pulled him towards me, my lips close to the side of his face.

"The fella in the photograph. You know him, yeah?"

St Claire snorted in pain. He coughed and spat out his reply. "Yeah, I know him."

"He a punter here?"

He nodded, his head brushing against my shoulder, the wig falling further across his face.

"He come here on his own or maybe with a friend?"

St Claire tried to turn his face away from me. I applied a little more of my tourniquet grip and listened to him gasp for air.

"How the hell would I know who he knocks about with?"

"I don't believe you." I wrung another inch of St Claire's flesh and bone between my fingers. Again he fought for breath, a thin string of spittle trickling from his mouth. I moved in and whispered in his ear, "Come on, just give me a name, man."

St Claire shook his head limply, his defiance ebbing away as I compressed his arm with a further crushing brace. He yelped in pain.

"It's Tick-Tock . . . the Indian kid in that photo is Tick-Tock's piece of tail."

"That's more like it, Perri. Now, gimme this Tick-Tock fella's given name."

"It's Moody . . . Jimmy Moody, but the hustlers in here call him Tick-Tock."

I pincered his arm one last time. "Why'd they call him that?"

St Claire rasped and coughed, his voice little more than a dry rustle. "Because the red-eyed freak turns up here like clockwork."

"Freak . . . why'd you call him a freak?"

He leaned forward, his face close to the edge of the table. He pushed the wig back on his head with his free hand and hissed at me hoarsely, "Cause Tick-Tock's an albino. The man only ever comes out after dark, along with the rest of this bloody city's ghouls. Tick-Tock likes his flesh dark and young. The young dark one in that photo was one of his favourites."

I let go of St Claire's arm and pushed him away. He recoiled into the corner of the booth, his face thick with perspiration. His eye make-up was smeared into black rings. He rubbed at his arm with a trembling hand, his cheek twitching. I stared back at him, wondering if he had any more information to give up. From his inflamed expression, I got the feeling that talk time was over. He straightened his wig and pulled himself across the seat towards the end of the booth.

"Whatta you looking at? You got what you came for, now piss off!"

I rested my back against the seat. "I'm gonna leave when I'm good and ready."

St Claire got to his feet. "That's what you think." He jerked a hand at the waiter, who came running. Perri pointed at a door on the edge of the dance floor. "Get Anderson. This guy's giving me a hard time."

I raised my palm to try to placate the waiter. "Take it easy."

He looked at me with uncertainty then back at a disgruntled St Claire, who stormed off towards the door. "Anderson . . . Anderson!"

Every head in the room jerked up when he yelled out the man's name. The door sprang open and a heavy-set guy with a shaved scalp and dressed in a tight-fitting penguin suit strode out. The big flunky's pee-wee eyes moved from side to side, looking for trouble. St Claire pointed at me. "Take that bastard outside and work him over. He's a peeper, trying to pump me."

I had time to run but lacked the inclination. Over the years I'd spent too long running from white thugs, and tonight I was in no mood to be legging it. I got up and went to meet Anderson and let loose with a sucker punch. His scarred head rolled away easily and I immediately regretted my foolish bravado. I tried with my right. He caught it on the forearm and moved in. His dull eyes shifted then he came at me fast. His first fist sank into my stomach hard. I dropped my guard and fought to take in air. The next heavy slug came into

88

my neck, below the ear. My legs buckled, the fight knocked out of me by two savage blows.

Consciousness went out in jangling discord, swallowed by a giant shadow.

CHAPTER
ELEVEN

I don't remember being dragged out into the night. I felt the rain pelting down on my head and a metallic taste in my mouth. I was pinned against a hard brick wall. Something equally hard was hitting me in the face. First on one side of the jaw, then the other. Every time this happened, my head bounced against the wall behind me. This sequence, the blow followed by the bounce, continued maybe three or four times. Each time the fist connected with my face, I felt a wave of blackness reach out inside my head. Any strength I may have previously possessed had been sapped out of me; my arms hung at my side, my legs felt inert and distant.

Anderson snatched at my lapels, yanking me forward, then slammed me back against the wall. I heaved and gasped for air as Perri St Claire's minder stuck two of his stubby fingers under my chin and lifted my head to line up his next slug. That's when I saw something over the big man's shoulder — a tall shadow had appeared at the mouth of the alley. The figure stood still then headed towards us. Anderson was too engrossed in his work to notice. The shadow straightened up behind him and swung one arm high in the air. The arm came down with a dark object swinging at the end of it. It made a sharp sound, like cracking walnuts, on the back of Anderson's head, and he dropped in front of me. I couldn't read anything in his eyes because only the whites were showing. I pushed his muscular body away from me, his carcass toppling backwards on to the sodden ground.

Dinah Henry squatted down beside me and looked at Anderson lying spark out. "We better git you the hell outta here. I didn't hit this bastard very hard." She waved a short leather cosh in front of my face then picked my hat up from beside Anderson's motionless frame, took my arm and dragged me to my feet.

"Let me know when you're gonna hit him hard; I wanna be there to see it." My lips felt swollen, my legs like remote and rebellious colonies of my body. It was just as well that I was having trouble standing up straight on them. I would have enjoyed kicking Anderson along the wet tarmac and out into the gutter then regretted it later — several years later.

Dinah put her arm under my elbow, pulled me towards the alley and walked me over to my car. We were halfway there before my brain caught up with my tongue. "Where the hell did you come from?"

"I'm your guardian angel fo' the night, didn't I tell you?"

Dinah propped me up against the side of the Ford while I rummaged inside my jacket pocket for the keys. I snarled back at the bouncer, "Cut the shit, Dinah. I ain't in the mood."

"Fool, git yourself some manners!" Dinah almost sounded hurt. "I came indoors to keep an eye on your sorry ass from up on the balcony. Good job I did too, cause you'd be like a pile a' ground beef by now if I hadn't stepped in like I did."

"Did I walk out?"

"More or less. You had some help from Anderson. When he took you out back, I came after you."

I rested my forehead on the edge of the car roof, my breath heavy in my chest, my mind whirring, the rain beating down on my back. I snapped my eyes shut and saw white spots dancing behind the lids before I levered myself up, fumbled getting the key in the lock then jerked the door open. I lowered myself into the driving seat with as much dazed concentration as I could muster. Dinah reached inside, snatched the keys from me, stuck one in the ignition and started her up. I slumped back in my seat, pumped the accelerator, then looked up at my new-found saviour.

"You gonna be okay to drive this heap?"

I nodded. "Just about."

Dinah shook her head doubtfully then reached for the car door to close it. I raised my hand to stop her. "I haven't thanked you."

Dinah shrugged. "Don't bother. When you git ta seein' that cousin o' yours, tell him Dinah says hi."

As I drove away, I looked in my rear-view mirror at Dinah Henry as she stood in the rain. She'd taken a real risk in sticking her neck out to save my butt, and I wondered what the future cost to her might be if word got out that she'd been my saving grace.

It was an unsettling rumination, one that my reeling mind was reluctant to linger upon.

92

The late-night traffic had dwindled to almost nothing as I slowly drove the short distance back to St Pauls and home. I went into the bathroom, took a bottle of TCP and some cotton wool out of the medicine cabinet and leaned against the sink to clean up the two small cuts above my right eye and lower lip. The antiseptic stung as I applied it to my broken skin, my eyes watering from the smarting effect. I stared at myself in the bathroom mirror and shook my head. The battered and bruised reflection staring back at me didn't look so healthy. In the past, I'd taken worse beatings, but that was then. Four years ago, I'd been a different man, my hide and my heart tougher, and deep down I knew I was getting too old to be going toe to toe with a professional thug like Anderson.

I looked at my watch; it was just after one. I'd been washed out and tired long before setting foot in the Moulin Rouge. Three hours down the line, I'd been beaten to a pulp and was fit to drop. I staggered back to the bedroom and undressed, throwing my wet clothes on the back of a chair and getting into bed without looking at the photograph of my late wife Ellie and daughter, Amelia, on the bedside table. In a way, it was a relief not to have to explain to them about the mess I'd got myself into again and what I'd been doing all day to earn a crust.

I closed my eyes, my shame and pain fusing together, sleep coming up around me like a high tide. As I drifted off, I heard the distant whisper of my wife's soft voice echo inside my head, her quietly berating words lulling me towards a deep and welcome slumber.

"You know, there ain't no fool like an ole fool, Joseph."

CHAPTER
TWELVE

Sunlight was blooming at the periphery of my closed eyes. It wasn't shining directly into the shuttered bedroom but glowing from the hallway and the unshaded window in the kitchen at the end of it. I took a deep breath that seemed to fill my entire body. Exhaling, I tried to sit up and winced in pain. I was weak but no longer dizzy. I lifted my arm and squinted down at my wristwatch: 8.20 a.m. Almost a lie-in, but not quite.

I slowly raised my head an inch or two off the pillow and watched the room swirl around me. I took another six deep breaths before I tried to raise my feet out of bed and failed. I sucked in another deep inhalation and this time succeeded. Instead of dithering any further, I hoisted myself off the mattress and opened the curtains.

The sun almost knocked me over. It was so bright that I had to sit back down on the edge of the bed. Sitting there, gathering my thoughts, my breath swimming in and out of my body, I let my lungs do all the hard work while I regained a little of my inner reserve. Each pant of air strengthened me, bringing me the will I needed to get me back on my feet and drag my bruised hide down to the bathroom.

Two minutes later, I lifted myself up. I was a bit wobbly but made it to the door without falling. It felt like a victory. One thing that kept me upright was the sharp pain below my right ribs. My abdomen and side were tender to touch and every step sent a sharp shooting sensation through my torso and down my legs. Rather than resent the ache, I told myself to welcome it, because with each step I was shocked back into clarity, a jabbing reminder that my blood was still pumping; that life, if not a certainty, was still at least a possibility.

I made my way along the hall with the honourable intention of getting myself cleaned up. Once I'd made it inside the bathroom, I looked into the mirror and wasn't impressed with what was staring back at me. Most of Anderson's blows had made impact on my jaw, neck and around my midriff. My lower lip was not as puffed up and the cut above my right eye swollen. My nose was thankfully unbroken and I'd lost no teeth. Small mercies I told myself. I sat down on the edge of the bath and picked up the bar of coal tar soap then turned on the hot tap and hoped there'd be enough water left in the tank for me to soak my aching limbs.

A half hour later I was scrubbed clean, dressed in fresh clothes and wishing that I was still laid up in bed. My stomach was in no mood to entertain the thought of breakfast, and the inside of my head felt like it was being sandblasted. I'd stumbled into the kitchen and mashed a pot of strong coffee then sat down at the table, chucked two aspirin into my mouth and spent the next ten minutes hunched over my mug, waiting for the damn things to kick in.

It took another half hour to bring me fully back into the waking world. I'd drifted briefly back to sleep and my next bout of consciousness was announced by a knocking at my front door. Whoever it was sounded pretty reluctant to stop.

Before I had a chance to haul myself up off the chair, the knocking changed to a steady pounding, and by the time I got down the stairs the hammering had grown even louder. I slipped back the deadbolt, yanked the door open and was immediately blinded by the intense sunshine.

"Looks like you could do with a pair of healing hands, old son," snapped a hard voice. I knew straight off the bat who it was and instantly regretted my decision to open up. My eyes winced blearily at the sun behind the familiar thick-set figure in front of me. "That's good of you to offer, Superintendent."

More of the West Country accent quickly followed. "Less of your bloody cheek!" Fletcher edged forward. "I need a word with you, matey."

I rubbed at my eyes, yawned then took a couple of steps back to let the copper inside before heading back up the stairs. My favourite boy in blue on my coat tail, I waited on the landing and directed him into the kitchen. "I was wondering when you'd be turning up again."

Fletcher smirked. "Missing me, were you?"

"Oh yeah, like a hole in the head."

The policeman glared back at me, his face registering about as much emotion as a loan shark listening to a hard-luck story. He looked around blankly.

"This dive run to a decent drink?" Fletcher glanced down at his watch. "Never too early, is it?"

I slouched back down on my chair then nodded in the direction of the cupboard above the bread bin. I watched as Fletcher took out a bottle of Mount Gay, reached for a glass off the draining board, then poured himself a hefty draft of the amber-coloured rum, deep enough for drowning puppies in. He shook the bottle at me.

"Have one yourself, old son. It looks like you could do with a livener?"

I gestured at my throbbing head. "I'll pass, thanks."

Fletcher shrugged and smiled. "That's a pity . . . I thought you fellas went a bundle on this stuff any time of the day?" The superintendent took a quick gulp of his bucket of rum, and I was glad to see him fighting down a splutter. He wiped his mouth with the back of his hand then stood in front of the sink, examining me and his glass of free booze. "So, what the hell happened to you?"

I rubbed at the back of my head. "I met something nasty in the dark last night sniffing around for you."

"Sniffing, you say?" Fletcher looked back at me, the mirth in his eyes gone. He knocked back the rest of the rum, sat the glass down and pointed a finger at my face. "Well, I hope your sense of smell is still finely tuned, because I need you to come and take a whiff of something?

"Say what?"

The policeman sighed. "That beating you took must have affected your bloody hearing." He walked back towards the kitchen door and prodded my shoulder with his thumb. "Get yourself a coat. I need you to take a little trip with me."

I stayed put. "Oh, yeah. Where to?"

"Never you bloody well mind where to. Just do as I tell you."

It was then I noticed that the man had no smell, not like other cops. There was no body odour or aftershave. He was a self-contained unit, with no scent or any kind of style — the perfect package for a hunter of men. At any other time, I would have stayed on my ass, but it wasn't as simple as me putting my head down and staying put. It wasn't wise to get bolshie when you've got a mean white copper holding the unspoken threat of jail time over your head.

When you know that's on the cards, a strong sense of self-preservation needs to kick in. I wasn't keen on the idea of continuing to be Fletcher's lackey, but anything had to be better than being flung in a cell and the taste of prison food. I'm not keen on humble pie, either. It gives me indigestion, but I swallowed my pride and did as I was told, though following the superintendent's demands didn't sit right with my gut, either. None of this prevented me from shooting my mouth off at him as I got up.

"Alright, I'll go with you. But I tell you this right now, if I don't like the way things smell, I'm walking away."

It was a serious threat, but the superintendent didn't care. He nodded at me and grinned. "That's what I like about you, Ellington, old son. You always come out your corner fighting."

Fletcher's easy manner made me think that this simple ride in a policeman's car was not going to end well. As we walked out into the street, I thought for a moment about backing out. But I knew that I couldn't say no to the superintendent's demands. For now, Fletcher was the king predator and I was one of his pack hounds. If I wanted to remain a free man, I was either going to point out the prey for him or fall victim to the snapping jaws of the rest of his savage minions.

CHAPTER
THIRTEEN

I always felt a darkness descend whenever I drove westward out of Bristol into the county. Travelling into Somerset, you pass from black and brown dreams into white realities. You didn't have to cover many miles to feel it. When a black person travelled away from St Pauls, he was in effect entering another world; one where people of colour were simply not welcome.

That undesirable feeling pervaded my journey as we travelled along the A369 towards the coast. Fletcher's unmarked Hillman Hunter seemed to be crawling. The curmudgeonly policeman was clearly uninterested in setting any speed records on our jaunt out, though it didn't matter much to me. There was little point getting any place in a hurry when I had no idea where I was going. Fletcher didn't speak or look at me while he drove. He didn't seem like the kind of driver who needed to keep his eyes on the road, so I was guessing he liked the idea of keeping me on the back foot or just felt awkward having some black fella riding along next to him. Either way, I got a strong feeling that wherever Fletcher was taking me, he still needed my help.

Ten miles down the line and I was starting to get some idea of where Fletcher's magical mystery tour was going. With the Severn estuary on the horizon, we drove for another three miles or so along a series of narrow roads down to the coastal town of Portishead. The streets were clean and the drunks were few. I counted three churches on the way into town.

Fletcher headed along the high street, following the signs for the harbour, finally parking by the Esplanade overlooking the sea. Next to us a half-dozen police cars were lined up in a neat row like they were on a second-hand car lot. The superintendent yanked on the handbrake, turned towards me and pointed across to the rear of a large wood-frame building on the other side of the road. "Once we're inside there, you speak when you're spoken to, and do as I tell you. Got it?"

I nodded. I knew my place, or that's what I wanted him to think. Fletcher was the kind of man who towered over his peers and liked to hear the words "Yes, sir" as often as possible. Bullish and upright, any straighter and the man's spine would have broken. Almost every boss I'd ever had was a white man, and he was either tall or very fat; intimidation being the first requirement of the job. This boss was no different. He liked his flunkies to toe the line, and for now, I was happy to go along with the façade.

Fletcher led the way. We headed across the well-kept lawn of a park towards a boat house, its entrance partially hidden behind two weeping willows. To the right was a small boating lake complete with flowering lily pads and beyond it a playing field and park. Uniformed police officers seemed to be milling around every square inch of the seafront gardens. Many more were gathered around a menacing Black Maria, its back doors slung wide open like the mouth of a hungry beast awaiting its sacrificial meal. The front of the cabin, its veranda, walls and doors had been cordoned off with thick rope. Every part of the wooden structure seemed to have been painted green, like the leaves and grass either side.

A black-haired, charcoal-suited copper was standing on the porch of the boatshed. When he saw the superintendent heading his way, he straightened up like he was about to greet royalty. As we closed in on him, I could see that he had the mannerisms of a small man, delicate and precise, but at the same time he was beefy. He may have had the poise of a gentleman, but his flinty eyes and hard jawline spoke of trench warfare replete with mud, blood and shit. I watched him scrutinising me from head to toe before turning to address Fletcher.

"Morning, sir. Didn't expect you back so soon."

The superintendent ignored the subordinate's remark and slung his thumb towards me by way of an introduction. "Inspector Leach, this is Joseph Ellington. He's a civilian who's been liaising with the local Indian community back in Bristol on my behalf." Fletcher pointed. "Show him what we've got."

Leach flexed the tension out of his shoulders and walked back into the boatshed.

I took a step towards the door and looked inside. That's when the putrid stench hit me. The smell made my eyes tear and my stomach rise. The boathouse was all but empty, bar a half-dozen tatty deckchairs stacked

103

up against the far wall. I stood thinking that I might have been in over my head. By the time I'd walked inside and was poised over the open wooden tea chest in the middle of the room, I knew I was.

Staring up at me was the bloodied and beaten face of a young man. It was the face of Nikhil Suresh. His head had been yanked forward, framed by his slender forearms, his body crushed into an almost perfect rectangle, stuffed deep down into the box. Printed on the side of the shipping crate were the words, *It Pays to Buy Good Tea*. I'd seen my fair share of dead bodies. Many of them had died under violent circumstances. But I'd never seen anything like what had been inflicted on Nikhil Suresh. His killer had treated him like a thing that needed to be hidden, not at all like a human being. The bones in his arms and legs were broken, his forehead crushed. It was a gruesome sight. But even then, in the presence of such awful violence and evil intent, I was compelled to keep looking. Something inside was telling me to wait it out, an intuitive kick to remind me that Fletcher was watching my initial reactions to the horror I was witnessing. I stared woodenly at the two coppers, who stood in hulking silhouette like gargoyles awaiting the breath of life. Leach gestured towards the crate.

"The superintendent tells me that you were conducting a private missing-person search on behalf of this chap's family?"

I nodded. Leach made a snuffing sound in his nose. "Nikhil Suresh." His tone was scornful. "You manage to trace his whereabouts, perhaps what he may have been up to before he ended in there?"

"Not a lot." I took a couple of steps back from the tea chest. The stink rising out of it was making me gag. "Suresh's father put me on to a guy called Fahad Kamani. He's a waiter at an Indian restaurant over at Stokes Croft. Kamani said that Nikhil liked to hang out at the Moulin Rouge."

Both policemen's faces turned dour. Leach's eyes narrowed as he looked at me. "You talking about the poofter palace out at Clifton?"

I lowered my voice. "That's the one."

"And what did you dig up in that rat hole, apart from a room full of fairies?"

I could feel my hands open and close at my sides as I considered my reply. I kept my answer short and sweet. "I was able to ascertain that Suresh had frequented the nightclub and that he met men while he was in there."

"So, he was a closet Nancy Boy, then?" chipped in Fletcher, his eyebrow cocked.

I turned and shrugged. "Who knows. I get the feeling Suresh coulda bin leading some kinda double life."

Fletcher took a half-smoked cigar out of his pocket and lit it. He inhaled deeply and let the smoke trail out of his mouth, then scowled into space for a moment before setting his gaze on me. "Anything else?"

"Yeah. I spoke to a drag queen called St Claire. He said that Suresh was involved with a man called Moody."

"Jimmy Moody?"

"Yeah, that's the fella." I watched Fletcher's eyes go flat as he thought.

"If that's the case, then our man back there in the tea chest was messing around with some very nasty people indeed."

Inspector Leach nodded in agreement then begin to knead the thick folds in the back of his neck with his fingers. He moved in closer to me, set his palm on my forearm and looked me steadily in the eyes. There were thin grey scars in his eyebrows, a nest of pulsating veins in one temple that hadn't been there a moment ago. "You sure you didn't cop a feel of anything else strange while you were in the Moulie?"

"What the hell you talkin' 'bout, man?"

The inspector grinned and pointed to the cuts on my face and stepped even closer. "Looks like you were either asking the right people the wrong kind of questions or none of those arse bandits fancied a touch of black."

"Enough of that shit!" Fletcher bellowed. Leach's eyes flickered away from my face, and fastened on his boss. Fletcher's intense stare went from Leach to me then back to Leach again. "Let's keep this civil shall we, gentlemen."

Leach nodded in reluctant compliance. He looked back at the tea chest then across to Fletcher. "To my knowledge, Jimmy Moody's no ponce." Leach then turned to face me. "He's a nasty piece of work, but as far as the word on the street has it, he's no shirt-lifter. Whatever your transvestite pal told you sounds way off the mark to me." Leach looked back to his boss. "I'll go pay Jimmy a visit, bring him in for a chat."

As he went to leave, he leaned towards me, his mouth an inch or two from my ear. I could smell cigarettes, booze and mints on his breath. "Forget Moody," he whispered. "Something tells me this is the kinda thing these fellas do to each other when they find out that one of their own's queer?"

I remained silent, my hands trembling, then turned and watched the policeman walk away. From his swagger, it was evident that Leach was confident he'd got under my skin. His parting words felt as much a threat as an opinion, and I wondered how much time would pass before he tried to give it to me between the shoulder blades.

Fletcher stuck his cigar in his mouth and went out to stand on the porch. I drifted on behind him, ignoring him. I'd perhaps taken three steps across the neat lawn outside of the boat house before the copper shouted me back.

"Where the hell do you think you're going to?"

I turned and gave the superintendent a vacant look. "Home. That's me all done here, man."

Fletcher slowly shook his head at me, his face flushing with aggravation. "I ain't bloody finished with you yet. You can forget getting paid by Suresh's old man to find him now."

The superintendent hooked his thumb back towards his car. "I've got another very important appointment for you to keep, old son."

I should have told Fletcher where to stick his appointment there and then, but defying the law would only get me deeper into trouble, whether of my own making or the kind that the police concocted to keep me under their thumb. Some men I'd known had died challenging their superiors; I wasn't a big enough fool to go down that dark road. So, I treated Fletcher's aggravation at me as some strange kind of balm. It would soothe my symptoms for a while, but deep inside, the disease was still there.

CHAPTER
FOURTEEN

Six years ago, a man called Earl Linney, a powerful Jamaican alderman, hired me to find a woman he knew. I found her, but she wasn't exactly what she seemed to be and a lot of people died. Part of that terrible search had brought me to the council house. Today, all those years later, I was back. Another missing person and more death. It felt like history repeating itself.

The government building was on College Green in the heart of Bristol city. It was a semi-circular four-storey building built from bricks of Portland stone. As big as the place was, it almost looked friendly from the outside, but once you got past the front door all that friendliness disappeared.

Fletcher parked the Hillman in the car park at the rear of the building then escorted me inside. We took the lift to the third floor and headed down an office-lined hallway with a spotless white-marble floor. At its end, a woman sat at a reception desk. Her blond hair was pulled back so tight that it pained my scalp just to look at her. She wore a grey businesslike jacket and dark horn-rimmed glasses. She squinted at me, a confused look on her face, clearly unaccustomed to a man of my colour being in the same rarefied air as her up on the third floor, then ignored me, focusing her attention on the superintendent.

"May I assist you, sir?"

"Superintendent Fletcher. I have an appointment to see Mr Castle."

"Ah, yes, Superintendent. Mr Castle is expecting you." There were a lot of *I* and *you* being bandied about, but very little *we*. I was starting to feel like the invisible man. I watched as the woman picked up a phone, held down a small red switch and spoke into the receiver. When the receptionist had finished, she got up and pointed out Castle's office for the policeman. "It's the last door on the left, sir." Fletcher thanked her and strode off. I followed like an obedient gundog awaiting his master's bidding.

A tall white man in his late fifties appeared in an open doorway. He was high-shouldered and elegantly dressed, handsome and seemed to know it. His thick white hair was carefully arranged on his head, as carefully as his expression. "Good morning, Superintendent."

The two men shook hands. Fletcher walked into the office, leaving me out in the hall. I didn't have to wait long before I got some of the same formal treatment, less the welcoming handshake.

"Hello, Mr Ellington. My name is Herbert Castle. I'm a special liaison between the mayor's officer and the police. Please do come in." He opened up his palm to usher me inside.

In Castle's well-appointed office, a little sunlight filtered through the heavily draped windows, but the room was lit by artificial light. Amid this, Castle looked rather artificial himself, like a carefully made wax dummy wired for sound. On a shelf above his right shoulder was a framed picture of a clear-eyed woman, also in her fifties, who, I guessed, was his wife.

Fletcher stood almost to attention at the side of Castle's impressive polished teak desk. It allowed him to remain dutiful in the eyes of his seniors, but still higher up in the pecking order than me.

I sat down in a large armchair covered in soft green leather and winced, the pain in my side from last night's beating all the more apparent now that the effect of the two aspirin I'd taken earlier had worn off. Oil paintings of the Bristol region, landscapes and seascapes, hung on the walls around me like subtle advertisements. Across from where I sat, a man in his sixties, with a bald pate, viewed me suspiciously from an identical chair. He wore a grey made-to-measure suit, his frame thin and bony, with long, tapered fingers and deep green eyes. He crossed his legs and smiled at me. He reminded me of a nasty-looking porcelain figurine that Aunt Pearl used to keep on her mantlepiece. He gestured his head towards me by way of a greeting.

"My name is Truttwell, Mr Ellington. I also work for the mayor. I'm not here in an official capacity. Just keeping an eye on these terrible events."

"Events?"

Castle interrupted. "Let's not get ahead of ourselves, shall we, gentlemen." He walked slowly around his desk and sat down in his high-backed Chesterfield chair. I watched as he opened up a drawer, withdrew a brown manila file and sat it down in front of him. I noted the word *CONFIDENTIAL* printed on the front cover in large red print.

Castle leaned forward and placed one hand on the desk's green baize ink blotter. When he spoke, it was in a calm, neutral tone. "Mr Ellington, I'm sorry to interrupt your day, but I believe we have a blossoming emergency, here in the city."

"Emergency . . . what kind of emergency?"

Castle's cheeks flushed slightly. He cleared his throat then looked across at Fletcher and back at me. "I think at this juncture, it's best that the superintendent appraises you." He slid the file to the end of his desk. Fletcher took a step forward and opened it up. Inside I could see a large black-and-white portrait photograph of a young boy. A white boy. Fletcher carefully picked up the edge of the photograph with his thumb and forefinger then walked across and handed it to me.

"This is James Peberdy. He was eleven years old."

I shifted nervously in my seat. "You say *was*?"

Fletcher nodded solemnly. "Yes. He's dead. His body was found on Portishead golf course by a greenkeeper nine days ago. He'd been strangled and bludgeoned to death then dumped at the bottom of a ditch. He'd been spread out on a bed of beech leaves and hidden with branches and a carpet of moss."

I looked at the face of the young child in the photograph, slowly shook my head and muttered under my breath. "Jesus." Fletcher ignored my muted reaction and continued.

"The boy had left his home in Woodhill Road, at 6.45 p.m. on the sixth of August and the police were alerted later that night when he failed to return home. A search party was convened the following day, with the community of Portishead hoping that the schoolboy's disappearance was some kind of prank. By that time, he'd been missing for over eighteen hours, but we believed there was still a chance that he would be found alive." Fletcher stiffened and glanced towards Castle, a grim look on his face, then back at me.

"We were wrong. It was noon on the tenth of August when the child's body was finally found. Nearby to where James was discovered, under some trees near the twelfth hole of the golf course, officers found a bloodstained oak branch broken in two. We believe the branch was used to kill him. Rather than allow the press to have a field day with all kinds of speculation and perhaps run the killer to ground, we came to an agreement with the boy's parents to keep a lid on things until we had something more concrete to work on. The Indian's body turning up overnight has queered the pitch for us, confidentiality-wise, if you get my drift?"

Fletcher stopped talking for a moment and looked at the two other men in the room, his body rock solid and tense. He turned to face me again, his gaze going to the photograph I was still holding between my fingers. "It was difficult enough to contain the news of the death of this poor Peberdy child. Now with another body turning up so near to where the boy was found, we have no other choice than to go public."

Castle quickly cut in. "I didn't know about the matter of this dead fellow, Suresh, until earlier this morning. The superintendent appraised me of both this latest very sad occurrence out at Portishead boating lake and your earlier involvement with trying to locate the dead man."

"I ain't following you, Mr Castle. What's the death o' this white boy gotta do with me?"

"Nothing directly, Mr Ellington. But with two murders in such close proximity, and in such a short space of time, it's believed that they may well be connected. Now I have the urgent matter of bringing all hands to the pumps, as it were. We each have jobs to do, don't you think?"

I put my hands on the chair arms and began to rise out of my seat. Fletcher took a step forward and gritted his teeth, and I dropped my ass back down on the green leather cushion, shaking my head. I looked at the council official behind his desk. His face had turned a pale shade of red, but his irked demeanour didn't stop me from speaking my mind. "Mr Castle, the way I see it, the po'lice, they gotta job to do. But not me. I'm just a citizen, a civilian. All I gotta do is pay my taxes and keep my head down."

Castle smiled and nodded. "You're right, of course. It's the superintendent and his men that have to bring

114

this killer to justice. But you know this city could use your help also, Mr Ellington."

"Me? I can't help you or the damn city. I ain't the police."

"But you can. I've been made aware by the superintendent here that you know all kinds of people in the community."

I felt the blood pumping through the veins in my temples. "You saying you think a black man killed this white boy and then Nikhil Suresh?"

Castle shook his head, then tried to placate me with a calming wave of his well-scrubbed hand. "Not at all, Mr Ellington. No one is suggesting anything of the sort. We all believe that you can ask questions of people who may be reluctant to talk to the law. People who may know something. Important information that could help the police apprehend a killer. We need every hand we can get on this, Mr Ellington. He held his hand out towards me, but I left it alone.

I shook my head. "No thanks. I'm in the middle o' my own business, man. I can't do nothing for you."

"Yes, you can," chipped in Truttwell. The mysterious aid with no remit got out of his seat and walked slowly across the office. He stood next to the superintendent, looked at him and jutted his thin lip out an eighth of an inch. "Fletcher here tells me exactly the kind of business you've been involved in of late. Most of it unsavoury." Truttwell gave me a moment, just to let his intimidatory oration sink in a little. When he spoke again, his upper lip was tight against his yellowing front teeth. "I'm talking about Parson Street Primary School.

Accusations of theft, Mr Ellington. I believe it's not the first time you've been accused of stealing?"

"You gotta be kiddin' me. Is that some kinda threat?"

Castle quickly got to his feet. "Of course it isn't, Mr Ellington. No one wants to threaten you. We all want the same thing here. We believe a man is killing people. Children. Whoever it is has to be brought to justice. That's all we want. We think that you could be of valuable assistance to both the police and the council."

I saw Truttwell barely restraining himself from licking his lips and breaking out in a grin. I watched him walk quietly to the window, lift back the edge of the drapes and peer down into the street. He knew that I had to go along with the program that had just been set out before me. Fletcher would have me inside one of his police cells quicker than shit through a goose otherwise.

Nikhil Suresh being found dead in a box in leafy Portishead was one thing. It would perhaps make a column and a half on page two of the *Bristol Evening Post*. But a white boy murdered was a different matter altogether. Butchered kids found within spitting distance of decent white folks' homes just wasn't on. The council and the police would be fearing a backlash on the streets from the growing ranks of the National Front as well as from its well-fed constituents in the suburbs. People needed answers to questions the authorities in this room could do without being asked. Politicians and the powerful at the council house knew only too well that voters would have their say come

116

polling day — that this year's great and good could easily be next season's gofers. Bad news meant jobs lost. A dead child whose murder had been hushed up for the convenience of the local constabulary signalled that the heads of the men in the office I was now sitting in would be lined up for the chopping block. The air we all breathed at that very moment was racist.

Castle stood straight and tall when he walked around the desk to join the superintendent. I rose up out of my seat to face the two men. Truttwell wouldn't even look at me. He kept his smug face towards the window. Castle held out his hand to me again. I reluctantly pressed my palm into his and we shook. "That's it for me then," he said. The council official gave Fletcher a cursory glance. "I am assured that the police and Mr Truttwell's department will give you all the help you need, Mr Ellington. I'm sure they will keep me appraised of your progress."

Fletcher escorted me out of Castle's office quicker than a speeding bullet.

As we walked back down the hallway towards the lift, neither of us said a word. Fletcher knew that I hadn't hit the streets to undertake this kind of work for a good few years. Since Chloe had come along, I had tried to bury that kind of life. Despite my earlier reluctance to assist, Castle and Truttwell's strong-arming had secretly set off a fire in my belly, one that I knew would be hard for me to extinguish. I felt like I was a policeman once again, and that long-lost feeling had put a spark in my step and reinvigorated my battered body.

The undesirable errand those three white men had just charged me with — to go looking for the killer or killers of Nikhil Suresh and James Peberdy — was, in truth, like coming back from the dead.

CHAPTER
FIFTEEN

Later that afternoon, I stood in Loretta Harris's kitchen watching as she fried pork sausages, black pudding and onions and heated up a saucepan of red beans and rice while Chloe and Loretta's son, Carnell Jnr, played together in the front room. After the day's disturbing events, I needed time to let what I'd agreed to do for the police and city council sink in. I'd hoped being with my friend would calm my nerves, though I knew that once I'd given Loretta the low-down on what had been going on, the beating I'd received the night before and my further involvement with the police, she would have something to say about the deep water I'd got myself in — and none of it would be kind.

Since moving to England, Loretta had been a true friend. Back when I was doing my thing as an enquiry agent, she had never questioned my motivations or the way I would sometimes earn a living out of other people's hardships and miseries. Always a pragmatist, my friend had a simple code by which she lived. Never turn on your friends, and never talk to the police. In my time, I'd broken both those sacred charters. Not only did I speak to the police, I was once one of their rank and file. Worse still, although I never deliberately went out of my way to hurt any friend, I had, years before, unknowingly caused great sadness to Loretta, and it was in no small part that I brought about the tragic death of her husband, and my old drinking buddy, Carnell.

A simple, innocent act of kindness one cold, foggy evening in the winter of 1965 had resulted in him being murdered by men intent on killing me. Yet Loretta had never blamed me for her husband's death, never once spoke ill of my involvement or shunned our friendship. Rather, in the intervening years, Loretta had shown such forgiveness, comforting me at a time when she was still grieving herself, and over the years, my friend went on to embrace our relationship in a way that perhaps no living soul would or should have expected.

It's fair to say that when the Almighty had finished forging the spirit and mortal embodiment of Loretta May Harris, he broke the mould.

In the past, I'd never worked directly for the police or the council house, though the local beat bobbies would sometimes have called me down to the station and threatened me before asking favours, and Loretta knew this went on. Usually a copper would have me wait on a cold metal bench while they interrogated some poor black kid who would try and bamboozle his inquisitors by answering their questions in broad patois. I never refused to help the police out in a situation like that; I'd rather have seen a man of colour walk away from a night in a cell unharmed and free than ignore his plight and have him languish in the cold for days, probably beaten to a pulp for his trouble.

I'd expected to be browbeaten by Fletcher back in that fusty office earlier today, but the other two men were highfliers, way above the superintendent's pay grade. Those fellas were more important than the one dead Indian they'd hauled me in to talk about. I was pretty sure that the murdered son of an immigrant cobbler would mean little to either man. But a white kid, slaughtered in a leafy suburb and on their watch, would be an entirely different matter. Once the press got hold of that unsavoury story, Herbert Castle and the police would need a watertight excuse for keeping it quiet. My meeting this morning was most probably the beginning of a carefully planned whitewash. Fletcher had hauled me to that office to become his own personal Uncle Tom; I'd been brought in to help sweep the police and council's unfolding mess under the carpet. The colour of my skin, my lower class based on my race, had once again made me an easy mark, and three men who had little regard either for my well-being or reputation had cleverly carved out a different path for me to tread. I knew as I'd walked away from that meeting that I was already being sold down the river, the sense of oncoming betrayal palpable.

I also knew that those same three duplicitous men feared a greater evil than simply their own personal downfalls based on secrets and lies or their willingness to employ a man of colour to do their donkey work for them. In the past year, the National Front's shows of strength in the city had seen the police and anti-fascists clash violently on the streets of Bristol, and I knew that

121

the likes of Herbert Castle and the man called Truttwell would be getting hot under the collar at the thought of further rioting, especially the kind of civil unrest that was incited by the news that a white child might have been murdered by someone with black skin.

Enoch Powell's "Rivers of Blood" speech in the spring of 1968 had lit a fire of hate right across the nation, and the febrile politics that had swept the country since then had never been more delirious than it was in the South West. I'd never been a follower of politics, though, and wouldn't have trusted a politician as far as I could have thrown 'em. My old mama used to say to me and my late sister, Bernice: "*Whoever you vote fo', dem government, dey always gonna win.*" Truer words I've never heard spoken.

The country's current economic woes and industrial unrest over the past twelve months had spawned political extremism on both the left and the right. Politicians on both sides seemed unwilling to recognise that something malignant was blowing in the wind, few were willing to heed the seriousness of the situation, few had taken seriously Powell's earlier bleak rhetoric. But black folk right across Britain certainly had.

For a long time, they had sensed the agitation and tension rising in the towns and cities, though most were impotent to warn those in power of the coming storm. Our soapbox had been kicked from under our feet before we'd had chance to stand upon it. I had always known racism, but the hatred and bigotry that the National Front was currently spouting on the streets was both scary and dangerous, ruthlessly exploiting white working-class fears over immigration to create a far-right threat that had been unseen in Britain since Oswald Mosley's times. The sorry fact that few in power wanted to address the rise of such overt intolerance left black folk feeling that *Jim Crow* laws were waiting for them, just around the corner. When Bob Dylan had said that "the times were a-changing" I doubt he'd have realised how slow that shift would be here in St Pauls or, for that matter, the rest of the mother country.

We all sat and ate supper in Loretta's small, white linoleum and waxed-maple kitchen, me and my friend at either end of an old Formica-topped table while Chloe and Carnell Jnr boxed us in at the sides. The prospect of some fine, home-cooked food had lifted my sunken spirits a little, but my earlier worries about hustling for the police, the dead white boy and the bloody image of the beaten corpse of Nikhil Suresh still continued to invade my thoughts.

Loretta and I spoke only a few, brief words to each other during the meal. When we had all finished eating, my friend went upstairs with the children and ran a bath for them while I washed and dried the dishes. When she returned to the kitchen a half hour later, I was already sat back at the table, pouring my second three-finger-length of rum into a glass. Loretta stood in the kitchen doorway, a bottle of Dettol antiseptic in one hand and an old brass tin with the words *First Aid* printed on top of it in bright red, italic lettering. She looked at the booze in the glass and shook her head at me. "Tek off you shirt," she snapped. "Lemme clean up those cuts on you face and see if you broke any of you damn ribs."

I did as she asked and removed my shirt and vest. Refusing any sort of help from Loretta was like putting a red rag to a bull — actions taken at your own risk. The consequences for rebuffing such rare acts of kindness were being met with a string of foul language and the back of her hand upside your head. I'd taken more than enough punishment this past twenty-four hours. Compliance was the wisest move.

I closed my eyes while Loretta worked. I could see shadows swimming behind my lids, my face flinching in pain as she dabbed antiseptic on the cuts and my bruised ribs.

After she'd finished cleaning me up, Loretta bound the lower part of my torso with a length of bandage, taping the fabric dressing tightly around my back. I watched as my friend slowly screwed the cap back on the bottle of Dettol. She looked at me silently for a moment, her brown eyes examining me intently. "Why the hell you gettin' yo'self messed up in this kinda shit again, Joseph?"

Loretta's voice was so unusually full of feeling that it took me a moment to decipher her words. I pulled on my vest then looked up at her and frowned. "What kinda shit you talking about?"

Loretta sucked air through the gap in her front teeth. "Don't be givin' me that blank look, fool . . . I'm askin' 'bout why you tekin' on the Babylon's toil like you doin'?"

124

I took a deep breath and felt a suffocating sense of fear before replying. "Woman, we already been through this nonsense. I either toe the line with Fletcher and the po'lice or I'm gonna end up in a lot more trouble than just being accused of thieving bleach from Parson Street School."

The muscles in Loretta's jaw tightened and her eyes glazed with anger. She cupped her fist in her palm, her knuckles as hard as pebbles under the skin. "Bullshit! The Babylon ain't gonna be givin' you no hard time over a few bottles of Ajax suds, and you know it. You just wantin' to be the white man's po'lice again. Pointin' a big ole stick at a heap o' damn trouble you got no bidness gettin' involved in."

"It ain't like that, Loretta . . . This job, it ain't exactly what I got in mind to keep the wolf from the door, you know. I just gotta do what Fletcher tells me . . ."

Loretta suddenly swung her arm into the air, the palm of her hand stretched out in front of my face. "I don't wanna hear that honky pig's fuckin' name mentioned in ma house again, you hearin' me?"

I looked down at the floor, all too aware that I was being scrutinised angrily. "Yeah, I hear you."

Loretta stormed across the kitchen, reached into the cupboard above the refrigerator for a glass then returned back to where the bottle of rum sat beside me. I watched as she poured herself a large slug and knocked it back before walking towards the kitchen door, mumbling a string of obscenities under her breath. The expression on her face suddenly became less rigid and intense. Her eyes stared along the hall

125

then focused in on me, and she flicked her head back up, towards the ceiling. "You know you gonna need somebody ta be lookin' after that pickney o' yours while you out playin' detectives agin. You can't be expectin' Gabe and Pearl to be having no little kid under their feet all tha time. They gittin' way too old fo' that shit."

I sniffed and nodded in agreement. "How'd it be if Chloe stays with you for the time being, just till I get things sorted with the boys in blue? I'll pick her up in the mornings, take her to school, spend time with her at night then bring her to you before bedtime."

Loretta shrugged. "You know it be fine by me. Bring tha child."

I smiled and held out my hand to touch Loretta's arm, but she snatched herself away from my reach. I suddenly felt weak all over. I had to swallow before I could speak. "I don't mean to cause you so much grief."

"Grief, he says . . ." Loretta started to shake her head again. "Sometime, Joseph, I don't know if you have any fuckin' idea 'bout the kinda heartache you keep bringin' to folks' gate doors. Sum'ting tells me you ain't ever gonna learn."

Her eyes moved thoughtfully over my face as though she were a protective older sister looking at a troublesome younger brother. And then she turned and walked away, leaving me alone in her kitchen with only the bottle of rum for company and a big question mark as to whether I had acquired any degree of caution or wisdom in the forty-ninth year of my life.

* * *

The moon was down that night, the sky black, and trees of lightning trembled on the southern horizon. At four in the morning I was awakened by the rumble of dry thunder and the flickering patterns of light on my bedroom wall. A tuning fork was vibrating in my chest, but I couldn't explain why, and my skin was hot and dry to the touch, even though the breeze through the window was cool. I heard sounds like the footsteps of men coming through the trees, the scrape of a prising bar being inserted between the front door and the jamb of my old home, then the screams of my wife and daughter as a fiery inferno suddenly erupted around them. They were the sounds of ghosts, because the men who had inflicted such pain and misery on those I loved dearest were now dead. Killed by my own hand.

I sat upright on the mattress, the sweat pouring off me, my mind still reliving the blind panic and the horror from all those years ago. Despite the passing of time, such cruel feelings were never far from my mind. Now, not a day went by that I didn't wish I could embrace my long-gone kin, rather than still be scratching those ugly night-time ruminations that plagued my sleep.

I rubbed my palms across my face then got out of bed and went across to my dressing-room drawer to take out the army-issue US Colt .45 I kept hidden under my work shirts. I slipped the heavy clip into the magazine and lay back down in the dark. The flat of the barrel felt cool against my thigh. I put my arm across my eyes and tried to fall asleep again, the nagging voice in my head reminding me that any pursuit for slumber would be hard fought.

CHAPTER
SIXTEEN

I didn't own a crystal ball and I possessed no special powers to see into the future, but my tacit prediction that all hell would break loose when news of James Peberdy's murder hit the streets panned out just as I'd imagined. The early edition of the *Bristol Evening Post* carried the death of the Portishead boy on its front page, the headline "All-Out Search for Child Killer" emblazoned above the same black-and-white photograph of the deceased child that I had been shown in Herbert Castle's office the day before. BBC Radio Bristol had been broadcasting the tragic details since sun up, and word of the child's grim demise was being spoken about on almost every street corner across the city.

Nikhil Suresh's brutal slaying had managed to find itself a few inches of column space at the bottom of page six. Little had been made of the fact that both victims had been killed in the same quiet coastal town, and few details of the manner in which Suresh had met his death were reported. The grisly modus of how his body had been found mutilated and mangled no doubt hushed up by the powers that be at the Somerset and Bath Constabulary.

The deal that Fletcher had offered me when we had left the council house yesterday afternoon had been very simple. "Go sniff about where my fellas are gonna hit a brick wall." In other words, the slippery copper wanted me to stick my neck out on the streets of St Pauls and Montpelier, asking the kind of prickly questions that people living in those neighbourhoods would rather not be asked by Bristol's finest. Most of the black folk I knew would rather have jumped off a cliff than speak to the Babylon.

I was pretty damn sure no black man had murdered Nikhil Suresh, and I could only hope that was the case for the child, though Fletcher and the men who pulled his strings at the council house clearly thought differently. Something told me that those men had some kind of vested interest in my poking around in my own backyard. Rather than a murderer, I got the feeling I was being sent out to find them a patsy. If the chump was black, all the better.

For now, most folk I would come into contact with and grill in the local area would be unaware of the Peberdy killing. That kind of news would take a while longer to filter out into St Pauls. Few in my neighbourhood listened to local radio or read the town rag, and it was rare to see a newspaper board out on the streets. The *Evening Post* was already disconnected from the city's black communities, another Bristol institution that black people didn't feel was for them, and they were already wary of telling the *Post* about any kind of news. They had a deep suspicion of a

130

newspaper that only wrote about black people when they committed crime, and they were right to be wary.

My instincts told me to stick with the Suresh killing. Stay on the same path I'd been sent down by Fletcher a few days before. Castle had instructed the superintendent to offer me ten pounds a day plus expenses to conduct my own enquiry. It was the very same daily rate that had been offered by Nikhil Suresh's father to search for his missing son. If I was about to pocket Castle's blood money, it was only right and proper that I finished earning what had already been proffered to me.

Detective work, sleuthing, snooping about — these are all inexact practices. My hunch to start at the beginning may have been a shot in the dark, another blind alley that would lead me nowhere. But for now, it was all I had. Something told me that I needed to head back to Cotham. Back to the home of Nikhil Suresh. To cross-examine his folks. Decent people who were bereaved. Grieving. Broken-hearted.

There had to be better ways to earn a buck.

CHAPTER
SEVENTEEN

The front door of Suresh's shoe repair shop was ajar, the CLOSED sign hanging centre stage in the door. Inside, I could just make out the flicker of candles burning and heard voices coming from the back of the store, chattering, busy words that I could not understand. I stood on the step and hesitated for a moment then knocked and waited, and knocked again, before I saw someone move from behind the counter and head my way.

An eye regarded me out of the shadows. The voice that went with it asked, "Yes?"

I stood back in the street as the door slowly opened. A young Indian woman, dressed in a long white sari, stared back at me. The eye was one of a cat-green pair set in an angular dark brown face. They burned back at me from deep hollows beneath heavy brows. She was of slight build, perhaps five-two in her flat shoes, and pretty in the hard way that poverty imparts on its denizens. I took off my hat and smiled at her.

"Is Mr Suresh about, please?"

The woman shook her head. "Uncle is not home. I am Keya, his niece. Can I help you?"

"My name is Joseph Ellington. Your uncle employed me earlier this week to look for his son, Nikhil."

The woman's nostrils flared. Her face sank towards the floor. When she spoke, it was barely more than a mumble. "Nikhil is dead."

"Yes, I know. I am very sorry for you and your family's loss."

The woman looked back up at me. Neither of us said a word for a moment. Behind her, an elderly woman walked slowly out from the shadows towards the door, coming to a halt a few feet behind the younger woman. She also wore a full-length white sari, her head covered in a long linen scarf. She was barefoot, her face partially hidden behind gold-rimmed glasses. She spoke quietly to the younger woman in their own language then stared at me. The language may have been foreign to me, but I could still hear the reluctance in the tone of her frail voice.

"My aunt wants to know why you have come to her home?"

"I'm an enquiry agent. I'm working with the police, but I'm not part of them. Mr Suresh paid me some money to see if I could find your aunt's boy." I hesitated, considering my next words carefully, then looked at the old woman. "Now, I'd very much like to earn what was given to me by hopefully finding the person who did Nikhil harm."

The younger woman repeated what I'd just said to her relative. I felt the old woman's fox-fire eyes focus in on me. A chill ran down my spine and raised the hairs along the back of my neck. I inclined my head in the hope of offering up a measure of unspoken respect then offered the briefest of smiles at the grieving matriarch before speaking.

"May I come in?"

My gesture had been a simple, silent expression of condolence, but it was all I had to give to a woman who spoke little or no English. One thing I knew was that people like the Sureshes and I had one awful thing in common. We both knew the terrible agony of losing someone we loved to unspeakable violence, and in feeling that pain learned to live with not quite enough and make do with somewhat less than that.

I followed the two women through the shop and upstairs. Nothing much had changed in the drab sitting room. The only difference since I'd last visited was that the almost perfect cubed space was now bathed in a murky haze. The curtains were drawn and the place had been lit with an array of different-sized wax candles. There was still the same musty aroma of stale spice and pungent incense permeating the air, and the padded chairs and sofa had now been drawn around the low coffee table. In its centre was a small black-and-white photograph of Nikhil Suresh. Around the frame, arranged in a circle, were torn rose petals of differing colours. A single large, church-altar-style candle burned at the side of the photograph, its flame dancing back and forth; its brittle illumination reflecting eerily off the glass. The young woman looked nervously at her aunt, then back at me.

"Would you like some tea, Mr Ellington?"

134

"No thank you. I don't want to impose. I'll try to be as brief as I can. I just have a couple of questions about Nikhil I'd like to ask, if that's okay?"

"My uncle and aunt have already spoken to the policeman yesterday. We both translated into Punjabi what the officers were asking aunty."

I smiled at the two women. "By chance, do you or your aunt remember any of their names?"

Keya nodded. "The man doing most of the talking was called Leach."

I nodded back. "Has Nikhil ever been in trouble with the law?"

The young girl quickly translated my question. The grieving elderly woman raised her left arm out in front of her, the palm of her hand rocking from side to side. She eyeballed me, her withering glare more than adequate an answer to my insensitive enquiry.

"Would your aunt know if Nikhil ever played golf?" As soon as the word *golf* left my mouth, the old woman twisted her face away, avoiding my scrutiny by concentrating on her niece.

I could tell that Keya had seen the same troubled expression on her aunt's face. When she asked my question, her tone seemed more reverential and measured. The old woman considered her niece's words for a long time. When she did begin talking, her voice was low, her speech hesitant. Keya waited for a second or two before telling me what had been said.

"No, Nikhil did not play the game. He pulled the cart for others, she thinks."

"You saying that her boy was a golf caddy?"

"Caddy?" Keya shrugged. "I am not sure what this word means."

I smiled. "A caddy is somebody who pulls a cart with golf clubs loaded up on it."

Keya nodded, then said with almost no hesitation, "Then that is what Nikhil was doing."

"Your aunt perhaps have any idea where her son might have pulled this cart?"

Keya repeated my question. The old woman remained silent and just shook her head in reply.

I looked over the girl's shoulder. "Could I look in Nikhil's room?"

The two women stood on the landing while I went through Nikhil's things. The room wasn't large enough for the three of us, with little in the way of personal possessions or decoration. There were box springs under a single mattress, with a drab canvas and leather trunk at the foot of it. From the looks of things, the trunk worked as both a night table and Nikhil's closet. The window that looked out on to the backyard wasn't wide enough for a man to squeeze through, giving the dead man's room the feel of a jail cell.

Nailed to the wall over the bed was a cork bulletin board. Tacked upon it were pictures cut from magazines, newspapers, books and comics; photographs and drawings of men, many of them in uniform — a policeman, a sailor, a fireman, a footballer, a soldier and, oddly, Superman. All of the men were young and white.

136

I looked around the room. Nikhil's bed was made and the oak floor swept.

"Did your aunt clean up in here?"

Keya spoke in Punjabi again, then back to me in English. The old woman was looking down at the floor, her head shaking slowing from side to side, and muttering under her breath.

The young woman seemed embarrassed. She shook her head at me and pointed a finger at the mattress. "She says, not really, Mr Ellington. Nikhil was always very neat and orderly. She only made his bed again after the police searched in here last night."

I gestured towards the wall. "That's an interesting bulletin board."

Keya repeated what I said to her aunt. Mrs Suresh kept looking down at her feet for a moment longer then stared up at the board before speaking.

"Nikhil didn't have girls up there, but he liked girls," Keya translated. "It's just that he looked at clothes and important people and he thought that was what it took to be something special here in Britain."

I glanced across at the trunk. "Can I take a look in the chest?"

Once I'd been told it was okay, I kneeled down and lifted the lid. Inside were balled-up socks, T-shirts, vests, trousers and underwear, all jumbled. I figured this was from the police search.

I looked at the old woman. "Did the policemen take anything from this trunk?"

The old woman shook her head then walked away back towards the sitting room without saying anything further. I got to my feet and a few moments later she returned with a black, leather-bound photo album, held tightly in both hands. She stood with her back against the hall wall, her body trembling, and glared at me, tears welling in her lower lids. As she passed the album over to Keya, a tear fell down her cheek and landed on the album's cover. Keya quickly wiped it away with the tips of her fingers then handed it to me.

I flipped through the pages. Most were recent colour photographs, all very innocent, mainly of Nikhil standing alone outside Bristol Zoo, or posing down at the harbourside, and one taken from the top of Cabot Tower. As I continued to leaf through the album, five black-and-white Polaroid snapshots fell from inside the last loose pages of the book. Three of the photos had been taken inside the Moulin Rouge nightclub. The glossy pictures showed Nikhil Suresh dressed in a wide-lapelled suit, his frilly shirt open to reveal his bare chest. He sat laughing on the lap of a white man, whose face was, by chance, obscured by Suresh's own head and shoulders. The man's pale hands were clearly visible, his arms wrapped around Suresh's waist, the fingers positioned either side of his groin. Secrets and lies, I thought. What family hasn't kept them or spoken falsely for them to remain hidden?

The fourth and fifth photographs took me totally by surprise. As I looked at them in dismay, I felt my mouth dry out and my insides flutter and knot. The last pictures had also been taken at Moulie, at the same time. They showed Nikhil Suresh up on his feet, a forced smile on his face, staring into the lens of the

138

camera with something like fear in his eyes. The dead man had his back to the bar, various balloons, paper-chain decorations and a huge Happy New Year banner hanging behind him. Standing either side, their arms draped across Suresh's shoulders, were two of the most powerful and dangerous men in Bristol.

CHAPTER
EIGHTEEN

One thing I've learned in nearly fifty hard years of living is that there's a different kind of death waiting for each and every one of us — each and every day of our lives. There're drunk drivers; train, plane and boat accidents; drowning in pools and rivers. There's banana peels; diseases and cockeyed medicines that are supposed to cure them; jealous husbands and wives with knives or worse in their mean hands to do their damn worst. And then there's plain bad luck.

Nikhil Suresh's murder had not just come down to ill fortune. The five Polaroid photographs in my inside jacket pocket were proof enough of that. Suresh had been keeping the kind of unsavoury and dangerous company that most hardened villains would have thought twice about. Three of the photographs were proof enough that the dead man was leading a double life. Suresh's mother, although unable to communicate that fact to me, knew the same. The anguished look on the poor woman's face had told me everything I needed to know. She'd been keeping a skeleton hidden in the closet for more years than she cared to remember, the arranged marriage yet another way of veiling her son's homosexuality.

Any good mother worth her salt knows their child like the back of their hand, and the woman had always known the truth about her boy, a secret I'm sure she'd have been more than happy to take to her grave. Nikhil's murder and the subsequent police investigation would more than likely uncover painful truths; destructive revelations that had a habit of bringing decent families like the Sureshes to their knees.

Once I got back to my car, I gave in to a kind of weariness. The two men standing next to Nikhil Suresh in that final photograph were both well known to me, and thinking about them was like trying to bring back a nightmare. Their names were William Ryder and Jah Rhygin, and as I stared at both men's faces, I felt a hot sensation deep inside my chest, like a flame punching a hole in a sheet of paper and spreading outward until it blackened everything it touched.

There was only a handful of pubs, bars or clubs in Bristol that a man like me, or any black or Asian person, was welcome in. I was pretty much used to having the front door of most boozers slammed in my face. But that wasn't the case with the Bamboo Club. When black folk walked into that joint, they knew they were walking into a place where they really were welcome. Didn't matter whether you were Jamaican, Barbadian or from any one of the other Caribbean islands we had originally hailed from — in the Bamboo, you were at home.

If you wanted to take a drink of rum or a pint of stout, perhaps chew down on a steaming plate of pigs' feet and rice and peas and listen to some fine tunes, then you headed for the Bamboo. Once your ass hit a seat, you were one hundred per cent relaxed — the Bamboo was our place, somewhere we could laugh, tell stories, play darts and dominoes, and we felt comfortable engaging in conversation in our mutual tongue. The familiar sound of patois rang about the place, the dialect and song of our childhoods.

It was just after two in the afternoon by the time I'd driven back to St Pauls and walked through the doors of the club. I made my way down a corridor and offered up a greeting to Norman Tandy, the elderly Barbadian doorman who sat behind a dilapidated lime-green kiosk, noisily slurping at a bowl of Brown Down chicken stew. The octogenarian gatekeeper flashed a greasy smile at me and waved me on into the inner sanctum of the club, then went back to eating his supper.

At the end of the hallway, I grabbed hold of two looped brass handles and pulled open the double doors. Inside, I immediately caught the attention of a half-dozen older punters, who lifted their faces out of their drinks to gawp. To some black folk: in St Pauls, I was still the Babylon. A former policeman and snoop who couldn't be trusted, an outsider who was to be tolerated rather than embraced. In truth, I didn't give a damn what any of them thought about me. I kept on walking across that dance floor, the sting of their razor-sharp stares burning into my back.

When I reached the bar, I leaned against the edge and looked back at the chary audience who had all

142

returned to supping their hooch before a sharp, sudden jab at the top of my shoulder jolted me from my eyeballing. I turned around to face the bar. Standing in front of me was the Bamboo's head barman, Garnett Downie. He sneered at me blankly, an air of impatience seeping off his barrel-shaped torso before folding his arms like a mean-spirited schoolmaster about to scold a pupil.

"What you havin', man?"

"Rum." I pointed over to the half-empty bottle of Mount Gay that sat on a glass shelf just behind his head. "Make it a large one."

Downie nodded, reached for the bottle and grabbed a crystal tumbler to pour the rum into. I paid for my drink and wandered over to the jukebox, chose a record and stuck a coin in. I watched as the record slowly dropped down on to the turntable and tapped my fingers on the side of the jukebox as The Maytals number "Bam Bam" began to play at a fairly low volume, then went and found myself a seat in one of the booths at the back of the club. I took a hefty swig of my rum and reached inside my jacket pocket to retrieve the photo of Nikhil Suresh standing between the two men. It was like looking at a cherub framed between two devils. A lamb to the slaughter, if ever I'd seen it.

Association with either of them was like taking a glass-bottomed boat ride through the city's sewer system. Blood, money and death were the only currencies they dealt in. The grisly manner in which Suresh's body had been found now started to make a little more sense to me. The dead man had been

143

associating with monsters, and he'd clearly gone on to pay a very high price for it. Never had the term *hanging with the wrong crowd* been more apt.

The first of the two was William "Billy" Ryder. We had crossed paths twice before in the past and I'd deeply regretted it both times. Ryder'd had the criminal action in Bristol locked up since the late 1950s, his sanction and charter underwritten by the family of vicious thugs he had working for him. This motley mob of crooks and heavies was referred to by the crime boss as *the firm* and few other villains were ever stupid enough to go head to head with them. Hence most of the prostitution in the city, fence operations, money laundering, gambling, shylocking, union takeovers, drug dealing and even game poaching out at Ashton Court became forever Ryder's special province. No street hustler, grifter, pickpocket, thief, dip, stall or low-rent con ever crossed him; not unless they wanted to find one of their limbs hacked off and hanging in the window of the local butcher's shop.

It was said that Ryder feared neither man nor beast, but I had it on very good authority that the criminal kingpin shuddered at and shrank away from the ghoulish enigma that was Jah Rhygin.

God Raging. That's what the name Jah Rhygin meant when it was spoken in hushed Jamaican patois. It was said that a succubus lived in the breast of the Jah and that malignant spirit gave him no respite. Those who lived in fear of his far-reaching wrath and his much-rumoured occult powers considered Rhygin to be the living embodiment of the Heartman, a creature

144

of the Bajan underworld, part human, part demon. The Jah's mantra to his fearful minions was simple. The world belongs to the strong, not the meek. The lion devours the foal, the falcon feasts on the sparrow. He who denies this, denies the might of the Rhygin.

I peered at the photograph for a moment longer then stuffed it inside my jacket pocket before knocking back the last of my rum. The spirit slid like velvet fire down my throat. The stark realisation that at some point I would have to face both of these infernal boogeymen hit me like a lead weight as I got to my feet.

I knew that, of the two evils, it was the Jah's altar that I would have to kneel at first.

CHAPTER
NINETEEN

I collected Chloe from Loretta's just after four and drove the short distance from my friend's house back home. The sky was bright and hazy, and the spotted patterns of late-afternoon light and shadow fell through the canopy of the oak trees and raced across Chloe's face. Her knees, white socks and patent leather shoes were dusty from play. I noticed that she kept looking curiously at the side of my face.

"Yeah?" I asked.

"Sum'ting wrong, Joseph?" she said.

"Nah, not at all."

Chloe shrugged. "Sum'ting bad happen, ain't it?"

"No, everything's fine, child ... and don't say 'ain't'."

"Why you mad?"

I shook my head. "Listen, I gotta go out again later, run some more errands for work. I want you to go stay with Loretta and Carnell Jnr till I got things sorted, okay?"

"How long I gotta be there fo'?"

"Just a few days while I help these fellas out."

"These fellas bad men?"

"No, they're not bad. Why'd you say that?"

Chloe's sullen face looked up at me. Her eyes were round and unblinking. "I heard Loretta shouting at you last night, talking 'bout Babylon. Is that what she calls bad men?"

I took a breath and let it out. "No, that's a word some people use when they're talking 'bout po'licemen."

Chloe looked at me curiously. Her voice was quiet when she spoke again. "You a po'liceman, Joseph?"

"No, no I'm not. I'm helping out some po'licemen, but just for a short time."

I watched her look into space, then she smiled. "Well, that's okay then, I suppose."

I turned in to Morgan Street and parked up in the shade across from the house, then pulled Chloe against my side and kissed the top of her head. I could smell the sun's heat in her hair, and, despite all the madness going on around me, for the briefest of moments felt truly content with my lot.

That evening, Chloe and I walked down to the Orange Grove café on Moon Street for fried chicken and steamed rice and peas. The air had become clear and cool, the sky darkening except for a lighted band of purple clouds on the horizon. We sat at one of the checked-cloth tables on a screened porch that looked out on to the road, and while we waited for our food to arrive, we watched the seagulls dip and wheel outside. We spoke very little during the meal, and I could sense that Chloe had more questions that she wanted to ask me, reassurances that she needed to hear, but for some reason chose not to pursue. I remained silent, not wanting to make matters worse, to unsettle or upset the child more than I knew she already was.

An hour later, the two of us headed back across St Pauls over to Loretta's place on Brunswick Street. Chloe held on to my hand, her tiny fingers hard and unyielding as they wrapped around my own. When we arrived, I opened up the gate, walked up to the front door and rapped on the glass panel in the centre of it. I squeezed Chloe against my side and looked down into her face while we waited for Loretta to open up.

A few moments later, she threw open the door, a joint hanging out her mouth; she was dressed in a purple velvet dressing gown and fluffy mule slippers. Her dark, oiled afro was tied up high on her head. She leaned against the door frame, took a big hit on her roll-up then blew a plume of grey ganja smoke out into the street.

"Where tha hell you two bin?" Loretta looked down at Chloe and winked, then shot me one of her evil stares. "I bin waitin' on this damn pickney to git here an' he'p me out. Carnell Jnr, he bin axin' me when this chil' gonna be knockin' on my gate do' for tha better part of t'ree hours. Little fucker bin driving me crazy. I was just 'bout to tear him a new ass'ole!"

I ignored my friend's ranting and reached into the inside pocket of my jacket and took out a small manila envelope. "Here, I thought this might come in handy."

Loretta stared at the envelope, then snatched it out of my hand. She tore open the top, pulled out the thin wad of cash and quickly rifled through the edge of the banknotes. "What's this shit fo'?"

148

I looked down at Chloe and winked, then back up at Loretta. "You gonna need a little dough fo' all those ice creams you gonna be buying, ain't you?"

Loretta stuffed the envelope into the pocket of her dressing gown and smiled at Chloe. "Joseph, you gone an' read my mind, brutha."

I smiled at Loretta as she took hold of Chloe's hand gently in her own, then kneeled down and gave the child a hug. I kissed her forehead and watched as her eyes began to dart from side to side before a veil of sadness fell across her face. I touched her cheek with my hand and got to my feet.

"Goodbye, little guy," I said.

"Bye, Joseph."

Chloe's eyes began to film. I bent down and gave her another kiss on the top of her head then quickly headed back down the path and out the gate. Out on the street, I turned to look back and watched as Chloe blotted her eyes with her sleeve. I started to call something to her, to leave a comforting statement hovering in the air that would somehow redeem the moment: an apology for going away, for deceiving her, but I stopped myself from uttering any such idle sentiments and walked on into the night. It was one of those miserable times where I realised that you have to release others and yourself to their shared pain and sadness and not pretend that pretty language can heal either.

CHAPTER
TWENTY

Victor Ellington was family. My cousin had always been a constant fixture in my life. He was a ladies' man, a philanderer, a fabulous raconteur, a stone-cold killer and probably the best friend I ever had, though he was really more of a comrade. He was the kind of man who stood beside you through blood and fire, death and torture. No one in their right mind would ever choose to live in a world where they'd need a friend like Vic, but you don't choose the world you live in or the skin you inhabit.

There were times when Vic had stood up for me when I wasn't even in the room or the neighbourhood. That's why black folk still rarely gave me any grief. To most locals living in and around St Pauls, I was still considered to be a white man's lackey, the former copper with a dubious past and a reputation for getting myself and others into trouble. But I was also kin to Vic Ellington, and so people had always backed away, seeing the ghostly image of my cousin hanging at my shoulder.

I lived in a world where many people believed the law dealt with citizens equally, but that belief wasn't held by my people, and especially not Vic. The law we all faced was most often at odds with itself. When the sun went down or the cell door slammed, the law no longer applied.

In that sort of cruel domain, faced with such prejudice and intolerance, it was easy to see how a man like my cousin had become as delinquent, immoral and felonious as he had. What was perhaps harder to comprehend was how Victor Ellington had evolved into the beast that was Jah Rhygin.

I have always believed the dead have a voice and inhabit the earth as surely as we do. I believe that they speak in our dreams or inside the sound of the rain or even on the static of a telephone call when there is no other caller on the line. To the police, Victor Ellington was very much dead. His apparent demise after falling to a watery grave below the Clifton Suspension Bridge five years earlier had been welcomed by the Bristol constabulary, who'd always viewed him as a slippery criminal enigma; a man who appeared to have the luck of the gods on his side and who had perpetually foiled so many of their attempts to put him behind bars.

Our community in St Pauls had grieved and mourned his passing at the time, but no funeral was ever held. Vic's body had never been recovered from the muddy waters of the River Avon, the local boys in blue wrongly presuming at the time that it had been washed out into the Bristol Channel and lost forever at sea.

Weeks later, I was to find out that, like Lazarus, Vic had in fact risen from the dead. He had miraculously survived the drop of two-hundred and forty-five feet

151

and was swept away into the night; his remarkable resurrection transpiring through his own gritty determination rather than any divine assistance from a celestial being. I had then watched him bid me farewell from the upper deck of the TSS *Camito* as it sailed out of Southampton dock in the early autumn of 1966.

When he returned to Bristol from the Caribbean three years later, his homecoming was as surreptitious and stealthy as his departure had been. Vic's comeback took the physical guise of a Jamaican Rastafarian. With his face scarred and covered in a long salt-and-pepper beard, his hair in long rope-like dreadlocks and his right eye now covered with a black leather eyepatch, he walked through the city's streets looking like a very different man to the one I, and so many others, including the police, remembered.

But my cousin had never been dead to me, even back then. Nowadays, although I saw less of him, and he lived under a different name to all but me and his parents, I still took him everywhere I went, even though he was rarely physically at my side. He was my barometer for evil, my advisor when no good man would have known what to say. Vic was proof that a black man could live by his own rules in Britain. Knowing that, it was easy for me to believe that my cousin, however seriously injured, could easily crawl up out of the Clifton Gorge and return to life whenever he'd damn well felt like it.

It was late, gone 1 a.m., when I finally left my house and drove down to the waterfront at Buchanan's Wharf, just outside of the city. I sat in my car and looked out at

152

the old grain warehouse that was Vic's headquarters. It was a six-storey Victorian building, its two ancient red-bricked towers standing guard over a blossoming criminal empire that was mantled by the legitimate business front of Redland Import and Export. My cousin always used to tell me, "You wanna hide sum'ting, then go hide it where every damn fool can find it!"

Vic was the only black man I knew who had managed to get himself a place in an all-white business neighbourhood and then remain as inconspicuous as a hibernating dormouse. He rarely went to bed before sunrise and, like most predators, he undertook both his bloodletting and business affairs after dark. If I were living the life I had promised myself, I'd have been back at home hours ago, with Chloe tucked into bed and my feet up. But that kind of cossetted world was a million miles away from that of my cousin's.

I was about to give my hot-tempered kin the third degree and I wasn't sure I was going to like what he'd have to say. Entering his shadowy realm to challenge him as to why he'd been pictured with a dead man and a fellow member of the Bristol criminal underworld would, I knew, create problems of its own. It was an unenviable and reckless predicament to find myself in. In fact, I was sure that if any other ill-informed soul had been foolish enough to give him the third degree on such a delicate matter, they would have found themselves stitched into a mail bag and dropped unceremoniously into the Severn Estuary.

It's no exaggeration: Vic was one of the most dangerous men I had ever known. And so I stopped to consider the implications of such high-risk activity before getting out of the car.

But in truth, these were impotent deliberations, wasted on rational thought or gut instinct. The tenebrous path that I was about to tread was one I wished I didn't have to take, but I knew at that moment in time that I had little choice in the matter.

Men like me rarely do.

You never went to the Redland building unless you were invited, though for a few privileged individuals, the door was always open. I was one of them. Once you found yourself inside the place, getting up to the top floor to see the Jah was not without its problems, even if you were associated by blood. Certain protocols had to be followed. Strict rules adhered to. It was easier to gain an audience with kings, queens and presidents than be granted the opportunity to bow before Vic's arcane alter ego, Jah Rhygin.

Smoke Billings stood at the alley door that led up to Vic's apartment on the sixth floor. Smoke had a heavyweight's physique and a tired, motherly face. His countenance was one of sad kindness, but I knew that he'd killed half a dozen men for money back home on Barbados before coming to work for my cousin. He wore a sixties-style, narrow-lapelled brown suit with a gold chain on his waistcoat and a crimson kipper tie, a red rose drooping from his buttonhole.

"Smoke," I said in greeting.

154

He raised his head a half-inch in salutation, watching me with his watery grey eyes.

"Looking for Vic," I said. I'd uttered those words so many times over the years that they had started to sound like an incantation.

"Not here."

"He needs to be found."

Smoke's nostrils flared wide as he tried to get a sense of my purpose. He took a deep breath and then nodded. "Brutha, you can tek an audience wid tha Jah six floors up if you stupid enuffta climb dem mean stair?"

I peered through the doors then walked past Smoke into the narrow stairway that would take me up to his master. When I neared the top, a large ebony door swung open and Vic's right-hand man Elijah Bliss came out to meet me. Bliss's skin was toasted gold. His features were neither Caucasian nor Negro. Bliss was over six and a half feet tall and he never smiled. I know that if he hadn't had the call from Smoke downstairs, he would have been ready to shoot me in the forehead.

"JT," Bliss said. "What's your bidness?"

"Lookin' for Vic."

Bliss looked over my head as if I wasn't there before setting his shark-like pupils on me again. He was wearing a navy-blue tuxedo with a powder-blue ruffled dress shirt. He leaned against the door that he guarded with his life and lifted one of his powerful shoulders towards me to prevent my access before adding a sarcastic, "You outta luck tonight, man."

155

I took a step towards the big man. "The Jah needs finding," I said, knowing that even this self-important and dangerous bodyguard would not want to cross his master when it came to meddling in the business of close family. He had to let me in, but he sure as hell didn't like it.

"You tooled up?" he asked, a god-like grin creeping across his lips.

I shook my head.

Bliss sniffed the air, considering, then decided I wasn't a threat and moved aside.

I walked past him into a room that took up the entire floor. My footfalls echoed on the floorboards, sounding my arrival, and I could feel Bliss hard on my tail as I made my way across the enormous room.

Vic was sitting behind a large, polished mahogany desk against the far wall. High brocade curtains behind him were opened to reveal a huge black-and-white framed portrait of Muhammad Ali. There was a brandy snifter half-filled in front of him that I knew contained his favourite Mount Gay rum, and splayed out across the green baize top, I could just make out a copy of *Mayfair* that was opened at the centrefold to reveal a near-naked blonde. A half-smoked joint smouldered in a cut crystal ashtray.

My cousin stared across at me but remained still, an icy, reptilian look on his face as I drew closer towards him. As I neared the antique Davenport, Vic lifted the reefer to his lips and inhaled deeply. I saw the red tip ignite in a fiery glow and watched as a grey cloud of hash smoke drifted up around me.

156

Vic sat back and wet the tips of his thumb and forefinger, pinching at the still-glowing end of the joint before flicking the stub across the room and slowly rising up out of his high-back sovereign seat to greet me.

"Well, cleaner man, wha' brings you inta tha lion's den after tha sun gone down?"

CHAPTER
TWENTY-ONE

"Damn niggah, who bin stompin' on you fuckin' lip?"

Vic rose up out of his chair, waved off Bliss then walked around his desk and shook my hand. He wore black, flared leather slacks and a black silk shirt, the first two buttons opened. On his baby finger, he wore a thick gold ring sporting an onyx Lion of Judah with diamond chips. His shoes were Italian leather, honed to a shine. My cousin eyeballed my beat-up face then tipped two of his fingers under my chin and lifted my head. "Dat's sum big-assed bruise you got goin' on there. Who give you da beatin'?"

"Some heavy over at the Moulin Rouge."

Vic raised an eyebrow. "Da queers' joint? Man, wha' da hell you doin' hangin' 'bout in a gussypa rat 'ole like tha' fo'?"

"It's a long story."

"An' you come t' me ta tell it?" Vic flashed his gold-capped teeth. The gesture felt as innocent to me as Eve's come-on in the Garden of Eden. He pointed at a plush-looking armchair opposite his desk. "Sit you arse down."

I did as I was told.

"Drink?"

"Sure."

Vic walked over to a teak cocktail bar, grabbed a glass and poured me a heavy measure of rum before sitting back at his desk. He laced his fingers together then rested his elbows on the green baize top. His one good eye was pointed in my direction, but he was looking inward, weighing up the situation in his head. The boyish grin on his face was meant to disarm me, but I wasn't fooled.

"How dat damn pickney you always got hangin' off ya shirttail doin'?"

"She's good," I said, feeling a smile of my own inch across my face. Even the presence of one of the most feral men I knew could not extinguish my delight in hearing his voice again.

"She wid Pop 'n' Momma?"

I shook my head. "No, I got her bunked up with Loretta and Carnell Jnr for a few days while I sort out a few problems I got going on."

"Problems . . . Wha' kinda problems?"

I looked down at the polished wooden floorboards, my head trying to formulate the right words. When I raised my head, Vic had shifted in his seat, so he now loomed over me. I felt a thin bead of sweat trickle down the back of my scalp and underneath my shirt collar.

"Spit it out, man. You ain't come callin' on me at dis time o' tha' marnin' fo' nuthin'." He took a sip of his rum. After he'd swallowed, I heard him hiss in satisfaction.

"I got myself mixed up with the law."

159

"Dat ain't no surprise. Babylon see a niggah walk outta his front door in a marnin' an' always tink he mixed up in sum'ting."

"I wish it was that simple."

Vic raised a powerful finger to his lips. "JT, I walk outta dis damn place every day an' I mixed up in sum'ting. Only ting I worry 'bout is if my shit gettin' mixed up at da top or not. You hearin' me?"

"Loud and clear." I knocked back a mouthful of my fiery liquor before continuing. "Thing is, I don't think you're gonna like hearing about what I need to ask you."

Vic shrugged. "Den don't axe."

"I don't have a lotta choice."

Vic let out a deep sigh. "Every fool gotta choice, man. Only ting he gotta git vexed 'bout is if he mek tha right one."

"Right choices and me, we've never made happy bedfellows."

"Don't I know it." Vic looked me in the eye and smiled. My cousin had read perhaps three books in his entire life, but he knew human nature as well as any psychoanalyst with a lifetime of experience. I believe that he knew why I was calling on him so late and revelled in my discomfort. "So, wh'appen?"

"My old friend Detective Superintendent Fletcher has got me over a barrel again."

Vic scowled. "Dat rasclat pig. I shoulda dropped his hide inta a hole years ago."

"Maybe so, but at the minute he's very much alive and well, and he's putting the thumb screws on me."

160

"Wha' fo' dis time?" Vic sat back in his seat. I could see a change come about in his previously edgy demeanour.

"A few days ago, I walked outta my job after a . . . a misunderstanding."

Vic scratched his chin. "Misunderstandin'?"

"Yeah, you know, the same bullshit, just a —"

"Different honky, right?"

"Yeah, more or less. Fletcher got wind of a police report accusing me of theft. He's cooked up some damn bum rap to get me to do his dirty work."

"Babylon got you fingsmittin' fo' him?"

"Cou'se he ain't!"

Vic sniggered and snapped the back of his hand at me. "Den git on wid wha' you come 'ere ta axe me."

I reached inside my jacket pocket, took out the Polaroid and leaned forward to slide it across the desk. "Fletcher got me looking for the fella, there in the middle."

Vic picked up the photograph and sniffed. He took a quick look then threw it back down in front of him.

"You find 'im?"

"Nope, I didn't, but the po'lice did, a couple of days ago. Found him stuffed into a tea chest out at Portishead. He was in a pretty bad way."

Vic ignored what I'd said and pointed at the photograph. "Where you git dis snapshot?"

"It was in a photo album he'd kept in his room back at his folks' place."

"Any more o' dem pictures got me in 'em?

"No."

161

"Babylon, dey know 'bout 'em?"

"Not as far as I know."

Vic smiled. "Good."

"The young fella, his name was Nikhil Suresh."

"Huh, uh . . . So?"

"So, I was hoping you could help me out?"

"How?"

"Well, for a start, I was hoping you could tell me how you got yourself photographed in a nightclub frequented by homosexuals, with William Ryder and a fella that's recently been found stuffed in a box with his head caved in?"

Vic shrugged. "Me an' Ryder, we got ourselves mutual business interests, dat's all."

"And these mutual business interests of yours perhaps involve the Moulin Rouge?"

"Dey might do." Vic offered me a sly grin. "Dey might not."

"That's some flimsy answer you giving me."

Vic shrugged again. "When you not gittin' da answers you lookin' fo', axe da man different question."

I could feel my guts beginning to churn. I was on tricky ground, and my cousin knew it. "What's going on in that picture, Vic?"

"Dat night, I wus pickin' up a New Year's gratuity that Ryder owed me. Nuthin' else."

"And why was Suresh in the photograph with you?"

"Dat fuckin' no-good cock rat was one a' Ryder's batty boys. Tha' boy woulda bin hangin' off a' Billy's frowsy dick all night befo' dat snapshot was teken."

162

"I heard there was a fella called Jimmy Moody that was into boys." I downed the rest of my rum and pointed to my face. "The night I took this beating, the Moulin's drag act told me that Suresh had his hooks in Moody, not Ryder."

"Tick-Tock Moody is Ryder's triggerman. Dat funny-up honky is fucked up. He a bullaman fo' sure. Moody's inta anyt'ing that breaths o' crawls. He'd a' bin da fella dat found dat Suresh fo' his chief. Billy Ryder, he don't like ta be seen chasin' after skinny-arsed boys."

"Can you think of any reason that Ryder would want Suresh dead?"

"I gots no idea, an', brutha, I don't care . . . Billy's the kinda goat-head honky dat don't fuck 'bout wid reasons. If da man gotta mind ta snuff outta fella, dey gone." Vic pointed at the photograph. "So, we all dun 'ere, Joseph?"

I nodded and reached across the desk for the Polaroid. Vic snatched it, held it up in front of his face and put his finger back against his lip. "Dis shit, it gonna die 'ere."

Without uttering another word, I looked on as my cousin took a gold-plated lighter out of his pocket and lit the edge of the print. When it had begun to catch, he dropped the burning photograph into the ashtray on his desk and watched it slowly melt and curl until all that was left was a small mound of fried plastic and ash. Vic got to his feet, walked back around the desk and rested himself against the front edge.

"Now, Mr Detective. Seein' as you is back on da beat
. . . I gotta me a question to axe you."

I cleared the frog out of my throat. "Yeah, and what's
that?"

"You evah 'ear of a brutha called CeeCee Buford?"

"Heard of him," I admitted. "Don't really know
anything about him, though. Hear he likes to back the
dogs and horses, plays poker, hustles a little pool in the
Prince o' Wales."

Vic began to laugh. It wasn't a guffaw or even a roll.
It was a calculated chuckle that only politicians and
killers had mastered.

"Dat's da fella, cuz. Anyt'ing else 'bout da boy spring
ta mind?"

I shook my head. "No, from what I've seen of him,
he seems like a small-time guy."

Vic smiled again. He always grinned when
misfortune was about to occur or had happened to
someone else. "Shit, you always got da right words
'bout folk, JT. Even if you don't know a damn ting
'bout 'em, you nevah say nuthin' outta place, you know
that?"

I nodded, accepted the compliment and waited.

"CeeCee, he a barman at tha Top Rank club over on
Nelson Street."

"Yeah? I didn't know that."

"I bet you didn't know dat tha fucka were a t'ief
neither?"

Vic pocketed a set of keys from his desk drawer, got
to his feet then curled a finger at me a couple of times.
"Come wid me. I got sum'ting ta show you."

164

I followed Vic out the door I'd come through earlier and down one flight of stairs. Bliss was waiting, standing like a gothic pillar in a chapel, outside a pair of metal swing doors, each with a fire-glass window set in the centre. On the other side of the doors I could hear a man sobbing. Vic gestured towards his lackey.

"We ready ta sort dis shit out?"

"Yeah, everyt'ing like you asked, Jah."

"Good. Dat's wha' I like ta 'ear." My cousin looked at me and smiled. "JT, you mindin' if I share sum'ting wid you? Put you straight 'bout me an' dat queer, Billy Ryder?"

Vic took a step forward and Bliss pulled one of the metal doors open and held it for the two of us to walk on in. Inside, a small black man wearing a metallic gold suit was sprawled over a wooden work bench, his arms outstretched and pinned at the wrists by two of Vic's beefy "associates". The man's trouser legs were saturated with his own urine, a yellow pool collected on the floorboards between his splayed feet. Vic winked at me then pointed at both the pool of piss then at the fella.

"You rememba CeeCee, JT?"

I remained silent. Buford wasn't so wise.

"Is dat you, Vic?"

"Sure is, brutha. You 'naw CeeCee, I always like a fella got a good mem'ry, cause nine times outta ten he's a smart fella who could 'predate a tough problem. Cause you know I got me a problem 'ere." Vic stood behind the man's spreadeagled body and slammed the toe of his shoe into one of Buford's ankles. Buford hollered out in pain while Vic walked round to face him.

"Shit, niggah, wha' dey got you wearin' down at dat fuckin' club?"

"I-It's wha' dey pay me ta wear, Jah," Buford stuttered.

"Dat right? Dey pay you ta fiddle me outta ma cash too?"

The barman's legs struggled not to give way as he craned his neck to look up at his accuser. "No, Jah . . . I ain't took a damn penny o' your money. I swear on my mutha's life!"

Vic sucked his teeth. "Don't be disrespectin' you mutha like dat. It ain't right. Fool, I know dat you bin dipping you fingers in what's rightfully mine. You bin tekin' a fair wad o' it, an' fo' way too long. Well dat shit, it gonna stop tonight."

"You got it wrong," Buford gabbled.

"No, CeeCee, you tha one got it wrong, brutha." Vic snatched at Buford's hair, yanking his head back. "Now, when you next see Mr Ryder, you tell dat honky boss o' yours dat da Jah, he don't like one o' his paid lackeys t'iefin' off a' him. Let 'im see wha' da Jah does ta fingsmittin' pigs dat tink dey can rob off me."

Vic nodded at Bliss. The big man walked across the room, selected two ratchet knives from a rack on the wall and returned to where Buford was being held down. He tested the point of one of the blades then drove it through the centre of Buford's right palm, pinning his hand to the bench. Buford screamed in

166

agony. I grimaced as Bliss repeated the process with the other hand and the barman fainted.

Vic turned to Bliss. "Stick a rag in his mout' an' leave him fo' an hour. Den, 'fo' you kick his arse out in the street, tell 'im if he ain't back at Ryder's skanky club selling my gear by tomorrow night, I come find 'im, and I cut his t'roat. Understand?"

Bliss nodded and Vic smiled, patted the unconscious Buford on the cheek and headed back over to me. He took a moment to wrestle the bunch of keys out of his trouser pocket, handed them to me then started to walk away, whistling to himself.

"What are these for?"

"Fo' you to git back inta that shabby office you still got over at ole Perry's gym."

I looked at the keys, shook my head and called after my cousin, "I don't need an office."

Vic blew out of his nose and shook his head. "Bullshit! You do if I say you do. Look, you a fly gumshoe agin, brutha. Time fo' you ta start actin' like it."

He walked away, leaving me in that godforsaken torture chamber with the stench of blood, piss and blind fear crawling up inside my nostrils. As he passed through the doors, he stopped, turned to face me and did something that I could make no sense of. He stared back me, muttering to himself, as though he was having a conversation with his own demons, those cruel comrades in arms that no one else could see. As he disappeared from view, I told myself that it was an illusion on my part, that it was fear and an inevitable reaction to the horrific scene I had just witnessed. I told myself that my cousin, the man who I had always loved and trusted, was neither deranged nor a monster.

I believed Vic was who he was, and that he had always been that way, ever since we'd been kids. He was violent, funny, bad tempered, sincere, honourable, tricky, courageous, lewd, treacherous and barbaric. Ultimately, he was a man who had laid down his life and killed for me, and I knew that he would do both again without a moment's hesitation, and that was what truly scared me about him.

CHAPTER
TWENTY-TWO

I got home a little after three, the grisly image of CeeCee Buford's hands being skewered to a work table burning inside my head, his screams and wretched pleading still ringing in my ears. In the kitchen, I drank a cold pint of water then put my face under the tap to cool down before drying it and resting back against the draining board, the pit of my stomach tight and knotted.

I touched at my bruised cheek and jaw and winced as I examined the still-puffed-up skin around my cheekbone. My eyes stung from lack of sleep; my tired limbs were aching with fatigue. I slowly slouched down the hall towards my bedroom, threw my clothes on the back of a chair and fell into bed. My head hit the pillow and I was quickly drawn towards a welcome slumber. My urgent desire to sleep had been swiftly granted, but as I often found, there was a high price to pay for such brisk repose.

I dreamed that I was a dead man in a coffin underground. Down where nobody could get to me, not the police nor Vic, but I could see everything and everyone. Chloe was playing with Loretta and Carnell Jnr in the small yard at the back of their house. My late wife Ellie and daughter Amelia were back home on Barbados, swimming in the azure waters of the North Atlantic Ocean. Across the street from the cemetery I was laid up in there was an old jail house. Inside, in a row of dilapidated, rusting cells stood all the people, living and dead, who had harmed my loved ones.

I had fallen asleep on my back with my hands on my thighs. I woke up in the same position. My earlier aches and pains seemed to have disappeared in that nocturnal imaginary grave I had just woken from, the cold earth leaching out my pain and the disquiet that had been nagging at my gut. The night's eerie sequence of images and events, while unpleasant to experience in a dream state, had offered some kind of restorative elixir upon waking, which I was grateful to receive.

I took a bath, shaved and changed into a clean white shirt and charcoal grey trousers, then made toast, scrambled eggs and enough strong coffee to keep my eyes open for the rest of the day.

When I was done, it was a little after 9 a.m. I went into the bedroom, slipped my jacket on then reached into the pocket to retrieve the keys that Vic had given me. I stared at myself in the mirror on the wardrobe door and weighed the keys in my hand before walking back down the hall towards my front door. As I opened up, I once again felt a deep-seated nagging hit the bottom of my belly.

I slammed the door shut behind me and headed outside, those damn keys beating against the side of my hip with every step, thinking there was a reason why optimism didn't come naturally to a fella like me.

170

Perry's Gym on Grosvenor Road was a place of legend. It had been a rundown two-storey joint in the heart of St Pauls where local fighters came to train and spar, and where Vic's criminal empire originated. Its original owner, "Cut Man" Perry, had long disappeared with his tail between his legs. Rumour had it that he had sailed out on the first tug that would take his sweaty fat arse back home to Jamaica after he got himself in hot water back in the winter of 1965.

Vic had viciously coerced Perry to sign both the deeds and his boxing gymnasium concern over before the corrupt trainer skulked off into the night. My cousin had then quickly developed the place as a front for his import and export firm and set me up a small office behind the gym's changing rooms. For a while, I ran a not-too-successful enquiry business, doing favours for those in our community that needed a friendly face to mediate for them; that was to say, I took on other folks' hardships, tried to sort them out and generally on any given day found myself going toe to toe with local hoods, money lenders and sharks, dubious landlords or the police and always found myself poorly paid for my trouble. The agency and Vic's involvement in the fight game had also offered a further legitimate front for his burgeoning criminal activities.

Nowadays, it was one of the best-looking buildings in the area thanks to an annual outside paint job, its front steps being scrubbed each Monday and a fresh and constant young membership of pugilistic men wanting to test themselves. I'd not set foot in the place for

171

nearly two years. It was easy to see why Vic had been so quick to hand me back the keys as soon as he got wind that I could be of possible use to him. I was back in the game, scouring the streets for the missing or the dead, which meant I was fair game.

A lowly assistant caretaker in a primary school out in Bristol's predominantly white suburbs was of no use to my cousin, but a man who was in direct contact with high-ranking police officers and council officials was a prize worth nurturing and protecting.

The brass plate outside the gym announcing where I had previously plied my trade had never been taken down. It was no bigger than the size of an index card and simply read "JT ELLINGTON. ENQUIRIES". Strangely, like the granite steps I now stood on, the plaque had very recently been given a thorough buffing, the sunlight reflecting off the gleaming metalwork. The main doors of the gym were already open and, as I climbed the stairs, I could hear the dull sound of leather hitting leather, the rhythmic hop and jump melody of feet lifting off the wood floors and the whir of skipping ropes that followed.

The nondescript interior of the old gym, with its leaky ceiling, had changed very little. As I walked in and up a small ramp, I spotted two rings next to each other, both with muscular black fellas sparring inside them. On the far wall, there was a row of heavy bags, some spare workout equipment and a speed bag. As in any boxing gym, there were, of course, plenty of mirrors.

None of the men currently working out took any notice of me as I strolled past them. No one else was around to greet me, though Vic had likely sent word for folk to keep out of my way.

My office was at the end of the hallway. I took hold of the brass door knob, opened up and flicking the light switch on. The bulb that glowed brightly beneath the ceiling rose illuminated a room that had, like the wall plaque outside, been scrubbed and polished to within an inch of its life.

I sat down in my chair, picked up the phone and put the receiver to my ear. I heard the familiar sound of a dialling tone purring back at me before I dropped it back into its cradle. I leaned back in my seat and shook my head in disbelief at how much work had been undertaken on my cousin's bidding and completed in such a short space of time. I smiled as I looked around the office and surveyed the spit-shined floors, the cherrywood desk with its battered typewriter and the old metal filing cabinet that sat by the door — which had stored more bottles of booze and spare shirts than it ever had paper.

I found myself musing over old times and the many shady individuals who had walked inside such a small and unassuming room and offered me their thirty pieces of silver to sort out various predicaments.

It was only when the telephone began to ring that I was yanked away from such reminiscences. I reluctantly reached across the desk and rested my fingers over the back of the handset, letting the bell ring a couple more times before lifting it up. Instinct had already told me that once I'd picked the damn thing up, whoever was on the other end was almost certainly gonna ruin my day.

CHAPTER
TWENTY-THREE

"Ellington?" the man's voice asked.

I hesitated for a moment, then said, "Yeah."

"It's Fletcher here."

My brow creased. "Man, how the hell did you get this number?"

"My desk sergeant took a call early this morning, that's how. He left a message for me to call you back on this number."

"Call me back? As far as I knew, this damn thing ain't worked for the better part of two years."

Fletcher sighed heavily. "Well it's working now, old son, so if you didn't leave the bleedin' message, who the hell did?"

"Beats me. I've just moved back into my old office while I'm digging the dirt fo' you guys."

"What a bloody carrying-on this is. Who you been pissing off?"

"Pissing off? Man, I ain't got the faintest clue what you're talking about."

"I'm talking about the fact that you gotta have been treading dog shit over somebody's best cream carpet to draw in all this attention so quickly."

"You've lost me, Superintendent."

"Oh, saints preserve us . . . How'd you ever get to wear a bloody police uniform?" Fletcher took a deep breath and blew into the mouthpiece. "Look, you prat, whatever you've been up to has clearly gone and rattled somebody's cage. In the past couple of hours, I've had an anonymous caller informing me how best to keep tabs on you and a request from Herbert Castle's office summoning you to his home as a matter of urgency."

"What the hell fo' now. I thought I was reporting to you?"

"Oh, you are, and don't you bloody well forget it," Fletcher barked. "Now, do yourself a favour and get your arse over to Castle's place pronto and then get back to me, understand. You gotta pencil handy?"

I quickly opened up my desk drawers, rustling about inside for paper and something to write with. "Yeah."

"Well, get this down."

I wrote an address for a place out at a village called Clutton and dropped the pencil on to the desk top. When Fletcher spoke again, his tone had become lighter, which made his next words all the more threatening.

"So, you got anything else to tell me?"

"Not a lot," I lied. I'd already decided that Fletcher didn't need to know about the Polaroids or Vic's involvement for a while longer, if at all.

Disbelief cracked in Fletcher's voice. "Well, you need to pull your bloody finger out and get a move on, don't ya? There's some very important people counting on you to come up with the goods."

"I'm trying my best, Superintendent."

176

"Yeah? Well try a bit fucking harder." Fletcher let his harsh words hang in the air for a moment then slammed the phone down on me.

Herbert Castle's hidden mansion in the Somerset countryside was less than a half-hour car drive from my home in St Pauls. The tiny village of Clutton might have been another world; one where the privileged and wealthy lorded it over the peasants scraping to make a crust in the rundown sector of the city that I'd just blown in from. I drove up to the house on a private road that widened at the summit into a parking apron.

When I got out of the car, I looked back over the Chew Valley and could just make out the sprawling suburbs around Bristol and the Clifton Suspension Bridge half-submerged in smog. I crossed over a well-tended lawn that circled a fishpond whose stagnant smell competed with the unmistakable and lingering farmyard odour that comes with living out in the country. The old-fashioned deep veranda at the front of the house was shadowy and uncluttered, and the polished boards creaked under my feet as I approached the front door.

From inside, a sharp sound split the silence, twice then a third time. I knocked the wood-panelled door and waited.

Three more high-pitched noises cracked out from somewhere deep inside the house, probably the cellar. Between them I heard the tap-tap of approaching footsteps, then a woman's voice spoke nervously from behind the heavy frame. "Is that you, darling?"

I didn't answer. I listened to a key turn in the lock, took a step back and watched as she opened up the door. The sudden, pinched look of surprise on her face immediately told me there was little chance of me becoming her "darling" any time soon. I smiled and watched as her slender fingers curled tightly around the latch stile before speaking again. "Oh, I'm sorry; I was expecting someone else."

I flashed my best doorstep grin. "My name's Ellington. Am I right in thinking this is the Castle residence?"

I got another chary look before the woman answered. "It is. What can I do for you?"

The woman's fingers tensed a little further. She was tall, still young, with a fine head of chestnut hair. Her body leaned awkwardly in the doorway, her malachite-green eyes searching my face suspiciously for a moment, the pupils suddenly looking through or beyond me, as if she was searching outside for someone she feared or loved.

I smiled again, this time a little less cockily and took a step towards the door. "Ain't nuthin' you can do fo' me, lady. I'm guessing it's most probably the other way round."

The woman stiffened and her face hardened as she eyed me up. "I beg your pardon."

"I have an appointment to see Mr Castle." I told her my occupation then peered over her shoulder. "What's all the noise about?"

The woman relaxed a little and slowly shook her head. "Oh, that's Daddy. When something upsets him, he likes to go down to the basement and loose a few rounds off at a target."

"He's shooting a gun?"

The woman shook her head again, this time with a little more vigour. "I'm afraid so."

"What's he firing down there?"

She shrugged then feigned an all-too-brief smile. "Oh, nothing dangerous. It's just some little air pistol he plays about with."

"In my experience all guns are dangerous, little or not." I pointed inside. "Would it be okay if I came in?"

The woman cleared her throat nervously, thought for a moment then opened the door a little wider, opening out her hand.

"Of course. Please do come in. I'm Ruth, Daddy's eldest daughter."

I thanked her, walked on in and watched as she shut the door behind me. It gave me a second or two to get a closer look. Ruth Castle was perhaps in her late thirties but looked younger, with thick hair chopped off in girlish bangs, which made her heavily freckled face seem wide. She wore white tennis shoes that looked like they'd just been taken out of the box and her dress hugged her slender figure. I looked around the impressive hallway and whistled. "This is some place you got here."

"Daddy seems to like it. I come up to visit from the city once a week, just to keep an eye on him."

I nodded and continued to look around. Inside, the air was unpleasantly stale. I could feel the huge structure both surrounding and hanging over me. It

179

was more like a public building than a home — the kinda place you go to pay a late tax bill or get a divorce.

"A police superintendent by the name of Fletcher called me earlier this morning. Your father asked that I pay him a visit."

The woman smiled again. "Do you undertake a lot of work for Daddy?"

"Nah, I've been asked by the police to assist the council regarding a somewhat delicate legal matter?"

Ruth suddenly averted her eyes, dropping her gaze towards her feet. My use of the word *delicate* had clearly unsettled her; she backed away like a shy child, walking to a door at the end of the hallway and calling down a lit stairway, "Daddy, there's someone here to see you."

A rough bass answered. "Who is it?"

Another shot went off below my feet.

"A Mr Ellington. He says he's some kind of detective, and that he has an appointment with you."

"Tell him to wait."

Five more shots sounded under the floor. I felt their vibration through the soles of my shoes. Ruth's body registered each one.

When they had ceased, she still lingered in the light from the basement stairway, as if the gunshots had been an overture to music that rang in her head and echoed along her nerves, holding her rapt. Heavy feet mounted the stairs, and she backed away from the man who appeared in the light. There was something strange about the look in her eyes as she moved, a mixture of

180

fear or hatred. The man ignored me and looked at his daughter with a kind of puzzled contempt.

"I know you hate the sound of bloody gunfire. You can always stuff cotton wool in your ears."

"I didn't say anything, Father." She turned back to me. "This is Mr Ellington."

Castle made a huffing sound. "I know who the hell he is, Ruth."

He pushed past his daughter and came to face me underneath the stuffed head of a stag that was hanging on the wall. The fussy civil servant seemed somewhat different since we'd last met. Gone were the rugged good looks I'd noticed at the council offices some days earlier, his sculpted features now replaced by a more haggard air. He looked like a man who'd received bad news, the kind that makes a fella shrink in his skin. His high shoulders were now bowed, his chest caving under a wrinkled velvet smoking jacket. White glinted in the reddish stubble on his cheeks and chin, and his eyes were rimmed with red. They smouldered in his head like the last vestiges of inextinguishable and ruinous passion.

Ruth gracefully slid herself between me and her father and began to walk further along the hallway. "I'm thirsty, Mr Ellington. Let me go and prepare us all some refreshments."

The councillor growled. "Don't start with the bloody hospitality routine, Ruth. This chappy is here on business."

She began to walk away but quickly stopped in her tracks when the old man bellowed after her. The young woman spun round on the spot like a scared squaddie on parade to find her father stabbing a finger towards her. "No bloody drinks, Ruth!"

Castle turned to me. "This way, Ellington."

I followed him down the hall and into a musty study that was adorned with portraits of rich dead white folk and floor-to-ceiling bookshelves lined with dusty leather-bound tomes that had clearly never been read. The old man stood at the far side of the room, his back towards a grey stone fireplace that looked like it had not seen flames for many a day.

"I'll keep this brief."

"That's fine by me."

Castle ignored my throwaway remark and leaned his elbow on top of the mantlepiece. "Have you made any progress since we last spoke?"

I shook my head. "Like I told the superintendent earlier this morning, not a lot. I'm just getting to grips with the case. There's a lot of ground to move over. Lotta folk to speak to. I'm just one fella who's out there trying to get a break when normally there'd be a dozen or more po'liceman knocking on folks' doors."

Castle considered me for a moment, took a deep breath through his nostrils, then continued, "Look, I understand the uniqueness of your present situation; however, I and my colleagues were hoping that you may have had something that could perhaps quell the fears of the general public and, of course, aid the constabulary in garnering them a swift arrest. I'm sure you realise that the clock is ticking. A child has been murdered, you know?"

182

The hairs on the back of my neck stood up and I took a couple of steps forward. Castle never took his eyes off me as I moved towards him.

"And there's also Nikhil Suresh's body cooling itself down at the morgue too, if you remember?"

Castle flinched. "Yes, of course . . . there's the matter of the young . . . Indian fellow to consider too." The bureaucrat's accent was pure top-drawer Bristolian, all the *h*s firmly in place as he spoke. I noticed that his left cheek had a slight twitch and the rest of his face seemed only to have two expressions — a mournful stare that made the average bloodhound look cheerful and a brief, cruel smile, the kind he probably thought was supposed to touch your heart. As far as I was concerned, Castle had only one touching feature and that was the contents of his wallet. Although I didn't realise it, I was about to find out just how deep those contents were.

"In light of the difficulties that you are facing, I and the council are aware of the enormous scale of the task that has been set you and I would like to address that right now." Castle swivelled his head slowly towards the door behind me as if he was concerned that someone else may be listening to our conversation. When he spoke again, his words were delivered in a more hushed timbre. "One of the reasons I wished to see you this afternoon was regarding the matter of remuneration."

I cleared my throat. "Matter of what?"

"Remuneration, Mr Ellington." Castle repeated the word carefully. "Something not discussed with you properly at our previous meeting. The council would like to offer you a fee for your services which we feel should reflect our gratitude for your continuing endeavours in this sensitive matter you have willingly undertaken on our behalf."

Castle stared at me for a moment, waiting for some kind of response. When I didn't give him one, he smiled to himself then continued with his patter. "Shall we say the sum of twenty pounds a day plus expenses and a bonus if you can successfully bring this awful situation to as swift a conclusion as possible and, of course, offer the police a realistic suspect?"

My right eye twitched thinking about all that money. "That's a lotta cash you're offering, Mr Castle."

Castle nodded. "I'd say it's money well spent, if you can assist our city to catch a killer, don't you think?"

"I think it's a very generous offer, and I'd be happy to accept."

"Good!"

Castle paced across his study, pulled open one of his desk drawers and withdrew a large manila envelope. He walked back to where I stood and held it out to me.

"Here's a week's payment in advance. I'll have my secretary draw up another payment if required and we'll settle any further debt with you when the job is all done and dusted." He nudged the envelope for me to take. I grasped at the edge, but the old man held on to it for a moment. "Keep the superintendent fully appraised, as before."

He let go of the envelope and gestured at the door behind me. "That will be all."

184

I stuffed the envelope in my jacket pocket and watched Castle walk back to his desk, then I turned to leave.

"Mr Ellington," he called.

I swung round. "Yeah?"

Castle sank down into a high-backed leather chair and placed his left hand on top of the desk. "As regards speaking to people, as you mentioned earlier . . . there's one door I'd like you to stay away from."

"Whose door's that?"

Castle gave me another one of his pencil-pushing smirks. "I think we both know who I'm referring to. Let's just say I'd like you to leave the great and good of Bristol's business community well alone during your investigation. I'm sure I don't have to illuminate further?"

I shook my head, my chin down low when it should have been held high. "No, Mr Castle, I got all the light I need for now, thanks."

I walked out of Castle's study and back down the hallway towards the front door. Ruth was nowhere to be seen. Outside, I took in a couple of deep breaths of fresh air and brushed my hand across the envelope in my pocket. A down payment for services rendered and no questions asked. Especially if I was considering directing any of my third-degree enquiries towards a certain Mr William Ryder. Castle had just protected the man whose pocket he was firmly entrenched in, and all for just twenty pounds a day plus expenses. The shady councillor clearly believed he'd just bought himself another chump. I wasn't about to burst his bubble by saying no to his fishy offer. For now, I'd see how the next few days played out. See if I could stay ahead of the game and bag me a bad guy.

Cheddar or blue, I thought to myself.

I needed to know with what kind of cheese William Ryder had just set his trap.

CHAPTER
TWENTY-FOUR

I felt dirty after being in the presence of Herbert Castle. My throat was tight after our conversation and I wanted to head back to St Pauls, hole up in a pub for the rest of the day and feel the comforting warmth of a couple of shots of rum inside my belly. Getting lost in a bottle wasn't going to wash with my grim overseer, Superintendent Fletcher, though. He'd demanded that I spill the beans on Castle, and I knew it was best to keep the copper off my back by keeping him in the loop.

But before I made the call, I needed to work out how much of my meeting with the sly council official I was going to detail. Accepting what I believed to be Castle's bribe money could be explained by saying that the council house had seen the light and decided to cough up a fee for my services. Fletcher wouldn't be happy that I was being paid by his betters, especially as he'd already gone to so much trouble to strong-arm me to do the council's — and his — dirty work. The superintendent's cooked-up theft charges had been put in place to keep me under his thumb. Castle's offer to pay me was in itself a double-edged sword. On one side, I now had a legitimate role in delving into the two recent murders; on the other, I was going to be treading on the toes of the Bristol police; white lawmen who wouldn't want me nosing in on their investigation. I had to tread carefully with Fletcher — he'd be scrutinising every word I said and having my movements shadowed once he found out I was on the council's payroll.

The superintendent being on my case was only part of the problem; getting him to play ball and let me do my job in the coming days was going to be another. I always believed that it was my psychological make-up that had made me a good detective. I was ninety per cent pragmatist and the rest was superstition. Fletcher wouldn't be interested in that — how I worked or where I'd picked up such skills. He'd originally wanted me to do his dirty work, to sniff out the whereabouts of a missing Indian fella, a problem that neither he nor the rest of his men had any interest in dealing with. When Nikhil Suresh turned up dead, his murder perhaps connected to bigger things affecting the great and good of polite society, the tricky copper clearly developed other plans for me.

From the moment Suresh had been uncovered, stuffed down deep in that box and carved up, Fletcher had moved me into position to continue with his donkey work. He still had himself a black bagman, a colonial to sniff out the bad guy for him from within the "community". The superintendent wanted an easy collar to keep the chief constable, the establishment and their many white voters happy, and I was reluctantly playing my part in upholding the status quo

188

for them. The whole situation stank to high heaven, and I was stuck at the bottom of a manure pile, not of my own making, having to breathe in its stench.

I know bad. I've been around the vile and the cruel, the rotten and depraved, for long enough. My gut was telling me that it wasn't a man of colour who had murdered either Nikhil Suresh or the young white kid, James Peberdy. Back when I was on the force in Barbados, dealing with crimes where a black man had been deliberately put in the hot seat by white rulers, I usually spent most of the investigation in the black parts of town and never the more salubrious white neighbourhoods. In the black parishes, a fella's friends, his loved ones, even those who hated him were usually there for us to grill and put the squeeze on. The crime any black fella was suspected of was almost always expected to have been committed close to home. Since the days of slavery, black folk had been crammed into slave quarters and ghettos, same-race marriages and schools segregated by locality. Once the perp was caught and in prison, his cellmates would be black, and in death it was always a congregation of black faces that would lay him to rest. I may have been over six thousand miles from home, but the facts remained the same. White folk were as happy here to let a black man or woman take the fall for them as they were back on Bim, whether they had committed the damn crime or not.

I stopped at a telephone box just outside of Clutton and made my call to Fletcher, only to be told by the

189

desk sergeant that he was out for the afternoon and would not be back until early the next day. I left a message for him to call me at my office in the morning and headed back up the lane towards my car, the sky overhead grey and crackling with dry thunder. I reached into my pocket for the keys and was about to cross the road when I saw Ruth Castle pass by in a flashy dark green Triumph. She looked back at me and a few yards down the road made a U-turn, almost running over an old fella on a bicycle. She sped back up the lane and stopped, her window down, the front windscreen spotted with raindrops and mottled dust. "I want to talk to you," she said.

"Go ahead."

Her eyes lighted on my old Ford. "Not here. Follow me into the next village. How about I buy us both a drink?"

I glanced down at my watch, my face burning with embarrassment. "I'm kinda tied up right now."

Ruth smiled. "No, you're not."

CHAPTER
TWENTY-FIVE

I tailed Ruth's car through a series of tree-lined country lanes for a couple of miles, unsure of what the hell I was letting myself in for. The voice in my head told me that I was heading towards a heap more trouble. It was a warning I knew I should have been heeding, but I was a sucker for curiosity, whether it killed the cat or not.

Another half-mile later, my eagerness to find out more led me into the village of Pensford. A few yards in, and Ruth hung a sharp left then raced over a crossroads before coming to a screeching halt on the gravelled frontage of a pub.

I saw a white flicker of lightning in the trees surrounding the George and Dragon as I pulled up. I stayed in my car long enough to watch Castle's daughter get out and rest her rear against the polished wing of her coupe. The heavy, wet-smelling air was criss-crossed with birds as I walked across to join her.

Ruth reached into a clutch bag, took out a cigarette, lit it and blew a plume of smoke up into the air. She wore patent leather spiked heels with flared Levi's and a loose white blouse that looked as if it had been touched with pink and grey watercolours. She smiled at me then pitched herself off the Triumph and extended her hand. We exchanged the briefest of greetings, her slender fingers sliding out of my paw before I had a chance to embrace them properly, then she flicked her cigarette into the road and pointed towards the pub.

"Shall we?"

We walked between a series of wooden benches, each positioned at right angles across the pebbled ground. In the centre of each of the outside tables stood a white sun umbrella, the word *CINZANO* emblazoned across the canopy.

As we approached the entrance, I saw a skinny old fella with work-weary shoulders sweeping out the spaces between the dustbins with a long-handled broom. He worked the ground frantically, wielding the brush in long stabbing sweeps. The man looked up and shot me a scowl then went on sweeping. Inside, the pub was as quiet as the grave. There was no jukebox or fruit machine, no friendly chatter, just a chilly atmosphere that would have been ideal for hanging meat up.

A couple of monastic-looking fellas sat at a brass-topped table nursing drinks. The two locals both offered me a dirty look before returning their gaze to the inside of their glasses. The pub walls were adorned in a crowded array of rural memorabilia, including mounted fox heads, stuffed animals and historic gin traps.

A woman stood behind the bar with her back against the till. She was tall, severe-faced, perhaps in her late sixties, and wore an ill-fitting flowered cotton dress with a motheaten, navy cardigan. It was a look of badly judged, coiffured dishevelment. Her thinning grey hair was tied neatly in a bun on top of her head and her face had been plastered from nose to chin with cheap make-up. She looked like she'd just been embalmed.

The woman slowly lifted her head from the copy of *Woman's Own* that she was reading, clocking me straight off the bat. Her face turned to thunder as we approached the bar, though she remained silent, glaring at me over a pair of half-rimmed brass spectacles. A cigarette hung loosely from her mouth, the long length of dead ash at its tip ready to drop on to the floor at any moment.

Realising that her cold demeanour wasn't having the desired effect, she slowly folded over the corner of the magazine page and placed it on a shelf underneath the bar. Then she took off her glasses, crossed her arms and rested them on top of the cash register before walking the short distance to serve us. Ignoring me, she focused all her attention on Ruth.

"What'll it be, madam?"

"I'll have a Cherry B with lemonade, please." Ruth turned and smiled at me. "What's your poison, Mr Ellington?"

I looked down the polished oak counter and pointed towards one of the hand pulls. "I'll take a pint of bitter, thanks."

The barmaid took a small brown bottle from a shelf behind her, lifted off the cap and poured the dark red liquid into a sherry glass. She placed the drink in front of Ruth then shuffled down towards a trio of ceramic hand pulls, giving me a withering look before drawing my pint and sliding the filled glass down the bar towards me. She then tugged a pristine white cloth from the cord of her apron and lay it on the counter next to her, before looking at Ruth, her lip curling.

"That'll be eighty-five pence."

As Ruth went to open up her purse, I held out my hand. "I'll get this."

I fished out some change from my trouser pocket and slapped the coins on the bar. I flashed a grin at the old woman. "Keep the change."

The barmaid said nothing. She covered up the money with the cloth, scooped it up inside the fabric then crossed over to the till and rang up the amount. I picked up my drink as the cash register's drawer shot out, the metallic sound clattering across the room. I stood and watched as the woman tipped my money into the drawer, her fingers never so much as brushing a single coin. She slammed the till shut with the palm of her hand, picked up her spectacles and went back to reading her rag.

I could feel Ruth's awkwardness as she led me across the lounge into the snug. The small room was nestled away at the rear of the joint and looked as off-putting as the front of the damn building. Brown carpets, brown walls and a series of tatty wooden chairs placed around three smeared, glass-topped tables completed the dismal effect. Ruth placed her drink down on one of the tables, then sat down, clasping her hands in her lap. She nodded at the seat next to her and I lowered myself into it. We looked at each other for a few moments before she spoke.

"You get a lot of that kind of thing, do you?"

194

"You talking 'bout the warm welcome I just got back there?"

Ruth nodded. "Hardly warm."

"I've had worse." I shifted in my seat before continuing. "Small-minded bigotry comes easily to some folk, Mrs Castle."

"It's Miss, and please, call me Ruth."

"I got the impression that you were married."

"Well that's a leap. How come?"

"When I heard you calling out 'darling' from the other side of that front door earlier, I assumed you was talking to somebody that you were close to."

"I was, and I am." Ruth chuckled to herself. "I thought that it was cousin Hannah calling on me. We sometimes play tennis together on the court behind Daddy's old spread. She was supposed to come over this afternoon for a knockabout. She didn't turn up."

"I'm sorry to have disappointed you."

"I wasn't disappointed." Ruth smiled then looked down at her hands for a few seconds; long enough for the average person to formulate themselves a lie. I took a sip of my beer and rested back against my chair.

"So, what is it that you wanted to talk to me about?"

I watched her carefully considering my words before she raised her head. "You said that you were some kind of detective working for my father?"

"Kind of . . . the Bristol constabulary have asked me to assist both them and the council house. Your daddy's one of the fellas who's running the show from up there on College Green. I'm just doing a little legwork for both the council and the po'lice."

"Legwork?" She sounded surprised.

"Yeah." I cleared my throat and said, "You know, other folk's dirty work."

Ruth tilted her head to the side. "You mean my father's dirty work?"

"Nah, more like the po'lice's," I lied.

"So, my father isn't in any trouble, Mr Ellington?"

"No, he's not in any kinda trouble, far as I know."

"So, the fee that he offered you, that wasn't to hush certain things up, was it?"

I raised an eyebrow. "Sounds like you've been earwigging round your ole' man's study door?"

Ruth's cheeks began to flush. "Daddy's house may look grand, but it has thin walls, Mr Ellington."

"If we're gonna be on first-name terms, how 'bout you call me Joseph?"

I took another slug of my ale and heard the voice in my head warning me again about curiosity killing the cat. Snooping had never killed this cat, I thought, but a pair of bluey-green eyes just might.

Against my better judgement, I let my natural inquisitiveness off the leash to run and sniff around. "What kinda things would a man like your father want hushing up?"

Ruth looked down at her feet and shrugged. When she fixed her eyes on mine again, they were glazed. When she spoke, her tone was brittle and matter-of-fact. "Rumours, Joseph . . . the sordid kind that ruin reputations."

"And is any of this hearsay you're talking about true?"

196

"Most of it."

"Powerful men often have powerful passions."

Ruth appraised my words with her stormy, sky-coloured eyes and sniffed. Then she shook her head ever so slightly.

"Uh-huh . . . Well, Daddy's many predilections will be his undoing, I can assure you of that."

"Predilections?"

"Women, Joseph. The loose kind."

I took a deep breath. "I'm sorry."

Ruth pulled her head back and sneered. I could see the tension knotting in her shoulders. "There's no need to be. I've known about his weaknesses for some time. It's always been his dirty little secret, or so he thought, even when Mummy was still alive."

"And you believe there's others that know 'bout your father's transgressions? People who would like to see him hurt?"

"Nice choice of words, Joseph." When Ruth looked across at me, some kind of wordless knowledge seemed to pass between us. When she spoke, it was as if what she was telling me was already common knowledge in my own consciousness. "I think someone has been hurting my father for quite some time."

After a momentary pause, she reached out a delicate hand towards my face and said, "It looks like you've been in the wars?"

"Oh, that's nuthin'."

Ruth let her hand drop back into her lap. "So, getting knocked about is an occupational hazard for you, is it?"

"Sometimes, if I'm unlucky."

"Are you unlucky often, Joseph?"

I smiled. "More times than I care to admit."

I stared into Ruth's eyes. She was certainly lovely to look at, beautiful in fact. Her skin was peppered with tiny freckles and her cheekbones were high, but her face was full enough that it didn't make her seem severe. Her eyes were either blue or green depending on how she held her head. They gave off a look of quiet vulnerability, a still gaze that I began to feel slowly melting away my usual wariness towards strangers.

Despite sensing the gentle thaw of my own guarded nature, the snoop in me just couldn't stop prying. What's the old saying? Ah, I remember now. Curiosity flayed the cat alive, ripped it apart limb from limb and listened to it scream before it killed it. That's the one.

I rested my elbows on my knees and laced my fingers, an unapologetic sinner at the gates of the house of damnation who was about to undertake the devil's inquisition, the vexing question on the tip of my tongue, aching to break the silence, ripe for the asking. I took another deep breath and when the words finally came out my mouth, they flowed with the ease of a liar delivering his deceits.

"Who'd you think could be out to hurt your father?"

Ruth bit her lip. "There's a host of people that would like to see him in the gutter."

"But there's one person in particular, perhaps?" I pressed. Ruth's eyes tightened and her nostrils flared. I almost felt bad about the pain that wrenched across the young woman's face before she spoke again. "Yes, there's one . . . a man called Ryder . . . William Ryder."

198

The worst kind of question to ask is the one you already know the answer to. The imprudent enquiry I'd just made was one I already regretted uttering.

That said, there were three important things that I'd just got out of my discourse with Ruth Castle. One was that I liked her very much, the second was that her old man was not to be trusted and finally, whatever his trouble was, it was deep.

CHAPTER
TWENTY-SIX

For some, even our darkest past moments are preferable somehow to those few interludes of peace and sunshine we may experience. Why? God only knows. I was normally content with the fact that life often threw me a curveball. This afternoon had been one of those rare occasions when I'd not struck out.

My unexpected rendezvous with Ruth Castle was both pleasurable and informative. Before I'd left the pub, she'd written her phone number down on the back of a beer mat and I'd promised I'd be in touch in a few days. There was something about Ruth that had charmed me, something I couldn't quite put my finger on. Perhaps it was just the way she looked at me, or maybe it was the aura of confidence and obvious beauty that had caught my eye. She'd been the first white woman to invite me to take a drink with her in public, and that certainly brought her up in my estimation, though I could well do without having a good-looking woman on my mind with all the crazy stuff going on. I didn't want to have to forget about my meeting with Ruth, but it was a safe bet that, for now, I could find plenty of ways to take her off my mind. Hearing that her old man was on William Ryder's payroll was one such way. It hadn't come as a great shock to know that someone had their claws into the shady councillor. I just wished it could have been some other thug.

Until a few days ago, my life had been relatively simple, but in a matter of hours my laid-back existence had turned into a nightmare, and all on the threat of a false accusation, a copper I couldn't trust and the offer of ready money. As a policeman, I'd been treading in murky waters for a long time, but even back then I was never in fear of drowning. Now, I had an edgy feeling that I was wading into hidden depths; an abyss that I may have trouble returning from. I'd always known that there was no easy way to rid yourself of a past you'd much rather forget. Lifestyles and habits may change, but deep down, the individual doesn't. No amount of money, sinner's prayers or booze offers that kind of peace of mind. Saying farewell to the dark side doesn't mean that the dark side wants rid of you.

And I was about to be reminded of that fact.

It was just after four thirty by the time I drove back into St Pauls. I got out the car and headed across Grosvenor Road towards Perry's gym; that's when I noticed the sleek blue Mercedes parked about twenty yards down the road, and the familiar huge fella leaning on it. Elijah Bliss clapped eyes on me, threw away his cigarette and quickly headed my way. I could see by the easy-going look on his face that my cousin's triggerman wasn't coming at me to cause trouble; that and the fact that he was wearing the kind of suit that made him look like a

201

chauffeur, which told me he was no doubt out ferrying Vic from one dubious meeting to another. I braced myself for Bliss's bullish jive and tried not to snigger at the brother's tight-fitting outfit. Bliss would have looked a lot more comfortable in a leopard-skin leotard, with his music hall weightlifter's build. He stopped in front of me and I shot him my toughest look, the sort that would normally make a lion blink, but Bliss wasn't impressed with my bravado.

"The Jah want a word, brutha." Bliss pointed at the Mercedes. "He waitin' in da car."

I lifted my wrist and flicked my eyes at my watch. "You ain't been hanging round long I hope?"

Bliss shrugged. "Dat don't matter none. The Jah don't find ya 'ere, he gonna root you out sum'place else."

I cocked a knowing grin. "Cou'se he is."

I followed the minder to the car. Every window bar the windshield had custom blinds fitted and pulled down. Bliss looked up and down the road then opened the back door. A cloud of thick smoke escaped, and the woody stink of ganja hit me as I peered inside.

Vic leaned forward, his features partially hidden in the reefer fog. "You gonna stand out in the street like a donkey's dick or you gonna climb on inside so we can go git us a damn drink?"

The secluded room at the back of the Beaufort Inn was always dark, even on a summer's evening. The dim wall lights and empty chairs made it the perfect place for Vic's kind of business. Dutty Ken shoved his head

202

round the door, bowing and grinning, his usual Havana stogie hanging from the corner of his mouth. "You fella's wantin' sum'ting fo' you tongues?"

"Bring us a bottle o' rum," Vic said softly.

"And a couple o' frozen glasses too?" Ken added, knowing my cousin's usual indulgence. The chubby barman kept a handful of squat liquor glasses in the freezer at all times, ready for my cousin's pleasure.

"T'anks, Ken." Vic said, flashing his gold-capped teeth.

I leaned across the table, my voice low as I spoke. "Whatever it is you want with me, perhaps it's best we talk about it back at my place?"

"Shit. This joint my fuckin' office, jus' like tha' one you got ovah at Perry's. You don't have ta worry 'bout Dutty Ken. He don't hear nuthin' an' he won't say nuthin'."

Ken brought our drinks. Under his arm was a square of white card. He put the bottle of rum and the chilled shot glasses down on the table and held out the card for Vic and me to see. The barman then went and pinned the special sign on the snug's door. CLOSED FOR A PRIVATE FUNCTION. That sign would stay up until Vic had concluded his business with me.

"Well?" I asked.

"Well what?"

"What's all the cloak-and-dagger stuff for?"

"I don't have ta hide from no fool."

"I don't normally see you in this neck of the woods — not during daylight hours anyway."

Vic grinned. He stared at the closed door, his one good eye bright. I watched him take a joint out of a silver cigarette box and stick it in the corner of his mouth, smelled the sharp sulphur of a struck match and then, a few seconds later, the sour scent of burning sinsemilla. Smoke wafted round my cousin's features, and his smile seemed to move with the sinuous wisps.

"It right wha' I bin hearin' 'bout Dinah Henry over at da Moulin da other night?"

"What about her?"

"Sum suckah tell me dat ole Dinah caved tha' back o' sum honky's head in wid a blackjack to save you stupid neck." Vic pointed at the bruises on my face and laughed. "Dat bitch dragging your raggedy arse outta sum alley had me laughin' an' strainin' so hard I gave myself a fuckin' haemorrhoid. Shit, dat ting bin stingin' me longer than when I got shot."

"Whaddya want to see me about, Vic?"

Vic nodded slowly. "To begin wit', dat photograph you bring me the other night." He slugged back a triple shot of rum then refilled his glass.

"Yeah, what about it?"

"You any nearer ta findin' out anyt'ing 'bout who kilt dat Indian boy?"

I shook my head. "No. I just keep hearing William Ryder's name being bandied all over the place."

My cousin grinned at me again. His dark skin and grey eye made him appear wraithlike in between all the smoke and the room's soft lighting. "Dat ain't no su'prise. Dat damn honky, he gonna have sum'ting ta do with dat coloured boy endin' up dead. Sure as God grew little green apples."

"What makes you say that?"

Vic crossed one leg over the other and shrugged. "I already tell you I seen tha way dat boy wus round Ryder da night dat damn photograph wus taken. Only be a matter o' time befo' dat queer honky git a flea in his ear 'bout sum'ting dat crazy boy did or said. Billy likes his bidness an' pleasure kept sep'rat'. Dat boy gonna be dead cause he didn't respec' dat fact."

"How come you know so much about Ryder?"

"JT," Vic said in an exasperated grumble. "You da one come ta me axing 'bout da fool. I'm jus' fillin' in da blanks fo' you."

"Come on, Vic. Cut the bullshit. What you angling at?"

My cousin's eyebrow rose, maybe just a quarter inch. When you're facing that kind of peril, you notice small gestures like that. I'd seen Vic in action. He could kill a man and then go take forty winks without the slightest concern. The eyebrow-raising meant that his irked feelings were in check and that he wasn't about to blow a gasket.

"Me an' Ryder, we got ourselves a mutual agreement goin' on."

"What kind of agreement?" I ventured tenuously.

"Da bidness kind. One dat's startin' ta git traitorous."

"You wanna expand on that a little for me?"

Vic took a hit on his joint. "Me an' da honky, we bin cuttin' dis city up fo' a while now. I got da herb, da booze an' every penny dat comes in an' out o' most o' tha clubs from 'ere ta tha Somerset borders . . . among other tings."

"And Ryder . . . what's he getting out of this deal?"

"Plenty, man! He got the cockrats an' da whores, all da knockin' shops . . . an' his gun runnin'."

"Guns?"

"Yeah, fo' da the micks."

"The who?"

"Da Irish Republican Army . . ."

"Ryder's selling arms to the IRA?"

"You betta believe it. Word is, he makin' a tidy packet outta it too!"

"And you'd like a cut of that action?"

Vic shook his head slowly. "Me got no interest in mekin' money sellin' shooters ta Paddies. It's Ryder other dirty bidness dat bin stickin' in ma craw."

That foolish thirst for knowledge I possessed was dragging me further down a dark road, one I could well have done without going down. I could feel myself being slowly lured in on what was most probably a fine web of lies and deceit, and Vic was like a spider, suspended in a dark corner, waiting.

"What kinda dirty business?"

Vic took in a lungful and held it for moment. When he spoke, his words were dressed in the heady fumes of grass. "Da snitchin' kind."

"Are you sayin' Ryder's a police informer?"

"Naw, am sayin' he wukin' fo' da fuckin' council!" Vic sucked air through the gap in his teeth and gave me a dirty look. "Cou'se he a fuckin' rat, you eediat! How

206

you tink he git away wid killin' sum poofter dat vexin' 'im if he ain't got da Babylon in his pocket?"

My mouth went dry. I drank the entire glass of rum in one swig, but it didn't touch that fearful dryness. Vic could see that he'd touched a nerve. He could smell my unease and suspicion like fresh blood dripping from a scared and wounded animal. It was time for him to go in for the kill.

"Ryder bin bredren wid da Babylon fo' lang while, brutha. He got himsel' plenty inside man helpin' out fo' sure. Ain't no big pinch goin' down in dis city wid out Billy Ryder helpin' da po'lice. Fellas like you friend Superintendent Fletcher fo' instance. Babylon leave Ryder's operation alone jus' as long as he feedin' 'em a line on some other poor ass'ole dat dey can bang up. Soon come a time when dat honky bastard gonna be snitchin' on me. Well, he can kiss me arse if he tinks he gonna tek me out at da neck. I want Ryder gone. Now, dat honky can either hang himsel' wid his own dotishness or am gonna he'p him hang himsel'. You git me?" Vic looped his arm around the back of his chair and snickered.

"An' you got to thinking that I'd be the kind of fella to help you tie the noose?" I said, raising my voice more than I wanted.

That took the smug smile off of Vic's lips. He leaned forward and clasped his hands. Many men who knew my murderous relation would have quailed at that gesture. But I wasn't afraid. It's not that I'm so courageous I can't know fear in the face of certain death. And Victor Ellington, or Jah Rhygin or whatever

207

the hell he wanted to call himself, was certainly death personified, but right then, I had the kind of problems that went far beyond me and my mortality.

"I was tinkin' dat I could point you in da right direction wid Ryder an' the dead boy. Perhaps help ya git da Babylon off you back too."

I glared across the table. "So that's why you handed over my old office keys the other night, got my telephone ringing again . . . made sure that Fletcher knew I was back in business. You saw all this madness coming, didn't you?"

Vic remained silent, biding his time as he enjoyed watching me trying to work it all out.

I pointed a finger in Vic's face. Normally, it would have been a very foolish thing to do, but I didn't care anymore. "You knew Ryder's had his Babylon lackeys on the Bristol force, knew they were probably covering up some kind of grief he got himself in to. All you needed was your own skivvy on the inside, some damn fool who could find out what that grief might be and use it against him, didn't you?"

Vic shook his head and then laughed. It was a real laugh, friendly and amused. For the briefest of moments, he looked like my cousin instead of a ghetto hard man who rarely seemed ruffled or human at all.

"JT, brutha . . . You may tink you 'naw me better than me mutha. Don't be frettin' 'bout wha' you tink I'm up to. Cause wha' you really need ta be tinkin' 'bout right now is how I can git you from outta all dat shit you up ta you neck in. Shit dat's risin' fast an' will pretty soon be creeping its way inside your mout'."

208

I looked down at the ground, my head spinning, my heart racing inside my chest.

"Alright," I said after the proper pretence of waiting. "And how do you plan to keep me out of all this shit?"

Vic sat back and blew another cloud of smoke up at the ceiling. He looked across at me with a plain face, the laughter gone. When he spoke, his voice became a whisper, like the slither of a snake over the nape of my neck.

"Well, fo' a start we can go pay us a visit to dat closet queen, Perri St Claire. If any fool got the dirty 'bout wha' Billy Ryder gits up to in an' out o' his bedroom, it's dat ponce fo' sure."

Vic lifted his head and sniffed the air as if he was nosing out the scent of distant prey. I imagined prehistoric wolves making the same gesture before they howled at men, women and children sat shivering in their caves.

CHAPTER
TWENTY-SEVEN

Some private detectives spend long nights in darkened rooms listening to and taking pictures of the people next door; they sit for days parked down the road from the homes of business cheats or adulterers, waiting to get the right incriminating photograph. Some high-end investigators are little more than pencil pushers who go through hundreds of pages of accounts and financial transactions until they find the one entry that frames the subject of their investigation.

That's not me. That's not how I worked. My puzzles had human pieces and no single resolution. I'm the kinda gumshoe who helps those folks struggling to help themselves. The fella with a gambling debt hanging over his head, the woman with a loan shark creeping on her doorstep. In my job, I might try to help find some missing fool who was last seen stumbling out of the front door of a boozer or a cat house, or recover a cheap family heirloom filched by a devious relative. Over the years I'd been involved in my fair share of bloodshed and mayhem, death and misery.

But in all that time I'd never caught a murder case. That was until a few days ago.

Now, I had two slayings on my plate, trouble snapping at my heels and that biting feeling in the pit of my gut that I was heading towards a whole heap more of it.

It was just after ten thirty. We'd left the Beaufort's snug via the back entrance, the stink of reefer following us out into the street. Driving out of St Pauls with Vic next to me, sucking on a joint, wasn't how I'd envisaged ending my evening. My cousin was eager to start digging up the dirt with me, partly because he liked the idea of tagging along with me to cover my back and partly because he wanted to somehow implicate me in his own current criminal activity. Telling him that I wanted him to play no such part would have put us at odds, and an angry Vic was like a grenade with a loose pin, a savage dog breathing down your neck. He'd already made his mind up that he wanted to draw blood and I'd have been a fool to have tried staunching that hot-headed desire.

I gripped the wheel, my heart beating so hard I could feel it in my throat. Vic was sour and silent. That would have been an unpleasant combination with any companion but with him there was always the threat of something bad going down. It was at tense moments like these when I could sense the violence he was harbouring. Dark thoughts would flit through my head, like flying leaves in a strong wind.

Vic wouldn't have been happy going into partnership with someone who could perhaps get the upper hand over him. He liked his trade alliances to be uncomplicated, no matter how tenebrous they were, seeking deals that he solely controlled and benefitted from. Getting chummy with a high-profile crook like William Ryder wouldn't have been something my cousin had undertaken lightly. The two men breaking bread and their mutual criminal organisations going into cahoots together would have been a short-term proposition for Vic.

Whoever had whispered the news that Ryder was a police informer into Vic's ear perhaps wouldn't have realised how quickly their intelligence would have sealed the crime boss's fate. Vic would have thought up some kind of foul play to inflict on the gangster. Something swift, precise and final. A hidden realm for Ryder to rest eternal within, his remains sunk in cold and lonely ground or at the bottom of deep water. For Vic, killing was a tool of the trade, hardly worth discussing, and he felt no need to explain or justify his reasons to me.

It took less than twenty minutes to drive out to where Perri St Claire lived. Vic had told me that the female impersonator was bunked up in a tower-block flat in the Redcliffe district on the southern edges of the city. Underdown House was one of three high-rises that sat on the corner of Commercial Road; St Claire's place was nineteen floors up. We parked on a side street close by, but before opening the door I turned to address my deadly passenger.

"How's it gonna pan out up there?"

Vic shrugged. "I'm jus' gonna let you talk ta tha muthafucka, dat's all."

212

Reading the subtle emotional changes in my cousin's face had been a lifelong study. Vic's eyes could shift from pleasantries to murderous intent with barely a twitch. Right then, a steeliness crept across his eye and the corners of his mouth.

"And you're sure St Claire's gonna be up there, where you say he is?"

"You tink I'm sum kinda eediat? Cou'se da fool is deh. You man Perri, he a creature a' habit. When he ain't crooning in dat queers' club, he tokin' up in his pit. Me man deal 'im t'ree ounce o' blow twice a week, an' he sum'time deal fo' me if it mean he can mek a few pound fo' himsel'. Ole Perri like da feel o' cash in his 'and 'bout as much as he do a fella's pick-pick." Vic winked then gestured towards the roof of the car. "He up deh fo' sure, stoned."

"And when we get up there, we play this my way, right?"

Vic smiled at me. "Shit, man I ain't 'ere ta mek nah trouble."

"Nah . . . cou'se you're not," I lied, hoping that Vic couldn't read me as well as I could him.

Underdown House was a 22-storey monstrosity that was crying out to feel the kiss of the wrecking ball. Shabby and rain streaked on the outside, the walls inside weren't faring much better. The lobby, if you could be generous enough to describe it as such, was thick with spray-paint messages, obscene slogans and incurable optimism about Bristol City football club. The lift was out of order, so we resigned ourselves to

213

giving the soles of our shoes a punishing workout on the concrete stairs.

It took us a good three minutes to climb nineteen flights then another two while Vic stood on the landing finishing the last of his joint. We walked down the spartan communal hallway to find the door we were looking for — number sixty-eight, white plastic numerals on chipped, canary-yellow paintwork. Classy, just like the fella that was hopefully shacked up inside. Vic put his thumb on the bell button, held it in for a while and waited.

"Who the hell is it?" a man's voice called from behind the door.

"Perri . . . It da Jah! Me man say you gotta bit o' urgent bidness you wanna t'row me way?"

"Business . . . what business?"

Vic put his face against the door panel and sighed. "Da kind me don't wanna be hollerin' 'bout outside on dis scabby landin'."

"I don't know what you're talking about, Jah."

"Bullshit! Don't keep me waitin'. Me drove out 'ere at dis fuckin' lousy time o' night on da promise dat you 'ad money in mind, an 'ow you bin tellin' me boy 'ow you an' me can mek sum."

The man stammered on the other side. "Money . . . what money?"

Vic began to hammer at the door with his open hand. "Don't mek me ha' ta come ta dat frowsy club you hang 'bout in. Open up dis fuckin' gate befo' I kick it in."

214

There was silence for a moment, then St Claire did as Vic had commanded. As he did, I could just make out the carving knife in his left hand. He saw me then took a moment too long deciding whether to slam or stab. In that split second of indecision, Vic booted at the bottom of the door and stormed inside, sending St Claire sprawling backwards. Vic drove the heel of his boot into the man's stomach then stood on his hand, kicked the blade away and yanked St Claire back up on his feet by the scruff of his neck. Vic slammed his fist into the man's face, snapping his neck backwards, the top of his head slamming against the wall. St Claire screamed; the funky, grass-tinted wind forced out of his mouth smelled like the final exhalation from a corpse.

I followed Vic as he dragged St Claire down the hall and through into the living room. The musky odour of marijuana struck at my face. Thick clouds of smoke filled every square inch of the place. Vic pinned St Claire to the lounge wall with the palm of his hand then stabbed a finger towards the TV set before flipping a light switch by the frame of the kitchen door. "Turn up dat ting!"

Vic shoved St Claire into the kitchen. I did as he asked then took a quick look around as I made my way back across the tiny room. A standard lamp lit up one corner; otherwise it was dark. Battered Venetian blinds hung at the window and the damp walls were papered in purple flock. A threadbare carpet that had once matched the colour of the wallpaper did little to improve the squalid feel of the place. On top of a shelf on the sideboard was a glass bowl. It contained a couple of pints of cloudy water and one small goldfish swimming frantically in circles.

In the kitchen, a bare bulb from the overhead fixture could hardly have been called a light. The floor was pitted linoleum; beige where it had kept its colour, grey where it had worn through. There was a card table for dining with a fold-up plastic chair. On the far wall, next to a small refrigerator were three empty shelves that were once cabinets, before the doors had been ripped off.

Vic spun St Claire round and dropped him into the seat. Gone was the wig, flamboyant sequin dress and the false eyelashes; what was sprawled out, quivering, in front of me was nothing like the creature I had encountered at the Moulin Rouge a few nights ago. Perri St Claire now had short black hair that hung down to his eyebrows in a greasy, unintentional fringe. He was wearing a bright yellow nylon shirt, vest showing through, dark grey flannels and brown slippers. His face was pale and smeared with his own blood.

Vic grinned his most evil grin at him. "How you doin', Trevor?"

I raised an eyebrow at Vic. "Say who?"

Vic smirked at me then thumped the top of St Claire's shoulder with his fist. "Dis 'ere is Trevor Furse. He only dress up like a cheap cockrat at da weekend. Ain't dat right, Trev?"

St Claire's face trembled with shock, his nose streaming blood, the split on his lip ridged up like a battered starfish.

"Jah, you know I don't answer to that awful moniker any longer."

Vic slapped St Claire so hard it knocked him out of his seat.

"Git da fuck up! You gonna ansah ta whateva fuckin' name I call you."

St Claire spat blood-tinged spittle on to the floor then scrabbled up on to his knees before heaving himself back into the chair. "You can't do thi —"

Vic grabbed St Claire's mouth and squeezed hard. "Don't you be tryin' ta mout' off ta me, boy." Vic pointed at me. "You gonna prick dem ponce ears o' yours back an' you gonna 'ear wha' dis man ovah deh gotta axe you. Understand me?"

St Claire tried to nod. I watched Vic tightening his grip on St Claire's face before letting go of him.

I took out the black-and-white passport photograph of Nikhil Suresh and hung it in front of him, real close, to get a good look at. "You remember me asking you about this fella the other night?"

St Claire squinted his watery eyes and nodded. "Yeah, I remember." I flinched; his breath was as stale as the room.

I shook the photograph at him. "You remember telling me 'bout a fella called Moody?"

He nodded again.

"You told me that the man in this photograph was Moody's 'piece of tail', yeah?"

"Yeah, that's right. What about it?"

Vic slapped St Claire around the back of the head. "Mind you mout'."

"Well I think that this Moody fella you put me on to was more of a matchmaker than a punter."

St Claire face whitened and twitched. "I got no idea what you're talking about."

"No? Well, I have it on good authority that your Jimmy Moody is the man who makes sure that a certain William Ryder stays happy when he pays a visit to the Moulin."

St Claire gave me a vacant stare. "Who?"

Vic's huge fist crashed against the side of St Claire's face, catching him squarely in the eye socket. St Claire's head sank, his chin grazing his chest. There was panic and anger in his voice when he finally spoke. "You're making a big twat out of yourself." He flicked his eyes towards Vic then back at me. "Getting Jah to knock me around ain't gonna help that dead Indian bloke. You need to leave all this shit alone. That includes me!"

"Who said anything about him being dead?"

Vic looked sideways at me. I saw his right hand slide out of his coat pocket with a leather-covered blackjack, an old-fashioned one that was shaped like a darning egg with a spring built into the braided grip. St Claire saw it too. He tried to raise his forearm but he was way too slow. Vic hammered the blackjack against St Claire's shoulder. He let out a howl of pain, clasping his palm hard against his collarbone, his eyes watering uncontrollably. The fearful expression in his eyes was unmistakable.

St Claire swallowed hard, shaking his head, drool seeping from the corner of his mouth. "Well, I seen it in

218

the paper, didn't I? All over the front page it was." A bead of sweat began to trickle down the side of his right temple. He stared nervously back up at Vic then looked around for an escape. When he saw there was no chance, he gave his attention back to me. "Look! Come on . . . for Christ sakes, there ain't that many Indian boys being carved up in this city, is there?"

"Tell me what William Ryder wanted with Suresh."

St Claire blinked and flexed his jaw. "Whaddya think he wanted?"

"You're treating me like I'm stupid." I glanced up at Vic and then back at St Claire. "And that's starting to piss the Jah off. Now, why don't you tell me what Ryder was up to with the boy?"

Vic stroked the leather across the back of St Claire's skull. His hands were shaking. Another drop of sweat fell from his chin.

"You know what he was up to," he answered, his eyes coming back to mine. "Ryder and that Indian . . . they were shacked up together."

"Shacked up . . . You saying that they were in some kinda relationship?"

St Claire pressed his hand against his shoulder and grimaced with a spasm that made his eyes close. He shook his head in exasperation. "Relationship . . . fling . . . having it off . . . Call it want you bloody well want. The two of 'em were at it like jackrabbits for months."

"And was Ryder still seeing Nikhil Suresh around the time he ended up dead?"

"How the hell do I know?" He swallowed and then took a deep breath. "Perhaps."

I put the photograph back inside my jacket pocket and squeezed my temples. "Perhaps . . . what makes you say that, Perri?"

"Ryder, he came into the club late one night a few weeks back. He had that Indian fella all over him then. They were necking in one of the booths, then all hell breaks out. Both of 'em arguing like a couple of old queens. Ryder was furious, screaming and threatening the coon about something or other."

Vic dug the tip of the blackjack into St Claire's cheek. "Watch who you callin' a coon, Trevor."

I stared up at Vic and shook my head, then looked back at St Claire. "What do you think they were arguing about?"

St Claire turned up his palms, his eyes like heated marbles. "I don't know! Look, you and the Jah can keep up with this crap all night if you want, but I'm telling you straight: that's all the dirty laundry you're gonna get outta me."

Vic chewed at his lip, his eyes smiling at me. He tapped his jaw with his finger like a drum then snatched St Claire off the chair and hurled his fist into the man's stomach. It was a deep blow, in the soft place right under the sternum. St Claire's face flashed white with shock. His mouth gasped and his eyes locked open. I called out to Vic to stop, but my words meant nothing to him. He grasped hold of St Claire's middle finger and bent it sharply. St Claire screamed. Then Vic jerked it backwards, breaking it. St Claire made a high-pitched gurgling sound and collapsed to his knees. Vic kicked him in the side and eyeballed me before taking hold of another finger.

"Axe dis fool agin."

"Perri, what were Ryder and Suresh arguing about?"

"I . . . I . . . don't fucking know . . . Something about some job Ryder had got him, that's all I know . . ."

Vic braced St Claire's finger between his own, applying a little more heft, then moved down to murmur his ear, "A job where, Trevor?"

Then he bent the finger further, snapped it back.

"Golf club!" St Claire screamed. Vic let go of his hand and he sank to the floor sobbing. "It was at a fucking golf club."

The skin on my face tightened as I saw the seat of St Claire's trousers soak with his urine; it began to pool around his shins and ankles and leak out across the linoleum. I kept pressing.

"Which golf club?"

Vic reached down and wrapped his huge fingers around St Claire's wrist, before lifting his arm into the air and snatching at the other hand. St Claire went into full-on panic, his knees and shins sliding on the wet floor. I tried to pull his hand away from Vic's vice-like grip but quickly gave up. He glared at me over his shoulder, stuttering in fear. "It was . . . it was . . . that private one . . . the one out at Portishead . . . Ryder's a member there."

In my mind, I saw the face of the dead boy, James Peberdy, and remembered where Superintendent Fletcher said the child had been found. *Portishead golf course . . . under some trees near the twelfth hole.* Vic was grinning at me, urging me to keep on at St Claire. I stood over the piss on the floor and got down on my knees by his side, resting the palm of my hand on St Claire's shoulder. He flinched.

"What was Suresh doing at the golf club?"

St Claire slobbered and made a moaning sound in his throat. His expression was opaque. He tried to make words, but they wouldn't come. Vic yanked on Perri's arm then pressed the sole of his shoe down against the backs of his broken fingers. Trevor, Perri St Claire, whatever the hell the poor man's name was, stared back at me, tears streaming helplessly down his bloodied face. When he finally found the strength to open his mouth and begin to speak, his voice was little more than a whisper.

"Please . . . please, I don't know . . . I don't. How many more times?"

A wave of nausea started to course slowly up through my body as I got to my feet and reeled out of the kitchen, lumbering back down the hall and out of flat. I stood shivering on the landing for a moment, my head and eyes stinging with shame and guilt. Then I heard another violent scream come from inside and felt the bile in my gut rise up. I clasped my hand over my mouth to try to stop myself from throwing up and hurried towards the staircase. My legs shook as I raced back towards the street, my knees weak, my mind racing along, trying to put together what I'd just heard.

Halfway down the stairwell, the chill night air suddenly yanked me out of my frenzied trance. I stopped and took a deep breath, holding on to the rail,

222

my skin clammy as it touched the metal. I closed my eyes for a second or two then began to tread over each concrete rung at a much slower pace, fearing that I was perhaps descending down into hell and that the devil himself would be waiting for me when my feet padded off the last step.

CHAPTER
TWENTY-EIGHT

The house was in darkness when I got home. It was a little after one. Out of habit, I looked in on Chloe's room even though I knew she was tucked up safely over at Loretta's. I stayed outside in the hall for a while, staring at the empty single bed, imagining that my adopted daughter was asleep underneath the blankets, sucking her thumb, her stuffed rag doll on the pillow next to her. I leaned against the door frame and rubbed my face. I could smell the scent of stale alcohol against my palm, a rancid odour that crawled up into my nostrils as if out of a dark well. I felt like I had aged a century, that someone had slipped a knife along my breastbone and scooped out all my vital organs.

I went into the front room, filled four inches of rum into a glass and knocked it back. The booze hit my stomach like canned heat. I gave myself a refill then took myself and the booze to my bedroom.

I undressed then sat on the edge of the bed in my underwear, trying to let go of the torment that was rattling around inside my head. My body was hot and the backs of my legs quivered, my skin clammy to the touch.

224

I held out my arms in front of me and shook them in the hope that it would help release the fatigue and anger that was bottled up inside of me, but I was genuinely jazzed up, wrapped so tight in my hide that it felt like a prison. I felt like a caged lion pacing inside his enclosure. My eyes stung; my breath was sour and trembled in my throat each time I tried to breathe.

I told myself that I needed to sleep, that hitting the sack would help me to shut out the persistent resonance of the screaming man inside my head and banish the feelings of guilt and impotence and the haunting image of Vic torturing a petrified Perri St Claire. But those tacit words of self-counsel were to go unheard. Instead I went into the dry heaves and ended up on my knees in front of the toilet.

When I was done, I fell back against the side of the bath. Inside my head there was a sound like the roar of the ocean in a conch shell. My body shook, flashes of colour popping like lesions behind my eyes. I began to sob like a child, and I didn't care. For now, I was used up, finished, as dead inside as I was the day the undertaker had dropped my wife and daughter's bodies into their graves.

I slept until seven thirty the next morning. The early light was grey in the street, then the sun came up red on the eastern horizon. I went into the bathroom with my empty rum glass, filled it with tap water and drank it down before getting myself ready for the day.

After some toast and coffee, I stood with my back against the draining board and worked out in my head everything I needed to do over the next few hours. First I had to update Fletcher on my meeting with Herbert Castle and lead him gently towards my suspicions about William Ryder. For whatever reason, perhaps simply dumb family loyalty, I knew I had to keep Vic out of the picture for now, so Perri St Claire's revelations would remain undisclosed. I needed to see Chloe, to hug her and tell her that I loved her. I needed to feel the warmth of my family and friends around me. I hungered for the innocent company of Aunt Pearl, Uncle Gabe and Loretta. I needed to forget about the carnage, the lies and corruption that were washing back, uninvited, into my life. Today, a phone call to the police and time spent with those I cared for most were my only goal. Whatever road I ended up on afterwards was fine by me as long as it didn't involve killing anyone or getting killed myself.

I stared out of the window, down into the small backyard below, my mind wandering all over the place. I began to daydream about the dead boy, James Peberdy. In my reverie, he was sitting peacefully underneath a row of trees. My friend Carnell Harris was next to him. Both of them were covered in blood, their clothes reduced to mouldy, tattered rags.

Then in the distance I saw Vic approaching across a lush green lawn. He was dressed entirely in black. He kneeled down between Carnell and the boy and began talking and laughing. Then he took a small Bible from the pocket of his long leather coat and began to read. The boy and Carnell just sat there listening while my

226

cousin recited from the scriptures. I saw him mouth the word *sinners*.

Above their heads I watched as hundreds of ravens gathered in the tree branches above. I knew that they were waiting silently and patiently for Vic to finish his sermon so they could descend and pluck the flesh from the two poor dead souls' bones.

CHAPTER TWENTY-NINE

There was a quarter mug of cold coffee left on my kitchen table by the time I was ready to hit the street. I'd taken my time drinking the bitter dregs, making my plans and trying to ditch the lurid vision that had crept into my subconscious. I still felt almost completely in the dark about what the hell was going on. I knew that two murders had been committed, that the men who had appointed me with the task of investigating these crimes could well be implicated themselves and that I'd been paid — and paid well — for all this confusion.

These muddled thoughts were yanked out of my head when I heard someone calling out my name as I walked out my front door.

"Mr Ellington?" a man said. There was an unusual accent to his words. It wasn't local Bristolian or deep country Somerset, not a copper's authoritative voice and it certainly wasn't black. The intonation was hushed and oddly unyielding.

I turned to see a man with skin the colour of freshly drawn milk and straight chalk-white hair that was too long for office work but nowhere near shaggy. Somewhere in his forties, the man had pink irises and deep red pupils that looked like they'd been painted on by hand. He was maybe five-eleven and strong the way good rope is, slender and knotted.

"Yes?" I said as the man approached me.

"My employer, Mr Ryder, would like to speak with you."

"And you are?"

The man came to a sudden halt, like a squaddie on parade. "I'm Moody."

"What, all the time?"

That got the man called Moody to smile. I could tell by the cast of his face that this was not a common occurrence.

"I haven't heard that gag before. I ought to write it down."

Moody lost the grin and took another step towards me. He wore well-shined black leather shoes, a black flannel suit and a white shirt that was buttoned up to the neck but sported no tie. He was, I could tell, deadlier than a pit of Cottonmouth vipers.

"What does your Mr Ryder want?"

With a slight gesture of his head he told me that he didn't know or, at least, wouldn't say.

"And when is this get-together supposed to be happening?"

"I can drive you there now." It came to me that he spoke English like it was a language learned by some erudite foreign scholar. Moody gestured down the street, where I saw a parked maroon Bentley Tl saloon. There was a half-dozen kids already hanging around the car. I wondered if there had ever been such a fancy motor parked up on my street.

I pointed down the road. "I got my Ford. It's parked a few cars behind yours."

Moody nodded. "Then you can follow me."

There didn't seem to be much room for reason or argument, so I went to my car and Moody to his. When the small crowd of kids saw him coming, they shifted out of the way without uttering a word.

The albino's dangerous bearing demanded such reverence.

We breezed our way out of St Pauls and over to the Avon Gorge Hotel on Sion Hill, just outside of the city. Moody pulled the Bentley up to the entrance, where a woollen red carpet connected the front doors of the hotel to the kerb. I pulled up after him and got out.

"Yes, sir?" a handsome, young blond lad asked. He wore the grey slacks, silk white shirt and red waistcoat of the Avon Gorge's valets.

"I'm with him," I said, pointing to Moody.

"Oh," the young man said. "The key's in the ignition," I told him.

When I strolled up to Moody, he turned and walked into the lavish hotel.

I followed.

The ceilings were high and the colours regal and tasteful. The paintings looked to be original, but I had no idea who they were by or in what era they were painted. Moody and I were the subject of many stares from the patrons and hotel staff, but no one spoke to, much less bothered, us. We made it to the gaudy, golden elevator doors and Moody pressed a button.

"Mr Moody?" a man said in such a way as to demand attention, not to greet or recognise. Foolish, in this instance, I thought.

The white man in front of us was reedy and well groomed. His dark navy suit probably cost more than most working black folk made in a couple of months, and his moustache was thin enough to slice ripe cheese. His commanding posture suggested to me ex-police or retired army officer, and of fairly low rank. I would have bet that for most of his career he'd been sucking up to his betters. He'd retired to do the same for the rich folk walking through the hotel's front doors, but he wasn't bowing down to no black fella.

"Just Moody," my albino guide replied.

"Who is your friend?"

"Mr Ryder's guest."

"His guest?"

A silvery bell chimed and the elevator doors opened; the tinging sound pealed in my ears.

"After you," Moody said to me.

The elevator operator was looking at the carpeted floor of the lift when we got on. "Floor?" he asked as he looked up. Moody sneered at him. "Oh, penthouse," came the reply.

The lift opened on a pulpit of a room, ten feet square, a closed door at its end. The only furnishing was a mahogany stand on which perched a vase with a couple of dozen lilies poking out of it. Moody surprised me by knocking on the door of the penthouse suite. I had expected him to press another damn button or use a key. A moment later, the fancy rosewood door swung inward and a bare-footed young man wearing a crimson jacket and black silk trousers bowed, as I guessed his Indian ancestors had done for generations, and backed away for us to enter.

The room we entered was more than a few hundred square feet, and it abutted another wall beyond. I could see a patio half the size of the room we were standing in, which in turn led out to a small balcony. The ceilings were almost the height of the hotel's reception downstairs, and the furnishings were expensive, beyond the imagination of the average Joe in the street.

In a large, winged leather chair, with its back turned to the window, sat a white man who looked to be in his mid-fifties. William Ryder, I presumed. The gangland boss looked every bit the part sitting there on his throne in an expensive Savile Row suit, his jet-black hair combed elegantly back from his forehead, a hint of Brylcreem keeping it in place. His face was chiselled and hard, with intense black eyes, which would have been more at home on a shark, set square in his face. A beak-like nose completed the look of a man renowned for his ruthlessness. He gave me the once-over before he turned to his associate.

"Mr Ellington, sir," Moody said coolly.

"Nice place," I said.

Ryder placed the tips of his fingers together in a gesture akin to prayer. "Have a seat." His voice was a warm growl, with the merest trace of an accent.

Moody pulled up a chair for me. It looked expensive but it was certainly inferior to the one that Ryder was sat in. The snow-white flunky stood at the side of me,

232

motionless, like a switched-off machine. A machine for hurting people. I got the feeling that one word from Ryder, one look, would set the albino working again. That thought made my hackles rise.

"Can we get you a drink?"

I was wondering how old a malt whisky I could get from the bar in a room like this. But I knew better than to try it on.

I looked up at Moody and shifted in my seat. "Er . . . no, thank you."

Ryder's eyes mimed regret. "You disappoint me." He leaned forward in his chair, raised his arm with a lazy swimming motion and clicked his fingers at his aide. "Moody. Go play. Can't you see you're scaring Mr Ellington."

Moody need no further instruction. He nodded obediently, turned and marched quickly across the room and out of the door, leaving Ryder and me alone in the makeshift throne room. Neither of us spoke for a minute, the crime boss only finally opening his mouth when he was happy that the silence was making me uncomfortable.

"So . . . do you have a first name, Mr Ellington?"

"Yeah . . . Joseph."

"Very biblical . . . You don't mind if I call you Joseph then?"

I decided to go with the flow. "That's fine by me, Mr Ryder."

"Good. You can keep calling me Mr Ryder for now . . ." He slapped his palm on the arm of his chair rhythmically a couple of times, watching me. His fingers were so long and thin and his nails so pink and clean that his hands looked more like those of a surgeon than a crook. "I want to thank you for coming to see me this morning."

"No problem. You got me a little confused why I'm here, though?"

"Just a little?" Ryder said with a mournful smile. He leaned across his desk to a sterling silver cigar box and selected a slender greenish panatela. "Care for a smoke?"

I declined his offer and watched Ryder trim the end with an antique cigar cutter. "Let's get down to business, shall we?"

Ryder warmed the panatela's slim length with the thin-blue flame of a petrol lighter before lighting the end. "You're a detective, yes?"

"Kind of."

Ryder's features were shrouded in blue smoke as he puffed his cigar. " 'Kind of' is a rather vague description of your occupation, don't you think?"

I shrugged. "The people who used to hire me normally weren't looking to detect much. Most of my work back then was doing favours for people. Helping folk outta trouble, if I could."

Ryder waved away a wreath of cigar smoke, flashing a diamond ring the Pope himself would have kissed. "You said 'back then'. I take it that you're longer in the favours business, Joseph?"

"Well, I wasn't until a few days ago."

"So, you've been drawn back into the world of offering benevolence to others, have you?"

234

"That's one way of putting it."

Ryder leaned forward and fixed me with a conspirator's grin. "Would you perhaps be in a position to grant me a little of that goodwill?"

"That all depends on what you are asking for, Mr Ryder."

"For you to turn a blind eye, perhaps?"

"What would I need to be ignoring?" I said, affecting an innocent stare.

"I believe Herbert Castle has already gone over that ground?"

"Ah, so it's your door I'm supposed to be staying clear of, is it?"

Ryder laughed and shook his head. "Is that how Herbert put it? That man, he has an artful way with words."

"Yes, he does . . . Called you part of this city's 'great and the good'."

Ryder sat back and gazed at me. "And a flatterer too." He licked his lips before continuing. "Back to the thorny matter of you paying no heed to people and things that don't concern you. Can I rely on your detective-like aptitude to brush aside what is of no consequence?"

I rubbed at my cheek with the back of my hand. "That may not be so easy."

"How so?" There was a sharp edge to his voice.

"Nikhil Suresh?"

Ryder's eyes tightened. He stared back at me and took at least fifteen seconds to consider the name I'd just mentioned. Finally, he said, "Word has it that you're being handsomely rewarded over at the council house for your investigation into Mr Suresh?"

"You talking 'bout Castle's bribe money?"

Ryder, his face slightly flushed, smiled. On him, it was more of a leer. "I wouldn't know about any bribe money."

"No? I think it's dirty money to keep me off your scent."

"Really? Well, it wouldn't be the first time you've been bought off to do that, Joseph."

"Sorry?" I said, my control starting to slip.

"You may not realise it . . . but we've crossed paths before."

I blinked. "We have?" I said, my heart racing.

Ryder became very still, like a snake about to strike down a victim. "Yes, your involvement with the Erotica Negro affair some years back . . . the late Terrance Blanchard — oh, and of course . . . Stella Hopkins."

I breathed slowly and cleared my throat. "I beg your pardon."

"Terrance Blanchard . . . he was an old friend of mine from back when I was advising members of the council house. Before his unfortunate demise, he'd expressed his concerns to me about your handling of matters regarding that terrible business with the missing girl, Hopkins."

I got to my feet. "Did he now?" I pushed the chair away from me with the back of my legs.

Ryder saw the hurt on my face. His eyes flicked away from mine to stare at the burning tip of his cigar, then came back to me again. "Yes, Terrance was a friend of

236

mine and Councillor Castle's, in fact. I believe Herbert frequented the Negro . . . many times."

My palms started sweating, heat rising up in my chest.

"And you . . . you ever pay that dive a visit?"

Ryder shook his head slowly, the skin around his eyes stretched tight, the pupils like onyx marbles. "I was never fond of dark meat, Joseph . . . if you get my drift?"

"Oh, I'm reading you loud and clear, Mr Ryder."

"Good . . ." Ryder drew the word out. "Because I wouldn't want you to get your wires crossed about me. Nosing around in my personal and private dealings, it could be a very dangerous thing to do."

I took a couple of shaky steps backwards. "I'll bear that in mind while I'm going 'bout my business. Most people who know me . . . they kinda used to me snooping 'bout where I ain't wanted."

Ryder huffed air out of his nose, a smirk crawling to the edges of his mouth. His eyes fixed on mine. "Funny . . . that's exactly what Stella Hopkins' mother said about you."

The ground seemed to tilt under my feet and my stomach knotted up as I walked away. When I reached the door, I turned on my heels and pointed an accusatory finger at Ryder's face. "Brother, somewhere down the line, my dirt-digging is gonna throw up the truth 'bout you and Nikhil Suresh. You can count on it."

Ryder's face tightened, his eyes still locked in on me, the morning sun catching in them like reflected firelight. The cigar between his fingers burned fierce. "Ah, the truth, Joseph . . . you'll find that to be an elusive quarry."

CHAPTER
THIRTY

I clocked the dark blue Rover parked across the street from the Avon Gorge's car park as soon as I'd strolled out of the hotel's front door with the valet. The driver had positioned the car close enough to the exit to immediately set the hairs on the back of my neck on end. The vehicle's engine was running. Its blacked-out windows smacked of it being an unmarked police vehicle and also made it impossible for me to get a look at who was inside. Whoever the unknown denizens were, be it the local fuzz or some of Ryder's cronies, they were clearly intent on making a very simple statement to me.

We can see you, you can't see us and we'd like to keep it that way.

I headed across the car park slowly, my keys already in my hand. I unlocked the door then leaned against the roof of the Ford and stared directly into the tinted windscreen for a moment. I was pretty sure that staring out the faceless occupant inside wasn't going to provoke them to confront me. Whoever was inside was far too shifty for that. What I did know was that somebody was trying to lean on me, and giving 'em the eyeball was my way of saying I wasn't gonna scare that easily.

I drove south-east out of the city and along the Bath Road towards the village of Brislington. If I was going to be followed, I thought I might as well take whoever was on my tail someplace interesting. While heading towards my next destination, I'd give the predicament I was in a little more thought.

All my present troubles had started with Superintendent Fletcher, and I felt that the solution would have to begin with him too. I needed a little more time to work out if the deaths of the young boy, James Peberdy, and Nikhil Suresh were definitely connected to William Ryder and whether Fletcher or any of his men were implicated in either or both of their killings. My gut instinct was crying out to me that someone, if not a number of officers on the Bristol force, would be entrenched within Ryder's organisation. Perhaps they were trailing after me in the car behind. The question was, who were they?

I knew I had acquired little wisdom with age. For me, the answers to the great mysteries that surrounded the criminal mind seemed more remote now than ever, and after my short time in the presence of William Ryder, I was no better informed on such unusual matters. I found it hard to accept that immoral creatures like Ryder became as powerful and as corrupt as they did. Here was a man who ran as vile and malicious a criminal empire as my own cousin did; perhaps more so. Who flouted the law and had corrupt police officers and powerful men at the city's council undertaking much of his illicit business for him. Ryder was clearly detached from most of the criminal acts undertaken at his behest and was equally casual to the suffering of the innocent affected by such iniquity. At the same time, here was a man who was often lauded for charitable acts and substantial financial contributions to both local government and fellow businesses. How the hell did he get away with it, and for so long? For me, this was the greatest riddle: to understand the nature of such evil and the way that it mingled with ordinary and upright society. Was there a diabolical force at work in men like Ryder, a satanic figure with leathery wings and the breath of a carrion eater in our midst?

In the past, the answers to such questions were often found in the wisdom of a dear friend. A kind soul who I would call upon, seeking advice from her sage mind on the ills of mankind and how I could better understand them. But that fount of such prudent, owlish knowledge had fallen silent upon her death eighteen months ago. Now, when such challenging matters troubled me, when the difficult questions I could not answer myself required deeper thought and remedy, I spoke only to her insentient remains.

I parked on the road outside of the Arnos Vale cemetery. In my rear-view mirror, I could see that the Rover, which had been glued to my rear, had pulled up to the kerb some fifty or so yards back on the opposite side of the street. Nobody was getting out and I could see from the exhaust fumes that the engine was still purring away.

I grabbed my jacket off the back seat and got out, ignoring my new-found companions, then headed through the heavy, wrought-iron gates and down a flagstone avenue past rows of headstones that stood erect in silence, like a sea of the dead. Some were crumbled with the weathering of the years; some were smooth with new black or gold scrolled writing set against pristine white marble and laid with floral tributes. Most, though, were overgrown and unkempt, their mourners most probably in the clay soil close by.

Mrs Pearce had died a little over five months after I'd returned home from Barbados with Chloe and Vic in tow. It had rained the day of the funeral. In fact, it rained all that week. During her interment, water dripped from the trees, ran in rivulets from the eaves of the chapel and formed brown pools that were filled with floating leaves. I remember the dull grey-green light of the sky and, most of all, the river of tears I shed that day.

What little family the old woman had stood over the grave in their printed cotton dresses and brushed dark suits as the vicar from the church she had attended for over forty years read the service of the dead while an altar boy held an umbrella over his head. Her relatives had nodded at me, and two of the ladies from her prayer-meeting group shook hands, but in truth I was a stranger among the many mourners in attendance. After they were gone and the last car rumbled along the tarmac and out of the gates, I'd stood under an oak tree and watched two council gravediggers spade the dirt over the coffin. One of them became impatient to get out of the rain, and he started to push the soil off the mound into the hole with his boot. I recalled walking out from underneath the tree's sagging branches and barking:

"Do it right, man."

For the next twenty minutes, I'd stood over those two fellas, the unmistakable odour of damp moss, mould and wet clay percolating through the dank air, watching every shovelful of earth they hefted into that hole in the ground. I listened to their faint mutterings of dissatisfaction and the sound of the clumps of mud and stones hitting the coffin lid. Only when the men had patted down the wet earth into a neat barrow and placed a small wooden cross at the top of the grave did I choose to leave the cemetery.

I'd trodden back up the path, my head hung low, with a deluge still swirling out of the sky, the water glistening on the concrete and bouncing off the black spiked fence that surrounded the graveyard. Above me, the dark clouds had seemed to be filled with electric lights, the wind resonant with the whispering of lost voices from those departed long past.

I snapped my eyes shut for a moment, eager to rid myself of the mournful reverie that was invading my thoughts, then looked down at the grave and felt a gentle shiver run through me. I opened and closed my hands, wiped them on my trousers then rested them on top of the granite headstone and stared down at the short epitaph engraved into the memorial slab.

Marjorie Ann Pearce
Born 24 October 1880
Died 19th August 1969
Generous of Heart. Constant of Faith

"Happy memories, Mrs P."

I could hear myself breathing in the silence. I counted the seconds, my heart twisting. When I spoke again, the words came in a crackle. "No flowers . . . just like you always told me."

I kneeled down on the grass beside the headstone, shut my eyes again and began to talk quietly. I told my friend about walking out of my job at the school. About embroiling myself once again in police business and with Herbert Castle at the council house, about the murders of Nikhil Suresh and James Peberdy, my earlier meeting with William Ryder and Vic's involvement, and about the unknown person or persons who had just followed me to the cemetery.

I left out nothing.

I told her about Chloe, about how much I loved her and how I was leaving my adoptive daughter in the care of Loretta Harris while I traipsed around the city digging into other folks' miseries. I told her about how Gabe and Pearl were doing, about the couple who had moved into her old home and how they were looking after her beloved garden.

Then I spoke about my unexpected chat with Ruth Castle and how, despite all the madness that was going on around me, I was still thinking about her.

I told my old friend how much I missed her.

I stayed by that headstone for what seemed like an hour, but in truth it could only have been a few minutes. I let the light come back into my eyes and got to my feet, wondering if my friend had heard my words.

I hoped so.

I heard the flapping of wings as I walked away from the graveside and headed back towards my car. At the cemetery gates, I could see the Rover still parked up on the opposite side of the road, only now the passenger-side window was down, the heel of a hand resting on the sill, fingers tapping the door panel.

Without turning around again, I got into my car and started it up. As I turned into the traffic, I saw the Rover pull out and hook back up on my tail. I drove slowly, eyeing up the vehicle in my rear-view mirror. I made my way into the city and out to St Pauls, the anonymous car winding behind me like a snake trailing its quarry.

CHAPTER
THIRTY-ONE

The phone was ringing when I got to my office door, but whoever it was had hung up before I got to the receiver. It was a harsh reminder that I had a few calls of my own to make. I threw off my jacket, sat down behind my desk and reached for the telephone.

"Bridewell Station," a woman's voice answered.

"Superintendent Fletcher, please."

"Hold a moment."

The phone rang.

"Fletcher here."

"Afternoon, Superintendent."

"Jesus . . . Finally! Where the fucking hell have you been?"

"Doing your damn legwork, like you ordered me to."

"Less of the bloody cheek. I've been calling you all morning." I heard the opening of a metal drawer and the rustling of paper. "So, whaddya got for me?"

"Stuff I don't wanna be telling you 'bout on a telephone, that's what."

"Stop pissing me about, son."

"I ain't goofing around here, Superintendent. I need to speak to you someplace the walls ain't got ears."

I heard Fletcher sigh deeply. "Fucking unbelievable. Who do you think you are? Shaft?"

"No . . . I think I'm a fella that's starting to feel a noose creeping round his neck. You wanna hear what I gotta tell you, then it needs to be face to face."

Another irritated sigh. "Right, meet me in the bar of the Three Sugar Loaves, Christmas Steps, nine thirty. And don't keep me bleedin' hanging about."

I could sense that the handset was about to be slammed down on me, so I spoke quickly into the receiver.

"Hey, are you having me followed?"

"No." Fletcher hesitated for a moment. "Why'd you ask?"

"Well, there's a dark blue Rover with blacked-out windows that's been sat on my arse fo' the better part of the morning. I thought it might have been a couple of your boys keeping an eye on me?"

"You should think yourself bloody lucky. If it had been my lads, they'd have had your arse down to the nick and sat in front of me by now."

"That's a comforting thought."

"Nine thirty, Ellington, and try not to bring whoever's in that Rover with you!"

The line went dead, the buzzing tone left whining in my ear.

I lifted my jacket from off the floor and reached into the inside pocket. I pulled out a beer mat and then dialled the phone number scrawled on it.

"Bristol Polytechnic," a woman's friendly voice said.

"I'd like to speak to Miss Castle if she's available?"

There was a brief pause on the other end of the line. "Miss Castle will be in student services at the moment. I'll try to put you through to her."

The next thing I heard was another ringing phone.

"Student services," a mature woman said.

"I'd like to speak to Miss Castle, please."

"And who am I speaking to?"

"My name is Ellington."

"Is this college business?" she asked.

"No, po'lice bidness," I responded to the operator's obliquely condescending attitude.

The line went dead for a moment, followed by a series of clicks then a soft voice that I'd been eager to hear again.

"Good afternoon, this is Ruth Castle."

"Good afternoon, Ruth."

"Mr Ellington . . . well, this is a surprise. It's good of you to call."

My lips suddenly felt numb. I cleared my throat before speaking. "You did say I should get in touch . . . 'bout us meeting up fo' that drink?"

"Yes . . . yes, I did."

"You free later on this week, maybe?"

"Why not later this evening?"

"I'm kinda tied up until way after ten."

"Okay, so why don't you come on over once you've untied yourself?"

"That's gonna be kinda late t' be callin' on you, ain't it?"

"Not at all . . . I'm a night owl."

"Well, if that ain't a problem?" I said nervously.

"No problem. I'm in Clifton Wood — forty-four Bellevue Crescent. Last terrace at the top of the hill. I'll see you later," she whispered before putting the phone down on me.

I finished scribbling the address on a scrap of paper and cradled the receiver, a smile creeping across my face. Then I held my finger down on the switch and dialled one more number. The line rang for what seemed like the better part of a minute. Finally, my call was picked up. I felt the beam on my face I'd been wearing disappear.

"Vic?" Instead of an answer I got a series of wet, rolling coughs.

"Yeah . . ." He coughed some more.

"It's JT."

"I 'naw who da hell it is!" He hacked. "How you doin'?"

"Better than you from the sounds of it."

"Nah, am good. Blazin' me herb, dat's all."

"We need to talk," I said.

"Den fuckin' talk!"

"Not now. Later on, tonight, after you've finished sucking on all that reefer?"

Vic laughed and wheezed at the same time. "Uh-huh . . . Mek it after midnight. Me 'ave a bit o' bidness need tekin' care o' first."

The line fell silent for a few seconds. Then I heard Vic breathing heavily on the other end. When he spoke again, his voice was sombre, his tone blunt. "You soundin' vexed?"

"That's cause I am. I'm getting the feeling I'm punching above my weight with everything that's going down."

"Dat right." My cousin was hushed again, but only for the briefest of moments. "You rememba wha' I tole you 'bout packin' befo' a fight, JT?"

"Yeah."

"Well, you do it, brutha."

Vic hung the phone up. His parting words were a thorn piercing my heart.

CHAPTER
THIRTY-TWO

It was a hair past four by the time I left Perry's Gym. I'd called Loretta before heading out and arranged to meet her and Chloe back at Gabe and Pearl's place just after five thirty. I'd been promising that we'd all get together for supper for days and I knew I couldn't put it off any longer. Loretta said she'd let my aunt know we'd all be over and that I could face the old woman's wrath for not telling her sooner when I showed up outside her door.

The Rover that had been parked further up the road earlier was gone. I stood in the gutter for a moment, staring at the empty space where the vehicle had been and wondered again who the occupants inside could have been. Not Fletcher's fellas if I was to take his word. Whoever had been following me since I'd left the Avon Gorge hotel had been determined to instil more than a little disquiet in me. They'd come into my own neighbourhood to reinforce that sense of unease and it had had the desired effect.

As I got into my car, I told myself that if I was going up against bent lawmen or organised crime, I should at least have the sense to be afraid.

A solitary raindrop splashed on my windscreen as I turned into Morgan Street and parked up outside my house. On the pavement, a parliament of magpies stood so close to each other that their tails were touching. They were staring off in different directions, watching each other's backs. I wished that I had the same kind of brother at arms to rely upon. All I'd ever had was Vic, and standing side by side with him was like pressing up against a bad-tempered king cobra.

When I got out of the car, most of the magpies took off immediately, though one of them cocked its eye at me, looking me up and down. Its hard bright gaze was sizing me up and no doubt labelling me a fool.

"What you looking at?" I asked it as I crossed the road. The bird answered by hopping into the street and flying on to the bonnet of my car. It pecked at the feathers under its wing for a moment, then returned its dark stare towards me and cackled. *One for sorrow*, I thought.

I unlocked my front door and walked inside. When I turned to close it, the bird was gone. I was certain that it had left bad luck as its parting gift.

I flicked on the immersion heater to warm up some water for a bath, then brewed a pot of coffee. While I waited, I wandered aimlessly around my little rented home, wishing that Chloe was with me and that I could turn back the clock and find myself just returning from a day's graft at Parson Street School — the carefree life of an assistant caretaker. How I longed to be back with my broom, sweeping the corridors and classrooms. There were worse jobs I could have been doing; it had

252

certainly been better than the work I was currently undertaking.

I looked at the bottle of rum on the dresser in the front room and ran my tongue over my lips. Vic always said that there were few things more beautiful than a bottle filled with deep amber rum. He said that the magic liquor shone when the light hit it, and that the colour reminded him of precious things like jewels and gold. He also said that rum "wus betta dan sum lifeless bracelet or damn crown!" I had to agree with him. Rum for most Bajan men was a living thing. Your friend when nobody else was around, the solace that held you tighter than any lover could.

I thought all that while standing over the bottle and I knew for a fact it was all true. True the way a lover's pillow talk is true. True the way a mother's arms comfort her child. But a rum mind couldn't think its way out of the problems I had. So I put the half-empty bottle out of sight in the dresser cupboard where it belonged and settled for a mug of Nescafé.

I soaked in the bath for twenty minutes then went into my bedroom to dress. I put on a fresh shirt and tie and my best navy suit, then fished out my Aquascutum raincoat and took my favourite penknife and some cash from my bedside drawer. I looked at the cubbyhole with its combination padlock next to my bed and thought about the last words Vic had said to me before he'd hung up the phone.

You rememba wha' I tole you 'bout packin' befo' a fight, JT?

I kneeled down in front of the locked recess and entered the combination into the padlock, snapping it free. After a moment's hesitation, I swung it open, retrieved a brown leather holdall, which I dropped on the bed, then began to take out the contents, laying them out in a neat row in front of me.

It was an eclectic array of items to retrieve from a travel bag, that was for sure. Aside from a change of clothes and some toiletries, including first-aid supplies, there was a sewing kit; an antique black-leather sap; a four-inch brass knuckleduster; a torch; a length of rope; a roll of five- and one-pound notes, amounting to one hundred pounds; and lastly a semi-automatic pistol, shoulder holster and four box magazines containing thirteen rounds apiece.

The items spread across my bed were what Vic liked to call a "fight or flight" bag — a collection of items that he recommended I secreted away in case I found my back against the wall and needed to make a swift exit. At the time, I hadn't questioned his reasoning — just put into place the things he advised. Now, I was still in the dark, unsure why he'd advised me to bring the dusty holdall out of cold storage and keep it close by.

Maybe my cousin was just being overcautious. Maybe he knew something I didn't.

Perhaps his sly and prescient words were little more than stern counsel to keep me on my toes.

Whichever way I cut it, I knew what Vic had said to me earlier should not be dismissed lightly. It was the

254

kind of artful advice I'd have been a fool not to take seriously.

Pearl and Gabe's house was smelling real good when I walked through their front door. The aroma of cinnamon and allspice wafted up the hall from the kitchen. Home cooking never smelled better. I hung my coat on the stand just as Chloe came running out the front room to greet me. Her hair was tied back in pigtails and she wore a white calico dress printed with pretty little red and yellow flowers. I opened my arms as she bolted towards me and hoisted her up on to my hip.

"Hey there, little guy. How you doin'?"

Chloe nodded, her eyes dancing with light and expectation. "Alright." She looked at me curiously, felt the side of my cheek and looked down in my face. "That still hurt?"

I shook my head. "Nah . . . not anymore."

Chloe took my chin and turned my head to face her. "Are we going home tonight, Joseph?"

I smiled and squeezed her hard against my chest, then looked over the top of her head towards where Loretta and Gabe were now standing at the top of the hall. I whispered into my little girl's ear, "Not tonight. But soon, baby, real soon. I promise."

I put Chloe back down and stroked her hair. I saw a smile grow at the edge of her mouth and eyes when Gabe called up to me. "You two gonna stand deh all night or you gonna come an' eat?"

I took Chloe's hand and we headed up towards the kitchen.

"How you doin', Aunt Pearl?"

"You don't need ta be raisin' you voice so high ta me, boy. I ain't deaf!"

My aunt pushed open the kitchen door with the rubber tip of her cane. She was a small woman, under five feet tall. Her light blue dress was old and faded. Over the dress was a wide white apron. The early evening sunlight coming through the window lit up the right side of her face to reveal the drooping corner of her mouth, from when she'd been laid low by a stroke. Her walnut-brown face had been cut in two by it, and the terrible after-effect of the palsy flowed down one side from brow to chin. But despite a slight slurring of her voice, Pearl refused to let the affliction best her. She made a gesture that would pass as a nod. "Come on in 'ere tha pair o' you."

Chloe and I walked through into the kitchen. It was my favourite part of the house. It always felt welcoming, the kind of place a family from the Caribbean could laugh and love in. It was a bolthole, a home where I was always made to feel welcome, and now Chloe and Loretta felt the warmth of that good cheer too.

Gabe and Pearl had rented the Victorian-built, brick terrace from the same landlord for the better part of twenty-five years. The yard out back was unruly. Long shaggy grass grew around a rusty old garden shed, and a half-dead crab apple tree stood at the back of it. Around the tree, in huge stone pots, grew snap beans,

256

cucumbers and bushy tomatoes. My aunt and uncle liked to be surrounded by things that were both bountiful and colourful, reminding them of their childhood days growing up back home on Bim.

Once I'd greeted everybody properly, Pearl wasted no time getting us all seated. "You ain't chirren — tek a chair if you wanna eat!"

We all sat at the big hickory table that stood in front of the old Aga; Gabe and Pearl opposite each other at either end and Loretta, Chloe and I pinched in at the sides. Loretta poured herself and Pearl a couple of glasses of VP sherry while Gabe dished up steaming plates of pepperpot stew from a big polished duchy pot. Pearl, despite not being as quick on her feet as she once was, was still a hell of a magician in the kitchen.

The old woman looked at my bruised cheek and shook her head. "Boy, whaddya bin up ta now?"

I looked into her face for a second, knowing that I was about to tell her a lie. Her eyes were full of sympathy or pity. I didn't know which. "It's nothing. I took a fall a couple o' days ago, that's all. I'm fine now."

I saw a dark reserve sweep across my uncle's face. Pearl continued to look at me without speaking again for a long time. While she did, she seemed to get older and older; her eyes were tired and there were deep folds in her face. It was like she was ageing in front of me and I was partly responsible with the worry I and her son had caused her over the years. The bulb above our heads was fluttering, maybe it had been the whole time, but right then I thought that if that damn light went out, she'd die.

After supper and we'd all helped with the washing-up, Chloe, Gabe, Loretta and I went into the front room. My uncle sat in the armchair and watched while the three of us played a few hands of Old Maid and Snap. Pearl, in the meantime, was resting her feet in front of the warm range back in the kitchen.

At around eight thirty, Gabe rose up out of his seat and called my name. "You gotta minute?" He hooked a finger at me then turned and walked out of the room without uttering another word.

"Sure," I called after him. I winked at Chloe and got to my feet. By the time I'd followed him out into the hall, the old man was standing at the foot of the stairs. "I want you ta do sum'ting fo' me, Joseph."

"Yeah, what is it?"

My uncle looked at me wearily. "When you next see ma boy, you tell 'im dat he needs ta come see his mama." Gabe hunched his shoulders and swallowed hard. "Tell dat fool ta come see her befo' it's too late an' she ain't 'ere no more."

I felt a lump rise in my throat. "Cou'se I will. You got my word."

I took hold of Gabe's arm and tried to steer him back towards the front room, but he refused to move. Instead he smiled at me. It was a rare gesture, one that made the hairs on the back of my neck stand on end. He rubbed at his eyes, blinking repeatedly, then gazed down at the ground for a moment before turning away and climbing the stairs. I watched him disappear on to the landing then heard his footsteps treading the boards above my head, followed by the sound of a door closing quietly.

As I went back down the hall, I heard a match strike in the kitchen and found Pearl lighting an old oil lamp. I watched her place the brass lantern in the centre of the kitchen table then mouth a short, silent blessing. Shadows jumped around the room as I stepped inside, a calm feeling setting in around me. I walked across to my aunt and gently put my hand on her shoulder.

"I gotta hightail it outta here soon, Aunt Pearl."

She turned and smiled then took a couple of steps towards me and touched my cheek with her palm. She had workwoman hands, not callused, but hard from a long life of doing for herself and others.

"I dreamed about Victor last night."

"Yeah . . . he come and say hi to you?"

Pearl smiled again. She had a strong superstitious streak, believing that the dead and those about to die could speak to her through dreams.

"Boy didn't say nuthin'. Dat fool was sitting in a chair in his bedroom, up deh." She pointed at the ceiling with her walking stick. "He jus' staring at the ground. I call out t' the child t'ree o' four time befo' he looked up at me. My boy wus cryin' like a pickney an' I couldn't do a ting 'bout it, Joseph."

Pearl's chest swelled with her breathing. She reached out to me and took my head in her arms and held it tight.

I didn't try to pull away.

CHAPTER
THIRTY-THREE

A heavy mist had blown in from the waterside down by the docks as I made my short night drive from St Pauls into Bristol. The roads were quiet and I was comforted to find that I didn't have my old friends in the Rover trailing my arse. I parked on the corner of Trenchard Street and headed across Colston Road and down to Christmas Steps. Above my head, an orange streetlight burned with no great intensity but was still just bright enough to light up the entrance to the sheer, stone-flagged street.

I made my way down the steps, occasionally looking behind me, the fear that I was being followed niggling inside my head. The Three Sugar Loaves was nestled away in the right-hand corner at the bottom of the road. Several overflowing dustbins and a few old packing cases thrown together in an untidy heap stood beside the door. I peered through the window to get a measure of the place then walked on in.

Inside, the Three Sugar Loaves was one of those boozers that the breweries hadn't ruined yet. Old and dusty with decent beer for its punters, it had a solid mahogany counter like you'd find inside a bank, framed with a flamboyant, etched-glass optic shelf. The bar was long, like a flattened horseshoe. It was a grand structure of curved pillars and ornate tiling, with Babycham glasses hanging upside down like bats from a polished wooden shelf over the back of the bar. The walls were covered with decorated mirrors advertising brands of nourishing stout, but between the mirrors were faded sepia photographs, taken when showbiz was still called music hall. It was an hour to closing time and the place was all but empty. Fletcher sat on a high-legged stool at the end of the bar. I walked across to him and waited for the barmaid to serve me.

"Pint of bitter, please." The barmaid gave me a dirty look and nodded. Fletcher slid a pound note across the counter. "He's with me, Else."

The woman reached reluctantly for a pint pot from underneath the bar, then yanked on the hand pull to draw up my beer. The superintendent nodded towards his empty glass. "Same again for me, and have one yourself."

"Ta very much." The barmaid ignored me and offered Fletcher a cheeky grin, took his money and strutted off towards the till. The copper smiled as he watched her sashay away. She was the sort of woman that went well with the pub. Plump, fiftyish, piled-up hair, low-cut satin dress, cameo brooch, Edwardian cleavage.

The superintendent glanced down at his watch. The barmaid handed me my pint and refilled Fletcher's glass. He smiled and thanked her, took a mouthful of beer and suggested we move somewhere a little more private.

The snug we ended up in was tucked away at the front of the pub and was little more than a booth with decaying Dralon benches and a matching headrest that ran the length of the back wall. Cigarette smoke hung over every inch of the room. The wallpaper could barely be seen for tatty black-and-white photographs of comedians, boxers and singers, all of them autographed just to let you know that the Sugar Loaves was once the place that big stars who'd appeared at the Hippodrome had supped. We perched ourselves at the end of the stall. Two drinkers, sitting side by side. He was a copper by trade and I was a criminal by colour.

Fletcher chugged back half his pint before speaking. When he finally addressed me, his voice was as shallow and bitter as his ale. "So, come on then. What's with all this bloody cloak-and-dagger stuff?"

"Cloak and dagger! Man, can you blame me? After what I been digging up this past couple a' days I don't know who the hell to trust."

Fletcher moved a little closer. He smelled of cedar and his face had been scrubbed so clean that it glistened. "Well, you can trust me, old son. You should know that by now."

"That right? Well, I ain't so damn sure."

"Tell me what you've got?"

I shook my head. "Nah, man . . . I gotta question fo' you first?"

"Well, let's have it?"

"Why'd you really come to me 'bout Nikhil Suresh?"

"What ya talking about?"

262

I swigged a couple of sips of my ale and carried on. "I'm talking 'bout why a fella like you would give two shits 'bout some Indian kid going walkabout, unless you got some kinda vested interest in his welfare?"

"Go on . . ."

"That boy sure as hell didn't go missing cause he was scared 'bout getting hitched to no overseas bride he'd never clapped eyes on befo'."

"No?"

"Nah . . . Something tells me you knew Suresh already, didn't you?"

"Maybe."

"Maybe? Come on, man. It didn't take that much digging fo' me to find out that boy was messing about with people he shouldn't have."

"What kinda people?"

"One of the biggest thugs in this city fo' a start."

Fletcher ducked his eyes in mock coyness. "Just the one, old son?"

I ignored the insinuation. "Suresh was up to his neck in something, I just ain't sure what. I'm pretty certain that he was having a homosexual relationship with William Ryder." I took the Polaroid of Suresh and Ryder together out of my jacket pocket and slid it across the table.

Fletcher picked it up, scrutinised it for a moment then raised an eyebrow. "Billy Ryder . . . well now."

"And my gut is telling me that Suresh was somehow involved in the death of the kid, James Peberdy, over at Portishead."

"What makes you think that?"

"Suresh worked over at the golf club . . . and Ryder, well he's a member there. I've got it on good authority that Ryder flew into a rage one night while he was at the Moulin Rouge with Suresh. Whatever Ryder was unhappy with Suresh about had gone down earlier in Portishead."

Fletcher grimaced as he pulled out a packet of Capstan from his jacket pocket. "You ain't painting a very pretty picture, Joseph." Fletcher shook the packet in front of my face. "You want one?"

I shook my head. The superintendent sat back, put a cigarette between his lips then lit it. He sucked on it enthusiastically.

"I don't think I'm telling you much you don't already know, Superintendent."

The copper frowned. "What makes you say that?"

"Hey, you ain't no fool; don't go treating me like one."

Fletcher squinted at my tone. "Some of what you've just told me is old news, some of it's not." Fletcher took another mouthful of his pint. "Ryder being bent has been whispered about for years, but he's always managed to keep it quiet. I'd heard otherwise."

"How'd you know?"

Fletcher inched himself across the seat towards me. "Nikhil Suresh was one of the best informers I'd had for a long time."

I was speechless for about thirty seconds. The revelation hit me like a bucket of ice-water. "Say what?"

"A couple of years ago Suresh was caught being a naughty boy again. He'd already got a criminal record,

264

mainly importuning for immoral purpose in a public khazi. Only this time our boy was found by a couple of beat bobbies who nabbed him with his trousers down in an alleyway with a reprobate name of Ralphie Clarke. The Indian was down on his knees at the side of the Top Rank club on Nelson Street. The Rank's always been the kind of scabby watering hole the likes of Clarke and Billy Ryder frequented. I was at the station the night he was brought in. When my lads braced him, it became pretty clear that Suresh liked the company of the criminal type and, sometimes, black fellas. It was me that got him off another hustling charge in return that he kept his ears and eyes open for me in joints like the Moulie."

"So, when he fell off the map, you thought you'd use me to root around in my own backyard. See if I could sniff out any queers who knocked about with Indian fellas, that kinda thing?"

Fletcher winked at me. "Yeah, something like that."

The policeman inhaled as much tar as he could muster from the Capstan before releasing the spittle-soaked end from his lips. He blew smoke out as he spoke. "By the time Suresh turned up dead inside that tea chest, we had the death of a child on our hands and I was getting the squeeze from the powers that be over at the council house to keep a lid on it till we had more to go on."

"Which brings me to Herbert Castle."

"You go and see him like you said?"

"Yeah, I went alright."

"Well?"

"Well, that old fella's more slippery than a barrel of snakes for a start. He had me on the council's books no sooner than I was in his damn office. I came outta his place with my palm greased and a wad o' cash in my pocket just to do his bidding, so long as I didn't go sniffing about in William Ryder's business."

Fletcher sat forward and rested his arm on the table. "Did Castle say that?"

"Not in so many words . . . but, hey, I know a bribe when it's being offered me."

"And you took it?"

"Like I said, I ain't no fool. Cou'se I took his damn money. I'm telling you 'bout it now, ain't I? Most of the people involved in all this crap are either on the take or bent. You sent that fella o' yours Leach to go see Ryder's right-hand man, Moody, straight after you showed me Suresh hog-tied up in that crate. Couple o' days later that albino is waiting for me outside a' Perry's Gym and drags me out to the Avon Gorge hotel to see his boss."

"When was this?"

"First thing this morning."

"And?"

"And he gave me some old shtick 'bout doing him a favour."

"What kind of favour?"

"The kind that Herbert Castle neglected to mention to me when I was standing about in his office. I needed to stay out of Mr Ryder's affairs, that was the short of it. Whatever it is you've got me into has got both those fellas messing their pants. Ryder told me that he used

266

to be a good friend of that son of a bitch Terrance Ryder and that Castle used to visit the Erotica Negro club, that sick dungeon I found Stella Hopkins in back in '65. Said there were plenty other powerful folk the law never caught up with back then who'd been down in that hellhole."

Fletcher stared down into his pint glass. "Old ghosts . . . who'd have thought you'd end up dragging that old hornets' nest back up?"

The past nightmares, the latent fears, the sadness in every corner of my mind came together for the briefest of moments to form a dark vision of the Blanchards' underground torture chamber. I snapped my eyes shut and opened them again to drive the poisonous image out of my head then took a deep breath and glanced out of the snug door towards the bar. It looked like we were the only two left in the place.

Fletcher stubbed out his cigarette in a glass ashtray. I shuffled in my seat, changing tack as I did. "You know anything 'bout Ryder being a grass for somebody on the force?"

Fletcher glared at me. "Not for a copper at Bridewell, I'm pretty bloody certain of that. Who'd you hear that little nugget from?"

I could see Vic in my mind, but his image quickly disappeared from behind my eyes. "It was a fella called Trevor Furse," I lied.

"What, that ponce who dresses up as a tart at the Moulie? Oh, this just gets bloody better by the minute." The superintendent cleared his throat then slumped back against the back of the bench, eying me warily.

"And along with everything else you've just told me, you think that Detective Inspector Leach is in Ryder's pocket, do you?"

"Who knows? I think somebody gotta be leaking out information to Ryder from someplace. Half your squad might be in on it . . . Who knows, maybe most o' them fellas at Bridewell Station are in on the racket. Fo' all I know you could be as thick as thieves with the man. I might be putting a noose round my neck just by telling you all this shit."

A disdainful look drew over Fletcher's face and he fell silent for a moment. I watched him painfully contemplate the possible crookedness of one or more of his own band of brothers. When he continued speaking, his voice was hushed and tinged with unease. "You really think I'm crooked?"

I shrugged and spread my hands out. "Man, fo' as long as I've known you, you've had fellas working alongside your arse that were as shady as a stash a' nine-bob notes. Why the hell should you be any different?"

Fletcher gave me a dirty look. "Then you don't know me half as well as you think, matey."

"That right? Well, tell me, Superintendent, what you gonna do 'bout all this madness?"

The copper's eyes were resolute. "I'm going to bring Mr Ryder's world crashing down around his ankles, Joseph, old son. That's what I'm gonna do."

He sank the last dregs of his pint and stuffed the Polaroid into his pocket. "And you're gonna help me do it."

The copper pushed his empty pint pot across the table and got to his feet, then put a hand on my shoulder. "I'll give you a call tomorrow before midday. Make sure you're around. I don't wanna have to come traipsing round half of Bristol looking for you. Got it?"

I nodded, gulped down my beer and stood up. Fletcher took a few steps back and looked me up and down, took in my Sunday best two-piece and grinned. "You shouldn't have bothered getting spruced like that on my account."

"I ain't wearing it fo' you."

"No . . . so it's a lucky lady then?"

I smiled but didn't say another word.

We headed for the door. For the first time ever, I felt like I was walking out of a public building into the big wide world with a white fella more like his equal than under his heel.

I didn't know it at the time, but it would be a short-lived sense of victory.

CHAPTER
THIRTY-FOUR

The night ballooned through the door towards the superintendent and me in a rush of damp, sulphurous air as we walked back out on to Christmas Steps. Mist hung in a dull, yellow skein below the streetlights and wove its way along the entire length of the scarped street. We stood in silence underneath the arched brick recess of the pub door. Fletcher's eyes fixed on mine; they became murky and veiled as he studied my face.

"You just watch yourself, matey." The policeman winked at me then took a cigarette out and stuck the unfiltered butt in his mouth. He raised his hand to bid me goodnight and took a step out from underneath the alcove, striking a match against the pub's wall.

The dull, wet *pfft* sound I heard came out of the blackness, the report no louder than the crack from a child's cap gun. Out the corner of my eye I saw a faint spark ignite from a barrel less than twenty yards away, the shooter firing from an odd angle, across the street, up high, perhaps out of a top-floor window. I bobbed and weaved back towards the protection of the doorway, my shoulders grazing the corner of the pub's entrance rather than finding any sanctuary. I twisted sideways back out into the street, hoping I'd be able to drag Fletcher down towards me.

The first bullet struck the superintendent in the shoulder like a brick wrapped in lead. I felt my breath explode out of my lungs and my knees cave towards the ground.

Above me, I saw Fletcher's body hit by a second shot, and he wrenched backwards in a single, savage jerk towards the door, the cigarette flying from his mouth. His arms instinctively shot out either side of him, his hands attempting to reach up towards his chest. Disorientated, I stumbled backwards, my head hitting the wall behind me, sending an explosion of pain up into the back of my skull, my ears thundering with the sound of my wildly beating heart.

My legs gave way and I dropped to the ground like a stone. Dazed, my head fell to my chest, my mouth turned bone dry.

I swiped at my eyes with the back of my hand, my breath heaving in my chest, then swallowed hard to clear the ringing from my ears, reaching out to cling to the brickwork next to me. I dug my heels in against the base of the stone step to steady myself and squinted out into the darkness. Across the street, I could just make out the silhouettes of two men moving from out of a doorway and beginning to run towards me. Both were dressed head to toe in black, their faces hidden by woollen balaclavas.

I clambered back to my feet, clawing at the cobblestones, and scrambled backwards down the steps until my shoulders connected against solid brick. One of the men raised a pistol in my direction. I froze and watched as he headed down the steps towards the road. The other masked man stopped for a split second to stand over Fletcher's body. He kicked the superintendent's leg with the toe of his boot before swiftly moving towards me.

The hooded figure circled around my legs, a suppressed automatic in his right hand. He glanced back up the street then took a couple of steps closer and crouched on one knee, pointing the muzzle in my face. My stomach constricted and my mind raced, searching for words that could perhaps turn my situation around — anything that could impose some measure of humanity on the masked individual. I could feel the adrenaline coursing through my system, my pulse leaping in my neck. I ran my tongue across my lips and tried to speak, but my petition became a tangle of rusty nails in my throat. I opened and closed my eyes before holding out my hand defensively in front of me.

I saw the man's index finger tighten on the pistol's trigger, then watched as he raised the barrel of his gun upwards towards the sky. The gunman pulled the trigger, the recoil of the pistol jerking against his wrist, the silenced weapon thudding next to the side of my face. I felt my arms and legs go limp, my insides burning as though someone had cored through every sinew and bone in my body with a machinist's drill.

The hooded man's gaze moved over my face before snatching a clump of my hair between the fingers of his gloved hand. He yanked me towards him and pressed

272

his mouth against my cheek. When he spoke, I could hear the hoarseness of his voice an inch from my ear.

"I can wait," he purred. "But no matter where you run to, you're mine."

The gunman slung my head back against the wall and rose to his feet. I watched him brush his knee with his palm then turn and disappear back into the night mist. Moments later, I heard a car door slam, the engine revving and tyres crunching over gravel out on to the two-lane road.

I looked back, up to where Fletcher's still body lay. I tried to call his name, but no sound would come from my parched throat. I swallowed hard again, the inside of my mouth tasting like battery acid, my breath foul in my own nostrils.

I held on to the wall, forcing myself up, and staggered back towards the pub door. I stood, unsteady, staring down at the superintendent. Fletcher stared back up at me, wild-eyed, frozen.

His mouth opened, his tongue clicking at the back of his throat. Blood and saliva ran down his cheek into his hair. I kneeled down beside him, as a priest might, reaching for his hand, his fingers cold and stiff between my own. His breathing was ragged, the colour was draining from his face.

I leaned over him, turning his head towards me. When he spoke, the mumbled word came out in a whisper, smelling of bile and nicotine.

"Joseph . . ."

I lifted Fletcher's head into the crook of my arm, supporting his neck, and saw the life swiftly departing from his face. His eyes opened wide, the lids fluttering like bruised flower petals, his last gasp a hot gust of air blown into my face. I watched the superintendent's gaze dilate and he was gone.

I remained motionless for a moment, lost in a jumbled-up world of my own, my hands trembling, my gut churning. The stink of scorched cordite seemed to grip at every square inch of air around me, the acrid tang coating the inside of my mouth and creeping down my throat. I twisted my head round when I heard the sound of raised voices coming from inside the pub, alerting me that whoever was on the other side of the door was perhaps only seconds away. I stuffed my hand inside the superintendent's jacket, yanked out the Polaroid then hauled myself up and bolted out into the street.

I charged back up the steps, taking them three at a time, the sound of the superintendent's voice calling my name over and over in my ear as I retreated into the inky gloom.

274

CHAPTER
THIRTY-FIVE

It had begun to rain heavily by the time I'd sprinted back up Christmas Steps and got to my car. I clambered inside, my body shuddering, breath ballooning in my chest, the smell of the superintendent's blood on my hands making me retch. Sweat soaked into my shirt and under my armpits, and nausea bit at my guts. The iridescent green hands on my watch said 10.37 p.m. The threat of death and the bloodshed I'd just witnessed had left me struggling to think straight. Every fibre of my being should have been screaming at me to get the hell out of town or over to Vic's joint, but all I could reason was to head straight for Ruth Castle's place like I'd agreed to earlier that day. I felt for my keys and fumbled to get the right one in the ignition, but at last I started the Ford up and pulled slowly back on to Colston Road. The rain clattered on the car roof and streamed down the windows, the neon signs above the pubs and clubs looking like blue and red smoke in the mist as I drove out of the city and headed over Clifton Wood.

The journey to Ruth's home took me less than fifteen minutes. I'd been looking in the rear-view mirror every ten seconds to check I wasn't being tailed again.

The stark realisation that Fletcher's murder had been orchestrated for me to take the fall was quickly sinking in. It shouldn't have come as any surprise that there wasn't an unmarked police car trailing me. Why bother to chase me down now? Apprehending a culprit so quickly, so near to the place of the offence, would look too much like a coincidence to any decent judge. If it was Ryder who wanted me taken off the board, he'd have organised a more hard-nosed method for the police to collar me. Once the boys in blue were on the scene back at the Three Sugar Loaves, the barmaid would soon be giving them a description of me, and the likes of Detective Inspector Leach would no doubt be brisk in putting out an all-points bulletin for my arrest. A decent manhunt would do the rest and the Old Bill would have me banged up in no time.

I'm sure that was the plan.

And I had every intention of spoiling it for them.

I parked in a side street opposite Ruth's home. She lived in a red-brick tenement row house that was connected to several others by a common porch and a shrub-filled front garden. I walked along the path to her front door. The rain ran off the roofs around me and spun like a vortex of wet light on the stained-glass window set in the centre of the door. I raised the brass knocker, let it fall against the strike plate a couple of times and waited. A few moments later I heard footsteps inside.

Ruth was smiling when she opened the door. Her hair was tied back in a high ponytail. For some reason, she looked smaller than when I'd last met her and she wore a pretty yellow dress and white kitten-heel sandals. I watched the swift change in her expression when she saw the state I was in. I moved towards her, eager to get in out of the rain then looked sheepishly down at my watch.

"Not too late, I hope?"

She shook her head, her face suddenly drawn, her eyes filling with questions that she didn't have adequate words for. She took a step out on to the path, looking up and down the street, before quickly moving back inside and ushering me to follow. "Come on in."

I stood in the hallway and waited for her to close the front door. When she turned to face me, her eyes fixed on mine. They were pensive, blinking once or twice. "What in the name of sanity has happen to you?"

"It's a long story . . ."

"Is it now?" Ruth looked at the blood on my coat then at my hands, the skin around her eyes tightening. She waited for a few seconds then gestured towards the stairs. "You better go on up. Second door on the right. You'll find everything you need in the bathroom to get yourself cleaned up."

I smiled and thanked her, then trudged on up the staircase like a scolded schoolboy.

I found the light for the bathroom and walked on in. The place was pristine, white porcelain shining from every angle, the scent of patchouli oil permeating the air. I stood over the sink, turned on the hot tap and used a clamshell-shaped soap to wash the blood from my hands. I washed my face then cleaned the blood spots from my overcoat before drying myself off and running my fingers through my hair.

When I returned downstairs, Ruth was waiting by an open door at the end of the hall. She held a crystal tumbler in her hand. As I approached her, I could smell the heady scent of the malt whisky inside it.

"I thought you could perhaps use one of these?"

Ruth handed me the drink and walked into her sitting room. It was candlelit and furnished with a modern-style armchair and matching two-seater couch. A polished coffee table stood centre stage and framed beach-scene prints hung on either wall. I stood in the doorway, watching as Ruth went over to the green-tiled fireplace and turned back to me with wide eyes. "So, come on then. Let the cat out of the bag?"

"Say what?"

"This was supposed to be a friendly get-together over drinks. Instead you turn up looking like you've been sleeping on a butcher's block. I'm assuming the blood isn't yours?"

I took a heavy hit of the whisky and shook my head. "No . . . A policeman's."

"Jesus Christ . . . what the hell have you done?"

"Not me." I took another swig.

"Then who?"

"Some guys in balaclavas jumped me and a copper called Fletcher. He ended up getting shot."

"Shot!" Ruth hesitated for a moment, her eyes narrowing, her face becoming more and more clouded.

She was struggling to take in what I was saying. "This policeman . . . is he . . . is he dead?"

My left hand balled into a fist and I inched a few steps further into the room. My legs felt weak, bloodless, cold. I glanced back across the room towards Ruth's face. My eyes met hers then I looked away again. There was a tingling in my throat, like a heated wire trembling against a nerve. "Oh, yeah. He's dead alright." I felt my heart drop as the words left my lips.

Ruth was quiet for a moment, then she said, "Why don't you sit down?"

I dropped down on to the sofa, then looked back up at her. The room was so quiet, all I could hear was the rain pelting against the window.

"Perhaps it would be a good idea to start from the beginning?"

So, that's what I did. I told Ruth how Fletcher had approached me, about my involvement in the police investigation on behalf of the council. I told her everything I knew about the deaths of Nikhil Suresh and James Peberdy and about what had happened on Christmas Steps earlier that evening. When I'd finished recounting my tale, I drained the rest of my whisky and looked back up at Ruth. Her eyes were unreadable in the dim light of the candles burning either side of her. I set my empty glass on the table, unsure if I should bring up the subject of her father. I had been candid about everything else. There seemed little point in holding back now. I swallowed.

"A few days ago, William Ryder told me that your father was a good friend of his and that he used to hang out in an illegal club. One that I had some nasty dealings with some years back."

Ruth's jaw set and I saw irritation flicker in her eyes. She stared searchingly into my face, her hand resting against the mantlepiece. "Illegal club . . . what kind of illegal club?"

I shrugged. "Some strange joint, out in the sticks, at a place called Cricket Malherbie."

"That still doesn't explain the sort of club it was."

"You told me that your father liked loose women, that there were rumours 'bout him, right?"

"Yes."

"Well, the Erotica Negro was a club where fellas like your father went so they could 'relax', if you get my drift?"

Ruth sat down on the edge of the couch and put her hand on my shoulder. Her face was a dark silhouette.

"Why'd you think Ryder said those things about my father to you?"

"You saying they ain't true?"

Ruth put her hands on her lap and shook her head. "No . . . I'm asking what you think he'd gain bringing my father into all this?"

"He wanted to rattle me, get my mind on something other than him. He was figuring to play me like he plays all the other chumps he controls. I think that's what he's doing with your old man. Your gut instinct 'bout him having his claws into your pop, well I don't think you're very far off the mark. I think he's in a heap o' trouble and Ryder's got him over a barrel."

280

Ruth's back stiffened. "To hell with my father! Whatever he's into now or has been up to comes as no surprise to me. He should have paid the piper a very long time ago. Now it looks like his indiscretions are coming back to haunt him."

"Maybe so . . . Look, trust me on this one. I think while all this crazy stuff is going on, you really ought to think about going someplace else. A friend's perhaps?"

"Why should I be chased off? Why should the sins of the father haunt me?"

"I ain't talking 'bout you being haunted . . . I'm more concerned 'bout you not getting hurt while all this madness is going down, that's all."

"I don't think it's me you should be worrying about. After everything you've just told me . . . after what's happened tonight, I'm more afraid for you, Joseph."

"If Ryder had wanted me dead, he'd have let his cronies blow me away earlier tonight. He wants me to take the fall for Fletcher being taken off the board. Perhaps even link me to the two other deaths I've been looking into. Main thing is, I'm still in the game."

"Is that how you see all this madness? A game?"

"Look, Ruth, a person has to act and think in a way that works fo' them. I can't control all this bullshit that's gone an' headed my way. I didn't deal any of it. In fact, I tried to deal myself out of this damn mess from the off. It just didn't work out that way. I either see Ryder's game out tonight or end up either in jail or with a bullet in the back of my head. It's as simple as that."

I saw the sadness in her eyes, and I took her hand in mine.

"The only thing I'm sorry 'bout is that I've come here tonight bringing my troubles back to you."

Ruth reached forward and touched me on the knee as though I were the one who should be consoled. "Perhaps the troubles you've brought could be the troubles I want."

"That might not be too wise, Ruth. Look, I shoulda known better. Soon as I walked up your garden path. It was wrong. I wasn't thinking like I shoulda been. Me coming here tonight just makes you an accessory after the fact. You knowing 'bout Fletcher being shot, 'bout me being there when he was. It ain't a good thing fo' you to be knowing."

Ruth's gaze continued to move over my face. "But I do know, and there's nothing else to be said about the matter. I believe what you're telling me is the truth. I'm not frightened to face facts. It's been a long time coming." Ruth's mouth parted slightly as she considered her next words. "I think my father has kept enough secrets and lies to last him a dozen lifetimes. I'm sick of living with my suspicions about the man, the years of feeling something was wrong but not actually knowing what. I'm tired of hiding amid my father's deceits."

I could hear the humiliation in her voice, see the shame in her face. I had seen the same look in victims of violence and crime many times, and it was almost impossible to convince them that they weren't deserving of their fate. I felt a sharp reply rise in my throat but decided to keep my own counsel about my ill feelings for Herbert Castle. I knew my response to Ruth needed to be more considered, kinder.

"Whatever he's done, now or in the past, that isn't your burden."

"That's not how the rest of the world might see it, Joseph. I've always known that Father's appetites would be his undoing. Better to be on the side of right now than be dragged down into the mire with him later, yes?"

I nodded slowly and dropped my eyes to the floor, heat rising in my cheeks, aware that Ruth's lack of sentimentality for her father's situation and possible fate was difficult for her to express. When she spoke again, I heard the brittle crackle of fear and uncertainty that often comes when a child speaks candidly about a wayward parent. One that they struggle to understand or connect with.

"So, what are you going to do?"

I looked up. "I need to go sort this mess out . . . try and set things straight."

Ruth took a deep breath and leaned across the sofa towards me. "Stay for a while longer." Her voice was a low whisper in my ear, her fingers like the brush of a bird's wing against my arm. She stood up and looked down at me.

I got up and put my arms around her, felt her body against me, felt it become delicate and close in my hands. I felt her hand under my chin and her sandaled foot curve around my ankle. I kissed her hair, and her eyes, and when she opened them again, all I could see was the electric blueness in them.

"Another time . . ."

Ruth put the palm of her hand on my chest and held it there. I could see a quiet sense of exasperation working its way into her face.

"One day you're going to have a quiet heart, Joseph."

"It's quiet now."

Ruth shook her head. "No . . . no it isn't. You're already thinking about the rest of the night. About the game and how you're going to play it. But someday there'll be no more games to play and you'll feel all that heat go out of you."

"Yeah? Well maybe I ain't made like that."

"Why do you think that?" she asked quietly.

"Because of the things I've seen. The things people have done to me and to those I've loved. Over time, I've been forced to learn some hard facts 'bout folks, 'bout the heat they've brought down on me and my family. 'Bout those cruel and unusual games we bin talking 'bout, and how those folks like playin' 'em to get their kicks."

I let go of Ruth's waist and took a step back. "I ain't prepared to be playing the kinda sport a man like Ryder wants me to no more. And I need that fire inside a' me to make him understand that."

We stood together in silence for a moment, Ruth searching my face with a look that was both hard and caring. I could feel the softness of her breast against my chest. I stroked my fingers against her cheek then stepped away from her. "I really need to get going."

284

I picked my coat up from the sofa and put it on.

Ruth followed me back down the hallway. She opened up the front door and I stepped outside. The air smelled as metallic and cold as brass. She smiled back at me. "You stay safe."

I nodded and walked a short way back down the path before turning to look back at her. "Hey, some kinda detective I am. I don't even know what you do fo' a living?"

Ruth smiled. "Schoolteacher."

My eyes widened. "Yeah, is that right? You think you could try and teach an ole fool like me a few new things?"

As Ruth gazed into my face, I saw her eyes fill with foreboding, as if she thought the dead might soon lay claim to me. "I could try."

For the briefest of moments, I thought about walking back and taking up her offer to stay. Instead I took another step further away.

"Think about getting outta town for a few days, Ruth. Go stop with a friend. Any place other than being around here at the minute. I really think it'd be for the best." I held out my hand. "I'll see you real soon."

It was a bleak way to bid a fond farewell to someone, but at that moment, it was the best goodbye I had to offer Ruth Castle. I walked away into the night, the rain hammering down on my head and shoulders, my heart beating like a clock that told time for both of us.

CHAPTER
THIRTY-SIX

Death comes in many ways. The grim reaper always has his way with us. And for that reason, *inevitability* is probably the worst word you can be uttering to yourself when the chips are down.

These were not the kind of thoughts I needed to be brooding over as I drove back into Bristol and down to Vic's place on Buchanan's Wharf. I was nervous to be out on the roads so late at night. There was no sign that I was being followed, but I was all too aware that the police might now be on the lookout for me.

I headed along the harbourside, pulling up in a side street close to the old warehouse. I cut the headlights, the downpour bouncing off the bonnet, the engine ticking, and sat for a moment, feeling as solitary as if I were sitting in the bottom of a dark well. I knew I needed my cousin's help to get out of the mess I now found myself in. But asking for Vic's aid was akin to making a pact with the devil.

I pondered that dubious fact for the briefest of moments before getting out of the car, opening the boot and reaching for the leather holdall I'd packed earlier. I slipped off my coat and jacket, fished inside the bag and took out the shoulder holster and pistol.

The weapon was heavy and cold in my hand. I dragged back the receiver, slid a round into the chamber and rested the gun back inside the holster before pulling it on. I closed the bag, lifted it out and locked the boot again. The air around me smelled of wet trees, torn leaves blowing in the wind.

I made my way out towards the harbour, staying close to the sides of the buildings along the length of the wharf. The River Avon was already starting to run high and wide, the rain striking the water hard, the air glowing with a misty yellow light six inches above the surface. I cut through to a cobbled avenue that ran along the back of Vic's warehouse then headed down the alley towards its guarded entrance.

I paused and looked around; that's when I saw that the front door had been kicked in. This was a bad omen. I felt myself sway, a rising sense of unease setting in as I opened and closed my hand, wiping my palm on my coat. My feet stayed planted on the pavement. I could have walked away, but I knew that there was nowhere else to go other than inside. I also knew that something was seriously wrong if Smoke Billings wasn't around.

I inched forward slowly and looked towards the stairs. Inside, the air smelled heavily of cordite. The entrance and stairwell were lit as usual.

As I made my way through the door and across the stone-flagged entry I saw Smoke's body stretched out on the ground to the left of me. I took a step towards him. He lay on his back, one leg bent under him, his eyes filled with black light. His lips were bright red, forming a wet clown's smile.

I stood over Smoke's body, gagging. I could smell dried sweat in his clothes, the oil in his hair mixing with the sour tang of blood. A round had cut off three fingers on his right hand, and a second one had entered his chest, just above his heart.

I stepped backwards and turned, staring out towards the alley before slinging my holdall to the floor. I stuck my hand inside my coat, snatched the pistol out of its holster and skirted backwards, raising it at arm's length towards the staircase. I edged towards the first step, breathing slowly and deeply, then stood stock-still for a second or two, took hold of the bannister for balance and eased up the stairs two at a time.

When I reached the first floor, I instinctively ducked down on my haunches, flattening myself against the wall, only rising back to my feet when I could see my way ahead was clear. I took another deep breath, felt the blood roar in my ears and slowly continued to climb the next flight.

On the second floor, I found another body. There was a pistol on the ground, close to where the man had fallen. I stepped slowly across the floorboards and looked down into the face of another of Vic's hired hands, a black fella called Miles Green. Miles's brown eye stared up at me; his other had been shot out.

I looked back down the stairs then continued to climb with mounting trepidation, my pulse racing, the pistol held out in front of me.

The third floor was clear, but on the fourth I found two more of Vic's men dead on the landing, lying in pools of blood. One man was sprawled against the wall, a hole the size of a cricket ball in the centre of his chest. The other man was face down with multiple gunshot wounds in his back. Whoever had slain the pair had been right at the top of the stairwell when they'd hit them.

Both of the dead men had been armed and ready when their assailants had rushed them. The fella with his back against the brickwork was still holding his gun. The killings looked like hurried executions rather than a full-on gun battle.

I pushed forward, clearing the fifth floor then heading up to Vic's apartment on the sixth. I put my hand around the door knob, turned it and let the door swing open. Inside, the office was bathed in full light. Furniture and glass were strewn everywhere, and bullet holes pockmarked the walls and ceiling. The room stank of reefer and gun smoke. The bloodied remains of two other men lay on the bare floor close to the centre of the room.

My eyes were struggling to take in the mayhem around me. The combination of fear and fatigue cut into my spirit like a cleaver. I wanted to back myself straight out, away from the butchery around me, head down those stairs and disappear.

I looked across the room and saw the body of another man right at the furthest end of the office. I swallowed hard and kept going, my foot catching on the neck of a broken rum bottle. I felt shards of thick glass crack underneath my shoe as I came to a sudden halt, a few inches from the remains. I stared down in disgust, muttering an obscenity to myself.

Elijah Bliss's body was stretched out across the top of Vic's desk. He'd been shot in both legs, just below the knees. It looked like he'd been strangled by hand: I could make out finger marks along his throat and neck. Whereas Miles had no expression on his face, Elijah's eyes and mouth were strained with fear. In my head, I saw the pale murderous face of Jimmy Moody, and imagined him throttling the life out of Bliss.

I stood back and holstered the pistol, thankful there was no sign of Vic. I'd entered the building because I was worried about him, and I'd believed he'd have done the same for me, but by anyone's reckoning it was a foolish idea to be hanging around the joint any longer. I wiped my sleeve over my brow, turned on my heels and headed back down the stairs. At the foot of the steps I snatched up my holdall and went for the door.

"Drop that."

I turned my face towards the voice.

A tall man dressed in the same black attire as the two men at Christmas Steps stood at the edge of the doorway. But his face was covered in shadow rather than a balaclava. He stood stock-still, his long coat open, his hands invisible.

"Get out here."

I dropped the bag on the ground, felt the breath go out of my lungs and my stomach sink.

"Boy . . . you got problems with your hearing? Shift your black arse out here where I can see you better."

I moved towards the doorway, my arms at my sides, the palms turned towards the gunman as he slowly backed away. I held up my hands then followed the man out into the alleyway.

"You must be looking for the same fella I am, yeah?" The gunman parted his coat and lifted a suppressed SLR rifle into the light. He grinned at me. "You can answer that question standing up. Or you can get on your knees and do it."

There was no way that I could reach for my gun. I told myself to stay calm, to try to think clearly. If the man had wanted to kill me, I'd already be dead. I lifted my arms a little higher, my gaze focusing squarely on the stranger. "I'll stay on my feet if that's alright by you?"

The gunman gave a sharp nod and lifted the barrel of his rifle a little higher. "So, where's the Jah?"

I shook my head. "I ain't got no idea, man." I gestured back towards the stairs then refocused my attention on the gunman. "All I've found back there are dead bodies."

"You're lucky you ain't one of 'em." His eyes fixed on mine. "I'm only gonna ask you one more time. Where's the Jah?"

"It beats me. I ain't seen him fo' days. I just turned up here on the off chance hoping I could score, that's all."

The man took a step backwards, shaking his head as he did so. I watched him raise the SLR and take aim,

291

the end of the silenced barrel sighted squarely in the centre of my chest. I felt a wave of panic course through my head and body — then, out the corner of my eye, I saw a brief flash behind the gunman's head, like a firework ignited by a match. At the same time, I heard a dull *pfufft* sound. The gunman heard it too. He widened his eyes, staring at me, the rifle still pointed at my torso. His jaw was hooked, his profile jutting out an inch or so more than it was a moment ago.

The first round had already punched through the man's throat before he or I had realised exactly what the sound was. Still holding the gun, he clenched one hand over the wound, blood congealing between his fingers. He made a choking noise, as if he'd swallowed a fish bone. I heard the sound again. The second round slammed into the back of the man's skull, exiting above his left eyebrow and showering the warehouse wall in blood, bone and grey matter. I watched him topple forward into a pool of muddy water, the rain falling on his back.

I snapped my eyes open and shut. I became aware of rainwater pouring down my face, soaking into my hair. I put my hand over my mouth to stop myself throwing up. My breathing was all over the place, my heart pounding. I fell back against the wall, my body shaking as I attempted to squeeze air into my lungs. Out in the street, I heard a cat meow. The wind gusted, clattering off the metal roofs nearby, and I stared down the alleyway towards the harbour front, watching as Vic began to walk slowly out of the shadows.

As he came closer, I saw his chest rising and falling, a scoped sniper rifle held out in front of him. He came to a halt at the dead man's feet, looked down and whistled.

"Shit . . . this boy ain't lookin too hot." He leaned forward and spat twice on the back of the man's head. Then my cousin stood erect, taking in my measure before winking at me. "Not bad fo' a one-eyed man, eh?"

Vic rested his rifle against the door jamb and looked inside. I watched his lip curl when he saw Smoke Billings' body lying on the ground.

He stepped back, took out a cigarette and lit it with a gold lighter, the smoke rising from his cupped hand as he stared back at me. The expression on his face was cruel and unblinking, a look that would have sent Lucifer himself into a cold sweat.

CHAPTER
THIRTY-SEVEN

There was a sharp pain behind my eyes as if someone had just hammered a nail into my temple. My heart was pounding away, my body quivering like a scared child. I'd barely had a chance to catch my breath in the short time it had taken Vic to run up six flights of stairs, assess the bloodshed dispensed against his crew, and return. He stood on the first landing motionless and silent, looking down at me, the savage light in his eye intensifying. It wasn't hard to read the deadly message on his face.

"Dat rasclat Ryder. I'm gonna 'ave his fuckin' carcass dripping blood by sun up."

Vic bit off a hangnail, spat it off the end of his tongue and walked down the remaining steps to stand in front of me. I put my hand on his shoulder. It felt like a lump of concrete. "I need you to calm down for a minute."

Vic wiped his hand across his mouth and gestured back towards the stairs. "Fuck calm, man! Dat pig, he gonna pay fo' wha' he done ta Bliss an' Smoke."

Now I took hold of Vic's upper arm. It hummed with pressurised energy. "Ryder knows we're family," I said.

294

Vic glared at me before shifting his eyes down to where my hand was. I let go of his arm and he pushed me out of his way.

"He doesn't trust you and I've been a thorn in his side since I started searching for Nikhil Suresh. Ryder had just one plan here tonight. He wanted me on the run and you and your boys never to see sunlight again. He already made his play against me earlier."

Vic gave a deep cough and spat a wad of phlegm at his feet. "Wantin' you on da run? Wha' you blabbamoutin' on wi' now?"

"Earlier today I arranged to meet Fletcher at the Three Sugar Loaves on Christmas Steps. When we walked out, somebody put a couple of bullets into the superintendent, dropped him in the street."

Vic stared at me in disbelief. "Some triggerman tek out da Babylon?"

"Yeah, there were two of them. Both in black, wearing balaclavas. They came outta nowhere. One put Fletcher on his back then stuck a gun in my face before they high-tailed it. Ryder's idea was to put me in the ringer for the copper's murder. They were packing some serious firepower too." I pointed towards Vic's sniper's rifle, which was resting against the door jamb. "One of the shooters was carrying something like that."

Vic walked over to the door, snatched up the rifle and slung it over his shoulder. He looked out into the alley at the dead gunman then back at me. "Looks like he ain't tha only honky I'm gonna be puttin' a bullet inta tonight."

I reached for my holdall, walked over to my cousin and pointed at the dead man. "Well, I think you started by drilling one of the city's finest."

I saw Vic's face tighten. I could almost see his heart beating against his shirt. He glared back down at the corpse. "He a fuckin' pig?"

"I'm guessing so. I think Ryder's got every corrupt po'lice officer in Bristol in his pocket. My gut tells me he's been using dirty coppers for years — that's why he's been able to pull off the two hits he's ordered tonight. The man's protected, Vic. He's protected by the po'lice, by local government and God knows who else."

I gestured again at the body. "That guy laying down there is probably more bent law. Same goes for the two that wasted Fletcher and threatened me earlier. Ryder's gonna know something didn't go down right when this guy doesn't report back to him. He's clearly got the jitters that I'm on to him about Suresh and he's now making it really clear that he wants to sever his ties with you once and for all. This guy's serious. He wants Bristol for himself and that means taking the two of us off the board."

Vic pointed a finger at me. "Let the fucka try."

A jolt of fear ran through my system and struck at my insides. "Man, he already is. Ryder's wiping the slate clean. He's come down this hard for a real good reason. This bloodshed ain't just about you two squabbling over who controls what. The man's hiding something and he wants his secrets to stay hidden. I wanna know what he's trying to hush up."

I remained motionless for a moment and chose my next words carefully, my palms sweating. "Vic, if you want to come out of this madness on the side of the righteous and with Ryder's empire in your back pocket then I need you with me, not going off on some damn killing spree."

Vic stared down at the floor for a moment, scratching the back of his neck, then gave me a quizzical look, his eyes lingering on mine as though he was trying to read my thoughts. "So, cleaner man . . . how you plannin' ta mek me top dog?"

I could see shadows and lights in Vic's face, like reflections that cling inside frost on a window. He took a step out into the alleyway, lifted his face to the rain and the breeze off the river, his true feelings walled up inside a private domain few dared to enter. He lit a cigarette with a battered Zippo and flicked the cap shut, then blew smoke out through his fingers.

"I'll tell you once we're out of this damn place." I looked down at Smoke Billings' body then headed back out into the alley, past Vic, and began to walk away.

I heard Vic make a noise that was somewhere between anger and exasperation. "Where da hell you tink you goin'?"

I ground to a halt, turning to face him. "To get my car."

Vic flicked his cigarette towards my feet, his one eye never taking its gaze off my face, a sudden grin breaking at the corner of his mouth.

"I got me a betta idea."

I followed Vic back into the warehouse and watched him hook his hands under Billings' arms and drag the body towards the wall, the dead man's blood smearing across the floor. Vic then walked over to the stairs and ran his hand along the wood balusters. In a panel underneath the skirting board there was a hole the size of an old penny piece. Vic put his finger inside and lifted the false wall out, exposing a wooden trapdoor in the floor. Underneath it was another larger door, this one cross-fitted with wide iron bands running around its edges, the rivets orange with rust. A metal ring was attached at its centre. Vic yanked on it and swung open the hatch then got down on his haunches, reached in and withdrew a large torch. He shone the flashlight down into the darkness and looked back up at me.

"Tell me that's not the sewer pipe down there?"

Vic gave a savage flick of his head towards the open hatch. "Git you arse down 'ere wid me."

I swallowed hard and followed him down a set of steep wooden steps. The walls were sweating with water, coated with lichen. I touched one of the wet stones with my hand, then wiped it on the back of my leg.

Eight or nine steps dropped us into a high-ceilinged subterranean alcove. The dense air around us smelled of mould and stagnant water. I pulled my holdall up close to my chest, unzipped the bag and fished around for the small torch inside. I switched it on and strafed a beam of light out in front of me.

"You gotta be kidding me. You know how much I hate being shut in."

298

Vic growled back at me in the dark. "Will you shut the fuck up an' keep movin'."

I shone my torch at the wall close to where Vic was standing, the weak glare skirting the side of his face. "What the hell is this place?"

"What you tink it is?" Vic shoved his thumb back over his shoulder. "Deh gotta be miles 'n' miles o' tunnels down in dis rat'ole. Back in da day, all dem rich honkies wus using it ta stash gear. Rum, spices, jewels, gold. All dat stuff dey bin thieving from folk back in the West Indies."

Vic turned and began to walk down the passageway. He called back to me, the earlier edginess in his voice all but gone. "Now it's a bolt'ole fo' bruthas like you an' me. Shit . . . who said nuthin' evah changes?"

I stayed close on my cousin's tail. The arched, red-brick channel was like a snakeskin turned inside out, slinking into the abyss under the streets around the docks. Whoever had built it tunnelled for the softest soil, not giving a damn about how straight the line was. Vic moved fast, kicking loose stones up off the ground. I matched his pace step for step, zig-zagging through a network of burrows, the dank stench coming off the walls clinging to my nostrils and making me gag.

As we pushed further along the shaft, the stone canopy above our heads began to lower. I felt my arms and the top of my head grazing the brickwork as the tunnel began to shrink around me. I could hear my own breathing, my pulse jumping in my throat, the unwelcome feeling of claustrophobia seizing at my insides. I could tell by the speed Vic was travelling at that he'd used the passageway to stay incognito many times before. That still didn't make me feel any better about being underground.

Another thirty yards or so and the tunnel began to open out again, the stone canopy above me rising.

Vic came to a sudden halt. Above him, a brick arch opened out into a small recess. He stepped inside the nook, shone the beam of his torch up a metal ladder that was fastened to the wall and began to climb. I moved into the opening and stood underneath, aiming the beam of my torch up towards the top rung. Vic reached above him to a circular manhole cover, placed his palms in the centre and pushed. I heard the access plate scrape over hard ground then watched Vic ascend the remaining crossbars and disappear. I shot up after him.

I stuck my head out of the hole, raindrops pelting the top of my head and face. Vic stood over me, offering me his hand. I snatched hold of his fingers and he pulled me out into the night. I stood at his side, shining my torch into the darkness. The weakening ray of light picked out white-painted brickwork. I took a couple of steps forward, lifting the torch upwards. As I did, the words *THE OSTRICH INN* stared back down at me.

CHAPTER
THIRTY-EIGHT

The Ostrich Inn was an old harbourside pub on Lower Guinea Street that had once been a haunt for sailors, dockside labourers and merchants who'd worked in the Port of Bristol during the time of the slave trade. Nowadays the Ostrich had become a very different kind of watering hole and its patronage was drawn from a more assorted band of folk. The place was more gambling den than pub, and you got in on account of your name, your clout and how much cash you were carrying in your hip pocket. You never went to the Ostrich unless you'd been invited. At least I never did. But for a very few people the door was always open. Vic was one of them, and that was because he owned the joint.

We entered the gaming house through the back door, crossing through the kitchen and out into the hall. A young black man dressed in a dinner suit and bow tie stood at the downstairs door that led into the bar. You could tell just from looking at his stocky frame that he was brawny and full of enthusiastic aggression. As soon as he saw Vic, he began to stride towards us, a perplexed look sprouting across his face.

"Everyt'ing okay, Jah?"

Vic shot him a hard look and nodded. "Yeah, Melvin, everyt'ing sweet. You got many punters still 'bout?"

Melvin gave a quick shake of his head. I noticed a wide, jagged scar at his throat, made all the more unsightly because it was lighter than his brown skin. "Nah, Jah . . . last ones crawled out 'bout ten minutes ago. Bin as quiet as the grave."

Vic sniffed and put his arm around the man's heavyset shoulders, drawing him in close. "I need you to go git me a motor from Brook Road garage. Sum'ting low-key."

The doorman gave a short grunt and nodded deferentially. Vic ushered him down the hall. "Git goin' now an' bring the wheels round back fo' me. Jus' leave the keys in the ignition."

"You got it, boss." The doorman bowed again and shoved past me, his eagerness to do his master's bidding evident.

Vic looked at me, his eye murky and unfocused. He pointed towards the door at the top of the hallway, then gestured towards the staircase behind him. "I'm gonna mek a couple o' quick phone calls an' come git you."

I turned quickly and took a step back. "Don't do anything without running it by me first, okay?"

Vic held out his hands, palms up. "Hey, man, back off. I jus' takin care o' bidness, dat's all. Ain't gonna mess wid wha'ever you plannin' okay?" A dark reserve flowed over Vic's face. I knew that he didn't have to utter a threat for me to choose my next words with care.

I nodded. "Fine," I replied, smooth and cool as glass.

"I'll be five minutes, dat's all."

I watched my cousin sprint up the stairs, the sinking feeling that gripped my innards hard to shift as I wandered down to the bar.

The interior of the club was dark, the air, curling with cigarette smoke, humid and musty. The bar was long and shiny black. I shook the rain off my coat, threw it over the back of one of the chairs and wiped my hands down the front of my trousers before heading towards the club's frontman, a fella called Claude Dabney. I'd known him from back home in Barbados and we'd never hit it off. He was a burly field hand who could work a machete all day long and then party hard until it was time to head back to his toil. We'd had an argument once, when we'd both been much younger, and I couldn't help thinking that I'd've probably died that day if it wasn't for Vic stepping in to rescue my hide.

Dabney was leaning back on a stool, propping himself against the wall next to the bar, a cigarette hanging between his lips. He smoked Strand filters, the cheapest, foulest brand that the Wills factory turned out. I guess he'd finished smoking it because he let the coffin nail fall to the floor when he saw me heading over. The dog end lay on the oak panel, smouldering and burning a black patch in the wood. The floor around Dabney's chair had dozens of burns in it. He was a nasty man who didn't give a damn about anything. His thick voiced crackled a greeting.

"Hey there, JT. Ain't seen you 'bout fo' a helluva while. Where you bin?"

I shrugged. "Oh, you know how it is, Claude. Just keeping busy, working."

"Yeah, you still cleaning up at dat ole schoolhouse?" There was a hint of a smile on his lips.

"That's me . . . still scrubbing away for the council," I lied.

"Uh-huh," Claude chimed. I could tell from the smarmy look on his face that he'd got a kick out of hearing me say that I was labouring for my white betters. His overeager grin was soon wiped away when Vic barked at him from the top of the stairs.

"Git you butt off dat fuckin' stool an' git me an' my man a couple o' pints o' Dragon."

Claude jumped up and darted around behind the bar, his sour body odour hitting me as he hurried past. He was wearing a worn frilled shirt and flared tuxedo pants, which were pulled high up over his waist by a pair of thick braces. He was in his late fifties and had the kind of beer gut that characterised the man's reputation for overindulging in almost every vice.

As he yanked on the hand pull, his belly strained against a filthy grey string vest that was trying to pop out where his shirt buttons were missing. His afro sat on his head like an old hat, and his face was unshaven. His cracked lips currently hid the gap where the two teeth that I'd punched out years before had once lived, and the dark circles under his eyes completed the look of a man in desperate need of a bath and a good meal. I sipped my beer and chewed the fat with him for a

304

couple more minutes until Vic stuck his head round the door and beckoned me over. "Bring dem pints o' stout wid you."

I slung my coat over my shoulder and carried the two jugs of ale out into the hallway. Vic was already waiting for me at the top of the stairs, beside an open door. I followed him up to the landing and walked inside.

"Tek a seat," Vic said, gesturing to a chair in front of a desk. He walked behind it and slumped down into a green suede recliner, putting his feet up next to a half-empty bottle of Gay's Rum. There was a pin-up calendar on the wall behind him where Miss August displayed her assets. The only other things in the room were a tall grey footlocker and a wooden chest. The floor was bare black-and-white-checked linoleum that was in dire need of a clean.

Vic sat back and stretched his arms out. I noticed the tan leather holster under his left arm. The muzzle of the pistol inside almost reached his belt.

I slid one of the pint pots across the table towards him and rested mine on the edge of the desk. Vic kicked his legs back off the top of the woodwork and snatched up his glass. I watched him sink the contents in a half-dozen swift gulps. He gasped in satisfaction, wiped his mouth and sat the pint pot on the floor. He looked at the rum, opened up a desk drawer and took out two shot glasses. He grinned and shook the bottle at me.

"One o' tha benefits o' wukin' fo' yo'self. Always have a bottle on tha table."

While he talked, he poured two measures of rum into both of the dimple glasses. He looked down at his watch, then back at me, the irritation in his eye sparking. "Okay, let me 'ear you masterplan."

"We need to go pay a visit to a fella called Herbert Castle."

Vic shrugged. "And?"

"I'm pretty sure that Castle's the keeper of a lot of Ryder's secrets, or at least the ones I'm interested in knowing about."

Vic knocked back his rum and refilled his glass. "An' where we find dis Mr Castle?"

"A place called Clutton, 'bout ten miles south of 'ere."

Vic groaned. "Nun, cow-shit country, agin?"

"'Fraid so."

"Every time you drag me inta you mess, we end up in honky wonderland. fo' once can't you pick a rasclat dat's closer ta 'ome?"

I took a draught of my beer. "Castle is a big hitter over at the Council House. He pulled in Superintendent Fletcher, put the thumbscrews on him to get me started looking for the killer of two people. I think he knows that Nikhil Suresh and a young white kid called James Peberdy are connected to Ryder in some way or other. I just need to find out how. Once we do, we got ourselves some serious leverage on your old business partner."

Vic poured himself another three fingers of rum. "Why'd Ryder wanna kilt sum kiddy. Don't mek no sense."

"None of this makes any sense, Vic. That's why we need to put the strong-arm on Castle."

Vic blew up his cheeks and let a long jet of air out of his mouth. "An' dis is your plan ta bring Billy Ryder ta his knees, is it?"

I nodded then gulped back another mouthful of ale.

Vic laughed. "Come on, JT, this is me you talkin' ta. You tellin' me dis is the best you got? We gonna sneak in through the gate do' o' sum ole white fella an' put da shakes on 'im?"

"Yep, that's exactly what we're gonna do. If we leave in the next half hour, we can be there well before sun up and creep the place."

Vic sank a third of his rum and draped his arm over the back of his chair. "Wha' if dis Castle fella ain't deh when we pull up outside o' his pad?"

I gave my cousin a blank stare. "That's a chance we just gotta take."

Vic finished the last of his liquor then got to his feet, fishing a small bunch of keys out of his pocket, before walking over to the footlocker and opening it up. I joined him and whistled as I stared at the contents. Resting at the base was a pair of cut-down, side-by-side Purdy shotguns and over two further shelves were two Beretta pistols, a Webley MK IV service revolver, a snub-nosed police Colt .32 with ivory grips, a sap and a leather blackjack, four pairs of brass knuckles, hand and leg cuffs, a short iron jemmy, half a dozen gas masks, and cartons of flares.

Vic looked at me and grinned. "You tink we got enuff inside ta go on wid?"

I watched Vic empty the contents of the footlocker into two heavy green army-issue holdalls. He whistled to himself while he stuffed the pair of shotguns into separate leather gun cases and rested the silenced sniper's rifle that he'd brought back from the warehouse on top of the bagged-up arsenal. He then took off his shirt and threw it across the room. He sniffed under one of his armpits and grimaced before bending down and opening up the wooden chest. He took out a black T-shirt and a lightweight army field jacket, pulled both garments on then looked back at the stockpile of arms on top of the desk.

"Gimme a hand lugging dis shit downstairs."

Vic snatched up the rifle bags and one of the holdalls, slung them over his shoulder and headed for the door.

I picked up the rest of the stuff and called after my cousin, hearing the quaver in my voice when I spoke. "Before we go, there's something I need to tell you."

Vic turned on his heels. "Yeah, git on wid it den."

"I saw Gabe last night." The silent moment that followed was one neither of us had chosen. I looked down at my feet and waited for Vic to speak.

Vic gave a heavy sigh. "Why you tellin' me dis shit now?"

"Cause I gave my word that I would, that's why."

"So, wha' dat ole goat 'ave ta say fo' himsel'?"

"Your dad asked me to tell you that you should go home. That you need to go see Pearl."

Vic frowned, his eyes searching my face. "Woman alright, ain't she? Her palsy not gittin' worse?"

"Vic, all I know right now is that they're both getting older by the day and you gotta go break bread with 'em sometime real soon."

Vic nodded his agreement and turned to leave. I followed. At the bottom of the stairs he turned back to me, his expression cool. "We ain't gotta worry 'bout none of our folks fo' now. I'm gettin' 'em all outta town fo' a while."

He began to walk down the hall towards the kitchen. I hollered after him, "What do you mean *all of them*?"

Vic drew to a stop and hesitated, then he turned back to face me, his hard, dark eye staring into mine. "Ah mean Gabe, Pearl, Loretta and the damn pickney. Dey all bein' shifted sum'place safe."

I could taste the bile rising uncontrollably from my stomach. My hand balled into a fist, my head reeling as though it had been slapped hard with a rolled-up newspaper. The inside of my mouth was as dry as a bone. In the distance, I heard a police siren ringing out and I scowled at Vic.

"Safe . . . what the hell are you talking about, safe?"

My cousin ignored my glowering fix and stuck a finger in my face, his tone almost a growl. "I'm talkin' 'bout mekin' sure none o' Ryder's boys git a chance ta mess wid our kin cause a' what's bin goin' down. Dat's tha call I made earlier. I got Dutty Ken and a couple o' his boys ovah at the Beaumont to go pick 'em all up."

My eyes were wide. I glanced down at my watch. "But it's after one thirty in the morning."

"So? You tink Ryder gives a shit 'bout wha' time o' day it is if he wanna kill sum fool?"

I exhaled and realised that my anger was quickly evaporating. "Where's Dutty Ken taking them?"

"Outta town," he grunted.

"Where outta town?"

"The smoke."

"London . . . why London?"

"Cause it ain't Bristol, an' I got bredren in Brixton dat can look out fo' em. Dat's why."

I was about to speak but Vic cut me off. "Now, we gonna git on the road befo' the cock starts crawin' or wha'?"

He didn't wait for me to answer, storming down the hall towards the kitchen door. I followed him, my tail firmly between my legs. By the time I'd made it out to the yard, Vic was nowhere to be seen. I headed towards an open gate at the side of the club, and as I walked out into the street, I heard my cousin curse.

"Muthafucka."

Vic was standing on the pavement underneath the orange glow of a streetlight. A bright red Ford Capri had been parked up outside, close to the main door of the club. I watched him curse again then pull a cigarette out and light it. He turned to me, his face like thunder.

"Just look at dis shit." Vic kicked at the car's tyre with the toe of his boot. "Didn't I say low-key?"

He hammered his hand against the roof, shaking his head. "Couldn't git nuthin' right till dey put the prick under six feet o' loose dirt."

I walked the length of the vehicle, my mouth agape. "Your boy Melvin, this what he thinks is inconspicuous?"

Vic sniffed the air belligerently, walked round the car and dropped the holdall and rifle cases in the boot. "It's gonna 'ave ta do."

"Have to do . . . This motor's gonna get us pinched before we get a mile outta town."

Vic climbed inside then leaned across and pushed open the passenger door while I unloaded the other bag and the sniper's rifle into the trunk and slammed it shut. When I joined Vic, he had an unexpected smile on his face. He turned the key, revved the Capri's accelerator a couple of times then winked at me.

"Black fella always gonna git pinched fo' sum'ting, JT. If it gonna 'appen, may as well be in a decent ride."

CHAPTER THIRTY-NINE

It was still raining hard as we drove out of Bristol and headed through rural Somerset to the village of Clutton. By the time Vic swung the Capri into a lane opposite Herbert Castle's place, the downpour was little more than drizzle. He turned off the engine and craned his neck over the top of his seat to make a quick sweep back up the road through the rear and side windows.

"You 'naw dat ole fool could 'ave sum hired 'elp inside his place."

"He could have. Let's hope not."

"I ain't hopin' fo' nuthin'." Vic slapped his hand against the gun hanging inside his coat. "You carryin' ain't you?"

I pulled back my jacket to reveal the butt of my pistol.

"Good." He turned to get out of the car. I took hold of his elbow, pulling him back towards me.

"There's something I've been meaning to tell you."

Vic shifted back in his seat to face me. "Yeah, wha's dat?"

"Castle, he has a daughter."

"Uh-huh, what about her?"

I hesitated for a second. "I seen her a couple o' times."

My cousin leaned back in his seat, rubbing his mouth. His interest peaked. "Seen her . . . you mean like on a date?"

"Nah . . . not a date. I just took a drink with her, that's all."

"Oh . . . dat's all?"

I coughed into my hand. "And I visited her place last night."

Vic was looking at me, shaking his head and grinning. "You fuckin' some white man's girl?"

"I ain't touched her, man."

"Naw . . . not yet, you ain't." Vic flashed a gold smile at me. "JT, you changin', brutha."

"How's that?"

"Fo' years you used t'be kinda uptight 'bout everyt'ing. Takin' dem little niggah jobs like gardenin' and cleanin' up. Now you shacked up wid a pickney, gotta nice place o' you own an' you lookin fo' a momma fro' the sounds o' tings." Vic started to laugh, slapping the palm of his hand on the steering wheel.

I yanked open my door and clambered out. Vic purred after me. "We gonna be hearin' wedding bells too, cuz?"

I stuck my head back inside the car. "I knew I should have kept my goddamn mouth shut."

I eased the door to and stepped into the road, the sound of Vic's muffled chuckling parroting away in my ears.

Vic and I were silent as we crossed the road and began moving towards the house. I could hear a slow-moving brook flowing in the distance and smell the damp stone and roses in the courtyard behind the hedgerow. Staying in the shadows the best we could, we worked our way up the long drive, a few feet apart, finally crossing over the lawn and sinking to our haunches underneath a large tree. Upstairs lights were on inside the house. I took my torch out of my coat pocket and ran the beam along the side wall before the two of us darted towards the rear of the building. At the top of the path Vic pressed himself against the wall then moved under a window and made his way through into the back garden. I followed, crouching down next to him in the darkness by the kitchen door.

Vic put his ear to the wood panel and listened for a moment then got to his feet. He reached underneath his jacket and took out a short iron jemmy. He opened and closed his right hand, breathing deeply and slowly, then slipped the crowbar around the edge of the door and began to prise the frame away from the jamb, working quietly, stressing the hinges back and forth against the screws until a piece of wood splintered inside and the lock snapped free. I froze, expecting to hear movement inside the house, but there was no other sound except the dull murmur of our breath and the splattering rain around us.

Vic withdrew the Beretta from his jacket and held the pistol out at arm's length, then pushed back the door. I shone the torch inside, raking the walls and

314

floor with the beam. Vic headed on in with me close behind. We walked swiftly through the kitchen and out into the hall, my heart thundering in my chest. Inside, the house was almost serenely peaceful. We pushed forward, Vic stopping at each door we passed, slowly opening them up and checking that no one was around. When we reached the lobby, I backed myself against the front door and looked up the stairs. I could see dust particles floating in the glow from the ceramic rose hanging at the top of the landing.

Vic's combing of the ground floor had indicated no sign of any police guards or Ryder's workforce. He pointed up at the ceiling, informing me he was ready to tackle the next floor. We tiptoed up the stairs, making our way past an open bathroom door towards the two bedrooms at the end of the landing. A dim light shone from the room nearest us. We crept along the carpeted floor, coming to a halt outside it. I turned off my torch and put it in my pocket before taking hold of the handle. Vic nodded and took a couple of steps back, the Berretta still held out in front of him. I turned the handle softly and pushed the door open. Inside, a bedside lamp offered some meagre illumination. I could hear the low-watt bulb crackling under its shade.

Herbert Castle was sleeping on his back, stretched out on an ornate brass bed, the breeze from an oscillating fan dimpling the sheets that covered his inert body. The air in the bedroom was thick with sweat, unwashed limbs and stale alcohol fumes. A bottle of scotch and a half-filled crystal tumbler sat on the nightstand by his head.

Vic crept across the room, picked up the drink and took a sip. As I slowly inched through the door, Vic grinned back at me, shaking the glass and mouthing the words, "This is some good shit."

Vic sank the rest of the whisky, rested the glass back on the table then leaned forward and placed the muzzle of his Beretta against Castle's jawbone. I stood at the foot of the bed and watched his face twitch, his eyes rolling under the lids. The councillor came to in the same way that an old cat might, slow and steady. It wasn't the kind of reaction I was expecting. I moved along the side of the bed.

"Good evening, Councillor."

Creases began to form across Castle's forehead, but otherwise he remained calm. "I suspect you know what that is sticking in the side of your face. You've probably got some idea of what it can do to the inside of your head too."

Castle's eyelids remained closed, his bare chest rising and falling with no irregularity, his hands folded passively across his stomach.

"You hearing me?" I asked.

"Yes, I can hear you," he whispered. He slowly opened his eyes but kept them directed up towards the ceiling. "How did you get in here?"

"Through the letterbox."

Castle lifted his head ever-so-slightly off his pillow, his gaze still pitched upwards. "Breaking and entering is a serious crime, Mr Ellington." The acid in his voice suddenly grew more corrosive.

"We know you ain't gonna be calling no law. That'd be way too embarrassing for the council if they started sniffing around your nasty hide." I gestured to the telephone on the bedside table. "I'll dial 999 for you myself if you like?"

"What do you want with me?"

I walked back across the room, pulling a chair out from a dressing table. I returned to the foot of the bed, turned the chair around, straddled it and folded my arms on the bentwood frame. "Same thing I've been wanting this past week or more. The truth about William Ryder."

I watched Castle blink. "I haven't a clue what you're talking about."

"Come off it. I know Ryder's got his claws into you. I just need to know how deep and why?"

Castle sniffed. "That's ridiculous."

"Enough wid dis shit . . . honky, jus' rememba who's holding the gun 'ere." Vic jammed the Beretta's barrel deeper into the old man's face.

Unlike my cousin, my actions were all bravado and I felt my palms sweating; I just had to make sure Castle didn't realise that. I cleared my throat and widened my eyes like a man trying to stretch sleep out of his face, then hit Castle with another question. "I want you to tell me about William Ryder and Nikhil Suresh."

"What about them?"

"What's the connection?"

Castle made a huffing sound deep down in his throat. "There isn't one."

317

Vic kept the muzzle of the gun square against Castle's face. I watched him apply a little more pressure before I spoke again. "That ain't true, and you know it."

Castle tried to shake his head, but the barrel of Vic's gun prevented him from protesting. "William Ryder is a well-respected member of the Bristol Chamber of Commerce, the city's esteemed Rotary Club, a benefactor of numerous charities, and a friend to many powerful and well-placed people in the city."

"You forgot to mention that he's also gangster."

Castle raised an eyebrow. "You've lost me. Gangster?"

Vic stuffed the muzzle of the Berretta under Castle's chin, forcing his head back. The councillor's eyes were as wide as a trapped animal.

"My cousin here is gonna spray your brains all over that wall unless you start talking."

"Have you gone m-mad?"

"Mad? You bet I'm mad. I've been mad ever since you tried to pay me off to keep out of Ryder's hair."

I watched Castle considering my words. There was no malevolent light in his eyes, nothing hostile about his behaviour. When he spoke, his words were evenly pitched and assured. "I really don't know what you're talking about."

"Sure, you do. You set me up and now you're trying to save your arse by spouting this 'I know nothing' bullshit. You've been lying since the first minute I met you."

"That's not true. My motives have been entirely honourable."

318

"Honourable, my arse." I gestured at Vic, with a flick of my hand to remove the muzzle of the gun from under Castle's chin. When Vic backed away a step, there was a small red circle where the steel had pressed against the man's skin. I rose up off the chair as Vic grabbed the councillor by the throat, yanking him upright, then pulled away the sheet to reveal Castle's naked body. His thighs and torso were covered with dense hair, like soft strips of fur, his phallus in a state of erection.

Vic raised the gun back into Castle's face. "You dirty ole fuck."

I looked down at the floor and blew air out of my nostrils, wiping the sweat off my forehead with my wrist. "This is the last time I'm gonna ask you this question nicely, Councillor. Give me the runaround and I'm gonna let my cousin here start doing the quizzing. And believe me, you don't want him getting in your face."

Castle stared at me arrogantly.

"Tell me what the connection is between William Ryder and Nikhil Suresh."

A long moist hiss emanated from Castle's throat. He calmly raised his hand, opening out his palm. "There is no connection, Mr Ellington."

I caught my breath, my reasoning to cajole and bluff the councillor a while longer, a part of me recognising that this was Ruth's father that we were manhandling. But Vic had already decided that enough was enough. In a split second, he stuffed the Berretta into the front of his trouser waistband then snatched Castle by the hair, yanking him up off the bed. He spun the councillor round, shoving him against the wall then pinning him by the throat before he drove his fist again and again into the man's face, sending saliva and blood stringing across the wallpaper.

He dropped Castle to the ground and kicked him, then brought his foot down with all his weight on the back of Castle's hand. Castle screamed out in agony, but my cousin was deaf to his piercing cry. Vic then reached down, hauled him up on to his knees and slammed his head back against the plaster.

"Dis shit you pullin' wid dis honky fuck ain't workin'. Lemme pop a bullet in his wrinkly ole dick fo' you. Git 'im talkin'."

I held up a hand to Vic and approached Castle. His eyes switched from side to side, and he flinched as I rested my hand on his shoulder.

"I know that William Ryder has a real hold over you. I know that you two go way back. All those Rotary Club dinners, charity balls, civic functions . . . those nights out over at Cricket Malherbie."

Castle's head sank to his chest. I kept at him. "You remember those nights over at Terrance Blanchard's place, don't you?"

I reached down and lifted Castle's chin up with my fingertips. His head came up to meet me as easily as an empty husk. "Surely you ain't forgot a joint like the Erotica Negro club, Herbert?"

Castle closed his eyes and pressed his trembling fingers to his temples. "I remember . . ."

320

"That's good. Now let me try and prevent you having another amnesia attack, so that my cousin here doesn't have to beat you to death."

Castle nodded weakly. "I'll tell you what I know about your well-respected friend, Ryder. Then you can try and fill in the blanks for me, okay?"

Castle nodded again, his watery eyes staring up at me. Blood and spittle ran down his chin and dribbled on to his pale torso.

"I have a photograph that shows William Ryder in the Moulin Rouge club in Clifton. That same Polaroid you can see Ryder getting real chummy with the dead fellow, Suresh. Now I know the two men knew each other. I know that they were likely to be fairly intimate. I know that Ryder got Suresh a job at the same golf club in Portishead where James Peberdy was found dead. I'm pretty sure that both the boy's and Suresh's murders are linked. Yes?"

Vic prodded Castle's arm with the muzzle of his gun. Castle gasped and nodded a third time.

"How are they linked, Herbert?"

I leaned forward. Castle's breath covered my face like a soiled, damp handkerchief and he mumbled to himself for moment before he began to speak.

"It was . . . it was all a terrible accident." Castle rubbed his eye with the back of his hand and blinked at me. "The Indian fellow, Suresh. He and Ryder had been . . . involved." Castle spat out the word *involved* as if was a piece of rotten meat.

"And?"

321

Castle breathed heavily, choosing his words carefully. "And by all accounts it was a rather torrid affair."

"How'd you mean?"

Castle coughed. Fresh blood trickled out his mouth, his slaver frothing around his cut lips. "You know how some queens get?"

"No, not really."

"There were petty jealousies, hysterical outbursts in public, all very unseemly behaviour."

"Unseemly behaviour? You mean like a man who pays for whores and visits private clubs out in the sticks so that he can indulge himself with the pleasures of the flesh — those kinda *unseemly behaviours*?"

Castle looked up and sneered. "I've always had a penchant for the darker meats, shall we say."

Vic leaned against the wall and pushed the Beretta into the side of Castle's skull.

"What do petty jealousies have to do with Suresh and a child being killed?"

Castle sniggered. "That's . . . that's exactly my point. None of this insanity would have happened if people knew how to conduct themselves in public."

"What the hell you talking about?"

Vic cracked the barrel across the top of Castle's head and the man hollered, his body falling forward. I caught him by the shoulders and pushed him back against the wall. He groaned and looked back up at me. "There was an argument, between the two of them . . . out at the golf club."

Castle spoke slowly, the words dragged out of the past and filtered through layers of secrecy. "Suresh had been drinking while serving behind the bar at the club. It was during an annual soiree of some kind . . . one that Ryder was attending. I'm told that during the evening, Ryder was getting rather chummy with one of the young waiters. Suresh didn't like it."

"Who told you this."

"Well . . . Ryder, of course."

"And Ryder, he always washes his dirty linen with you, does he?"

"If . . . if it's to his advantage, yes."

"Carry on."

Castle ran his tongue along the inside of his mouth. "The event finished during the early evening. When Ryder was leaving the club, Suresh approached him as he was getting into his car. The fellow was uninhibited, speaking freely about William, and in an unsavoury manner which other members may have heard."

"What did Ryder do with Suresh?"

"By all accounts he was assisted into the back of Ryder's car and driven away. Rather than have the fellow screaming like a banshee on the backseat, Ryder had the car stopped and the two men got out to settle their differences during a walk."

"You expect me to swallow this? Cut to the chase, Herbert."

"Swallow it, spit it out; I don't give a damn. It's the truth."

Vic jabbed the muzzle of the Berretta into Castle's ear. "Enough wid the attitude. Do as the man say an' cut ta the fuckin' chase."

Castle's eyes flickered. "While the two men were walking, at some point they settled their differences. And they . . . they . . ."

There was now considerable fear in Castle's eyes. I cracked the knuckles in my right hand for emphasis. "They did what, man?"

"Kissed."

I frowned. "I don't understand?"

"Who in their right mind would, Mr Ellington?"

"Talk sense, man."

"When they were embracing . . . they were seen."

"By who?"

"The boy . . . the boy Peberdy . . . he saw the two men kissing. He'd been out collecting golf balls. He . . . he stumbled across them during that intimate moment."

"And Ryder killed the child cause he'd seen 'em kissing."

Castle continued to speak in almost a whisper. "No. No . . . not Ryder. It was Ryder's right-hand man, James Moody, who killed the boy."

I looked at Vic, not quite able to take in what I was hearing. We'd spent the last few minutes trying to get Herbert Castle to talk. Now, with his head bowed, I couldn't make him stop.

"Ryder said he recognised the child. Said the boy was a pupil at the school that Ryder's a governor at. He'd seen him during assemblies, that kind of thing. When William tried to approach him to try and placate him, the boy ran. Ryder panicked and sent Moody after him. Moody caught the boy, the boy struggled and that's when Moody hit him."

324

My tongue suddenly felt several sizes too large for my mouth. I fought to get my words out.

"Hit him . . . that kid was beaten across the back of the head with a length of wood."

Castle looked up at me; there were actually tears in his eyes. "It should never have happened . . . it was a mistake . . . a tragic accident. When Moody returned, he'd finished the child off and dumped the body. Suresh became hysterical again. Demanding to know where the boy was, what had happened to him? From that moment on Ryder knew that Suresh would give the game away. That he couldn't trust him to keep silent. He was sure at some point, sometime in the future, that Suresh would betray him and talk to the police. It was a risk that Ryder simply wasn't prepared to take. Ryder had Moody dispose of him . . . to prevent Suresh from blowing the whistle."

Castle swayed on his knees for a second then slumped forward, his forehead grazing the carpet. I watched him fall on to his side and curl up into a naked ball. His sobbing echoed around the room. I pitched backwards, my legs like jelly, then dropped on to the edge of the bed and stared over at Vic. He gave Castle a dirty look as he writhed at his feet and shook a cigarette out of a packet.

"Man kilt the chil' ovah a damn kiss?" My cousin shook his head then walked towards the door. "Dat's gotta be sum o' the most fucked-up shit I evah heard."

His parting words reverberated inside my head like a curse.

CHAPTER
FORTY

I guess I should have felt relieved to have finally heard the truth. To know that I could put William Ryder in the bag for ordering the murder of Nikhil Suresh and his involvement in the killing of James Peberdy. I had enough credible evidence in Castle's confession to put Ryder and his minder, Jimmy Moody, away for life. In fact, all in all, when the sun rose later that morning, it should have been a fine day.

But that's not the way things were about to pan out. Getting to the truth had been one thing, being able to inform members of the Bristol constabulary, and find men on the force who I could trust, was going to be another. Both Vic and the councillor were about to remind me that nothing in life is that easy, even when you think you're holding a winning hand. Sitting on that bed, listening to Castle bawl and whine, I thought my problems were all but over.

I couldn't have been more wrong.

When Vic returned to the bedroom, he was carrying a pair of handcuffs and a roll of duct tape. His face tight with anger, he dropped the cuffs on to the floor in front of Castle then began to root through the drawers, gathering up clothes and underwear. He slung them on the bed.

"Git dressed."

I pulled Castle to his feet and handed him a pair of underpants and trousers. "Best do as the man says."

Castle nodded and stumbled backwards against the wall, his body odour rising into my face. He righted himself then fumbled to get his feet into his skivvies and draw them up to his waist. He looked up at me nervously, his eyes searching mine. "You need to listen to me, Mr Ellington."

"I do? 'Bout what?"

"Ryder called me last night. He was furious. He said that if you were to contact me in any way that I was to let him know immediately. Told me that if I didn't cooperate that I . . . and my family would face terrible consequences."

I saw the tears forming in Castle's eyes again. "What kinda consequences?"

Castle shook his head. "He wouldn't say. But he advised me to inform you that if you were to approach me, that it was in all our best interests to call him forthwith . . . He said that I was to impress upon you the severity of failing to reach out to him."

I looked at my cousin. "Did he now?"

Vic caught my eye and nodded towards the phone. "Call the prick. Find out wha' he playin' at." He turned to Castle, clicking his fingers. "Gimme my man Ryder's number."

Castle pointed at an address book on the dressing table and swallowed before speaking. "It's in there."

I threw the councillor a crumpled white shirt, which he only just caught in his shaking hands, then leafed through the Rolodex until I found Ryder's number. My call was answered after a half-dozen rings. The gangster's voice was easy to recognise, his tone brittle and matter of fact. There was no rise and fall in his pitch. No expression of being irked at the ungodly hour I was calling. "Yeah, who is it?"

"Ellington."

There was a moment's silence on the other end of the line.

"Ah, Joseph. Good to hear from you. Burning the midnight oil, eh?"

I felt my pulse pounding at the side of my temple. I took the phone away from my ear then quickly replaced it. "You could say so."

"I take it you've spoken to our mutual friend, Herbert?"

I looked across at Castle. "Yeah, I have. I'm with the councillor at the moment."

"Are you now? At this time of night? He can't be very happy about losing his beauty sleep."

"I don't really care."

"No, perhaps you don't. Neither do I. That said, it is rather fortuitous you two being together and calling me whatever the hour."

"It is?"

"Oh, yeah, very much so. Just gimme two ticks, Joseph, will you?"

The line hummed. I pushed the earpiece closer to my face and heard muted voices and a series of rough shuffling sounds.

"JOSEPH."

When Ruth Castle hollered my name, I felt my throat tighten and the inside of my mouth go dry. My hand flexed at my side, my eyes smarting with rage and fear as I heard Ruth being snatched away from the phone. A couple more seconds of static crackled into the receiver before Ryder spoke again.

"Now, you're going to do exactly what I tell you, understand?"

Ryder's instructions seemed to last forever, his orders given with a calm, almost military precision. When he'd finished speaking, Ryder broke the connection, leaving the dialling tone trilling in my ear, and I slumped back down on the bed, shaking my head. I propped my hands on my knees, then squeezed at my temples and stared at a spot between my shoes before looking up at Vic.

"He has Ruth."

Castle groaned. I turned and saw the colour that had been slowly coming back into the councillor's face begin to drain again. His washed-out eyes never blinked, wide with a grim knowledge that was lost on everyone else in the room.

Vic shrugged. "Who you talkin' 'bout?"

"Castle's daughter."

"So wha'?"

I pinched my eyes with my thumb and forefinger and dragged myself up off the mattress, took Vic by the elbow and guided him out on to the landing. When I spoke, my voice was low, the words fluttering with agitation. "Ryder says, I don't do as he asks and the girl's dead."

Vic made a huffing sound and pulled his arm out of my grasp. "Fuck 'im."

I pressed a finger into Vic's chest. "I'm being serious, man. He wants the photograph I have of him and Suresh together and he's demanding that we deliver Castle back to him later tonight. He needs the councillor to continue to keep things sweet for him with the police, the press and anybody else who might be sniffing about after the shit hits the fan."

My face was burning, the words I needed to say sticking deep in my throat and finally leaving my mouth almost as a whisper. "Ryder says he'll hand Ruth over, unharmed, if I bring him the councillor and . . ."

Vic scratched at the back of his scalp. "An' wha', goddamn it?"

"And you."

Vic nodded, his jaw clenched, his mouth tight. "Man's axing fo' a lot, ain't he?"

I began to nod, staring briefly down at the floor before refocusing on Vic. "Ryder says that Ruth, Chloe and me, we can leave town. That Ruth can go her own separate way, and the child and me, we can get lost someplace else. He told me that he'll arrange for Suresh, James Peberdy and Fletcher's murders all to be pinned on you in some way or other. My guessing is that after tonight he ain't gonna let you be around to plead your innocence, either."

330

Vic rubbed his chin with two fingers, his face twisting towards mine. "Where's dis shit s'posed ta be goin' down?"

"Ryder wants to make the exchange at Glenside."

"Wha', the nuthouse?"

"Yeah . . . Out at the chapel at the rear of the hospital. Ten thirty this evening."

Vic looked at his watch before heading back into the bedroom, snapping his fingers again. I watched him pick up the telephone and dial a number. He turned around, gave me the thumbs-up and grinned.

I dreaded to think what was coming next.

CHAPTER
FORTY-ONE

Vic made several more telephone calls before we left Herbert Castle's home, each of them cryptic and brief. I knew from past experience that it was pointless trying to quiz my cousin. Grilling him while he was hatching some kind of plan would simply make him clam up more. I might as well try speaking to the wind for all the good it would have done me. Whatever he was up to would be unveiled only when Vic was good and ready to tell me about it.

Once the councillor was dressed, Vic roughhoused him into a chair, handcuffed his wrists and taped around his mouth and the back of his head. While my cousin went to collect the car, I fished a coat out of the wardrobe and hung it over Castle's shoulders. The old man's eyes were lit with fear and a faint haze from the whisky he'd been drinking before retiring. His cheek and nose were swelling up from the beating Vic had given him, the skin above his left eye blossomed with a dark purple bruise.

I frogmarched him downstairs and we stood and waited in the lobby, the councillor staring down at the floor, shivering. I heard the Capri's wheels kicking up the gravel as it pulled up outside the front door. By the

332

time I brought Castle out, Vic was leaning against the back of the vehicle smoking, the headlights dipped, engine still running. My cousin opened the boot and gestured at Castle with a flip of his head.

"Git you honky arse in deh."

Castle hesitated and mumbled frantically underneath the gag, then, panicking, stumbled backwards into me. Vic shot forward, reaching for the man's shirt collar, and yanked him savagely towards the open boot, his head and the top half of his body swiftly pitched over the edge. At the same time, I reached down and grabbed hold of his legs, tipping him inside.

Vic slammed the lid shut, leaving Castle to kick and babble, then got in the car and waited for me to join him.

As we headed back down the shingle drive, I looked at the dashboard clock; it was a little after 4.30 a.m. We pulled out of the gates and back down the lane and made our way out of Clutton. I wanted to say something to Vic, to try to get him to open up to me, but I couldn't find the words. I just looked out of my window, staring up at the streetlights, their glow casting shadows through the trees, whose wet branches blowing in the wind reminded me of my long-gone childhood adventures — nights spent with my late sister, Bernice, and Vic. I recalled the three of us running between the trunks of cypress woods on Barbados, laughing, happy, unaware of the sadness that would be bestowed upon each of us in the years to come. It was odd to find myself thinking of my childhood at such a chilling and uncertain time; I had no explanation as to why.

Dawn was little over an hour away, the diminishing night sky still allowing us the ability to travel on the sly. Vic drove quickly but carefully, choosing to stay on as many country lanes as possible to avoid any unwanted police attention. From the direction we were going, I knew that our destination had to be pretty close to Bristol. I just had no idea exactly where Vic was taking us.

We crossed the River Avon at Keynsham then headed north through quiet suburbs for a good thirty miles, bypassing the city and St Pauls. At Frenchay, we headed north-east for another six or so miles until we reached a signpost for a place called Hambrook. Vic headed through the centre of the village, finally reaching a fork in the road on the outskirts where he turned on to a tree-lined dirt track which led us down to a wooded area and, next to it, a small house. As we closed in on the place, the Capri's headlights picked out the whitewashed walls and bay windows of a small cottage.

Vic swung the car underneath the overhanging branches of a row of trees then turned off the engine. It rattled under the bonnet for a moment, and he looked back at the building.

"What's this place?"

"An investment."

I saw him smile to himself. "What you talking about?"

Vic pushed open the driver's door and began to climb out. He twisted his head back towards me.

334

"Bought it fo' Pearl an' the ole man 'bout six month ago."

"You're kidding me?"

Vic rested his arm against the top of the door frame. He looked back inside, shaking his head solemnly. "Nuh . . . Said dey din't want no part o' sum'ting paid fo' wid blood money."

Vic looked over at the cottage, then back at me. "Suppose dey hadda point."

He flipped the cigarette he'd been smoking in the car to the ground in a shower of sparks, kneaded his hands together and forced a smile. "Com' on, luvva boy. Gimme a hand ta git you father-in-law outta the trunk."

The air smelled of flowers and wet grass as we walked Herbert Castle down the path towards the rear of the house. Above us, the clouds were marbled with early morning light, the trees filled with the faint chatter of birdsong.

Vic brought the councillor to a halt next to a wooden dovecote then reached up inside the coop and retrieved a tobacco tin. He opened it up, took out a set of keys then tossed the tin over a thick privet hedge before walking Castle to the rear of the cottage and unlocking the door. He pushed the councillor inside and I followed, the earthy stink of damp catching my breath.

Vic walked across the room and flicked a switch on the far wall. I coughed at the back of my throat and squinted across the sparse kitchen. I looked around and shook my head.

"What's that damn smell?"

335

Vic shrugged. "I dunno. Previous owners I suppose."

"Previous owners . . . What the hell were they, grave robbers?"

The kitchen was the worst kind of housing nightmare. Bare, wet plaster ran from ceiling to skirting board. The linoleum floor was filthy and cracked, cobwebs feathering along the jambs of the window frames and the hearth hadn't been touched for years, ash from its last fire peppering the charred remains of wood. A chipped double-bowl farmhouse sink sat underneath a cracked tile sill and next to the draining board stood an old gas cooker that was in dire need of condemning. I exhaled a long jet between my lips.

"No wonder Pearl didn't wanna move in."

"Shit, whaddya want? Place got power, 'n it's got gas goin' through the pipes. Nobody said nuthin' 'bout the joint bein' fuckin' five star."

Vic turned on the hall light then spun Castle around on his heels and shouldered him out of the kitchen and down the hall. We climbed a narrow staircase, turning left at the top. Vic stopped abruptly halfway down the passageway and kicked open a door. He knocked on another light and I walked forward and peered in.

"Don't tell me, the last owner died in there and hasn't been touched since."

Vic gave me a hard stare. "Shut the fuck up an' let's git dis honky bedded down."

"Shouldn't we send a canary in first?"

A confused crease appeared across Vic's brow. He pushed Castle inside. As I entered the room, I thought it was well-carpeted then realised the pile beneath my feet was a threadbare Berber print with strips of doubled-over cardboard behind the matting acting as underlay. The curtains were grey winding sheets and the bed looked like a medieval mantrap. Dirt clung to the walls.

Vic pulled the tape away from Castle's mouth and pushed him down on to the stained mattress. The councillor stared up at the two of us, fear prickling in his flat eyes. Vic kicked at the foot of the bed to make sure he had his prisoner's full attention then stuck a finger into Castle's face, and I watched as his slight frame sank into the box springs.

"You feel like you wanna scream an' shout in 'ere, you go right on an' do it. Ain't nobody gonna 'ear you."

When we left the room, I felt a flare of shame ignite inside of me and the back of my neck became prickly and hot, as if someone had just struck a match against my skin. Despite my earlier flippant banter with Vic, the idea of holding a man — Ruth's father to be precise — hostage felt wrong. The idea that I was on the good guys' side never felt further from the truth.

I followed Vic back downstairs and into the kitchen. While he went back to the car to bring in the holdalls, I ran the tap at the sink and waited. I heard the old pipes whistle and chug and when the faucet finally gave way, the water didn't flow but spluttered, spitting out in chaotic bursts of cold liquid which was orange and dirt-flecked. I put my hands underneath the tap then splashed my face with a couple of palmfuls, drying myself with the sleeve of my coat.

When Vic returned, he dropped the bags on the floor and propped the rifles against the wall, his face set with exertion. He rested his back against the draining board and lit a cigarette, inhaling deeply.

"So what now?" I asked.

Vic's eye lingered on mine for a moment before letting a column of grey vapour rise out of his mouth. He held the cigarette in his lips and grinned. "Now I wait fo' me breakfast ta be delivered."

Just over an hour and a half later I was standing in the living room of the cottage looking out the front window at a pair of Land Rovers heading down the path towards us. The two vehicles banged over the ruts in the road, throwing dust up into the air that drifted into the fields either side of the track. I called Vic in from the kitchen. My cousin slouched up beside me, his favourite pewter hipflask in his hand, and laughed to himself, then grabbed hold of my arm, hauled me out into the hall and flung open the front door. I saw his face sober as he watched the two heavy-duty motors pulling up alongside his Capri. Vic's eye fixed on my face before raising the hipflask to his lips. "Weddin' party's 'ere, brutha."

I stepped out on to the porch, the air so heavy with ozone that I could almost taste it, my head not quite believing what my eyes were now seeing. Speechless, I watched as the nebulous silhouettes of all three men came fully into view.

Walking towards me were Vic's island buddies, Everton "Bussa" Worrell, Grantley "Bitter" Lemon and the young Bajan who I'd only ever known as Dead Man. Early morning sunlight lit their slow-moving frames from behind. They gathered around Vic and me like gothic gargoyles, a trio of deadly executioners, who lived in the knowledge that certain death always followed in their wake.

CHAPTER
FORTY-TWO

My cousin may have been a closed book to most, but I knew Vic was sure that death could come for him at any time and in any way, almost all of which would be bad. I was sure that the horrors he'd both inflicted and witnessed had impressed on him how lucky he was to still be alive, but he'd never admit that fact to me. Living the kind of unrighteous existence that Vic did brought him close to the unpleasant reality that the dark angel was never far from his side, eager to squeeze the breath from his chest and the light from his eyes — perhaps when he least expected it.

Like my felonious kin, my own experiences of death had taught me that its grasp was never far away. Its unwelcome, indifferent presence stalked the good and the bad, clinging to the bedsheets that stuck to the ailing bodies of the injured or ill, shadowing the strong and the weak alike. Deliberating those harsh realities now made me realise why I was once again in the company of three of the most ruthless killers to walk the face of God's green earth, and why Vic had resurrected them from whatever Hades they'd lain dormant in to once again do his bidding.

I could count on one hand the number of people who have ever truly frightened me. My cousin was one of them, but Bitter Lemon had to be right at the top of that list. As far as I knew, I was only one of a few select people who knew his real name, and I would never say it aloud, much less write it down. A childhood friend of Vic's, for nearly two decades Bitter had been the man the professionals went to when they wanted somebody dead. He could kill anyone, anywhere.

If you needed it to look like an accident, there was a heart attack, mugging gone wrong or car accident in the offing. If the body needed to disappear, it would never be found. No one wanted to hear that Bitter Lemon was after them. If word got out — and it rarely did — their reactions were many but predictable. Some ran. Others bought life insurance and settled their affairs. A few went to the police and sought protection, but in the end, they all died.

I knew this because I'd once walked a beat back on the island where Bitter had plied his cruel trade. He was fearful legend, a baneful myth more than mortal man, and on a bright August morning I found myself sitting at a battered dining-room table in a remote part of Gloucestershire in the company of this fearsome liquidator; a brutal soul who I now called my friend.

The men had carried their bags and enough armaments to start a small war into the kitchen and I'd greeted each one of them warmly. Vic, however, was more interested in finding out what Bussa had brought him for breakfast. My cousin nudged the Bajan in the arm with his fist.

"Well, com' on?"

Bussa scratched his thick-set neck. "Come on, wha'?"

"Gimme me fuckin' breakfas', man." Vic held out his hand indignantly.

Bussa retrieved a selection of foil-wrapped parcels from a rucksack between his feet and handed one to Vic. Vic tore it open and shoved two pieces of sliced white into his mouth, chewed a couple of times then spat it out. He glared at Bussa, shaking the limp bread in front of him. "Wha' the fuck is dis shit?"

"Fried Spam."

"Fried wha'? I look like da kinda fool ta you eats cold fried Spam?"

Bussa shrugged. "I dunno . . . Look, me an' the boys bin on the road since befo' four turty. Where'd you tink me gonna fin' you a bacon sarnie from at dis time o' the mornin'?"

Bitter covered his mouth with his hand, his huge shoulders rolling as he desperately tried to mute his chuckling. Vic flung the sandwich against the wall, glanced at his watch then set Dead Man in his sights.

"Go find sum'place round 'ere dat can cook us up sum bacon an' egg sarnies."

Vic stuck his hand into his back trouser pocket, pulled out a wad of cash and unfurled two crisp £5 notes. He threw them across the table. The young Bajan yawned and stretched, then got to his feet and kicked back his chair, grumbling to himself. As Dead Man headed towards the kitchen door I looked across at Bitter Lemon, a grin creeping across my face. My cousin set his thorny eye on me. "Wha' now?"

I held out my hands. "Hey, I wasn't about to say a damn thing."

"Dat's a wise move, JT."

Vic sniffed and took a swig out of his hipflask then slouched back against the wall like a sullen youth. I saw Bitter Lemon kick playfully at the toe of Bussa's boot. He winked at his friend, the two men trying desperately not to snigger, then winked at me before turning to Vic with a big grin.

My cousin sucked air through his teeth and swore under his breath. Bitter's white teeth and grey eyes sparkled at his old friend. Then the three men roared with laughter, their guffawing unbidden from deep within their chests. I bit my lip but quickly followed suit, my chuckling as loud as my friends', the brief respite a welcome relief from the knowledge that by day's end we'd have spilled enemy blood or lost our own lives.

I looked across at Vic; it was great to see him as I'd remembered him when we were kids. He was relaxed and calm, the killer inside hidden beneath a blanket of good humour, his sunny disposition egged on by the comforting warmth of the Barbadian rum coursing through his veins. I believed at that moment that I would one day be compelled to give up my life for my cousin and when the time came, I would go gladly.

Even so, I shivered at the thought.

I couldn't remember the last time my head had hit a pillow. My eyes stung and watered, my limbs ached and my frazzled brain was wracked with fatigue. While we'd eaten the breakfast supplied by Dead Man, Vic had continued to laugh and tell jokes, showing none of the exhaustion I was suffering. Bussa had supplied everyone but me with cigarettes. They all smoked, drank rum and the three men talked about their new lives in the UK and their fond memories of our time on the streets back home.

At around nine thirty, Vic became serious again, his face flat, the humour and mischief he'd been displaying minutes earlier gone. He sat down at the head of the table, lit a cigarette, then clapped his hands once to get everybody's attention and looked across at Bussa.

"You brung me dat map I axe fo'?"

Bussa sucked the last life out of the thin reefer that was stuck at the edge of his mouth before nodding. He threw the butt on the floor, stubbing it out with his heel, then heaved himself out of his seat and walked across to one of the kit bags.

Bussa tramped back and handed Vic the map. "Dis wha' you wantin'?"

"Uh-huh, dat's tha fella."

Vic snatched the Ordnance Survey map and began to open it up. He looked at the mess strewn across the kitchen table and barked at Dead Man, "Man, git rid o' dis shit."

The young Bajan jumped to his feet and gathered up the piles of crumpled serviettes and greasy brown paper bags that littered the table top. He rolled the paper into a huge ball, held it above his head and chucked it into the sink.

Vic gave him the evil eye. "Sit you scraggy arse down, you eediat."

Bussa and Bitter drew up a chair either side of me, Bitter with a wink at me. At over six feet tall, he was a big man, 350 pounds of granite-like muscle, his shaven head like a bowling ball perched on a thick neck, his arms a maze of purple prison tattoos. I still couldn't believe that he was actually sitting next to me. Lethargy, the worry of what Vic was up to and the earlier shock of seeing the three men again had stunted my normally inquisitive nature, but now I stared at Bussa, my brow creasing tightly. "How the hell are you all here like this?"

The big Bajan chuckled to himself. "Bin 'ere a while, now, JT."

Dead Man chipped in. "Yeah . . . Vic, he brung us ovah ta Brixton, Christmas o' sixty-nine. Cold as a muthafucka, it wus."

Bitter nodded in agreement. "Sure wus."

Vic stood up and spread the map across the table. He was looking at me, shaking his head and grinning. "Dese fellas 'ere are lookin' afta me Brixton interests. Got dem London suckahs flat-footed an' blind, ain't we?"

The three men nodded in unison, each grunting in agreement.

Vic put his palms either side of the bottom edge of the map and stared down at it then looked across at me. "Right, you show me on 'ere whe' dis Glenside place is?"

I got to my feet and peered over Vic's shoulder at the map, running my finger over it until I found the area I was looking for. "Here."

Vic leaned in closer, studying the terrain on the map, picking out where his advantages would be in territory we'd never trod over before in daylight, let alone at night. He looked up at me. "We gonna need ta be set up befo' dat muthafucka Ryder an' 'is boys show."

Vic scrutinised the map again and circled the hospital's chapel with the tip of his index finger. "Dead Man, you gonna need ta be hidin' you arse in dese trees out by dis ole church. Looks like deh plenty o' ground fo' you ta git lost in."

Dead Man nodded, grinning at his boss.

"JT, me an' you, we do jus' as Ryder axe. Go meet 'im at the chapel, ten thirty sharp. Bussa and Bitter gonna be close by befo' the heat gits turned up." Vic looked at the map again. I watched as he carefully studied the ground then stabbed his finger down. "We tell Ryder dat 'is man Castle is stashed in dis place 'ere."

I looked at the spot Vic had indicated. "Snuff Mills?"

Vic nodded. "Yeah . . . ole mill 'ouse down by the river. Plenty o' tree cover too."

"What about Ruth? Ryder's gonna want to see her old man before he hands her over."

Vic shrugged. "When the muthafuckas show up we see wha' dey do wid her. If she out in the open with

Ryder, it meks tings easier. If not, den we play it by ear."

"Play it by ear? Is that the best you got?"

"JT, don't sweat it, brutha."

"Don't sweat it? We're talking about a woman's life here."

Vic shook his head and reached for his hip flask. He could sell snow to an Arctic explorer and an electric blanket to the damned so why the hell shouldn't he be able to flog me a half-assed rescue attempt?

Vic saw the doubt cross my face but still pushed on with his sales pitch. "To begin wit', we gonna be eyeballin' Ryder when he shows up. Once we know how he's plannin' ta play tings out, we can tink 'bout how we git the girl off 'im, an' do it real quick."

I pinched at my temples and shook my head. "It all still sounds pretty thin to me."

Bitter got to his feet, walked over to one of the holdalls and pulled out a long black pistol. He returned, dropping the gun on the table in front of me.

"Dese beauties gonna he'p mek light work o' dem honkies."

I reached over and picked up the gun then looked up at him. "What is it?"

"Dat deh is a Welrod Mark One."

"Silenced automatic shooter," Vic interrupted.

Bitter nodded and pointed at the gun in my hands. "Dat ting, it can knock a fly off a bucket o' shit in the dark."

"We got L1 A1 self-loading rifles; dey silenced too."

Vic turned and pointed back at the bags stowed on the other side of the room. "Brutha, we got ourselves flares ta light the fuckin' place up an' mo' firepower tha' you can shake a damn stick at. Dat girl gone be fine, trus' me."

He walked around the table and stood next to Bitter without breaking eye contact with me then lifted a cigarette out of the pack in his shirt pocket. Bitter struck up his Zippo lighter and put the flame underneath the tip of the cigarette. Vic cupped his hands around the blue and yellow flare and sucked on the smoke before he reached over and put his hand on my shoulder.

"JT, man, you lookin' dead beat. Go git yo'self a few hours' shut-eye in the car. All dis shit gonna mek mo' sense once you rested up."

I looked down, my eyes straining to focus, then handed the gun to Bitter and got to my feet, stumbling off balance. The Bajan caught my arm and righted me, and I slowly walked across the kitchen and out of house, my head fuzzy, as if it was filled with cotton wool. I headed down the garden path back towards the Capri, struggling to put one foot in front of the other. I felt lost and scared, like a man out of time and place, with no castle to which he could safely return.

I woke a little after three thirty to the sound of bullfrogs croaking by a pond close to the house. I'd slept without dreaming, my mind and body surrendering to slumber like a worn-out toddler after a day's play.

I took my holdall off the back seat and went back inside the house, cleaned myself up at the kitchen sink then took the fresh clothes from my bag and changed. Bitter, Bussa, Dead Man and Vic had all been sleeping during different parts of the day, each taking turns to keep an eye on Castle upstairs.

At sunset, I stood on the porch and witnessed a change in the weather that was spookily audible, a sucking of air that drew the leaves off the ground and out of the trees and set them soaring into the sky, flickering like hundreds of yellow and green butterflies about the fields at the side of the old building. I could see a curtain of rain marching towards me, dissolving the western horizon into smoke plumes that resembled the outflow from an iron foundry. When I went back inside, I found Vic standing in the hall, a half-drunk bottle of rum in his hand. He smiled at me then gestured towards the front door. "Whaddya really tink ta dis ole shack?"

I shrugged. "Take some hard work, but the place could shape up pretty good."

Vic nodded slowly. "Well, I ain't gonna be needin' dese damn tings no mo'."

He reached into his pocket, drew out the keys he'd retrieved from the dovecote earlier and threw them over to me. I caught them and Vic turned and began to walk away.

Just as he was about to disappear through the kitchen door, he called back, his voice low, as if he didn't want anyone else to hear his words. "You an' dat pickney be jus' fine 'ere. Mek a proper 'ome fo' the two of you. Sum'place safe, like you used ta 'ave"

I stared at the keys in my hand then looked up to speak to my cousin, but he was gone, the kitchen door closed.

The rain was hitting hard against the window panes when I checked in on Castle. He was lying on the bed, his cuffed hands resting on his lap, ankles crossed. When he saw me at the door, he raised himself up, shuffling his body up the bed so his back rested against the headboard.

"Travel time?"

I looked at my watch — it was just after 8.30p.m. "Not long now."

"I don't expect it's going to be a pleasant trip, Mr Ellington."

I shrugged. "I suspect you'll be riding in the boot again, that's for sure."

Castle swung his legs off the bed. "Do you mind if I use the bathroom?"

I shook my head. "Come on."

I walked him out into the hall and down to the toilet. "Leave the door open."

He walked inside and looked back at me while he urinated loudly into the water. His face looked strangely composed, pink in the fluorescent light, as though he had surrendered both to the situation and the release in his bladder. Out of decency or revulsion, I suppose, I looked away from him. The trees were thrashing against the windows and through the edge of

350

the shades I could see the sky outside flicker as lightning leaped across the sky.

When he'd finished, I walked Castle back to the bedroom. He slumped back down on the mattress and stared up at me.

"What will happen to my daughter?"

"Nothing, she's gonna be fine."

Castle shook his head. "You really don't know William Ryder, do you?"

"Know him well enough to know the man can't be trusted." I took a step back towards the door.

"And what kind of man are you, Mr Ellington?"

"What I am ain't none of your damn business."

I turned to walk away, but Castle called after me. He fixed me in his gaze, his brown eyes sleepy and expressionless. He looked drawn and haggard, his clothes wilting with perspiration, but though he seemed defeated, the old man refused to keep his mouth shut. "I get the impression that there is more going on with you and my daughter than you are prepared to admit."

I swung round on my heels and moved in closer to Castle. His body shrank back across the bed as I approached. "Whatever may be going on between me and Ruth ain't got a damn thing to do with you."

Castle glared up at me and rasped, "But I'm her father . . . I have a right to know."

My hands clenched into tight balls, and I felt tiny beads of sweat prickle on top of my scalp. I rolled my shoulders, trying hard to keep calm. "Man, you gave up that right a long time ago. The kinda things you've done in the past, the lies you told, secrets you've kept. There ain't no daughter in the world would want to know you as their kin."

Castle went quiet for a moment, his eyes studying me. His face softened. "Do you pray, Mr Ellington?"

I shook my head, watching Castle chew at his lip. As he was about to speak again, his mouth snapped shut, his face immediately turning pale.

"The honky . . . he stays 'ere."

I turned to see Vic standing behind me, a pair of leg cuffs attached to a chain in his hand.

"Say what?"

Vic snatched my lapel and pulled me towards him. He put his face close to mine and whispered in my ear. "You heard me. Dat ole fool deh, he gonna be you best alibi after we finished our bidness wid Ryder. Ain't no way I'm givin' 'im up ta dat ponce. You need ta come away from all dis shit clean."

"But what about Ruth?"

Vic took hold of my forearm and squeezed it tightly. "I tole you, the girl gonna be fine. You gotta truss me, brutha."

Vic let go of my jacket then pushed past me like a freight train. As I stumbled backwards, my cousin was already backhanding Castle across the face, making him yelp out in pain. He shoved him back on to the mattress, grabbed one of his legs, snapped a cuff around his ankle then yanked the long chain across the room, attaching the second cuff through one of the bars of the cast-iron radiator.

Vic pointed a finger at Castle's quivering face. "You move off dat shitty ole bed an' one o' my boys downstairs gonna come up 'ere and dey gonna shoot you in the foot."

Castle flinched and bit at his bottom lip, his shoulders trembling.

"Dem fellas, dey 'ear you movin' agin, dey gonna come back an' take a knee. Honky, you keep shiftin' 'bout, time me an' my friend 'ere git back, deh ain't gonna be nuthin' left o' you. Understand?"

Vic slapped Castle around the face again then turned and dragged me out of the bedroom, slamming the door shut behind him. As we began to walk back along the landing, I heard Castle begin to speak, his voice quickly becoming louder, his words that of a prayer.

"God be merciful to me a sinner . . ."

I caught hold of Vic's arm and the two of us stopped at the foot of the stairs and continued to listen to the incantation.

". . . and make me to know and believe in Jesus Christ. I am utterly cast away. Lord, I have heard that thou art a merciful God, that thou art willing to bestow grace upon such a poor sinner as I and I am a sinner indeed. Lord, I take this opportunity to pray for the salvation of my soul. Amen."

Vic waved his hand dismissively in front of his face. "Shit . . . Dat ole fool really tink his god gonna look out fo' him? Honky axin' the wrong dude. He only got me now to save his white ass." Vic nudged me in the side with his elbow. "Com' on. Leave dat sukkah ta 'is prayin'."

And that's what we did. We left Herbert Castle and his sinner's soul for God to save.

Walking back down the stairs, I knew the only salvation I needed to concern myself with was that of Castle's daughter, Ruth. That was all that mattered now. I knew that someday I'd probably have my own sinner's prayer to commune to a higher power for the terrible things I'd done, and those I was about to do.

But at that moment in time none of that kind of thinking really mattered. In the next hour or so, I was ready to go out and kill my fellow man.

A man named William Ryder.

CHAPTER
FORTY-THREE

The moon looked like a sliver of burnt pewter inside the clouds. Rain twisted out of a purple-tinged sky, the white flicker of electricity in the trees surrounding the Glenside chapel making me think of the summer storms I had known growing up as a child. Vic had wanted the advantage of surprise, and he took it.

We'd driven into woodland a half-mile away from the hospital then walked in the dying light through dense thicket until we'd reached a steep bank that overlooked both the hospital and the little church. Vic set Dead Man up with the supressed, night-vision sniper rifle in a tangle of hazel and hawthorn on the boundary of the grassy incline, while Bussa and Bitter had wandered off into the undergrowth, positioning themselves with their silenced rifles and flash grenades closer to the chapel. Vic and I had remained on the slope, a vantage point that allowed us to just make out the road that ran along Glenside.

The wind sprang to life, blowing a heavy gust into the treetops around us. The rain pelted at my face, soaking into my hair and slowly seeping through the fabric of my coat. Vic pulled the collar of his army jacket up around his face, lifted the Welrod pistol out in front of him and inched closer towards me.

"Ryder gonna be here early."

I looked out into the blackness. "What makes you so sure? He's a cocky bastard. I thought he'd wanna put us on edge, keep us waiting?"

"Nah, we bin 'ere fo' ovah an hour, so we ain't on the back foot. Ryder, he be a fool if he didn't wanna scout out tha place.

"Once we know how many fellas Ryder's brung wid 'im, our boys can choose deh own targets. Stick ta wha' I tole you to do. You jus' keep Billy talkin'. Stall 'im fo' as long as you can. Try 'n' find out where he got the girl an' git her out so we can see her. We'll do tha rest, got it?"

"Yeah . . . I got it."

Vic squeezed the back of my neck and whispered into my ear, "Everyt'ing gonna be fine, brutha."

I lowered my eyes and didn't reply. I wasn't sure I believed Vic's assurance. I knew what was at risk, and what I had to do. I told myself to ignore the canker burning inside me, the fear nipping at my guts. I looked back out at the approaching blackness, resigning myself to the unalterable fact that you cannot hide from evil.

A few minutes before nine thirty we saw the headlights of three vehicles turning into the driveway of the hospital grounds. They made their way along the tree-lined drive before heading away from the main buildings and out to the edge of the coppice surrounding the chapel. Vic quickly moved down towards a grassy depression at the rear of the church. I listened to the car doors opening and saw the thin beams of torches ignite then sweep and search to treeline. Six men circled their motors, followed by the familiar frames of William Ryder and James Moody. The two men stood between the beams of the car headlamps. I took a deep breath and began to walk slowly down the embankment towards them.

The wind and rain gusted across the slope, blowing me backward, then there was the sudden glare of a torch being shone into my eyes. As I began to raise my arm to shield my vision, a man bellowed at me.

"Keep those hands at your sides, sonny."

I obeyed the command and took the last few steps down on to flat ground, my hands palm out at my sides. I saw the barrel of a rifle sweep out in front of me followed by the gunman, dressed top to tail in black, his face hidden by a balaclava.

"Hold it there."

The gunman circled me. I felt the tip of his rifle briefly touch the back of my skull before the man began to pat down my body in search of a concealed weapon.

"He's clean."

The gunman pushed me forward towards where Ryder and Moody stood. Three torch beams strafed the grassy ridge and the wooded area around me.

"Joseph, good of you to come out of hiding. There's a lot of policemen looking for you. In light of that fact, I'm very pleased to see you being so prompt."

Ryder wiped his face with a white handkerchief and brushed the rainwater out of his hair.

"Least I could do, all things considered."

Ryder nodded and took a step towards me. He wore a buttoned up woollen coat, the satin stripe on his dress trousers glinting in the light of the car headlamps.

I gestured at Ryder's feet. "I didn't know we were dressing for the occasion?"

"Very witty, Joseph. I have another late engagement to attend after we've concluded our business this evening."

"Another dodgy club?"

Ryder sneered, then twisted his neck to peer backwards for a moment before returning his gaze to me. "Did you know that we're standing very close to a little piece of your own personal history, Joseph?"

I shook my head. "No, I didn't. But I'm sure you're gonna tell me all about it."

Ryder looked at Moody and grinned. "You were right about this lad's mouth, Jimmy. Proper little smart alec, ain't he?" He refocussed his gaze on me, the rain lashing down between us. "You remember Alice Linney . . . Earl's missus?"

"Yeah, I remember her."

"Well, old girl Linney's locked up back there in that nuthouse. They moved her out of prison some time back. Apparently went stark raving fucking mad, she did. I hear that she used to repeat your name, over and over again. Day and night, so they say."

I shrugged. "That's good to know."

Ryder laughed under his breath, his expression now blank. "Here we are, the two of us, standing in the pissing rain, our pasts intertwined by that crazy old girl.

358

She brought Stella Hopkins, Terrance Blanchard, the Erotica Negro club and me right into your little world. Who'd a' thought it, eh?"

He changed tack. "Where's Castle?"

"I need to know the girl's safe first."

"Ah, the bait, of course. My fellas have had their eyes on Miss Castle for a while. Thought she might be useful to me if you started bracing her old man with difficult questions. Seems I was right to heed their advice."

"Nothing like a bent copper to put you right."

Ryder sniffed and turned his face into the breeze. "Very true, Joseph. Very true."

"Where's Ruth?"

Ryder waved his hand towards one of the masked men standing by one of the cars. He opened the rear door and dragged Ruth out into the open. Her hands were bound with thick rope, her mouth covered with black tape. Ryder took another step towards me. Moody shadowing his every move.

"I've been very accommodating, Joseph. We have an agreement to settle. Let me see Herbert Castle and that trumped-up ponce of a cousin of yours, and you and that wench there can piss off back to where you came from and never look back."

I felt myself swallow hard, my body trembling. I raised my hand ever so slowly and pointed towards the treeline. "The two of 'em are down at the old mill house at the back of this wood behind you. Vic says if you want him, then you gotta take your honky arse down there and get him."

Everything that happened in those next few seconds seemed to take place in slow motion. Ryder turned and looked into the trees before shifting his stare towards his right-hand man, then back to my raised hand. Moody moved towards his boss, one hand going inside his jacket, the other reaching out for Ryder's sleeve. When the two men's eyes met, the look on Ryder's face was one of equal bemusement and panic.

I heard Moody scream, "It's a hit. It's a fucking hit. Get her out of here."

Then all hell broke loose.

I hit the ground and rolled towards the hedgerow as the first of Dead Man's silenced rounds *thropped* past and cut through the head of the gunman nearest to me. I scrambled into the undergrowth, rolling out on to the other side. I dipped low on my haunches and saw Ruth being pushed back into the car, seconds before another silenced bullet hit that man in the side of the neck.

Ryder had already spun on his heels, his back covered by Moody's heavy frame, the two men darting towards one of the cars as the next two shots from Dead Man's sniper rifle took out another two of the gunmen. Bitter charged out of the thicket at the rear of the vehicles, fell to one knee and sprayed a series of short bursts at the back of one the cars, blowing out the tyres.

To my left, Vic bolted like a banshee down the edge of the embankment. As he ran, I saw him rip the cord at the base of a flare and toss it into the air, the night sky and wet turf around him instantly glowing with

360

bright phosphorous light. He fired off a couple of rounds as he zig-zagged across open ground, closing the space between himself, Moody and Ryder, the silenced Welrod pistol extended in front of him.

I shot out of the scrub at the same time I saw Bussa spring out of the trees next to the chapel, moving with remarkable agility for a man of his age and size. He dodged and weaved towards the cars before dropping to the ground and throwing my pistol at me. I watched the gun flip across the grass at the same time as Bussa rose up and lifted the semi-automatic and its suppressor with both hands, aiming with his arms fully extended. The last of the hooded men did not seem to realise how quickly their situation had reversed as Bussa ploughed towards them. He shot one man in the throat and the second in the face. They both fell to the ground, making no sound inside the rain.

I snatched up the pistol then heard the sound of a car backing across the wet ground. I saw Moody behind the steering wheel, dropped to my knee, aimed and let off two quick rounds. One tore into the car's engine block, but the second spiderwebbed the driver's side window and blew out the windscreen. It hung down like a crumpled glass apron as the car careered backwards, whipping the grass underneath its bumper and spinning divots of mud from under the tyres.

The car seemed to slow as it made a wide arc across the grass towards the woods. It lurched on its back springs as Moody shifted down, righted the wheel and hit the gas again. Bitter and Bussa raced towards the car, firing low, blowing out the front and rear tyres on one side. The car accelerated and spun to the left under another hail of gunfire before skidding into a corridor of trees. I saw the back end flick round and sink over the edge of the coppice before dropping down into a gully behind the treeline. There was a crash of metal and a bang as the car fell into the darkness, its headlights shining up at the sky.

Vic ran to where the car had fallen with me hot on his heels. Bussa and Bitter were already climbing down into the gully. Vic and I separated at the edge of the shallow trench and he pulled the cord of a second flare and held it out in front of him. The car had slid rather than toppled, and the rear of the vehicle dug deep into the earth. Three of the doors were yanked open.

Vic climbed down and opened the back door then looked up at me, shaking his head. I could hear the trees creaking in the wind as I pointed my pistol out in front of me and scrambled down the bank to join the three men.

Vic handed the flare to Bussa. He walked out into the coppice, raising the torch at arm's length, its radiance picking out a narrow footbridge. Bussa dipped the flare towards the ground; deep foot tracks led towards the bridge and along the muddy bank. Vic scanned the wood, the Welrod held out in front of him. He stabbed his hand at Bitter, ordering him to head for the river and over the bridge. We followed, my hands shaking, my legs like lead weights.

The slats on the bridge were soft with rot, a couple of them bursting under our weight as we crossed. The river's surface was dimpled with water dripping from the trees, the rain raising the level. A line of dried flotsam ran along the bank and weaved along the edge like a grey cobweb. Bitter was waiting on the other side, sunk down on one knee and peering into the trees in front of him. The flare in Bussa's hand was dimming, the night air around us becoming darker by the second.

We moved along the bank at speed before heading for the thinning underbrush on the other side of the wood. Vic and Bussa were out in front with me, with Bitter bringing up the rear. Three hundred yards or so into the wood, the river snaked back around us and we had to cross over a shallower stretch of water, the flare now all but extinguished. My eyes struggled to adjust from light to darkness again as the final flickers burned away.

Ahead of us I could hear the sound of faster-running water. As the thicket thinned and we came out into open ground again, I could make out the shape of a large building ahead. To our left was the river again, its fast-moving stream broken by a series of weirs.

As we made our way down towards the building, the rumble of the water became deafening. I doubted that Ryder or Moody wanted a duel under the trees. Both were creatures of guile, and I suspected they would be waiting where they had the best advantage. My head was throbbing and my palms were sweating around the grips of the pistol.

We pushed forward, Vic ahead of us, his arm waving in a silent order that we should spread out. I saw an electrical flash in the clouds. It leaped across the sky and for a second lit up the area around us before we returned to a blue-black darkness. Then I heard something move in the water behind us, the crinkle of leaves underfoot.

Bussa turned. The shooter behind me fired only once.

The report was like a starter gun at a track meet. The round caught Bussa high, blowing his forehead apart like an exploding watermelon, Vic screaming his name as the dead man fell forward into the water. I dipped to one knee as Moody broke out from the edge of the coppice and came running towards me with his gun out in front of him, firing. The first round skirted the side of my head, the second clipping the ground to my right.

Out of the corner of my eye, I saw Bitter running forward, his feet churning in the leaves, his rifle slung low as he fired. I heard the SLR click, then fail to discharge a round. Bitter flung the rifle into the air and kept running.

Moody managed to get off a single shot before Bitter was on him, hooking his hands behind the other man's back, crushing Moody's body against his own. I heard a single shot and saw a flash of light between their bodies. Bitter staggered and lifted Moody into the air, then the two of them toppled backwards to the ground. I heard the gun fire a second time and watched Bitter get slowly to his feet, ripping the pistol from Moody's hand and holding it by the grip, pressing his other hand against his side.

Moody shifted on the ground. Bitter cursed and stamped his foot against Moody's chest before emptying the rest of the gun's magazine into the man's alabaster face. When Moody was dead, Bitter turned towards me, his mouth open, his breath wheezing out of his throat. I saw the hesitation in his next few movements, then he dropped to the ground.

Vic called after me. My ears were ringing, the air tannic with the smell of burnt gunpowder. I got to my feet, the world feeling like it was tilting sideways, and staggered towards him, my heart seizing up with panic, my breath coming short. My cousin pointed down at the brownstone building at the foot of the river.

"Dat fucka gotta 'ave Castle's girl sum'place down deh. Ain't no place else fo' him ta run."

Vic pulled the magazine from the silenced Welrod, saw it was out of ammunition and dropped it at his feet. He removed his Berretta from its holster and chambered a round.

"I'm gonna head round back, see if I can smoke the bastard out. You cut across the water 'n' head toward the front o' the place. You mebbe able ta pick 'im off if the fool meks a run fo' it."

I nodded, my throat tight, my words unwilling to escape from my mouth. I watched Vic run back into the undergrowth before making my way back down the riverbank and heading downstream.

At the edge of the final weir, the moon broke through from behind a cloud; a solitary band of cold light shining through the canopy behind me. I remained motionless for a moment and looked down on an old mill house I'd mentioned to Ryder earlier. I sank down low and crossed over the shallow weir to the other side of the bank, then ran down a muddy track and through a clump of trees, the branches whipping against my face.

My knees sagged suddenly as I broke out of the treeline and headed down the short embankment that ran along the side of the mill. I came to a halt at the edge of the building, my pistol outstretched, my finger resting on the trigger. I took a couple of deep breaths then swung round to the front of the building, scanning either side of me. Vic was nowhere to be seen.

I looked back up the path, across the river and over towards the edge of the coppice. To the left I could hear water sluicing through the slow-turning mill wheel. I took a step back then edged towards the door, my right leg lifted slightly to kick it open.

That's when the odour hit me. The stink of sweat, mixed with blood and fear.

I turned and looked into the face of William Ryder. He was standing less than ten feet away from me, a revolver raised in his right hand. He was bleeding from a wound at the top of his left shoulder, his face nicked with glass cuts. In front of him stood Ruth Castle, still bound and gagged, her eyes wide with fear and tears streaming down her face. Ryder stepped forward, pushing Ruth in front of him.

"Drop it, Joseph."

I felt a coldness like a fist in my stomach and let the pistol fall at my feet.

Ryder waved his gun at me. "Now kick it over towards me."

I punted it across the ground. Ryder pushed Ruth forward again, the revolver now held at my face.

"Where's the Jah or Vic or whatever else you lot call that bastard?"

I swallowed hard, my eyes pitching towards the ground before focusing back on Ryder. "Your man Moody got him."

Ryder coughed. He cleared his throat before barking at me again. "And Moody?"

"He's back there in the woods with a face full of bullets in him."

"You do that?

I nodded.

"So it's come down to this, has it? Me and you chasing an eye for an eye?"

"Looks like it. We're all that's left — everyone else is dead," I lied.

"This one ain't yet. And she's a real handful. Not like her old man. Where is he?"

Ryder clenched his hand around the back of Ruth's neck and shook her. I heard her mumbled sobs from underneath the gag. There was a raw, skinned area above her left eye.

"Vic stashed him someplace safe, till you handed over the girl."

Ryder inched a step closer, his hand tightening around the back of Ruth's neck. "You're gonna take me to her old man. No more fucking about."

"And then what?"

Ryder looked at me with a lopsided grin. "Who knows?"

I opened out my hands, raising them slightly. "Let the girl go first, then I'll take you to Castle."

Ryder sniffed the air and shook his head.

"For Christ sakes . . . please."

Ryder pushed Ruth out in front of him, his small and crooked teeth clenched as he raised the gun to eye level and sighted it at the back of Ruth's head. "Be a bit of a shame to have to do this," he said. "But it looks like that's just the way it is."

Ryder pulled back the revolver's hammer, his finger tightening around the trigger. He took a side-step to his left, pushed Ruth out to arm's length and looked into my eyes.

Then behind me, for the briefest of moments, I heard a faint sound, like a strand of broken piano wire whizzing through the air. The blast hit Ryder in the sternum, knocking him backwards, sending his gun flying and Ruth falling towards me. As Ryder hit the ground, he made a whooshing sound, like a man falling down a step he hadn't seen. I grabbed Ruth by both arms, drawing her up to my chest and backing away towards the mill house.

Then I saw Vic walk out from behind the water wheel, his Berretta raised. Ryder was shoving himself across the wet earth as Vic walked towards him, trying to pull himself upright. But Vic put his boot on Ryder's back, bringing the man to a sudden halt. A crimson trickle ran from the edge of the gangster's mouth. Vic grabbed hold of Ryder's coat collar and pulled him upright so he sat in the mud, one hand pressed against the wound in his chest, his head lowered as he stared at the blood on his palm. His breathing was ragged, the colour draining from his face.

368

Vic took a step backwards, raised the Berretta and held it at the side of Ryder's head, then just as Ryder had done moments before, thumbed the hammer back.

I tore at the tape around Ruth's mouth and drew her towards me, tucking her face into my neck. Vic stood with the gun directed at Ryder's face, and the rain beat down on the two men for what seem like an eternity. The pistol in my cousin's hand never wavered.

Then I saw Vic look up out towards the treeline before reaching into his trouser pocket and pulling out his Zippo. I watched him flip the lid, strike up a flame then wave the lighter above his head. He lowered the gun to his side and began to walk towards me. Ryder looked up into my face and grinned.

He was still smiling when the silent bullet delivered from Dead Man's sniper rifle lifted his head up towards the heavens. Ryder's brains and bone blew out behind him and spattered across the sodden earth, his arms flailing into the air, his fingers outstretched as if he was grasping for the last heartbeats of life being snatched from him.

I watched his body drop back into the dirt and a puff of smoke drift up from his mouth like a dirty feather. It curled into the air then drifted back to the ground like a damned soul being summoned down into an infernal abyss.

Epilogue

Winter came early that year, the snow falling as harshly as it did when I'd first came to Britain.

The cold weather was an unpleasant reminder of the night, seven years earlier, when Earl Linney had strolled up to me as I sat with an empty beer glass in hand in the Star and Garter on Brook Road. On that icy night, with a blizzard blowing outside, his offer of easy money to go find his niece, Stella Hopkins, had been the bitter catalyst for the dark journey I undertook, one that led to the deaths of many and a sadness that I rarely speak of — one that continues to gnaw at my spirit all these years later.

Nowadays I look at snowfall as an unwelcome emissary. A chilly messenger of foreboding and a stark reminder to me that the Heartman, that evil spirit born of Barbadian folklore, was never far from my side.

After the madness of that night out at Glenside, I returned to the cottage at Hambrook and drove Herbert Castle out to Bridewell police station. I was held, without charge, for three days while Bristol city police braced me. I handed over the final Polaroid of Ryder and Suresh together. It seemed that Superintendent

370

Fletcher had left enough official documentation in his files to corroborate much of the evidence I gave the cops.

Detectives were brought in from out of town and they investigated my claims and questioned Castle. He slowly gave up everything he had on William Ryder and James Moody, and in so doing implicated himself in the duo's criminal activities as far back as 1963. The councillor was finally arrested a week later and charged with conspiracy to pervert the course of justice, malfeasance in office and a raft of other serious offences that took the clerk at Small Street magistrates two minutes to read out in court.

Despite the grilling the police gave me, I never gave up the Jah, as they called him, insisting that whoever had come to my aid had finished off Ryder and Moody for their own personal ends. I maintained that my part in the whole sorry affair had been simply to extricate the truth from Herbert Castle and assist in the handover of the councillor to Ryder and the subsequent safe return of his daughter, Ruth.

Of the six men found dead in the grounds of the old psychiatric hospital, three were found to be serving police officers, including Inspector Keith Leach. The rifle lying next to his body was found to be the one that had killed Fletcher. The rest of the masked corpses were men in Ryder's employ. Ryder and Moody were charged in absentia for the ordering and subsequent murders of Nikhil Suresh and Superintendent William Fletcher and for Moody's killing of James Peberdy.

During the weeks that followed, I attended the funerals of the child and the two men. I spent time with the Suresh family and returned the money given to me by Nikhil's father. I'd not earned a penny of it. All I brought to him and the family was the tragic news of their son's death. It wasn't my proudest moment.

The service for my friend, Everton "Bussa" Worrell was held at the chapel in Brunswick cemetery in St Pauls a fortnight after his death. Vic had his ashes flown back to the last of his relatives still living on Barbados. I'm told that they scattered his remains at Ragged Point in St Philip Parish, close to the chattel house that he'd been born in.

Bitter Lemon and Dead Man disappeared off the face of the earth. Many weeks later, when things had died down, word got back to me from Loretta Harris that Bitter was making a full recovery, the injury to his side a mere flesh wound. Loretta went on to tell me that both Bitter and Dead Man were set to return to St Pauls to oversee Vic's now expanding Bristol operation. It was a piece of hearsay that I chose not to query. The less I knew about my cousin's future criminal activities and his formidable associates, the better.

And me . . .

In October, Chloe and I moved out to the old cottage on Quarry Barton Road in Hambrook. Each day I drive the seven miles back into St Pauls for Chloe to attend school. We may be country folk nowadays, but I saw no reason to take her away from her friends and the community she had grown to love and feel safe in.

372

I don't do favours for folk anymore — well not the kind that are gonna get me into trouble, anyhow. I took a job working for the Bristol Bus Company, at their place out on Marlborough Street. I help maintain the depot, wash and polish the buses, keep the garage looking good. It ain't detective work, and I'm grateful for that. It's honest graft, and most of the time, I keep myself to myself. The money I earn just about pays all the bills, puts clothes on our backs and food in our bellies.

I spent the rest of the autumn using every spare penny I had left in the bank to do up the old house. It's a pretty little place, with a decent garden, hedged at each side, that looks out across the Gloucestershire countryside. It doesn't offer the brilliant azure views I remember from growing up on Bim, but it's someplace that I'm happy to call home. A rural dwelling perfect for bringing a little one up in and, as Vic had promised, it feels safe. When I lock up at night, I clasp the key in the palm of my hand knowing that nobody can take the old place away from my child and me. It's a helluva feeling.

Aunt Pearl, Gabe, Loretta and Carnell Jnr visit us often. Pearl brings over food or I'll cook. We all sit in the kitchen, eating, drinking, laughing and telling the kind of tales that always evoke happy memories of sunnier climes spent on the faraway Caribbean paradise we all miss.

Ruth and I continued to see each other after the dust had settled. It wasn't easy getting in touch at first; my gut reaction was to stay away, the memory of her father's indiscretions and arrest overshadowing my understanding of her true feelings towards me. We took things slow at first — the occasional walk across Clifton Down was followed some time later by our first date out together. We promenaded along the pier at Clevedon eating fish and chips out of newspaper. We take each day as it comes, and what will be, will be. I'd never expected to find love again in my lifetime, and the two of us being thrown together during such a terrible time has been a very strange blessing. In my experience, fate is often cruel, however its hand has been much kinder towards me than I ever could have imagined.

As for Vic . . . My scoundrel cousin returns to see me when I least expect it, usually as the sun dips in the sky and the evening shadows help mask his approach.

Vic is still Vic. Once a crook, always a crook. I'm aware that his "business" interests now take in much of Bristol, a great deal of London and large swathes of the rest of the country. Nowadays, I choose to see him as my kin, and not a criminal. It's a naïve thought but one that allows me to sleep better at nights.

As secretive and cunning as he always was, I am ignorant as to what part of the world he dwells in, but sense that it is remote and covert and that the company he keeps will be as lawless as he. Vic did keep his word about reconciling himself with his estranged parents, though. He ate humble pie and, one afternoon in late September, went and broke bread with the two of them. Rumour has it that when he walked through the front door of Pearl and Gabe's home on Banner Road

374

you could hear his mother's overjoyed weeping at the bottom of the street.

Sometimes when I least expect it, Vic will surprise me. I'll find him standing outside the kitchen door, a box of knock-off Mount Gay rum in his arms, a joint hanging from the corner of his mouth and a grin on his face that could charm the devil himself. At twilight, we stroll down the river that runs at the back of the house and fish for brown trout like two old duffers who have no need to share war stories or talk about bitter memories, more interested in watching the sunset and knocking back our hooch than anything else.

As it grows dark and we sit quietly on the bank, listening to the sound of the birds chittering and the water flowing past, I sometimes look across the other side of the river and out towards a spinney that's nestled at the corner of one of the fields. Often, I hear the laughter of a little girl playing, hear her giggle as she runs through the long grass and then a familiar woman's voice calling out the name: "Amelia."

I sleep soundly at night without nightmare or reverie, my beloved family close around me, both in the real world and behind the thin, white veil of the next.

Acknowledgements

A Sinner's Prayer is a book that was never meant to be. As early as 2003, I had a story arc outlined in a series of journals. Each story would feature a Bajan former police officer, Joseph Tremaine Ellington, and would be told over three separate novels: *Heartman, All Through the Night* and *Restless Coffins*. The final novel in the trio was published in early spring 2018 and, in truth, back then I knew there was perhaps one more tale left to tell.

The book you now hold in your hands is most certainly the finale, the end of the road for my old mate, JT. I've been asked by many kind readers, "Why stop at four?" and "Surely there is so much more to tell?" and "There's still life in the old dog yet." While it's truly heartening for a writer to hear such enthusiasm for the characters he's created and readers' requests for more books featuring them, I knew it was time to bid "adieu". I felt a strange responsibility to Joseph, Vic, Loretta, Gabe, Pearl and little Chloe. Over the course of a quartet of stories I've put each of them through more than enough grief and, with the conclusion of *A Sinner's Prayer*, I thought it time to offer my old Barbadian and Bristol friends a small measure of peace.

It's never easy to bid farewell to characters who have existed in your head and heart for so long and I will miss Joseph and the gang very much. I know their spirits will remain within me, and there'll be times that I'll find JT tapping at my shoulder asking, "Hey, when we getting back to work?" It's going to be difficult to ignore such an ardent request, but resist I must. There are pastures new to seek out, new characters to create and, I hope, great stories to tell. In the meantime, I won't close the door on Ellington completely. That would be unkind. If he was to return in the future, it would be in a very different incarnation. We'd need something new to say, something fresh and exciting. "Never say never," I hear you say. We'll see.

I wanted to take the opportunity to thank all the wonderful folk who have been standing by my side, supporting, caring, grafting since *Heartman* was published in 2014.

Thanks to Philip Patterson, my long-suffering literary agent at the Marjacq agency. Phil saw something special in *Heartman* and JT at Crimefest in Bristol in 2013 and ran with it. Since then, it's been an emotional rollercoaster of a ride, and I wouldn't have missed a moment of it. I'm pretty sure Mr P. may feel differently. I am blessed to be represented by such a great team at Marjacq, to be part of a stable of brilliant authors. My gratitude also extends to the formidable Guy Herbert, Sandra Sawicka and Leah Middleton.

The superb Edinburgh-based Black & White Publishing has published each of the novels. A huge word of gratitude to Campbell Brown and Alison McBride and to the entire B&W team.

I doff my cap to my fellow crime writing buddy, Tony R. Cox, who has offered a keen eye over the early manuscripts of three of the novels. His old journalist's hawk eye and pedantry for poor grammar has been invaluable. He's a true friend. Thanks, mate. I also owe a great deal to John Martin, former librarian, CWA Dagger in the Library judge, crime fiction historian and author of the invaluable *Crime Scene: Britain & Ireland*. John has been at my side from the off, appearing at book launches and making my life so much easier in front of an audience. A gentleman of the first order, I'm proud to call him my friend. Once again I must tip my hat to my oldest and dearest friend, Ken Hooper, crime fiction historian, book collector and master of all things Noir and to my fictional Bristol police superintendent namesake and my real life compadre, William "Bill" Fletcher.

I've been aided by a marvellous raft of reviewers and bloggers, all of them fantastic and all so supportive over the years. Cheers to: Linda Wilson, Sharon Wheeler, Abby Jayne Slater, Noelle Holten, Sarah Hardy, Richard Latham, Graham Paul Tonks, Amanda Oughton, Liz Barnsley, Robin Jarossi and to the stunning crime fiction maestros, Ayo Onatade, Ali Karim and Mike Stotter at *Shots* magazine.